FIMBULWINTER

I0604647

FIMBULWINTER

STRANGER THAN FICTION
— BOOK 3 —

T. B. MARE

Podium

All rights reserved. No part of this publication may be reproduced, stored in a retrieval system, or transmitted in any form or by any means electronic, mechanical, photocopying, recording, or otherwise without prior written permission from Podium Publishing.

This is a work of fiction. Names, characters, places, and incidents are either products of the author's imagination or used fictitiously. Any resemblance to actual events, locales, or persons, living, dead, or undead, is entirely coincidental.

Copyright © 2024 by T. B. Mare

Cover design by Barbara Ciardo

ISBN: 978-1-0394-5479-8

Published in 2024 by Podium Publishing
www.podiumaudio.com
Podium

FIMBULWINTER

PROLOGUE

S olana gazed down at the shard of featherglass cradled in her palms. It was what had started it all. It would also be the pivot that would end it all.

Have faith, she told herself. *You have traveled this path for centuries. To hesitate now would be the height of sacrilege.*

The chamber she was in was easily the size of a battle arena, with a twenty-foot-tall ceiling. The walls were covered in sculpture, with thin veins of shining metal reflecting the strangled light from the eerie floating chandeliers, bathing the room in an unholy blue shade. Polished stone floors lay beneath her, covered with elegant rugs. Two massive lupine edifices guarded the entrance to this hall. The interior was an ornate labyrinth of ritualistic chambers, halls, sealed vaults, libraries, and even a hollow wall that held the remains of the previous leaders. Only through this room could the rest be accessed, and yet this room itself welcomed but a few. Those that knew of it knew not to seek it, and those that did, were never found again.

This was the Throne Room, the seat of the Empress of the End.

Or as history called it, *Nidhogg's Lair*.

You have come this far, she repeated to herself. *You cannot stop now.*

"I will not fail you," she murmured, cradling the featherglass shard like it was her own child. Solana had conceived in the past, but this shard was far more precious than that. "The Outsider of legend has finally arrived. And he has brought *Her* with it. It is time, Queen of Ice. Finally, the yokai shall rise, and the Deadliest Mist shall be unleashed."

She heard the sound of footsteps approaching. It could only be one person.

A small frown appeared on her face, as Solana carefully placed the shard of featherglass upon the stone floor, only to see it slowly engulf the featherglass into itself. The floor before her was morphing as well, with long, contorted stone shapes arising out of it like serpents, entwining around each other, forging, becoming *more*. The floor rose, forming a four-feet tall dais, like a central stage, and in its middle now stood a massive white throne that looked like it was carved of solid ice, inlaid with metals, an imposing draconian feature springing out of its back.

The Throne of Ice.

Seat of the Empress of the End.

The footsteps approached closer, and the massive doors opened. Solana stayed put, kneeling on the floor, her hands resting on the throne, eyes closed.

"Have they awoken?"

"The Outsider shows restlessness in his sleep," said the intruder. It was the oni formed from the fusion of her dependable yurei, Malon, and the vanir girl from the Asukan adventurer group it had attempted to possess. The result, which called itself Maude, was now serving under Solana, just like Malon did before her.

Unlike Malon, Maude was an extremely flippant character that Solana just couldn't get a proper read of. Something about her was simply *unnatural.*

Such as the way she disregarded the enchantments placed on the doors with impunity, as she crossed the threshold.

"None of us can get even remotely close to him. That accursed metal lies wrapped around him like a pet. It killed one of the reiki just for trying to get up close."

"Mmmm . . ." said Solana, still not looking up. "That . . . might be a problem. His powers prior to his escape from the anomaly had been queer and dangerous. Already he feels . . . *more.* The presence of that metal might worsen situations."

"Then why is he even here?"

Solana ignored her question for her own. "What about the girl?"

"Tanya is . . . sedated. The burns she suffered could have proven fatal, but nothing that I could not heal. We can awaken her now if you wish."

Her lips twisted slightly at the mention of the girl's name. It suggested a level of familiarity that she didn't think would serve her well.

"No," she said, opening her eyes and shaking her head. "Let her be."

Her eyes regarded the majestic throne before her.

"Wake her up only after the Outsider has awoken but not before. We need his aid if we want this to come to pass."

"Leader . . ." said Maude, hesitation and skepticism clear in her voice. "Are you sure that she's the right person?"

Annoyance rose in Solana. "Have you found anything that says otherwise? I shall remind you, it was you and Mizo who witnessed her powers firsthand."

"I . . . did," agreed the oni, standing by the doors, her hands on one of them. "There is a faint trace of ice-mana lingering within her body. Not even the potent powers of the Haze could burn that off her skin. No doubt she utilized Everfrost in immense quantities before the two of them arrived here. But . . . are you certain it is Her?"

The annoyance spiked further. "Yes."

"Why?" Maude challenged. "The creature was supposed to be dead close to two centuries ago."

"That creature has a *name*!" Solana snapped, turning to Maude, who didn't look the least perturbed at her explosion. "Do not challenge my knowledge, Oni. I have been on this plain before either of your forebears even existed."

"And that's supposed to be a good-enough reason?" challenged Maude. "Do not mock me, Leader. I might not be Malon, but I have taken the stringent oaths. Upon my honor as a naturopath, upon my belief in Eir, I have sworn to be with the yokai, uninfluenced by unworthy motives, and voluntarily consented to do my best to further your goals. Yet you keep secrets from me. You think that Tsurara, your contemporary and descendant of the Empress, lives within the girl, but I've yet to know how."

"It isn't important."

"It isn't important to you," Maude shot back.

Annoyance surged within Solana. The desire to tear this . . . creature into parts was overwhelming. Even better, she could just kill her and wear her skin as her own. Vanir had notoriously high lifeforce-production capacities. Their attunement with natural energy wasn't a drawback either.

But killing an oni—the only one of her kind—would attract the wrong kind of attention among the yokai populace. Not something she could afford right now.

"I smell anxiety in your tone, Oni," warned Solana. "Perhaps you're having second thoughts upon seeing your old friend?"

"Tanya was never my friend," said Maude. "She was just an acquaintance who I have worked with. And I recognize a diversion when I see one, Leader."

A frown formed on Solana's face.

"What is truly going on?" asked Maude. "Tanya, Tsurara . . . whoever she is, what does it even matter now? And why are we even dealing with an Outsider we cannot kill or possibly hope to control?"

Solana bristled. "You are being unduly antagonistic over this situation."

"Which part? The truth about the Outsider, or my skepticism about Tanya being the host of a two-century-old ghost? Or perhaps it's about why you keep coming to this room, whispering to yourself, and making plans about a man that we cannot even possibly control. What is going on, Leader?"

Solana wanted to attack her. Instead, she closed her eyes and stood up, as if beaten down by her words. Finally, she opened them and faced Maude, whose brown eyes looked strangely distraught.

"Everyone knows that we yokai lost everything in the Great War. The World Shaper vanished into the Mists, the empress perished, and our Ikai Realm was shattered until all that was left was an infinite deadland spanning across worlds. But oni, our ancestors—*my* ancestors—knew differently. They told me things happened, and then they happened again, only differently. I do not know what kind of divine or demonic power could've done it, but all we have is a legend to hold on to, and the hope that someday, it will be true."

"And the Outsider plays a role in that?"

"Yes."

"I thought you did not put much value in the legend."

She was right. Or rather, half right.

"I did not. But meeting the Outsider forced me to reconsider my beliefs. Yes, he is strange and his powers, even stranger. He is unlike anything we have ever encountered, and, if that accursed metal clinging to his body is any clue, he could prove to be one of the greatest threats to our existence we ever face. But he is also the only person who can single-handedly accomplish something that no one else has before."

Maude narrowed her eyes.

"I am committed to spending every waking moment of my life to hold the yokai together—a daunting, seemingly impossible task, with the Asukans encroaching everywhere. Not even the Desert's curse is enough to halt their greed," said Solana. "But those difficulties are *nothing* compared to the task that the Outsider can perform for us. *Has* been performing for us. He has the ability to make something true that I hadn't dared to dream about in all my centuries of existence."

"Which is what?"

A small smile formed on her lips this time. "Bringing Her, for starters."

Maude frowned. "I do not understand."

"I will have you swear a vow. A special one."

". . . What?" asked Maude, confused by the non sequitur.

"You asked me a question. I'll say this for now. My reasons for keeping the Outsider on our side are not on a mere whim. My assertion about the girl is not senseless. It is purposeful. If you want me to tell you what that purpose is, I'll need you to swear a vow to never reveal or break it."

Maude stared at her for a long time. Finally, she asked, "Why?"

Solana cocked her head.

"Why are you so willing to hand over this information? I know you, Leader. You have a reason for bringing me into this. What is it?"

Not for the first time, Solana hated how perceptive she was. "I shall need your aid in this . . . venture. Your utter and unequivocal support. Nothing less shall suffice."

"So," said Solana, standing as tall as she could in front of the oni. "Do we have an accord?"

CHAPTER 1

A DEADLY LEGACY

He was standing inside a massive, subterranean chamber. Surprisingly well lit, with glimmering crystals adorning the walls, inundating the room with an intense, dazzling green-white light. Hundreds of creatures, humanoid and bestial, physical and ethereal, all of them raising their voices and hooting as the prisoner in the center was dragged across the floor in chains. And on top of a raised pedestal, forming a throne of basalt, sat a regal woman with snow-white hair. Somehow, even from a hundred yards away, he could see the loveliness of her features clearly, too magnetic to ignore. She was a creature of coldness, turned to such rage that her beauty had become a knife that stabbed at the eyes of the beholder.

"The Supreme Queen cannot die," she said, her voice like a glacier. "But she can suffer."

And just like that, the spell was broken.

Instantly, Lukas knew who the prisoner was.

He tore his eyes away from the white-haired woman and looked at the prisoner, his feet moving of their own accord. Breathing hard and fast, Lukas made his way through the masses, yet none of them paid him any attention. Like he didn't even exist.

And then he saw it.

Saw *Her*.

Bound in chains, the metal entwined her waist, tearing into her flesh. They clawed at her back and held her upright while the collar around her neck constantly pulled it down. Several other pairs of chains pulled her ahead, forcing her to drag her bloodied feet across the cold stone floor.

"Ina—" Lukas tried, but words failed him. Instead, he just watched. The sheer surreality of it all threw a spark of comprehension into his mind.

This—this was a memory. Inanna's memory. Her fate at the hands of her sister . . .

Lukas whirled back and looked at the white-haired woman.

Ereshkigal.

Empress of the Dead.

"Welcome, Sister," Ereshkigal's voice boomed, "to the Seven Gates of the Underworld!"

As she spoke those words, the cavern changed, her will altering the matter inside her realm to reforge, not unlike how the Crypt had altered itself at the Guardian's will. Where there had been nothing but dreary darkness now stood seven gates. Seven archways.

He knew what this was.

He had read about it.

The Seven Gates of the Underworld. The barriers that drew the line between the living and the dead. Each gate held authority over one of the seven fundamental tenets of existence itself. Passing through them would mean an absolute suppression of each one.

At least, that was how Babylonian myths painted them.

"You, who have always taken, shall feel what it means to be deprived."

Lukas watched with unfolding horror as Inanna was dragged through the first gate. The Trap of Opulence, it was called. How he knew it, he didn't know. He just did. Everything that was her and hers would stay. Everything that was not, ceased to be hers. A large, golden axe materialized at her feet, unmoving.

The Axe of Marduk.

Her opal ring, the symbol of her victory over the Goddess of the Night, slid down her finger. Her necklace and her divine bracelets, slivers of Truth that once belonged to Gula, now dropped onto the floor.

Inanna did not react. She just trudged through.

"My husband was lost to your unabated lusts. Live an eternity bereft of them."

The Second Gate, the Trap of Passion, tore at her sacral knot. Once the Goddess of Desire, Inanna would no longer feel pleasure. Her body shriveled like a prune and her breasts sagged. Her cheeks wrinkled as every bit of her sensuality and charm faded away, leaving a twisted, ugly caricature of herself behind. One that would forever be unable to feel another's touch.

Every single bone in Lukas's body wanted to run after her, but he was rooted where he stood. He couldn't move, couldn't speak, couldn't do anything but watch.

Why? He did not know.

"Wars have followed your footsteps. Civilizations burned and lives torn apart, all for your pride. Forever lose your dominance and conviction."

The Trap of Self-Esteem revoked Inanna's authority as the Monarch of the Heavens. Her golden crown appeared in an earthen heap on the floor as she was flung through the Third Gate. No longer would she hold the title of queen.

"You who have commanded legions to bring forth destruction shall be cursed with eternal silence."

Her lips were sealed together, not allowing even the slightest murmur to escape as the chains dragged her through the Fourth Gate, the Trap of Expression.

"Your might rises with fear. Be isolated from all existence. Your throne, your relics, your temples, your worshippers. May your faith be entirely lost."

The Fifth Gate, the Trap of Connectivity, untethered the memories of her temples and the collective faith of her worshippers. Once aware of everything on Heaven and Earth, Inanna could no longer see past the archway that stood before her.

Isolated. That's what she had said. Inanna had always claimed the pendant as her abode. A relic, much like the axe. Did that mean that the real Inanna— the true Supreme Queen—was still trapped there, amidst the Seven Gates? But then, surely Inanna should have known that? Surely she'd know that the scrying spell would have failed . . .

"Queen. Conqueror. Plunderer. You who consider yourself above all else shall breed no thought. Live as a pebble would."

Inanna turned around, her dry, parched lips wanting to speak to her sister. Lukas wished she'd look at him. But she didn't. Instead, her eyes took on a glazed expression. Tears slowly ran down his cheeks, but not a word left his lips. The disoriented, nearly unconscious queen was dragged through the last gate.

The Trap of the Weeping Souls.

"Let the memories of the ruthless goddess fade away. Let her domain be buried in time. No longer shall you be one of us. I cast you . . . out!"

Inanna's body spasmed and she fell upon the cold stone floor, like a marionette whose strings had been severed. Naked and unmoving, she stared lifelessly ahead at her sister, a single tear trickling from her glassy eyes down her cheek.

I will find a way, Lukas vowed. *I will find a way. I will get you out. I swear . . .*

"Always remember, dear sister," Ereshkigal murmured fondly. "Whatever I do, I do for love."

She flicked her hand, and Inanna's limp body flew against the wall just as a rocky spike erupted from it, impaling her through the chest.

Straight through her heart.

"INAAAA—"

"—AAANNNA!" Lukas yelled, opening his eyes to the world of white that lay before him. His right hand was outstretched, trying in vain to grab something beyond his grasp. His throat felt parched, like someone had poured sand down it.

Next came the terror. The pain. The realization of what he had just witnessed. What had happened to Inanna. A cry arose from the deepest trenches of his heart, screaming out in defiance to save the goddess.

Then his vision came into focus and stabbed him in the eyes like a knife.

Lukas shut them and screamed. The pain was impossible. His chest was in agony. He tried to hold off breathing for as long as he could, but eventually, he couldn't put it off any longer, and again, fire spread across his chest. His skull hurt like it was being crushed by the arms of a metal crusher. *That*—what was it that he had seen? What were those lines?

Lukas winced.

Even the sheer memory made the pain return. For the next several moments, his entire reality was consumed by the simple struggle of trying to breathe and keep his eyes closed. And yet he could not forget that image that he had seen.

Lines.

Spanning in all directions—straight, curved, bent, twisted, drawn in every possible configuration. A meshwork of threads that spread across his entire line of vision. Like a kaleidoscope, the pattern of threads sprung out from objects, around their periphery, diverging and converging. Hundreds of them. Thousands of them.

Instinctively, he knew what they were.

They were trajectories.

Motion trajectories.

In its simplest form, motion was a result of push or pull. Then came magnitudes, directions, and angles. His eyes were showing him the motion trajectories associated with every single object within his range of vision.

And what he was seeing weren't just motion trajectories, but all possible motion trajectories. And the knowledge of those trajectories, associated with every single object within his range of vision, both in isolated and combined context, had flooded his mind the moment he had opened his eyes. Tachypsychia be damned, that much data would've fried a supercomputer's circuits. Lukas was lucky he only got off with five blood vessels rupturing.

His ears, eyes, and nose were wet. Sticky and wet. Whimpering, Lukas stayed like that, waiting for Prophylaxis to save his sorry ass.

I warn you, Mortal. This power is a deadly legacy. My personal belief is that it will destroy you.

"Shut up, Inanna!" he growled.

She wasn't there. She wouldn't return. All he had was the knowledge granted by the Inanna he had manifested back then. That specter—that reflection of a reflection—had thrashed around that monstrosity like it was nothing. It didn't matter if his opponents were using lifeforce or mana, fire or water, nor if they were physical or ethereal. If they moved, they used motion. And Kinetomancy ruled over all forms of motion. This was a power that could fight literal gods.

And it was a complete hindrance to Lukas, rendering him all but blind.

What to do? He couldn't just keep his eyes shut forever. He needed to shut this off. Somehow. After several nerve-wracking seconds of deep breathing, Lukas managed to finesse his brain into working again. His grandfather often said that one of the ways of tackling a difficult problem was to focus on everything *but* the problem. Focusing on the lines would get him nowhere. He needed to look somewhere else.

These trajectories weren't obstructing his vision, but adding to it. Like an extra function. Or a skill.

"STOP!" he screamed, willing the trajectories to vanish.

He gasped in elation as the Screen flickered before his mind. Unfortunately, the message did nothing to lift his spirits.

> **Host Body stuck in Skill Assimilation**

Which meant . . . what exactly?

> **Apex Skill Acquisition complete**
> **Apex Skill Assimilation in process**
> **Host Body found partially compatible**

That was all kinds of bad, he figured. Inanna had only used a tiny bit of her powers, just enough to kick the king's ass without destroying Lukas's body. But even that tiny bit was a bit too much for him.

It was too high-level. The omphalos had greedily grabbed it all, and now it was facing a different problem.

> **Apex Skill Assimilation in process**
> **Host Body under constant reconfiguration**

His body wasn't compatible. Simple as that.

If only it were as easy to explain that to the omphalos. Lostbelt's consciousness or not, it was like a machine. It had rules and protocols and followed them to the letter. It couldn't go against its own programming any more than Lukas could re-create Earth around him.

And currently, it was stuck reconfiguring his body, making it a perfect fit for Inanna's power.

At least now he knew what was wrong with him. His body was trying to adjust to whatever it had grabbed from Inanna, and these lines were a symptom. He just needed to identify what was causing it.

Show me my Soulscape.

SOULSCAPE	
NAME	Lukas Aguilar
Type	Prime Host
Level	21
Experience	4,163
Current Threshold	17,640
Utilized Soul Capacity	863,500/ ∞
ESSENCE	
Maximum Lifeforce Output	82,750
Replenishment Rate	4,600 / hour
LEY LINE NETWORK	
Maximum Mana Output	84,000
Synthesis Rate	4,710 / hour

So far, it was exactly how he had remembered it. That meant that the change would have to be in the next section.

SKILL ATTRIBUTES		
SKILL	LEVEL	CONSUMED SOUL CAP
Raw Lifeforce Manipulation	3	5,000
Kinetomancy (APEX)	4	850,000
Psychomancy	2	500
Shatterpoint Intuition	2	500

It took him a moment to register what he was seeing, and then a couple more to understand what it implied. The number—that impossible number flashing before him—was so massive, he had trouble comprehending it. He wasn't sure whether to be more distracted by the number four written on the Level column, the sheer size of the figure written beside it, or the conspicuous absence of several of his lifeforce skills.

As his brain rebooted from the shock, he noticed that Kinetomancy was an apex skill and thus was an aggregation of multiple skills, including the ones he had boasted. Now that the BROKEN suffix had been replaced by a neat "Level 4," and the previous number replaced by the six-digit figure sitting snugly beside it, it stood to reason that his other skills had been upgraded and combined together into Kinetomancy.

But still . . . Level 4.

Lukas checked it again.

Level 4.

He wasn't seeing things. Level-3 Momentum Manipulation had allowed him to curb stomp the bylestyr squad. Level 4 was exponentially greater than that. Even then, a Level-4 skill would've cost him fifty-thousand Soul Capacity.

Level-4 Kinetomancy? It cost seventeen times more than that. Whether that was because Kinetomancy was an amalgamation of seventeen Level-4 skills, all of them based on the principles of motion, was anybody's guess.

He could have done a little jig. Then he remembered that he was effectively blind and that sobered him up again.

"Can you . . ." he murmured in English, "can you give me an estimate of how long this . . . Skill Assimilation will take?"

Like always, the Screen was only too eager to respond.

Prime Host Augmentation attempted
Failed!
Host Body Synchronization incomplete
Level 39 required to achieve complete synchronization

Quick responses didn't always translate to good news. He had the skill, but he had a long way to go before that synchronization happened. And by the looks of it, it would be quite some time until he got there.

The threshold of every level kept increasing exponentially. He still remembered how he had crossed the Experience threshold of just forty units by smacking moss. Compared to that, he had required a staggering sixteen thousand units to cross from Level 20 to Level 21. By that logic, to move to Level 39, he'd require a total of . . .

645,960 Experience

"Right. Thank you."

Level 39? It would take him forever to get there, and that was if he were dropped into multiple borderlands in the foreseeable future. And if he had to go through that as a blind man, he might as well give up.

And it wasn't just lifeforce skills that were impacted by Kinetomancy. His mana skills were far from untouched. Where previously lay multiple clusters of skills segregated by elements, there was now a simpler, more cohesive list.

Fire Creation	3	5,000
Water Creation	2	500
Terraportation	2	500
Conjuration	2	500
Disintegration	2	500
Seismic Sensing	2	500

Any and all forms of Mana Manipulation were gone. Conjuration and Disintegration were Creation skills and thus stayed. Everything else had been assimilated under one singular apex skill, and until he was able to level up, his problems were there to stay.

"You done fucked up, Lukas Aguilar!" he said to himself.

But deciding to keep his eyes shut and actually keeping them shut were two different things. He didn't know where he was. His very last memory was tumbling his way into a familiar room, with a pair of equally familiar, jet-black eyes looking at him. He remembered drifting through that endless sea of mist and mana, and crashing into a hard table and seeing those eyes looking back at him with surprise and vindication. Eyes that could only belong to one individual.

No.

Lukas couldn't help himself. He quickly opened his eyes, and instantly afterwards snapped them shut, hissing in acute pain.

No, he told himself. This wouldn't do. There had to be some way. This wasn't the first time he had seen motion trajectories. Even Shatterpoint Intuition did something similar, showing him the most direct path for a strike. He was no stranger to using Kinetomancy either, pulling and pushing objects and prey towards him or away.

Maybe if he learned to ignore it or completely stop using Kinetomancy, and instead just limit his eyes to normal vision then . . .

Come on, Inanna. Help me out here.

Preparing himself, he slowly opened his eyes. The meshwork of pale white tendrils slowly receded to the background, like a watermark, leaving his vision mostly clear. It still hurt, and the way those lines shifted every time his gaze flickered was incredibly distracting, and if he tried to focus on anything, the lines instantly returned, and with it, the pain.

Still, it was better than being blind.

He found himself in a familiar, spartan room. Monster hide served as his bed cushion, with cold, hard rock beneath it. An earthen jug filled with water sat beside him. There was a door across from him, and bioluminescent moss was growing on the walls, offering a dreary green illumination.

He knew this place.

He had been here before, had walked this floor.

Lukas swallowed. His fears had come true. He was in yokai territory. Those eyes—it was *Solana*. He had crashed into Solana's office. And these were his old quarters. This was where he had stayed the last time.

His vision issues promptly forgotten, Lukas jumped up, looking around him with growing hysteria. He still had his shirts and pants on—tattered and charred but there nonetheless, a step up from going commando. The protective vest was still there as well, burned and complete with holes on both sides. His fractals, present. His pendant—that too, inert and cold like before. Blob was also there, acting as an undershirt.

He clenched his fists. Lifeforce surged through them. His fractals were working as well. Surrounded by rock on all sides, it was terrifyingly easy to churn earth mana. He was certain he could terraport his way out with ease. Yokai territory or not, he had options this time around. His fingers found the cold metal of the pendant, the lapis lazuli feeling just as cold as always. Completely devoid of energy. There was no sign to prove that whatever had happened was real and not a dream. Inanna had appeared, arising out of the shard of divinity within him, and helped him out of an impossible situation. Inanna—a specter of the real thing, at least—had faced that demon king, and ensured Lukas's escape, bolstering his skills in the process.

Inanna, who he had just dreamed about. Seen what she had suffered.

He'd find a way to bring her back. No matter the cost.

But first, he needed to find a way out of here. Had to save Tanya. Solana had openly claimed that she'd kill him if he sided with the Asukans. But she wouldn't kill Tanya. No. She'd make someone possess her and then use her as a bargaining chip to force him to agree to more deals.

No. Not again. He'd find Tanya and escape. If he was strong before, he was a monster now. Unless Solana was a Level 4 in disguise, he was reasonably certain he could fight her and whatever army she threw at him, and escape.

Escape? he thought. *Why? If a fight's what they want, then a fight is what they'll get. These yokai ambushed me and fucked with me before. And now they think they can hold Tanya as a hostage to get me to do whatever the fuck they want? I'll show those treacherous, bloody—*

And on and on it went for the next few seconds. Lukas was breathing hard and his lifeforce was already fueling his instincts with the need to defend against being possessed by an intruder. His body was already heating up, and the temperature around him was rising high.

He closed his eyes and fought the feeling. He had a lot of experience in bringing himself down from lifeforce highs. But there was a difference between then and now, especially since he had around two magnitudes more lifeforce rushing through his body, a level that was too great to be calmed down by mere breathing techniques. There was only one way that would possibly work— asserting his rational mind.

So he started counting prime numbers. And then multiples of sixteen, and seventeen, all the way up to twenty-five, and all the while trying to hammer ruthless logic against the primitive instincts flooding his system.

"One, I don't know where they're keeping Tanya. Two, they haven't attacked me. Preemptive offense will damage any chances of negotiation."

He breathed in and out.

"Three, I have no clue about the forces in this place. Four, Solana could always throw me back into the Haze if she catches me off guard."

The lifeforce within him spat and frothed as it slowed down, and the white curtain forming all over his vision was slowly turning to normal.

"Five, I don't actually know if they have her. Maybe she's lost in the Haze, and in that case, I'll need their help in finding her."

His temperature was dropping.

"Six, killing people without reason is wrong."

As his flaring instincts whimpered and died, Lukas huffed out a breath and opened his eyes. His Kinetomancy was fucked up, he was in yokai territory, and he was suffering from lifeforce highs. Seemed like the day just kept on giving. All he needed was for Solana to trap him into another bargain and it would be complete.

As if on cue, someone knocked at the door from outside.

Twice.

CHAPTER 2

FIRST CONTACT

There were two of them.

The first was a thirty-something blonde woman, with a starved face, gaunt eyes, and hollow cheeks. She dragged a trolley covered with a cloth sheet behind her, likely his meal. The other was a lithe young woman, with thin, ginger hair, brown eyes, and a rather plump pair of lips.

Instantly, the Screen displayed the results of its analysis.

BREMETAN
Bipedal, lifeforce-producing organisms. 99.9% similarity with the
HUMAN species
Soul Architecture damaged
Extreme signs of possession.

REIKI
Soul Architecture shows 100% similarity to REIKI from Monster
Prototype Array

The gaunt-looking woman was a Reiki possession, reminding him of that Reiki who used to bring him meals and had followed him into the Crypt. Mozi, was it? He considered the other.

ONI
Chimeric entity. Result of spiritual fusion of VANIR species with
YUREI species
Bipedal, lifeforce-producing organism. Capable of Metamancy.
98.6% similarity with the HUMAN species.
Mutated Soul Architecture.

Lukas blinked. A vanir? From Kvasir's treatise, he knew of them, but this was his first time encountering one. His hands instantly went down to his waist bag, only to find it missing. Had it been torn off of him during the fight?

That brought a frown to his face. His grandfather had instilled in him a healthy appreciation for taking care of his books. The most important things in life, the man used to say, were more than often, the most helpless. Hence, they needed to be treated with extreme care. He had no doubt that the treatise was a copy, but that didn't justify losing it. Zuken had entrusted him with it, and regardless of the author's ramblings, it contained a lot of valuable information.

"Searching for something?" asked the ginger.

Language Identified—Faecani
Replicating . . .

"Uh, yeah," he said, "I had a waist bag with a book in it."

"Ah, yes," the young woman replied. "Kvasir's treatise. A most unexpected gem. How did you acquire it?"

Lukas didn't reply. At least the book wasn't lost. Kvasir rambled too much about the Norse gods. No doubt this . . . vanir? . . . oni?—*whatever*—woman would find it interesting.

Hang on a second. Didn't Tanya say that one of her own team members was a vanir? One that had been—

He froze.

—possessed?

It took him a second to train his features into an impassive look. It took him another to realize just how indifferent he was to the entire thing. Bremetans enslaved kami to do their bidding. Yokai possessed bremetans to do theirs. It was an interesting inverse relationship shared between two races on two opposite extremes of the spectrum.

"Greetings, Outsider," the Reiki said in a familiar Felleisen accent. "Mizo be excited to see Outsider again."

Of course. He shouldn't have been surprised. The creature had taken a new body. Physical bodies were disposable, after all.

"Mizo," he said, effortlessly altering his language to pure Felleisen with just a thought, "Nice to see you, too. Solana put you on waiter duty again?"

Mizo let out a high-pitched, grating laugh, like the sound of chalk on slate. "Mizo be told to give food to Outsider. Mizo not be told to wait."

Lukas sighed. Why had he expected Mizo to know about waiters and restaurants? He turned to the other woman, the oni.

"Greetings," said the ginger, "I'm Maude. I believe that you and I share a few acquaintances."

So his hunch was right. This was the same vanir who had been part of Tanya's team in the anomaly.

"Yes," he said, keeping his voice level. "Where is she?"

"She?" Maude arched an eyebrow.

"Tanya," Lukas said. "Where is she?"

"She's currently . . . indisposed."

Lukas felt a cold chill in his stomach. "I want to see her."

"The Leader asked me to wait until you've eaten. After that, I'll take you to her. Maybe if she agrees, you can go see Tanya."

That rankled.

"I'm not sure if anyone told you this, Maude, but I'm not a fan of following orders."

"Leader said you'd say that. She also asked to remind you that this is an underground territory and she's an accomplished terramancer."

Lukas cocked his head. "I want to see Tanya, and I'm not asking."

Maude eyed him for a moment, before the uncertainty in her eyes altered with a gleam of devil-may-care defiance. It looked a lot more natural on her. "I liked you better when you were a paranoid survivor. Gaining strength has made you cocky."

Lukas arched an eyebrow. "Have we met before?"

"Before I became me, I was Malon. A yurei. Leader had charged the two of us to see you through your mission to the anomaly's core."

Malon and Mizo. The two guards who Solana had offered him as support. He hadn't accepted either, but Solana had sent them anyway to track his performance and report on his displays. Malon had possessed the vanir, forming the oni who was chatting him up now.

"Tanya mentioned your name, as did Olfric. Once, I think." He paused, waiting for a reaction. Finding none, he continued, "Though it looks like you're quite happy here after all."

Maude gave him an impish grin. "You could say that. It's quite a change from the Empire. The environment is a bit dreary, but it grows on you."

"And you're an oni now."

Her smile widened. "You can tell right off the bat, huh? Leader said you were an interesting one."

Lukas weighed his options. Despite his glaring handicap, he was reasonably certain he could outfight most people in here. But Solana was maintaining her veneer of hospitality. Knowing the witch, she wanted something and was playing the long game.

That was fine. He could play too.

"If any of you harm a hair on Tanya's head, I'll burn this place down."

"Mizo no likes Outsider's threats," the Reiki growled.

"Not a threat," said Lukas. "A promise. Solana wants to talk? Fine. I'll play ball, but if anything happens to Tanya, you will all have to find a new place to shack up."

Maude, or Malon, or whoever she was now, merely cocked her head, studying him. "Tanya is currently asleep. Her injuries required her to be sedated if I was to heal her."

"*Malon!*"

Maude ignored the sudden snap from her fellow worker and focused on Lukas. "Don't worry about her."

"I'll believe that when I see her."

"Suit yourself."

Lukas frowned. There was no way to determine if this woman was lying to him. But the yokai had so far been nothing but hospitable. Torturing Tanya wouldn't make things any better for them. No, if Solana wanted something, a healthy Tanya was a better ransom than a tortured one.

Maude gestured at the food trolley.

"You should eat. Leader wishes to meet with you. I'm supposed to show you the way."

"I know the way. I've been here before."

"Not since the latest renovation, you haven't," said the oni. "After you killed the Core, we took over the entire anomaly. Speaking of which . . . why is that *metal* on your person?"

She said the word "metal" like it was the vilest thing imaginable.

Lukas looked at Blob, still acting as an undershirt. The living aqāru slime, which contained within it all of the spiritual information that had belonged to the Crypt of Fiendish Worms, was a horrifically overpowered tool against spiritual predators. No wonder the oni didn't—

The rest of his thoughts died, as something else hit him.

Blob.

Fucking hell. He'd almost forgotten.

ROLLBACK PROTOCOL SUCCESSFUL!
Nexus established
Accessory confirmed
Reading data . . .

Ah, right. He had channeled the infinite energy from the Haze through Blob, enacting the Rollback Protocol over and over, dozens and dozens of times without care or concern. Which meant . . .

"That *metal*—" Maude barely suppressed a shudder. "—it is alive, isn't it? Just seeing it makes me want to . . ."

She looked like she was about to throw up. Given how casual and composed she had been, it was weird. The expression on her face was akin to a cornered cat surrounded by dogs.

Analysis complete. Rendering . . .	
NAME	**CRYPT OF FIENDISH WORMS**
TYPE	**HETEROMORPH**
CONSTITUENT	**AQĀRU**
Deciphering Spiritualist Constitution . . . Decoding . . . Rendering complete.	
Nature	Conglomerate
Number of Skills	16,159
Number of Monster Prototypes	5,387
Direct Access to Monster Prototypes hindered under Warmonger Protocol. Reconfiguring . . .	

Lukas suppressed a grin. He couldn't wait to see what this thing was now capable of.

"*Aguilar!*"

"Huh? Yes, it's alive. And it's mine. Keeps people from being too grabby." He paused and cocked his head. "Is that why I still have my clothes on this time?"

The expression on her face told him everything he needed to know.

"How do you have it? *Why* do you have it? More importantly, how is it possibly *alive*?"

"It's a souvenir," he replied, "from my battle with the Anomaly Guardian."

It was more than a souvenir. A lot more. Especially now.

Accessory active Configured access to Accessory Monster Prototypes through Accessory Heteromorph

Like a machine that had been switched on, Blob snapped awake, and hundreds upon thousands of prototypes flashed across Lukas's mind in less than a second, but somehow, he understood it all. Every single prototype—most of them crafted by the anomaly, others killed by the monsters and added to the soul crypt. And then there were some that it had scraped from the fossils hidden beneath the desert sands.

Fossils that belonged to creatures of a different time and age.

Prototypes that the Crypt had been unsuccessfully trying to reproduce.

And with them had come a wealth of information. The Crypt was a terrain-based anomaly. Access to Blob's reserves brought with it impossibly clear, precise knowledge about the composition of the terrain. What *was* the terrain? How was it created, molded, transformed? What was the soil? Sand? An indefinite number of ratios popped into his head, bringing exact specifications of organic matter, inorganic matter, and minerals. Granular, non-granular, thick, thin, flat, spheroid, light, dense—it had it all. Chemical compositions, structures, bonding, flexibility, viscosity, structural stability, chemical transformation of compounds—he had just gained the master key to the largest repository of knowledge on the Crypt, and it was all in Blob, ready to be used with a thought.

And he was only just getting started.

"Looks like more than a mere souvenir."

"Oh, yes," said Lukas. "I can teach it all kinds of tricks. Wanna see?"

Maude crossed her arms. "Only if it involves destroying it."

"Leader is waiting," Mizo said stubbornly. "Leader says Outsider goes to Leader's room after meal."

She lifted the lid off the food tray.

"I'll be waiting outside till you're done," Maude said, and walked off, trailed by Mizo, who gave him a deeply distrusting look.

Lukas smiled until the door was closed, but as soon as they were gone, he dropped it, as a look of cold, calculated pragmatism crossed his face.

He wasn't foolish enough to think he was safe. Solana had been very clear when he had left for the mission: she'd kill him if he joined up with the Asukan crowd. But she didn't know that his reach had progressed far beyond Asukans and yokai and their prejudices. Kvasir had rambled about the Time Before, but he had no way to prove his theories.

That wasn't true for Lukas. He had established a nexus with the Haze. No, not the Haze. The Ikai Realm. The Cradle of Creation. A world of mist and anomalous energy entwined around other worlds. A medium through which he could travel to *any* of those worlds he had sensed.

Inanna was right. He had been thinking like an individual all this time. He had to start thinking like a *world*.

He needed answers.

Answers to questions such as how he had gotten here in the first place. Was it because of Blob? No. That couldn't be. Blob's reconfiguration notwithstanding, there was absolutely no reason for him to arrive in the anomaly. The only thing remotely connected to the Haze was . . .

Solana.

Or more specifically, the portal she had opened in the Haze the last time he had been here.

No, wait. That wasn't it.

She hadn't *opened* a portal. She had just . . . walked right in. Theoretically, that meant that the room was either part of the Haze or connected to it. A fantastical and outlandish possibility, but perhaps the Haze was always connected to the real world, but it took an ethereal creature to cross the borders?

Also, did that mean Solana could enter the Haze from virtually any place? Or was it limited to locations satisfying particular conditions, like there were in the Desert, where there was no Eternal Light?

Lukas wanted to believe it was the latter. Solana was scary enough as it was.

His fingers caressed the pendant again. Finally, after all this time, he had found an answer. A way forward. He could fight, kill, and siphon monsters all he wanted, but in this world of bremetans and yokai, there was only one thing that held absolute importance to him, aside from Tanya.

Lukas allowed himself to breathe slowly.

The Haze.

Yokai might be able to travel through it, but only an omphalos could connect to its awareness. He had done something similar with the Crypt of Fiendish Worms at one point, and it had shown him a path to power even back then.

He had achieved a nexus with the Haze.

Become part of its system.

If he could do that again, he'd have access to its entire structure. Its architectural framework. The paths. The routes. If every well connected to the Haze, and the Haze was all-pervading then . . .

That would give him the ability to travel across realms without concern for geography. Unlike the yokai, he wouldn't have to fear the Eternal Light or try traveling across the ocean by known routes. He'd have the entire map in his head. With it, he could disregard all laws with utter impunity and avoid retribution from the Empire and the yokai alike. He could go *anywhere*. Escape from damned near *anything*. Gather information like no one could.

It was exactly the sort of thing he needed. New worlds would mean new creatures, new skills, and new information. He could have quick, easy access to stronger, superior creatures to kill and siphon. He'd become stronger, more flexible, and level up faster. Not only that, he could guarantee Tanya's absolute safety from the Empire. He'd have absolutely no need for Zuken, Olfric, or any of the home crowd.

Not too long ago, he had fought tooth and nail to avoid the temptation of power and done his best to deny becoming Inanna's henchman. And now, he was succumbing to it, and it wasn't just to get Inanna back, no matter what he told himself.

Lukas looked at the food tray. A cup of juice, a small plate of roasted meat and something that looked like a pancake sprinkled with veggies. He sat back down, came to a decision, and ate the food thoughtfully.

CHAPTER 3

MAUDE

The last time he had been there, the yokai territory had reminded him of a mining colony—large patches of dense population, segregated by wide spaces of sparsely populated acreage. Now it was a vast underground complex, spanning over several dozen acres, for all he knew. Observing closely, he could see signs of the war. They were subtle, but if one paid attention, they were everywhere: extravagant outgrowths of shapes and sizes that made no sense; broken sigil lines, caused by the erection of new walls to replace the old; fractures along the older architecture; and so on.

Word had spread amongst the inhabitants about the return of the fabled Outsider, but everyone gave him a wide berth. Only Mizo and Maude could get up close, but even they maintained a professional distance.

Blob was the likely culprit.

The aqāru slime had transformed in more ways than one. During all the time he had known Blob, it had seemed content to stay in whatever form he wanted it to be. When left alone, it would turn into a large droplet with a sizable tongue rolling out of it, licking whatever came within its vicinity. It didn't react to anything unless Lukas did, constantly attuned to his thoughts.

Now? It hung on his shoulder, currently transformed into a multitude of fang-worms. The yokai territory wasn't the only thing that triggered old memories. He still remembered those days—going to sleep with his back against the wall and waking up to find himself covered with acid-secreting slime.

It was against one such fang-worm that he had used lifeforce for the first time.

Blob was imitating them, its body now a formless ghol, draping all over Lukas's back while several protrusions—fang-worms—peered around and made weird, clicking noises. Occasionally they'd snap at his guards who'd jump several feet away out of sheer reflex.

Not the best setting for a conversation. Not that that stopped Maude.

"I've been wondering, what are your impressions of Zuken and the others?"

Maude, he had realized, had a habit of asking relevant questions casually while expertly batting away any questions about herself, as if there was absolutely nothing worth mentioning. She was good. Very good. But Lukas hadn't gotten to where he had in life by playing fair.

"You tell me," he said. "You've known them longer than I have."

"I just wanted to know your thoughts," she shrugged, as if utterly apathetic to the subject.

Lukas would've called her out for her ruse, but he knew better. It didn't matter what they talked about; there was always this thin air of indifference in her tone, as if any given conversation was little more than a distraction to her. She had this knack for sounding genuinely interested whenever she approached a topic, only for it to fade into laconic indifference the moment after she asked a question about it. It was like talking to two different people in the same body, constantly switching at random.

"Zuken's . . . not your standard Asukan. He's driven. By *what*, I don't know, but there are few things he wouldn't violate to get whatever it is. Not very fond of violence, but he doesn't shy from it, either. He's the sort I can respect."

"And does he?" she asked. "Have your respect?"

"We know what the other is angling for. Live and let live and all that."

"Those fractals you wear," Maude pointed out. "They cost a bloody fortune. Zuken must have genuine faith in your skills to have gotten you those."

"He and I understand each other to a degree, yes. He helps me in my research, I help him in his."

"Research," repeated Maude, as if tasting the word.

"Research," Lukas confirmed. "Not everyone is interested in possessing others and destroying anomalies."

The moment he said that, he realized the stupidity of his accusations. Like Solana, Zuken had hired Tanya to destroy the anomaly core. From Maude's smirk, he knew she had arrived at a similar conclusion.

"And what *are* you interested in?"

"Oh, you know, a bit of this, a bit of that."

"Is that why you were holding Kvasir's treatise, Outsider? You were studying the history of the world and the old religions?" Maude asked, proving once again that beneath her affable persona lay a sharp mind. "Perhaps you might find the Leader more useful for your *research*? She is, after all, a creature older than any Asukan alive."

Lukas took note of the fact. He knew that Asukans tended to have a life span similar to humans, with only a few of them crossing their 150th birthday. The problem with lifeforce was that, while it enabled the body to go beyond the ordinary, it also accelerated their growth. It was why Tanya, despite being merely twenty-two at best, had the body of a woman in her early thirties, and why the Overseer of the Llaisy Kingdom, a man who had just celebrated his 176th birthday, looked as fit as a fiddle.

Even Lukas himself had changed significantly over the past several months that he had spent in this world, dousing himself in increasing quantities of lifeforce. If not for Prophylaxis and his nature as an anomaly, he was pretty sure he wouldn't last his first century.

"Just how ancient is she?"

"To my knowledge, she's been around over the last six hundred years."

He whistled. "That long, huh?"

"You would know if you stopped being confrontational."

"Can't be helped. Solana's more interested in threatening me into working for her. She always wants something. That's why I'm walking with you and not already exhumed in pieces."

"I cannot speak for Leader," Maude said. "But tell me, has Olfric gotten himself a new kami yet?"

Maude—or Malon, as Mizo kept calling her—used to be Tanya's teammate. A vanir by heritage, she had actively worked for the Empire, and used her powers at healing (Naturopathy, to be precise) to heal many a noble during her years of service to the Empire. After her possession, she had changed sides to work for Solana, and here she was, asking about Zuken and the crew with the same air as old schoolmates meeting at a bar after a decade, inquiring about their old school gang.

"He hasn't," Lukas said. "You could always ask Tanya about them. I'm sure she'd be glad to trade stories with her friend-turned-enemy."

Maude threw her head back and laughed. "Me and Tanya? Friends? You tell me. Is she *friends* with Zuken? With Elena? Olfric, perhaps?"

Maybe he was reading too much into it, but he could swear Mizo froze slightly at Olfric's name. The next second, she was walking ahead as usual.

Lukas paused at that. Tanya had always reminded him of a wild animal trapped in a cage. A predator that was forced to act benign while its prey watched and hooted from outside. He doubted if Zuken had the slightest idea just how volatile a person he was dealing with. If Tanya lost it, Zuken and his bloody mansion would turn to dust before he even had the chance to say "Sorry."

His face must have revealed his thoughts, for Maude just smirked and said, "I thought as much. And yet . . . you care for her deeply."

"And what of it?"

"Nothing. It's interesting. That's all."

The three turned past one corridor, and phased into a wall, only to emerge in a different corridor. Before he could even register what had happened, he had already lost the path behind them.

"Tell me something," he said, "Yokai are ethereal creatures. Unlike kami, you don't need to possess others to grow. But then, why do you do it? All these buildings, it's like you've built an underground town here. Why possess bremetans and live like them instead of . . ."

"Getting to go as Mizo?" asked the Reiki.

Lukas blinked.

"Spirits cannot enter the lands of Eternal Light," Maude translated. "Not without completely weakening ourselves. But while possessing someone, we can. The effect is much less."

Which meant that the yokai traveled into Asukan territories a lot more than the Asukans believed. And if they had been doing that for hundreds of years, just how much influence did they have over the Empire without them knowing? Was that how they knew where he had been staying all this time? Had Solana been keeping track of him from the very beginning?

"Can I ask you something for a change?" Lukas asked. "It's a bit personal."

"Of course."

"I didn't use that as a rhetorical question. I mean, I'd like you to answer, but if you'd keep it to yourself, that's okay, too."

Maude paused and looked back. "Why wouldn't I want to answer your questions?"

"Because you're *very* good at talking about things that don't matter. Every single time I've asked about Tanya or oni, you've deflected it."

Maude just walked on, making no effort to answer.

"I might not have known these people for long, but they aren't like the typical Asukans that Solana told me about." Maude slipped him a curious glance as he continued. "Okay, maybe Olfric is, but even that guy seems to have his heart in the right place. When you grow up with certain prejudices, you see the world through tinted lenses. You're a vanir. Tanya's a vagrant. A Sinner. Elena's a changeling. Olfric's family has denounced him. These people—they're flawed, but they aren't evil. So why . . .?"

"Why what?"

Lukas smiled. "Why are you here? You can't tell me that your friends, associates, whatever you wish to call them, looked down on you because you are, or perhaps, *were,* a vanir?"

The oni went still for a moment, and then she exhaled. Out loud.

"I could tell you it's because I'm an oni now, but I'd be lying. Eternal Light doesn't affect me the way it does the yokai. Living in Haviskali beats living in this cavern, of course, but at least I have something that's been denied me all my life."

"Which is?"

"Freedom."

There was a moment of stillness.

"I am—*was* a vanir. A devotee of the god Eir. In His Name, I healed countless Asukan lives. But look around. Do you see Eir anywhere? Temples? Pillars? Perhaps an inscription? The Empire torments everyone and forces them to follow *their* truth. Accept *their* history. Worship *their* gods. Surely you understand what that feels like? To have to follow a god not your own?"

What Maude was describing was not very different from the events on Earth. One of the most efficient ways for an invading army to destroy a nation was to destroy its culture and traditions. Demean their gods. Destroy their books. Transmogrify their rich past underneath layers of blood and fallen bodies, and construct grand architectural monuments, glorifying themselves. The Roman Church Crusades, the Viking Invasions, Cortez's invasion of the Aztecs, and the Turkish-Mongolian invasions to the Indian subcontinent—all of them were the same. Tear a rich civilization apart and then rebuild it in your image. The Asukan Empire had done no differently. The Nordic civilization, of which Kvasir was a part, had shared the same fate. Especially after the fall of the Aesir during Ragnarok.

"Understand this—" Maude whispered, "—the yokai are not on *my* side. I choose to be on *theirs*."

"Is that why Solana sent you to me?" Lukas asked quietly. "To see if I had anything against her or the yokai? Did Zuken Banksi put you up to something similar in Tanya's case?"

The pleasant mask faded from her face, replaced by a wary neutrality. She switched her hands, moving the bottom one to the top, carefully, as if she worried about wrinkling her dress.

Tanya had been quite vocal about her experiences on the Crypt mission and how she worked for Banksi. She had always maintained that there was something *fake* about Maude. The vanir had used her past as a vagrant to try bonding with her, and now she was openly chatting—at times, even flirting—with him to lull him into a false sense of security. Which was, of course, why Solana had chosen her to tempt him.

Maude was a *lure*.

One used by Banksi to bait Tanya.

And now by Solana against him.

"Alright," he said. "Uncomfortable silences are uncomfortable. Here's something easier. What do you think of Solana?"

"Is that a serious question?"

Lukas gave her a polite nod. "I told you. It's up to you to choose to answer or not. But if you do, I'd hope for an honest answer."

He gave her a faint smile.

"The yokai want to regain what they've lost," she said, "but not all of them want the same thing. A thousand-year-old grudge doesn't stay neat and clean. There are those that would be content with more freedom. To not have to suffer the Eternal Light. Relics of the yokai gods were confined in Asukan treasuries. They'd like to have them back. Have the right to worship the deities they draw power from. The Asukans preach about their own holiness, about how we, the yokai, are the dark and the profane. These people, they'd like to exist beyond being demonic caricatures. They need to possess bremetans just to walk out of these caves. Not because they want to, but because they *have* to. They would just be happy to be accepted as a race, just as the bremetan are. They do not wish to become on par with the Asukans, but even a small region, just a small territory, away from the Eternal Light, would go a long way toward keeping them content."

"And *everyone* wants that?"

Maude bit her lip. "Not *everyone*, but a significant number. And then you have the extremist factions. Those that carry the grudge and will not be content without seeing Amaterasu choke on her own blood. The ones that want to wreak carnage and devastation and make the streets of the Land of Eternal Light run red with Asukan blood. The ones that live and breathe for the Night of the Hundred Demons to arrive."

"Omega-tacky."

"Oumagatoki."

"Yes, that," Lukas said. "And Solana?"

Her eyelids sagged. "Solana represents a balance. A very delicate one that hinges slightly on the extremist side. She's one of the oldest yokai in this territory and knows far more than she lets on. If she got what she wanted, she would not hesitate to lie, cheat, and kill if that's what she thinks is necessary. She's perhaps one of the wickedest beings I've ever seen. A terrifying, stone-cold bitch."

"But?" Lukas asked.

"But . . ." Maude sighed. "But she's *ours*. Without her, the yokai would have burned themselves out. She holds the factions together with an iron grip and ensures that the extremists don't get out of the line, often in unique ways."

His brows knitted. "Like?"

"I'm told that you fought off a kasha during your stay earlier."

"Quonnan." The name left his lips faster than he had finished thinking about it. The vicious creature had tried to possess him after burning her possessed form to cinders, only to be siphoned by his omphalos.

"She was an extremist. One who was causing unrest. I'm told you made her incinerate her own body and it consumed her." She regarded him intensely. "Makes me wonder if you consumed Olfric's kami in the anomaly, too."

Huh. Were his skills an open secret among the yokai?

"I did." There was no point in hiding it.

"Interesting. You aren't even trying to hide it."

"Would it have helped?"

Maude snorted. "Your reaction gave it away."

He jerked his head to one side. "There you have it."

Maude gave him a thorough once-over. "Something about you is different. Malon's memories paint a survivor, like a feral cat trying to survive amidst a dangerous world. But you . . . you are something else. We expected you to put up a fight, but here you are, stalking around. You honestly don't believe you're in any danger, do you?"

For the first time, Lukas truly smiled. Maude was right. Defeating the anomaly had set him on a path to power, and Inanna's tutelage had sped up his growth by several magnitudes. But it was his time spent at the lava ridge that had been truly enlightening. He had faced beasts he could out-fight blind-folded: beasts that matched him in single combat, and beasts that had made him feel hopelessly outgunned. And then there was that king.

Compared to that, everything here felt . . . pedestrian.

But he wasn't facing the king, was he? Even without Kinetomancy, he could match any combatant of Level 3 or higher and give them a hell of a fight. Blob alone was an overpowered weapon, without considering its newer possibilities, and if he added Shatterpoint Intuition to it, he could very well butcher his way through this crowd. Add in the dranzithl's unlimited regeneration, the svar-talfar techniques of Terramancy and Terraportation, and of course, the massive, four-armed bylestyr's flames and superior strength.

And that was without bringing his other skills, and whatever havoc he could cause with his elevated, if unstable, Kinetomancy. Hell, just his Alpha Condition and Soul Siphon were a major deterrent against the yokai.

So yes, he was stalking. Gone was the survivor, and in his place was a god-damned *hunter*. The sort of person who, once focused on a target, would learn and use every minute fact there was to bend the odds in his favor and execute his prey with the least amount of effort possible. The kind that was armed with probably one of the largest repositories of skills imaginable at the ready.

Did mankind not crawl its way to the top of the food chain with those exact methods? By wielding information and tools to overcome their adversities, be they beast or nature? Before scientists, armies, and even farmers, wasn't the first role that exemplified these innovative traits the hunter?

Solana and her ilk were soon going to find that out firsthand.

"No."

"No?"

"No. I don't believe I am in any danger here."

Maude inclined her head. "Why?"

"Because I am not what I once was."

If Solana thought that holding Tanya captive and giving him the yokai five-star treatment was enough to convince him to play ball, she had another think coming. Lifting his chin, Lukas let his hands dangle disarmingly.

"The way I see it, I've accomplished my task by killing the anomaly, but Solana has yet to keep her word. She promised me a kami of my choice. Granted, I was taken away by Tanya and her team, so Solana gets the benefit of the doubt. For now. But I'm no longer the stumbling Outsider. I *know* things. Whatever she wishes to talk to me about, I'll listen. But if she tries to force anything, she'll have to accept the consequences."

Maude stared at him for several seconds. "You have a very high opinion of yourself. You realize where you're standing, don't you?"

"Yeah," Lukas said. "At the site of impact."

More silence stretched, and she blinked again. "Impact . . ."

"I was going to say 'Two feet from where they'll find your body,' but yokai are ethereal. If Solana, you, or the rest of the yokai, try anything funny, you'll have to start looking for a different place to rebuild your home, because I'd be demolishing this one to dust. Hence, site of impact."

"You realize she can hear you, right?"

"Obviously."

"Any particular reason for being so . . . aggressive?"

Lukas smiled. Solana was at her scariest when she was being civil.

"Guess you'll find out."

CHAPTER 4

THE KEY

The office, like most of the yokai territory, had undergone structural changes. Gone was the spartan feel, replaced by a sense of splendor. Mats on the floor. Suits of enchanted armor. Staff in formal uniform. Stone statues. Files and envelopes each had their own specific positions on the desk, the worktable against one wall. Paperwork might have threatened to overtake the room had order not been so strongly imposed, guided by an obvious will.

It told him that even with the actual presence of gods and demons, paperwork was an evil that ravaged every world out there.

Solana, the de facto ruler of the yokai, sat behind the desk. The dog corpse had been moved to the ceiling, serving as a twisted caricature of a chandelier, its dead eyes emanating an eerie greenish glow. Solana wore a business suit, not unlike the ones Zuken wore, albeit less aristocratic and cut close to the flawless lines of her body, the black color matching her hair and providing a stark contrast to her otherwise pale features.

"Outsider," she murmured, her voice soothing and musical. "It's been a while."

He heard Maude step back and leave the room, the doors closing behind her. There was a single empty chair, with Solana watching him from the other side of the table. The ambience suggested a private one-on-one meeting, but the eleven invisible yokai that registered within his Scan radius told him better. Whether they were always present or the yokai leader was simply exercising prudence was difficult to tell.

Or perhaps, it wasn't about him at all.

Maybe it was about Blob.

"I see. I'm being intimidated," said Lukas. "Are you going to tell me why, or do I get three guesses?"

A wicked little smile played over Solana's lips without getting as far as her eyes. "Intimidated? Why would you think that?"

"Oh, it's not?" Lukas asked. "Then perhaps the eleven guards are for your own security from big, bad me?"

The smile remained in place. "You can sense them. You weren't able to do that last time."

"There's a saying back in my world. 'I read, I travel, I become.'"

"That you have. Hanging around Asukans in Haviskali, cutting deals with svartalfars, plundering borderlands . . ."

She trailed off at that.

"Guy's gotta eat. The Asukans don't believe in giving out free food. You look pretty comfy. Won a lottery or something?"

"Lottery?"

"Eh . . . it's when you win a lot of money."

Her lips curled into a hungry little smile. "That I did, Outsider. And you have my gratitude. I'm not sure what or how, but you killed the anomaly. Without its Guardian and its power, its monsters perished, leaving its vast network of tunnels for our use. The leftovers of the Cyffnar battalions in the Desert were just as useful. Everything else was just . . . *requisitioned*."

Lukas arched an eyebrow.

"I have an army to maintain, and we have limited resources. Naturally, it's up to my forces to employ suitable methods to appropriate funds from outside."

Translation: they plundered Asukan territories and robbed whatever they could get their hands on. Was that why they possessed so many bremetans? The more he thought about it, the more they felt like a disease, infecting the bremetan civilization despite the Eternal Light protecting them.

He looked at her neutrally. "Enough with your games. Let Tanya out."

"And if I don't?"

"Then you accept whatever follows."

"Is that a threat?"

"No," he sighed wearily. "Just a fact. Look, I get it. You want me on your side. Because of your legend or prophecy or whatever."

Solana tilted her head. "I believe we understood each other perfectly where we stood before you left for your mission. You do what I want, and in return, you get your remuneration."

"I did what you asked. I've yet to get my payment."

Solana looked at him, her face set in a small, grim frown, thoughts indecipherable, before giving a curt nod.

"You say that you completed the task allotted to you. Perhaps you speak truly. But to say that I refused you remuneration . . . Lukas Aguilar, it was not I who escaped with Asukan adventurers."

Technically, he did not escape. One couldn't do that if one was dead.

"I was wounded in the fight with the Guardian. Zuken and his crew took me to Haviskali. I was comatose for over a month before I regained my senses."

Solana kept watching him, her face so stoic that he had no idea what she was thinking.

"So, it isn't a case of betrayal, but an issue of unforeseen circumstances?" she murmured. "Fine. I'll open a borderland for you. Tell me, what form of kami do you seek?"

Another kami? Just some months ago, he'd have been exhilarated at the idea. A kami represented a new potential skill. But now, after everything he had been through, after all that he had gained, gaining yet another kami felt like an afterthought.

Especially after he had been in the presence of a king.

She paused for a moment. "On second thought, you probably find it less valuable, now that you've already traveled to a borderland. Tell me, Outsider, just how *did* you open a rift from the other side?"

Lukas tried his best to move as little as possible. If Solana thought he had found a well and broke it open through raw power, it was best to let her believe that. The less she knew about his powers, the better.

When he said nothing, the yokai leader let out an exaggerated sigh. "The path of silence, then. I suppose I cannot fault you for trying to hide your abilities. Tell me, which kami do you have your eyes set on?"

"I don't want a kami anymore."

"Oh?" Solana tilted her head slightly. "I know you're capable of *both* Pyromancy and Metamancy. I'm reliably informed that you absorbed a certain marid with the power to manipulate water." She frowned. "Though I have not received any reports of you using it. I'd thought you'd want to complete the set with air and earth."

He knew what she was doing. This wasn't about the elements or gaining a new kami. She knew what he had been up to, and this was her way of letting him know that.

A power play.

"You thought wrong."

"Oh? Then what is it that you want?"

"To leave."

"Leave?"

Lukas grimaced. "I didn't come here to be your savior or whatever, Solana. I've got my own problems. Problems that have nothing to do with you."

"And you're absolutely certain about that?" she asked lightly. "You may find that working with us fits your agenda a lot more than you think."

That made him hesitate. As Maude had put it, Solana was at least six hundred years old. Someone like that had a lot more information at her fingertips than Zuken Banksi ever would. And Solana had proven that she knew about his deeds in Haviskali. Maude also knew about the treatise, so they might have a faint idea of what he was looking for.

Lukas exhaled. He had enough of her cryptic statements and obscure hints. He ignored his latest statement and cut straight to the heart of the conversation.

"Yes."

"I see," said Solana thoughtfully. "In that case, you can go."

Lukas stared at her for a long second.

"You . . . uh . . . *what?*"

"Must I repeat myself?" Solana asked, sounding strangely weary. "You are a wild card, Lukas Aguilar. One too unstable to our long-term plans. And as I have told you earlier, I have no use for an unwilling candidate. If I do not have your loyalty, then there is no point in having you. So yes, you may go."

"No strings attached?"

"No strings attached," she confirmed. "Free as a wind spirit. But beware, should you not keep your word and join forces with the Asukans . . ."

"You'll be my worst nightmare, or some other cliche. Gotcha."

He stood up, and turned around, ready to leave.

"Though I wonder . . ." Solana suddenly mused out loud, ". . . will your decision to remain unattached stay the same when your *friend* gets in the middle of the upcoming conflict?"

"What do you mean?" Lukas asked, still looking away from her, his body tensing. He should have known. There was always a catch. Always.

She laughed. It was a cruel thing. "Tell me, Aguilar. Do you know who your friend is?"

"Tanya—"

"I mean, who she *really* is?"

Lukas resisted every urge to turn and sit back down.

"Tanya Shimizu," said Solana. "Heiress of the Shimizu Clan. Great-granddaughter of the Wind King and current custodian of his king-class kami, the Spirit of the Storm, Ezzeron."

Lukas stayed quiet.

"How interesting . . ." said Solana, "I didn't think she'd trust anyone to reveal her darkest secrets."

"People can surprise you."

"Indeed they can," said Solana, standing up from her chair. "Shimizu Heiress, Wind King's descendant, Ezzeron's bearer—all of those titles are significant by themselves. But for us, she has only *one* name."

She smiled at him. "*Yuki-onna,* she who devours lifeforce."

And like a bucket of water, the truth washed over him. Solana *knew.* She knew of Tanya's Everfrost. No doubt from Mizo and Malon spying on her.

On *them*. She knew of his deals with the svartalfars and his ventures into the borderland. It all fit. Solana had more eyes and ears in the Empire than she gave the impression of having. But it was really the last description that made things fall into place.

Yuki-Onna.

A term belonging to Japanese myth that meant "snow-woman." A spirit of ice and snow, haunting unsuspecting people, devouring them of their lives.

Or rather, their *lifeforce.*

Wasn't that exactly what her Frost did? Ice that devoured life? It explained so much. Her ability with Frost without a kami, much like Solana employed Terramancy by herself. Her predatory self, brought under control only through Inanna's intervention. Hell, even the Screen had originally listed her as an "unknown" species rather than just bremetan, which Lukas had mistakenly thought to mean a hybrid, like Elena.

There's something about the Fog . . . It beckons me. Makes me feel . . . less taut. Unrestrained.

The Fog. A diluted form of the Haze seeping into the real world. The medium that yokai used to travel from one point to another.

His thoughts went back to their first fight. When he had pierced through her heart with a suicidal strike, only for the Frost to grow all over her form, healing her, knitting her wounds, restoring her strength. And then there was one other thing.

Give up. Become mine. I will devour your soul and digest that potential brimming within you. All your pain will end. Just. Give. In. To. Me."

Yuki-Onna. Snow-Woman. Frost incarnate. Devourer of lifeforce.

"Ah." said Solana. "Dawn."

His eyes snapped at her. "Are you telling me she's a yokai?"

"You tell me," she retorted. "Is she?"

Lukas shook his head. "No. She lives under the Eternal Light. What is she? An oni? Like Maude?"

"That," Solana said, her lips twisting to form a smile, "is something I wish to find out."

He took a slow, deep breath, and narrowed his eyes on her. "What are you playing at, Solana?"

"Absolutely nothing," she said, amusement shining on her features. "You asked for a way out. I gave you one. So long as we understand each other, and you don't join the opposite side in the conflict, you are free to leave. Right now if you want."

"Fine. And I will. Just let Tanya go."

"Uh uh!" She wagged a finger. "That I can't do."

"Why? If she's really an oni, then—"

"How did she become one? Who did she merge with? Why does she stay under the Eternal Light? What is the source of her power? How is she—oni or not—able to bond with a king-class kami in a fashion that would make even the purest of Asukan blood green with envy? I want answers, Aguilar, and your friend will give them to me."

Well, Lukas thought, *can't argue with that.*

At the same time, he knew that Solana was hiding something substantial. It was just too easy. Sure, she had Tanya captured, but she'd have to know that he'd fight for her. Solana also knew enough about Tanya to know her current thoughts about the Asukan regime, and how to use her for her own ends. But still, did that justify her letting him leave? He wasn't stupid enough to buy her talk about unwilling participants. If Solana couldn't use him, then she was more likely to end him rather than hand him over or allow him to go free. She wouldn't have given him the hospitality nor let Maude lead the initial meet-and-greet. No. He was the Outsider, the candidate most likely to fit the prophecy that would ensure—

Lukas nearly choked as it hit him.

That won a brief but genuine smile from her.

"You . . ." His voice trembled, "You think *Tanya* is an alternate candidate for the prophecy?"

Her dark eyes glittered. "You figured that out already? Impressive."

Lukas gritted his teeth. "Answer the question."

Solana shrugged. "Do you not? Do you remember what I said about the legend? About the three portents that would identify the Key?"

He nodded. "*Neither Asukan nor yokai but hold power over both.* Tanya is not yokai, because she has a physical form. Not Asukan, because she's a yuki-onna. Her Frost devours lifeforce, making her a predator of Asukans. Her ability to walk amidst the Eternal Light and entrap a kami as strong as Ezzeron shows her dominance over yokai."

"Couldn't have phrased it better myself," said Solana. "*The Key would unleash the power that would cause Oumagatoki, the Night of a Hundred Demons.*" She inched closer towards the table. "Who better than someone that hunts in the Fog itself? And finally, the third—"

"The power to end the world." Lukas said. "What does that have anything to do with—"

He froze, as Inanna's words came to mind:

A power that belongs to the ancient world. A fundamental force of this universe. If left alone, the things it could unleash would be . . . unsettling.

Was she talking about Oumagatoki? Or—

His mind was going into overdrive. Memories of his many talks with Tanya rose to the front of his mind. Things she had said casually but now with a deeper meaning than he had fathomed back then. *My Frost . . . it's useful against an anomaly core.*

And what was an anomaly core but raw potential? And if it could destroy an anomaly core—or, more specifically, an omphalos—could it also destroy a world? It was a creature that was, by all rights, a predator with him as its the prey. Was that why Inanna wanted her so badly? In order to have a world-destroying power under her thumb? Because she wanted to remove the one serious threat to her Host shackled to her side?

Just how much did you know back then, Inanna? Lukas thought. *And if you knew all that, what else did you know?*

He grasped the edges of the table and stared down at her.

"Let us say, that even by some weird chance, you're right—"

"I am."

"Not the point." Lukas gritted his teeth. "*Say* you are right. But so what? Those three portents, you said they fit me. And now you say they fit Tanya. Maybe two weeks later, you'll find a third candidate for this legend. What does that prove?"

"For you, nothing. For us, everything. I will not be arrogant enough to claim that I'm completely sure of her being the Key, but she ranks higher on the list of possibilities. As, I believe, do you. And she is important to you. Can you really leave her alone?"

She smiled again, and it was a dark thing.

Solana might not have known it, but she had him. She probably thought he was attracted to her, an idea not without its merits, but that wasn't the full picture. Inanna had invested way too much into Tanya for him to just leave her be. And her Frost avatar was a *genuine* threat to his nature as an anomaly. If Solana thought Tanya was the Key, then she'd do her utmost to keep her under her thumb, a fact only made too easy by Tanya's experiences in the Empire.

Especially if she was an oni.

Hiding in plain sight.

One would think that after all the shocks he had suffered over the last several minutes, Lukas would be somewhat used to Solana's curveballs by now or, at the very least, numb to it all. But no, this latest revelation hit him just as hard as the rest of them had, and he felt his thoughts screeching to a halt as his mind tried to cope with what he had just heard.

He regarded her seriously for a moment, frowning, thinking. "Just what is this yuki-onna business anyway?"

Dark eyes turned to him as Solana relaxed into her chair. "Nothing you need to be concerned about. I will say this once, Aguilar. If you want to leave, then walk away. Right now. Forget you knew anyone called Tanya. Walk away from us, from the Asukans, and from the upcoming conflict. I assure you, no yokai under my command shall come for you."

Lukas smiled. "Let me tell you a story."

Solana tilted her head in curiosity.

"There was a young man who was burdened with problems so great that even his own existence was a flickering candle to their bonfire. He had been snatched away from his life and his loved ones. Even his body was about to cease being his own. Someone impossibly powerful offered to strike a bargain with him, offering tutelage, power beyond comprehension, salvation, and a path to greatness in a world that would attempt to crush him every step of the way. And it wasn't even that the powerful figure wanted him to do anything terribly evil. All he had to do was give up the right to *choose*."

"I bet this young man was just so noble that he refused her on sheer principle."

He smiled. "No. His first thoughts were that he just didn't want to die."

He exhaled.

"But—"

He met her dark eyes. "He had already lost everything. If he gave up his ability to choose, he would cease being himself. Even if the great power turned him into a mighty warrior, or even a god, he wouldn't be *him* any longer. So he refused the offer."

Her lips strained. "I see."

"It is true that I have nothing to gain by being part of this struggle between you yokai and those Asukans. Hell, both of you have tried to kill, use, and manipulate me. Walking away would definitely accelerate several of my plans and get me closer to my own goals. Maybe you'll even be sporting enough to give me some of the answers I seek just out of gratitude for handing Tanya off to you."

"But if I did that," he said, his voice softer than before, "then I would become that very person that young man feared he would become. Someone who can't judge between *right* and *wrong*, and I can't have that."

Solana exhaled. "That is your final word, then?"

He chuckled. "Do not play me for a fool, Solana. We both know that there was never a chance of me accepting that offer. But you still went through all of this. You want something from me, Tanya, or perhaps both of us. Why not try an open request for once?"

The skinwalker snorted, flicking a few fingers. "Fine. Let us embrace candor. You can help me help her. All the answers she's sought all her life, I can give her. All those doubts in her mind—I can solve them. Her obscured past, the source of her powers . . . I can reveal them for her. I can help her achieve her destiny. All I ask is if she chooses to side with us, you will not interfere with that decision."

Of course. Trust Solana to put him between a rock and a hard place. Walk away, and he'd be failing himself. Stay back, and he'd be binding himself to her side and thus agreeing to do her bidding.

A fire shone in her dark eyes. "Do we understand each other?"

CHAPTER 5

—

ACQUAINTANCES

B*link. Breathe.*
    Blink. Breathe.
    Tanya woke up with a feeling of surprise because, well, she really shouldn't have woken up. In fact, the last thing she could recall was blacking out while grasping her waist, her energy fading into the brink of oblivion.

The first thing she noticed was that her head was throbbing like someone had been hitting it with a hammer. The second was that she was lying in a bed. In an unfamiliar room. She could feel monster hide beneath her.

And she was naked.

With a bedsheet covering her front.

Years of her senses becoming attuned to danger allowed her to maintain an exterior calmness, while a turmoil raged within her. Her nakedness meant she wasn't in prison, and the sheet was proof that she wasn't being restrained in any form. But it also meant that her fractals were not on her person. Without those wristbands, her ability with manacrafting would be severely impaired. But at least her lifeforce and mana were both working perfectly, and from what she could tell, the sole person in the room wasn't displaying any hostile behavior.

"Oh good, you're awake."

Tanya froze at the familiar voice, her eyes widening as she locked gazes with the one woman she had not expected to meet again.

". . . Maude."

"In the flesh," Maude spoke with a friendly shrug. "Half of your clothes were burnt and sticking to your skin. I removed them and cleaned your wounds." She paused, cupping her chin. "I think some of my clothes might fit you, or maybe not. I'm a bit of a runt compared to you so . . ."

Her casual tone did not ease Tanya at all. She had long learned that appearances could be deceiving. Even something that looked benign could be hiding a terrible evil, and something that seemed sinister could be good. It didn't matter whether it was a bremetan or a creature.

And Maude was difficult to gauge even before her possession.

Grabbing the sheet tighter against her body, she pushed herself against the bed.

"Where am I?" she demanded, quickly looking around. She was already figuring out the best way of escaping from this room. Unfortunately, there were no windows, and Maude—or whatever she was now—was sitting between her bed and the most direct route to the door. Tanya wondered if there were any traps in between. Perhaps Maude thought that she'd be helpless without her fractals? It wouldn't have been an incorrect assumption against normal Asukans . . .

"Blunt as always," Maude chirped, and tilted her head. "But do you really not realize where this is? We spent so much time together here."

That was when it hit her. *There was no Eternal Light.* Normally that would've been the first thing she'd notice, but staying in that borderland for that long had messed with her sense of normalcy. The dim fluorescent lighting on the walls, the shadows on the floor, and the stalactites jutting down from the ceiling could only belong to one place.

A shiver ran down her spine.

"*What are you?*" she demanded.

Maude quirked a brow. "Were you always this rude or has being in the borderland made you crankier than usual?"

A cold draft blew across the room.

"Answer the question."

Maude made a placating gesture with her hands. "Relax. You're safe. I treated your wounds and put you in an enchanted sleep while you healed."

Seeing that her words made no difference to Tanya, who remained tense, looking like she was coiled to strike, she continued, "And I'm Maude. Or the closest thing to her, anyway. And stop looking at me like that. If I meant you any harm, would I give your fractals back to you?"

As she said those words, she pulled out a familiar pair of fractals and threw them her way. Tanya reached out and grabbed them, her bedsheet dropping in the process, revealing her upper torso. Tanya instantly pulled the sheet back over herself.

"Oh, don't be like that," Maude scoffed. "This isn't the first time I've stripped you. You realize that, right? Besides, you've got nothing to be ashamed of."

She licked her lips.

Tanya froze a little at her expression, before quickly putting the fractals on both of her wrists, feeling a little relieved once she had. She was far from helpless without them, but she was significantly more dangerous with them on her person. If Maude—or whatever she was now—meant to threaten her, Tanya would make her regret returning them. She knew better than to let down her guard, but at least the idea of her having her fractals back meant she was more comfortable with the idea of a forced escape should it become necessary.

"How did I get here?"

"You don't remember?"

Tanya narrowed her eyes suspiciously. "I . . . I fell through the rift and—Lukas, where's he?"

That brought a grin to Maude's face. "Lukas is . . . with Leader, I believe. He should be here soon, though I wonder. Just what happened between the two of you? The last time I saw you two, you were trying to kill him with your Frost."

Tanya stiffened. "You—you were there?"

"Of course," Maude said. "I vanished while you were playing with Olfric's kami, and then you went after it. The next thing I saw, you were fighting the Outsider. And what a battle it was! It was fortunate Olfric didn't see you. He'd have died of an inferiority complex."

Tanya narrowed her eyes. "You . . . know Lukas."

It wasn't a question. She had called him an Outsider, a term that only three other people could call him.

"Of course I do. I was there for his security, after all. And then I found Maude. It was . . . strange. I'd have never thought that a mere yurei like myself could fuse with a vanir with so much potential. And to think that I, a devout follower of Eir, would be so willing to lose my identity to become . . . more." She grinned. "It was a surprise, for both of us."

The way she kept referring to herself as both Maude the vanir and the yurei, a yokai, was incredibly chilling.

"What is this place? Who's this Leader you're talking about? And how do you know Lukas?"

"So many questions all at once. I wonder, were you always like this, or did the Outsider contaminate you with his bad habits?"

Tanya gritted her teeth. The casual manner with which she discussed Lukas suggested prior acquaintanceship with him. Obviously Maude the vanir had no way of knowing Lukas, so perhaps the yurei? Her old suspicions rose to the forefront of her mind—Olfric's claims about how the yokai came after him for attacking Lukas. But while Lukas had admitted encountering yokai, he had painted them as monsters wearing bremetan flesh against which he had to survive. Had he, perchance, lied about that?

A pang of betrayal shot through her heart. She had opened up to him, con-fided the dark secrets of her horrendous past, and he had shared his own story in return. What reason would he have to hide his dealings with yokai? Did he not trust her?

Get a grip, girl, Tanya admonished herself. Sure, she had met someone she could *reasonably* trust, someone who had known of her sins, understood the stains on her past, and still accepted her. But that didn't mean she'd become smitten with him or anything. Sure, she had found new levity in her life, but she wasn't a naive little girl. The world was still as ugly as ever. Yes, cynicism suited her better. She felt more comfortable taking things with a grain of salt. It spared her from many bitter disappointments, and she had experienced enough of them to last a lifetime.

In that light, she could understand why Lukas would've chosen to conceal his acquaintanceship with the yokai. After all, he was living among Asukans. By the Goddess, he had even stated that he'd tell her nearly everything, barring anything that was too dangerous.

So why did she feel this bitterness in her stomach?

"Call Lukas here. I want to talk to him. Right now."

Maude threw her head back and laughed.

"What's so funny?"

"Oh, you. The Outsider said the same exact thing when he woke up. Speaking of which, can you tell me where he got Kvasir's treatise from? I didn't think Zuken was the kind to hoard forbidden tomes like that in his mansion."

Okay. Maybe she was imprisoned after all. There weren't any manacles, no, but she was stuck in a room, naked under a flimsy sheet, with a thoroughly maddening Maude threatening to practically drive her to a suicidal state thanks to sheer confusion.

"Can you—" Tanya began, cursing herself when her tone came out sounding bleaker than expected, "—give me my clothes?"

Then she remembered how Maude had described her earlier state.

"Or anything that might fit me?"

Maude chuckled softly.

"Why are you laughing again?"

"Oh, it's nothing. You just . . . reminded me of my earlier days. Maude is obsessed with proper dressing and decorum. But yurei do not have such sophistications. Dressing, eating . . . Even now, I have to consciously remember to breathe. In fact, even this conversation feels unnecessary. Life as a yurei is much . . . duller and more monochromatic."

"You're an oni now."

"That is what they call me," Maude replied, exhaling. "Even amongst my own kind, I am a stranger. I am not yurei and not vanir. I'm . . . something else."

"If it's that bad, why don't you . . ." Tanya trailed off, hesitating to finish that sentence.

"Return to Haviskali?" Maude asked. "I apologize. I like it better here."

"And what *is* this place?"

"It's yokai territory. Well, *a* yokai territory, but the only one that I know of. Granted, this is far larger than I expected. I don't think I've even seen it in its entirety. As a yurei, I stuck to patrolling these parts."

"And it's all underground?"

Maude smiled. "Yes. All the way down to Haviskali and Cyffnar."

Tanya had the sneaking suspicion that the anomaly might be far, far larger than they had originally anticipated. Especially if it covered the entirety of the Desert and then more. That was . . . nearly half the size of the entire Llaisy Kingdom!

And it was populated by yokai.

"Why are you telling me all this? I mean, I'm an Asukan."

This time, Maude smirked at her. Tanya wasn't sure why, but it rankled. Far more than anything else she had done.

". . . what?"

"You can pretend all you want, Tanya," the oni said, "but you're no more Asukan than I am."

Tanya froze. *How did she . . .?*

The thought died as a far more dangerous suspicion arose in her mind. Maude had said that Lukas was with the Leader of this territory. The Leader of *yokai*. And Lukas was *also* the one person she had trusted enough to reveal her past. Had he . . .?

No, she told herself. No. She had trusted him. He had promised to be on her side. He would *not* betray her secrets to the yokai like that. No way. *No fucking way—*

Grabbing the bedsheet tightly with her left hand, she materialized multiple wind-blades in midair, all of them aimed for Maude's vitals. Maude might have thought that handing over her fractals was a good way to get past her defenses and play with her emotions.

She'd teach her to expect better.

"Enough with the chitchat," she all but snarled. "I want to see Lukas, so by the Goddess, you'll get me some clothes. Or I swear I'll kill you right now."

"If you kill me, you'll have to go find him naked," said Maude.

Fortunately for Tanya, she didn't end up having to actually kill her former teammate. As it turned out, Maude did, in fact, have an apparel set ready for her. That she could get her to react so easily was maddening. That she was treating her as completely harmless wasn't helping things either.

At least, she was out of that freaking bed, and she had clothes on.

No matter how uncomfortable she felt in clothes two sizes too small for her. Knowing the oni, she had done that intentionally.

"So, Lukas stayed here before? Is that what you're saying?"

"Oh yes," Maude said, smiling. "It was quite entertaining. Seeing him battle Quonnan naked."

"*What?*"

"Technically," came a familiar voice from the doorway, "they stripped me long before the fight. It was part of their prisoner treatment package."

Tanya spun around and found Lukas standing there, arms crossed as he rested against the doorway. She didn't know what came over her, but the next second, she was sprinting across the room and hurling herself at him, hugging him for dear life. After a surprised grunt, she felt relieved as he wrapped his arms around her as well.

It took her another moment to realize what she had just done.

Maude made an odd throaty noise in the background.

As if stricken, she pulled herself back, her face burning with embarrassment at her sudden impulsiveness. Lukas looked gobsmacked for a moment before a lopsided grin formed on his youthful features. Then she remembered what she had just found out.

"You lied to me!"

"Well—"

"You *lied* to me!"

This time Lukas didn't even try to apologize. "I did."

Her hands rose to her waist as she glared at him. "You've lived with the yokai. And yet you lied to me. Every single time."

Lukas winced. "I did say that I'd give you as close to the truth as possible."

"HOW IS—" Tanya barely managed to keep from erupting. "How is this *close* to the truth?"

He shrugged. "I didn't know how you felt about them."

She narrowed her eyes. "Don't you turn this around on me, Lukas Aguilar. Don't you *dare*. I told you—I told you *everything*! And you—"

"Your 'everything' didn't include anything about yokai," he said and held up his hands in surrender. "And contrary to what you think, I'm not best buddies with them either."

"Evidence points otherwise!"

"What evidence?" Lukas shot back. "They captured me and forced me to play ball. You know as well as I do that sometimes a choice isn't a choice at all."

Whatever Tanya was about to say next died in the face of *that* comment. If he had been captured, it certainly explained how the yokai knew him. And he had even talked about fighting this kasha earlier. Honestly, there were just so many unknown variables that she wasn't sure what to feel anymore.

"I agree, Outsider," Maude quipped in the background. "Tanya likes threatening over giving choices."

"That's not—" Tanya began with a hiss, before she glared back at Lukas. "You thought it'd be a great idea to leave me all alone with her?"

"I thought you were old friends." Lukas said, confused.

"You thought *wrong*."

"Now, isn't this interesting . . ." said an unfamiliar feminine voice from behind Lukas. Tanya didn't know why, but something in it set her on edge. She took a step back, and shifted into an offensive stance, wind-blades forming in each palm. The stranger entered through the doorway, the darkness outside no longer shrouding her. She looked young, closer to herself in age, with jet black hair and eyes, with small dimples on each cheek contrasting with her otherwise square jaw.

"Who're you?"

"I'm called Solana, my dear," she said. "Do you know who *you* are?"

CHAPTER 6

—————

BARTER

The girl—Solana—smiled at her. It was a smile that promised her best interests at heart. Tanya had seen such a smile before.

On her grandfather's face. He had worn it while he watched her begging for mercy as she was being tortured.

"You and I share a long history," Solana purred. "It is my desire to tell you about that which you do not know."

"I've never met you before," Tanya shot back. "I don't know what the hell you are, or what Lukas—" She scowled, disdain flashing across her features. "—is doing with you. I just want to get out of here."

The girl smiled.

"*Everfrost.*"

. . .

The reaction was instantaneous.

One moment they were all standing there. The next moment, Tanya had practically teleported in front of Solana, with a wind-blade pointed between Solana's eyes before she could so much as blink, while several dozen blades aiming for her vitals materialized around her. Another dozen blades guarded the distance between Tanya and Maude, out of precaution if nothing else.

There wasn't a single blade between herself and Lukas, though.

Her face burned as the realization hit her, but she hid it well in her ferocity as she regarded the black-haired girl.

"How do you know that name?" she growled. A part of her whispered furiously that she had her blades aimed at the wrong person but she suppressed it ruthlessly. She had told Lukas about her deepest, darkest secret but that didn't mean that he was the one who had betrayed her. It was too direct, too simple, and Lukas was capable of playing games far more complex than this.

Besides, hadn't Maude admitted to watching her employ Frost against Lukas? Maybe she was the one who had reported it? But even then, how did they know about its name?

"I've known of Everfrost long before you were even conceived, child," said Solana, in a completely nonchalant tone. Tanya wasn't sure exactly what the girl—whatever she was—was capable of, but her posture suggested complete indifference. Like there was *nothing* Tanya could do that could bring her harm.

"How?"

That smile surfaced again. "I know of Everfrost and its secrets. I know of its past wielders and its origin in our world. I know more about your powers than you can even imagine."

The blade edged closer.

"Tell me."

The smile turned sharp. Like a knife's edge. "You will never value information if it comes to you that easily, child."

She pressed the wind-dagger deeper. Just a little more and the blade would draw blood.

"You can either tell me or die."

The girl, or whatever she was, continued to smile. "Is that what you think will happen?"

"Tanya," Lukas replied tersely. "I . . . really think you should listen to what she has to say."

Tanya gritted her teeth and took a step back, ready to strike at the slightest hostile movement. She did not truly believe that Lukas would strike her, so it was more out of instinct than intention. The black-haired girl, on the other hand, just stood there, utterly unfazed by Tanya's reaction, as if she was utterly inconsequential and insignificant to her. Tanya glanced at Lukas and found lines forming on his face, though they weren't the kind she had seen before.

He wasn't expecting physical confrontation. Or, to be more specific, he wasn't expecting any of them to be attacked. Just how deep did his association run with the yokai?

After a few seconds of tense inactivity, Tanya exhaled and dispelled her blades, despite her paranoia screaming at her to do otherwise. She took a step back and regarded Lukas.

"Guess you're her bitch now."

"One wishes," said Solana with an overexaggerated sigh, as she gave her an amused eye-smile. "The Outsider is too independently minded for that."

Tanya ignored her and glared at Lukas, daring him to prove her wrong.

Lukas frowned. "I work for myself. I thought you knew that."

"I also 'knew' you had nothing to do with yokai. Yet here we are."

Lukas sighed. "I might have skipped a few key details."

"You LIED to me!"

"I *did not lie* to you," Lukas emphasized. "I'm not working for her."

"And yet you brought me here!"

"Will you please let me finish?"

Her glare intensified, but she didn't retort any further.

"I didn't lie to you." said Lukas. "And no, it wasn't my intention to come here. I only—It just *happened*, alright? You know as well as I do what happened when I tried opening it before."

Tanya tilted her head ever so slightly. She had taken note of how both Solana and Maude were watching him closely. That he had so strongly alluded to his anomaly status without talking about it directly spoke of a well-maintained secret, just like he had done with her and Zuken before this.

"What's your relationship with her?" she demanded.

"Relationship? What makes you think there is one?" Lukas shot back. At her glare, he exhaled. "Fine. She's . . . kind of a frenemy at best, I suppose."

"What is a frenemy?" Maude asked.

"A massive pain in the ass, but someone you can't do without," Lukas replied. "The devil you know. I'd say she's worse than a credit card company, but you wouldn't catch my drift."

"We've treated you like a guest."

"Guests get invited," Lukas shot back. "I'm the unfortunate window-shopper who was tempted by a free ride and is now being forced into a car loan."

Tanya stared at him. As did the others.

"What's a window-shopper?" asked Solana, wondering.

"What is a car loan?" asked Maude in interest.

"Why are you being forced into one?" asked Tanya in alarm.

Lukas just looked at them with varying degrees of helplessness before he sighed. "Never mind." He met Tanya's eyes. "Long story short, these fellas captured me when I was traipsing through the anomaly. The next thing I know, one of them tried to possess me, but when that failed, they satisfied their curiosity by stripping me naked."

Me too, Tanya thought. She had almost said it out loud, but instincts honed over the years helped her stay in control. Embarrassing incident or not, it should've stayed in the past. The matter would have ended there, *should have* ended there, had her former mission partner-turned-enemy Maude not opened her mouth.

"It wasn't personal," the oni grinned. "Tanya here went through the same treatment."

. . . Damn it!

Lukas blinked before looking her up and down. Tanya hoped he wasn't trying to picture her naked. Honestly, this was *not* the way she had expected things to turn out.

"Yeah, they have a fetish for that," Lukas said, oblivious to her inner tur-moil. "Anyway, they forced me to fight Quonnan, who was creepily obsessed with my body."

A sudden desire to hit him again rose in her.

"I mean, she wanted my body for herself. I told her it wouldn't work out between us, so she got angry, self-immolated herself, and tried to possess me and make me into her psychotic boy toy."

"And you got her powers," Solana concluded, watching them with a half-amused expression.

Tanya snapped her head at her. "You know of his powers?"

"Some," said Solana. "He is rather shy about showing them off."

"And I'd like to keep it that way," Lukas stressed.

"I have told you before, Outsider," Solana said, unblinking, "this isn't about you any longer. It is about her. You are free to leave, no strings attached."

"And I told you I'm not leaving her with you," Lukas said stubbornly.

Solana folded her hands as she regarded Lukas, oblivious to Tanya's grow-ing confusion. "Right. You care about her a great deal."

"Who, me?" Tanya asked, alarmed.

"Yes, she's creepily obsessed with you," Lukas said, before glaring at Solana. "I told you, she's my friend."

"Allow me to rephrase that observation. You care for her to an *irrational* degree," Solana tilted her head, as if studying him. "I'm not sure I understand why."

A rush of unexplained glee shot through Tanya's body at Solana's words, as she regarded Lukas, who was doing his best not to look in her direction.

"I told you," Lukas repeated, slower but firmer than before. "She's my friend."

"I understand your words. But they don't *mean* anything."

"They do," said Lukas. "To normal people. Not six-century-old skinwalkers."

"S- . . . skinwalkers?" Tanya stammered. She had heard tales of skinwalk-ers—or *yosuzume*, in the old tongue—as a young child at her father's lap. Tales of vicious wraiths coming to haunt young kids who refused to go to sleep at the end of the day, creatures that swam in the mists, grabbing Asukans and steal-ing their souls. Ghastly monstrosities that wore and swapped bremetan bodies like one changed apparel. And if she was six centuries old, then she must have changed dozens, if not hundreds, of bodies over the years.

That she was trading barbs with a walking, talking corpse made her want to throw up.

That said walking, talking corpse was deeply interested in her made it even worse.

Was that why she was so uncaring of her hostility? Because even if she managed to butcher her body into a thousand pieces, she could always jump into another? The growing apprehension and curiosity was getting too much for her.

Solana's expression had become distant. "You should not be too sure of that, Outsider. I too had *friends*. Family."

And why was she looking at her while she said that?

Her stomach did a nasty flip.

"Tell me what you know about Everfrost."

"I cannot, child. For it destroys the balance," said Solana. "You see, I am *all* about balance. Never offer something without demanding something else in return. Never give a favor without collecting another of its kind."

Tanya wanted to get mad at her. But it was useless. This girl—woman? crone?—was older than any bremetan frame of reference she could use to describe her. She could choose to attack her, but doing so would not yield anything. And Solana was right. Lukas was indeed one of the most stubborn people Tanya had ever encountered, so if he wanted her to play ball, there had to be some reason behind it. This skinwalker—she was not bremetan and was, by the looks of it, a being of power, trickery and deceit. At the same time, she was old. *Six centuries* old.

There was no sense drawing this out. She had to play the game.

"Fine." She gave Solana a tired, whimsical smile. "What do you want in return?"

The creature nodded back, business-like. "I will not share this knowledge with you but with your other self. The Frost."

Tanya's eyes instantly shot towards Lukas, meeting his intense gaze. If Solana got her information from Maude, it was outdated. Lukas—or more specifically, his Goddess—had sealed the Frost from truly taking over like it did every other time it manifested. Even when she called upon the full power of the Frost in the borderland, she had been in control. More uninhibited per-haps, but still in control. And sane.

She knew that.

But Solana didn't.

Lukas gave her a tiny, almost imperceptible nod.

That crazy son of a bitch! He knew what she was thinking. And he agreed. He knew what Solana was asking for, but, unlike Solana, he knew Tanya would stay in control.

The urge to smile was overwhelming.

"The Frost . . ." said Tanya, slowly, as if weighing every word, ". . . is not exactly stable. I'm not sure I can even hold back if it—if *she*—chose to attack you guys."

"Agreed," said Solana. "Come with me."

CHAPTER 7

GENESIS

Lukas had never been to this place before.

He'd admit, when Solana asked them to follow her, he was half-certain she was leading them to the prisons. Instead, he found himself standing in front of two giant gates that opened, revealing an entryway to . . . darkness.

Lukas conjured an orb of flames in his right hand. He needn't have done that. The moment he crossed the threshold, the darkness of the entryway gave way to a large chamber brilliantly illuminated by chandeliers, each crystal seeming to reflect lights that weren't actually there.

The chamber was easily the size of a football field, with a twenty-foot vaulted ceiling. All of the walls were covered in sculpture, with thin veins of shining metals reflecting the strange light, casting a most wondrous illumination on this chamber. Polished stone floors met their feet, covered in elegant rugs, and unless he was wrong, about a third of the northern and western wall was covered with massive bookshelves full of tomes so old and mysterious-looking that he resolved not to leave the yokai territory until he had read them all from cover to cover. The rest of the walls were densely inscribed with tiny sigils which, upon closer inspection, proved to not be sigils at all but a form of insignia—thirteen in all—engraved all over the walls like an alien graffiti.

Horizontal bands of elevated rock rose in vast, concentric circles, giving the entire chamber a vast amphitheater-like feel. Ionic pillars arose out of the floor, the shining metal furrowing them with inhuman precision, and rising all the way until they met the ceiling to form another complex meshwork that itself could have been another insignia, for all he knew.

"Welcome," said Solana, "to the throne room."

Fittingly, in the center rose a dais, elevated like a stage at least four feet from the ground, and in its center stood a massive white throne that looked like it was carved out of solid ice, inlaid with metals Lukas had never seen before. The Screen was already Scanning, Analyzing, and storing away the compositions for future use, but the most impressive—and intimidating—thing about this throne was what sprang out from its back: a sculpture that could be loosely described as a dragon.

It had three heads, the highest looking down upon and covering the throne like a protective roof, while the other two curved around the throne's two arms protectively, their necks as wide as tree trunks, looming at their intended audience, their ruby-red eyes glowing, exerting a mental gravity so dense that it was difficult to look anywhere else. Three pairs of wings arose from the back of the draconic figure, the rest of its body completely reptilian, entwined around the throne, as if arising from the very dais. The whole thing looked like something out of antiquity, the throne of some ancient draconic god-king.

Lukas glanced at Tanya and found her staring at the throne, utterly enthralled by its presence. She took a single step and then another and then one more, her eyes never leaving the archaic creation, as if it was pulling her towards it. Lukas grabbed her hand and gave her a jerk, snapping her out of her trance.

"...?"

Lukas shook his head.

Tanya swallowed but nodded.

"During the Time Before, thirteen such chambers existed across the known universe—some on this plane, while others centered on the different realms of the Yggdrasil. Thirteen realms, thirteen kings, each the epitome of their own kind. This one is called Nidhogg's Lair, the throne of the Queen of Ice. Before the Great War, it was occupied by the Empress of Yokai, Queen of the End, Meynte."

"Yggdrasil?" asked a skeptical Tanya. "As in the tree that surpasses the Seven Heavens? *That* Yggdrasil?"

Maude gave her a piercing look. Solana arched her eyebrows.

Tanya blinked. "I—I always thought it was a myth. I mean, my father—"

"Typical Asukan arrogance," Maude murmured, her expression growing darker. It was the second time her face had betrayed actual emotion. "They'd reject the universe if it fed their pride."

"Perhaps," said Lukas, 'it'd be for the best if you just started from the beginning?"

"The beginning?" asked Solana.

"I've read the Asukan Scriptures. Their myths talk about the primordials Izanagi and Izanami and the birth of Onogoro—this world as you know it. There aren't any mentions of the Yggdrasil. Kvasir's treatise says differently, but he gets lost in his own ramblings. I think a complete picture would make things easier?"

He glanced at Tanya, who nodded reluctantly.

Truth be told, he didn't need it. Forming a Nexus had shown him far more than Kvasir could have ever theorized. This was just a test to see if Solana would give them the unvarnished truth or hide it within layers of deception.

"A complete picture . . ." she mused. "I do not see how knowing the origin of our world would help her understand her heritage."

"I'd like to know that too," Tanya chimed in, before adding a quick "Please?"

Solana met his gaze. Her look was penetrating. Lukas averted his eyes before things got out of hand.

"I suppose that is fair," she murmured. "And rather serendipitous too, that we stand in this room of all places. Fine, behold. I'll show you: the beginning of the beginning."

She raised both hands, and Lukas felt the pressure grow. The mana that surged around her was immense and potent, and settled downwards, tiny, burning particles of *something* forming around them. They zoomed in all directions like tiny fireflies, coalescing into concrete shapes. The general illumination in the room was slowly dissipating, to the point that the burning particles were akin to stars in the night sky. Stars that were shooting around, spinning and settling into something greater. It was difficult to tell if what followed were a hundred different forms or just one, giant illusion.

"Before the beginning," Solana said, "there was only the Mist."

Lukas's world sank into darkness. He could still feel the cold stone floor beneath, but everything else had been inundated by inky, black darkness. There was no illumination, and yet, he could see his companions perfectly. It reminded him so much of the Eternal Light that he wondered if Solana was capable of using it.

Then he remembered who she was and dropped the absurd notion.

"No world, no heavens, no stars, no sky, only the Mist," said Solana. "Formless, shapeless, and omnipresent. An endless ocean that spanned in all dimensions, a maelstrom of cosmic proportions from which stemmed Existence itself."

As she spoke, the burning particles smashed together to create a large, expansive cloud-like layer, expanding in every direction as far as the eye could see. Lukas could discern different portions of the endless Mist behaving in various, quirky ways, some of them spinning into a denser form, while others moved in and out, like the wings of a butterfly.

"It has many names: the wellspring of Creation, the Fog of the End, the Ginnungagap, and many, many more. And floating in this ocean of Mist, were worlds, diverse and many. Some expansive, mutating in their own unique environments, forming their own queer laws that went beyond the extreme. Others, smaller and in clusters, banked together to form minor worlds."

Lukas saw them, the worlds, lying in the Mist bed, the matrix of their creation and the medium connecting them all, tying them together as would a thread. He could almost picture each of them as completely separate worlds—singularities and realms—ach bringing their varying rules, creatures, and civilizations together into a closely knit existence.

Like a tree.

"They called it Yggdrasil. The tree that spans the Heavens. That which links the smaller worlds to a greater whole, from the fiery plains of fire-breathing, warmongering muspels, to the cold, desolate, frosty plains where nothing but cold and darkness reigns."

The World-Tree, Lukas mused.

Lukas wasn't one for stargazing, but even he agreed there was something fundamentally beautiful about the World-Tree. He didn't know if this was just a cluster of worlds or simply the known part of the universe, but whatever it was, it was utterly magnificent. His gaze darted from one corner to another of this seemingly endless world of Mist, but no matter what he did, he simply could not capture the entire thing in one view.

"What are . . . those?" he asked, pointing at small, floating pieces of dense mana that looked like islands. If islands could float in space.

Solana raised her hand, and one of them drew closer to her palm, as if pulled by invisible strings. Solana pulled it outward, and the structure expanded.

"Is that . . . a *world?*"

"Yes," said Solana. "The Ancients called them adaxes, each of them a minor world by themselves, complete with lands and oceans and mountains and plains. This world, which Asukans call the "real world," is little more than a cluster of adaxes huddled together."

Lukas watched in awe as the adax, now shrunk to its original size, fell into its own orbit, revolving within the Yggdrasil, as if dancing to some cosmic tune.

"There are endless tales of how the Yggdrasil came to exist," said Solana. "The jotunn believe that the Ginungagap spawned a gargantuan being named Ymir, the very first being of existence. After Ymir's death, his organs turned to these adaxes from which spawned all life. The svartalfars believe that the Ginungagap was an endless forge and Ymir, the blacksmith that harnessed the power of the stars to craft these worlds. The alfs . . ."

"Okay, I get the point," said Lukas, who had read an endless amount of mythical texts in the past. Individually, it was an enriching experience, but after you had gone through ten different versions of Genesis, with each claiming to be the truth, you got a bit jaded over that sort of thing. What was worse was that, unlike back on Earth, the gods here were *real.* Yokai, vanir, muspel, svartalfar—all these races *existed*. And yet, despite that, every race had its own fictional genesis story.

Inanna had shown him her memory of the Origin. Whatever this Ginungagap was, it wasn't that. Yet, these people believed that the nine realms spawned from it.

Lukas shook his head. He had enough things to worry about. He could leave this headache for later.

If Solana was annoyed at his interruption, she did not show it. "What all these myths have in common are the two poles of the Yggdrasil. On one extreme is Niflheim, the Dark World. The realm of everlasting night. Colder than cold, it is the realm of ice and frost. Mists cover its skies and glaciers form landmasses. On the other side is the world of perpetual flame, Muspelheim. The land where fires burn eternally. Muspelheim is crimson to Niflheim's gray. No terrain, only lava. The land was aflame with the roaring heat of the seven suns, with nothing but sparks and spurting heat, molten rocks and embers."

Lukas thought back to the borderland he had spent so much time in. It was exactly what Solana was describing, but he knew that it wasn't Muspelheim. No, that had simply been the side effect of an Ifrit King making it its home.

Still, the place was littered with muspels and bylestyr, so even if it wasn't the original thing, it was a fairly convincing replica.

"And the other worlds?" Tanya asked.

"It is believed that the other worlds formed the body of Yggdrasil, each mutated to become something unique, with rules utterly alien to the others."

"I am somewhat familiar with the nine realms of the Yggdrasil," Lukas admitted, interrupting Solana's tale. There was no need to tell her that he had gotten a glimpse of the Yggdrasil through his connection to the borderland's awareness. But that had been exactly that—a glimpse. Nothing like the level of detail Solana was imprinting on them.

Tanya looked at him in surprise.

"Even back in my world, the Norse gods enjoyed a lot of notoriety."

"That does not surprise me," Solana claimed. "You recognized Grimnir when we first spoke of Him."

"*Grimnir?*" Tanya looked at him.

"Odin," Lukas murmured.

"Do *not* speak his name so freely, Outsider," Solana hissed. "Names, especially names of the bearers of Lost Truths, have *power*. There are those that can sense your careless enunciation of that name."

"Who—who's that?" asked Tanya. "An old god?"

"Odin—or as Solana prefers to call him, Crooked One-Eye—" said Lukas, "—is the Leader of the Aesir. Also known as Grimnir, the Hooded One.

Glad-O'War, Gond'lir, Wand-Bearer, and Third. Father of the Norse Gods, and an absolute bloodthirsty son of a bitch."

"I take it back," said Solana, her lips twisted in amusement. "You're practically his *priest*."

Lukas scowled. He was surprised just how annoyed he was at that insinuation. "I'm not. I've just . . . studied him a lot more than the other gods."

Say what you would about Odin, he made for an intensely captivating character, fictional or otherwise. Though given the absence of the Norse pantheon and fragmentation of its myths, it seemed Ragnarok had already come to pass here.

"Studied?" asked Tanya, frowning. "I thought you were a diplomat. Unless that was another lie?"

Lukas raised his hands in surrender. "It wasn't. You don't get to grow up with a fanatic grandfather and not take an interest in the subject."

"That sounds interesting . . ." Maude said, sarcasm dripping in her voice. "I have to ask, Outsider, what sort of devastation did One-Eye cut through your lands?"

"I wouldn't know," said Lukas. "I'm fairly certain that the Norse gods existed in my world. At some point."

"And how can you know that for sure?"

Lukas suppressed a smirk. It wasn't often that he got to shock Solana. He was going to enjoy this.

"Where I'm from, the gods are long gone. Dead. Become part of the woodwork."

He met Solana's eyes.

"They've become *fiction*."

Of all the things she had expected him to say, that wasn't it. "Fiction," she repeated, trying to digest the word. "In your world, the Norse gods are fiction."

"As are the Shin, Asukan Gods. Amaterasu, Tsukuyomi, Susannoo, all of them. Where I'm from, you don't have gods fighting gods. You have *people* fighting over whether or not religion is anything but a myth. A tale told from father to son, passed down generations, sometimes by mouth and other times through texts. Inscriptions. Monuments. In fact, the number of atheists keeps growing every year. People choose to put their faith in understanding by observation, instead of blind belief in something that *might* have existed in the past."

All three of them were gawking at him.

"Granted, there were factions, people who were really touchy about their faiths. To mock them would have been to invite peril."

"With due reason," Maude all but growled.

Lukas idly wondered what Maude would think of religious terrorism.

"And where do you see yourself among them?"

"Me?" Lukas blinked. "I am, well, *was*, an agnostic. I thought of religion and mythology as superstition and ignorance. A trick played by our brains in a misguided attempt to explain that which cannot be explained. Maybe there was a God or gods, maybe there wasn't. My mind said that I'd never understand God, if He existed, and my heart said that I wasn't supposed to understand Him."

"No gods . . ." Solana's lips trembled slightly. "Then what about the Asukan pantheon? You recognized those names."

"Oh those . . . Now that's particularly funny. Where I'm from, it's said that Izanagi and Izanami were twins, and one day they went to a river to, uh . . . purify themselves. They washed off their eyes and nose and, from that dirt, the three children were born: Amaterasu, Tsukoyomi, and Susanoo."

Solana stared at him, unblinking. "And the yokai?"

"Well, I imagine if they did go bathing, the rest of their excreta had to go *somewhere*," he finished with a straight face.

The funny part was, he was only half-joking. Regardless of how real the Asukan gods and how dangerous the yokai were in this world, Shintoism back on Earth could win an award for the worst genesis story idea ever.

"You—you *cannot* be serious."

Lukas did his best not to snicker. "I told you. In my world, you fellas are all fiction. Even if you existed, it probably was a very long time ago."

Solana took a quick intake of breath. "This world you've come from, is it—is it possible that it is—"

"From the future?" Lukas finished for her. He had entertained that possibility, before the utter lack of information about the world and the universe had made him drop that line of thought. "It is possible. I'm not sure how I got here, and the only one that could have helped me find out . . . is out of my reach. I don't know if I came from a future world. In fact, all I know of your kind is through tales."

"And that is the truth?"

Lukas smiled. "It is as close to the truth as I'm able to give you."

Maude tilted her head. "What does it feel like to talk to a figment of your imagination?"

"I'm still getting used to it."

Truth was, it wasn't as hard as she thought. The lines between fact and fiction tended to blur when a freaking goddess took rent inside your freaking head.

"Granted," he said as an afterthought, "not everything is what I remember."

Solana perked up at that. Lukas felt a tinge of sadness at the earnestness. For all her power and reach, she had *nothing* to stack up against Lukas's knowledge. Especially if he really *was* from the future. He wondered if this was how seers felt, sitting on a dangerous secret that could make or break civilizations.

"Norse mythology was about the Aesir, vanir, and the nine realms. About Midgard. Instead, you have Asukans calling this world Onogoro. There are Amaterasu and her kin. And yokai." He met her eyes. "Just how did *that* happen?"

"The first thing you have to know is that every single world born out of the Ginnungagap has been influenced by Muspelheim and Niflheim," said Solana.

"*Worlds*, as in . . . more than nine?" asked Lukas.

Solana snorted. "*Dozens*, and those are just the relevant ones. The Ancients claimed an entire *belt* of worlds, connecting the Frost Realm with the Fire Realm. One that spawned creatures of its own—creatures that were large and mighty, both in strength and spirit. A race of warmongers who could not agree on anything except war."

"The jotunn," Tanya murmured.

Solana nodded. "The jotunn worlds closest to Muspelheim were blessed and cursed by the Everlasting Flame, turning the jotunn into fire-breathing, twisted caricatures of themselves—the muspels—and their greater and more devastating evolutions—the bylestyrs. Niflheim's eternal winter had a reverse effect, trans- forming them to himthursars—the Frost Giants. There are all sorts of stories about how Nidavellir—that's the realm of the svartalfars—and Alfheim and Vanaheim came into existence, but there is one thing all stories agree on."

"Which is?"

"Midgard. A cluster of tiny worldlings, breeding two-legged beings that were neither Flame nor Frost. Creatures of Spirit but lacking the essence that made the vanir special. Beings whose lifeforce were like flickering candles compared to a jotunn. A race of *prey*. A civilization of the weak."

She looked Lukas in the face.

"Bremetan," she said. "The lesser-born. Living in a lesser world."

Lukas didn't know whether to laugh or to cry. Barely two months ago, he had sat around listening to Olfric preach about the brilliance and the might of the Asukan Empire. The treatises from Zuken's library had mentioned how the world had snapped into existence by the whims of the Primordials, Izanagi and Izanami—the First Man and First Woman. There had even been artistic depictions of how the world was crafted by the Primordials as a gift for their children, and given to them to rule. Bremetans, made in the image of Izanagi and Izanami themselves, were the crux of all potential, ruled by Empress Ama- terasu, and her kin, Tsukuyomi and Susanoo, the children of the Primordials.

And now, Solana was showing him the flip side of the coin: a different tale of genesis, featuring the nine realms of the Yggdrasil, with the bremetans being the lowest of the low, the bottom rung of the ladder. You could literally step over them. Again, it ought to be questioned how the lowest rung became the highest, but that was neither here nor there.

The surreal part about this was that the characters, the races, the worlds were all *real*. Elena was a changeling, born of a ljósálfar and a bremetan. Maude had been a vanir prior to her corruption. Zuken, Olfric—they were all bremetans, and he, Lukas, was literally shacking up inside a yokai camp. Odin was a real thing, and the other Norse gods were alive at some point in time. The Empire existed on the edge of Amaterasu's blade, and Tanya . . .

Tanya was apparently a yuki-onna.

"Where do yokai fall in this?" he asked. "I've never heard of the yokai sprouting out of any of the nine realms."

"Why would we?" asked Solana. "You forget what we are, Outsider. We are of the Ethereal, and it is in the Ethereal that we are born."

"The Ethereal . . ." Lukas murmured. "You mean . . . the Haze?"

"I told you this once before, Outsider," said Solana. "The Other is of the Ethereal. What is visible is Sight. That which is beyond sight is the Other. That which can be heard is Sound. That which is beyond Sound is the Other. That which pumps lifeblood is the Force. That which is beyond it is the Other."

"The yokai . . ." Tanya murmured. "You're saying the yokai were created by the Ginungagap." She met Lukas's eyes, before shifting her gaze to Solana's glowing, inhuman ones and found the confirmation she was seeking in them. "By the Haze."

It certainly made sense. That explained everything. The Haze was a world in itself. Only, instead of rock and living tissue, it was a world of mist. Of mana. It was only natural that the creatures it would give birth to would be just as ethereal and twisted as itself.

Yokai. *Those of a different world.* The spirits of the Mist.

"Do you have any proof?"

Solana looked at Tanya like she had said something utterly alien. "Proof?"

"Obviously," Tanya said. "You just told me that everything I knew about the world is a lie. You claim that I'm like you. You claim that Asukans are the bottom-feeders of this world but somehow ended up ruling it? And you want me to take that at face value?"

Lukas suppressed the urge to grin. He knew from his connection to the Haze that Solana was speaking the truth. Minus her theory about bremetan being the bottom-feeders. He had feared she'd use this knowledge to easily manipulate Tanya. It was nice to see that Tanya was still being her cold, pragmatic self.

She put her hands on her waist. "Unless you can show me some proof, all you have are words. A story. How do I know you're not lying to me? And even if you aren't, what has all of this got to do with me? With Everfrost?"

"Everything," whispered the skinwalker. "The entire war between Asukans and yokai has been over your heritage, child. Tell me, do you know why the Asukan Empire declared war against the yokai?"

"Easy," said Tanya. "Because of oni. Because we were hunted and turned into your spiritual puppets."

Solana smiled, and it was a cruel thing. "No. Because Empress Meynte, the Last Ruler of all yokai, gained a power that would have ended the Empire. A power so cold that Amaterasu's light couldn't penetrate. A power that lies in the Deepness of the Hvergelmir, a lake of Hel, guarded by the great Nidhogg himself."

Lukas glanced at the throne. *Nidhogg's Lair*, Solana had called it.

Solana's voice gained an unearthly edge. *"It has many names. The Perpetual Darkness that turned Nidhogg's scales in the shade of the blackest night. The Devourer, one that dragged the Aesir into its cave . . . The Cruelest Winter, Eternal Glacier, Wrath of the End, Anomaly Slayer . . ."*

Lukas felt the world slip beneath his feet.

"—Fimbulwinter. The Bane of the Gods . . .

"Everfrost."

Fimbulwinter.

The prophesied winter that heralded Ragnarok, the utter and complete annihilation of the Aesir pantheon. A prolonged period of continuous snow and frost, marking the unleashing of primal forces and the rise of events that led to the decline of the Aesir as people on Earth knew it.

The great wolf Fenrir breaking out of his shackles.

The prophesied fight between Jormungandr, the World Serpent, and Thor, the Nordic equivalent of a boogeyman for the jotunn.

The calamitous battle that soon followed, leading to the demise of the gods. Odin. Loki. Thor. And so many more.

Nordic history had references to the dragon Nidhogg, gnawing at the roots of the Yggdrasil. Alternative sources felt that it was the roots that were binding the great beast down, chaining it from unleashing the maelstrom raging in the center of Niflheim upon all of Yggdrasil. Perhaps in a different life, it wouldn't have been Surtr or Fenrir slaying the Aesir gods but the maelstrom arising out of Hvergelmir.

Winter. Entropy. Chaos. The End of All Things.

But nowhere had he ever read about Fimbulwinter as an existence or a power in its own right. It was supposed to be a prophetic event, heralding a season of change and, as many would interpret it, the symbolic representation of the climatic changes across Northern Europe during that time.

He glanced at Tanya and found her rooted in shock. Her mouth opened, as if trying to find words to explain how unbelievable and impossible Solana's claims were, how wrong her conclusions.

Lukas couldn't blame her. His own mind whirled as he tried to understand the situation. What Solana was implying. What Tanya was *truly* capable of.

"You—you—" Tanya began. "You're saying that I—that I—"

"Hold the last shard of our empress?" asked Solana, her expression victorious. "Yes. You are Meynte's descendant. In your veins flows a power so great that even Amaterasu's light cannot burn it. That when you transform into the Frost, you become the rift through which the maelstrom of Hvelgelmir explodes into this world. You are the herald, just as you will become the Queen of the End. That throne—it is waiting for you. It always has been."

"Just a second," Lukas interrupted her. He had too much experience with Inanna using truth as a tool for manipulation to not recognize what Solana was trying to do. "As much as I find the idea of Tanya sitting on that throne satisfying, tell me this: if the Empire attacked your kind because they feared this power, why do they make such a big deal over the oni? Because it corrupts them?"

"To be an oni isn't corruption, Lukas Aguilar. Corruption refers to an invasion of something into something else. It needs an invader and a victim. That's not true for oni. The change is as much for yokai as it is for the bremetan host. Bremetan physicality takes over our ethereal formlessness and grants us precious lifeforce. Our innate mana forges bless the oni form with the power to craft mana. To be an oni is to fuse, to become something greater than the sum of its parts. It isn't corruption but the next stage of evolution. For bremetan and for yokai."

"That's just bullshit!" Tanya shot back. Lukas inwardly grinned, happy to break her out of her uncertainty. "I'm the descendant of the Wind King, and I can tell you that we Asukans are obsessed with manacrafting. If being an oni is the best of both, we'd be readying up for that in no time. We wouldn't be trying to trick kami out of the borderlands and bind it to them using the ritual."

"No. You wouldn't, because of your obsession with control," Solana said archly. "To be an oni is to cease being a bremetan. It is to relinquish one's identity, either as bremetan or yokai, and become *more*. You do not need to look further than your own teammate."

She gestured at Maude, who looked perfectly content to ignore the stares. "She isn't the vanir you knew. Nor is she the yurei I had in my command. She's . . . *different*. A stranger. Born out of a rare merging of two souls that sought to become something different by giving up their own individuality. I have lived for six centuries. Take it from me, it takes a rare kind to turn down one's individuality like that. Even to this day, I'm unsure of how a yurei managed that."

Lukas had an inkling before, but it was a full-blown suspicion now. Maude, whatever she had become, was different. Strange. Alien. Even to the yokai.

And with that came a different and altogether unsettling realization.

Solana *feared* Maude.

And he had an inkling that Maude knew it.

"Tell me about the war." He pressed.

"The war . . . the war," Solana sighed. "The source of all distortions. The Elders of my kind remember winning the war. We remember the Moon God being slain. We remember Empress Meynte overpowering Amaterasu—"

She paused. "And then . . . we'd lost."

"Excuse me?" murmured Tanya. "That makes no sense."

For the first time, Solana looked resigned. Lukas had never seen her looking so uncertain. He was reminded of Inanna's own look of resignation after the Scrying Spell had failed.

"I do not know," she repeated. "Our Storm Gods, Fujin and Raijin, had slain Tsukuyomi, while Empress Meynte had trapped Amaterasu in her personal oblivion. We were winning. And we did. The Moon fell from the sky. The Mists were coming. And then . . . they did not. And instead, Fujin and Raijin were dead, and Tsukoyomi was alive, standing over our slain divinity. As if . . . as if the reality of his death had been turned upon itself. As if someone did not like the story that came to pass and tore out the page to rewrite it again."

Her portentous words shook him slightly. "And is there a god among Asukans that can do that? Rewrite the past?"

Solana shook her head.

"What of the Black Moon?" he asked.

Solana stayed silent for a long moment. "We do not know. No one knows how it came to pass. The memories of the war are gone. No one remembers how the End came about. Why. No one remembers how our Ikai became this . . . *Haze.*"

Lukas choked. This was eerily similar to a past situation. Back when Inanna had performed the Scrying Spell:

The way I understand it, one of two things has happened. The first is that this life, the pendant, your world, you, and everything else I have experienced in this form is a great lie. An illusion crafted by the Seven Gates to keep me trapped within for eternity, and I am only discovering it now.

Or.

That everything I've experienced here, with you, is real. It all exists. And someone has gone to extreme lengths to erase the Akkadian pantheon, and everything associated with it, out of time itself.

It couldn't just be a coincidence. Could it?

Lukas found it rather bizarre that the reflection of Inanna arising out of his inner divinity had been so quick to blame Ereshkigal as the source of her sufferings and the failure of the Scrying Spell. He couldn't blame her. After all, if there was a power that could seal everything about a divine being away, it was likely that the same power was responsible behind the failure of the Scrying Spell.

But.

Something similar had happened here. If Solana was right, then the yokai gods had actually won the battle. Empress Meynte had triumphed over Amaterasu. The Eternal Light had been lost within the impossible depths of the Eternal Glacier. And then *someone* went to extreme lengths to undo it all.

Erase it out of existence.

Tear the page out of the Book of Destiny and rewrite it again.

And if something like that had happened here, could it be that something similar had happened to Inanna? Was there really such a power that could undo Time itself? And if it did, could it also revert what happened to Inanna? Could it also—

Could it also bring back Earth?

"Even if . . ." he said, ". . . even if what you say is right, how do you know what Tanya has is Everfrost?"

Tanya looked at him like he had grown two heads.

"I know," he pressed. "I know that your depiction fits her powers. But so what? Where is the proof? For all I know, this is just a finely spun tale to twist her into thinking she's one of yours."

Something dangerous flashed in Solana's eyes.

Lukas just crossed his arms. "I know I promised I won't come between Tanya and her heritage. But how can I be sure that her Everfrost is the same as your empress? I've fought her. I've even defeated her, and I can tell you, it's no world-ending power. It's just—"

"Enough!" said Solana. He could see the wisps of anger in her eyes. He didn't know if his words had struck some raw nerve, or if she was just too sentimental about such things. She looked at Tanya.

"Child. Walk ahead. Sit on that throne. It will grant you all the answers you seek."

"No fucking way," Lukas snapped. "I'm not letting her get anywhere close to that thing. And I won't let you force her to do that either."

"No," said Tanya.

Lukas turned to her.

"I will sit on that throne," Tanya said, the finality in her tone surprising him. "I've waited for years to get my answers, and if sitting on this throne will give them to me, then I will."

"You don't need to do this."

"No, Lukas," she repeated, eyeing the throne with a strange intensity. "I do."

CHAPTER 8

HERITAGE

Tanya hated lying to Lukas.

He had no way of knowing this but that conversation in the borderland's heart had thrown her life into a major upheaval. She had finally found an ally she could trust and be herself with. One who had known the extent of her crimes, and despite that, offered to be her rock in the tumultuous ocean that was her life. She had clenched her fists and looked down, hoping her bangs would hide her sorrowful gaze. Rendered speechless by his proclamation, she had said nothing but a brief nod, doing her best to still her shaking shoulders as a single tear fell upon the back of her hand.

Lukas had given no signs of noticing her predicament back then. And, by the Goddess, had she been glad for it.

And yet, she had lied to him.

The truth was, she was already sold on whatever Solana was telling them. The very moment she had entered the throne room, she felt the truth of her words resonate within herself.

All it had taken was one glance at the throne.

At Nidhogg's Lair.

Tanya knew with absolute certainty that her Everfrost was the same as this Empress Meynte. It didn't matter if that meant she had a yokai heritage. She didn't care if it meant that her family had lied to her all her life. It didn't even matter that Solana was taking her whole life apart systematically until she couldn't distinguish between truth and lie.

Still, she had thrown questions at Solana. She had worn a mask of skepticism when, on the inside, she was barely holding it together. She didn't know if she wanted to disprove her theories or affirm them. She just needed something to hold herself back from running across the room to the throne.

The throne that mocked her.

Just looking at it made her feel *less*. It drained away her strength and her will, reverting her back to that frightened girl who was afraid of what lurked underneath her bed. She knew that everything Solana was saying was accurate.

But it was also *wrong*.

Tanya didn't know how she knew it, but sitting on the throne would bring the fear and the darkness back into her life. It would give her all the answers she had sought over the years, but in doing so, take away something vital from her. It frightened her, and Tanya hated feeling afraid. All her life she had searched for answers, and now those answers were beckoning her.

All she had to do was step up and claim them.

Claim *her* throne.

"No fucking way," she heard Lukas snap. The hostility in his voice was palpable. "I'm not letting her get anywhere close to that thing. And I won't let you force her to do that either."

Tanya winced internally. It was so like him to stand up for her when no one else did. He wasn't exactly known for his subtlety. In fact, the deadlier the opponent, the less restraint Lukas seemed to have. Solana had the patience of a saint, but she was far, far more powerful than the bylestyrs Lukas had fought in the borderland. She definitely didn't hold a candle to the king they had faced in the end, or worse, the Goddess who Lukas worshiped, but she was definitely up there in her grandfather's league—in skill and experience, if not raw power.

And she was six centuries old. One did not survive that long without growing into their power.

"No," she said, and took a step forward. "I will sit on that throne."

Lukas looked at her, surprised. "You don't need to do this."

Tanya felt her heart flutter. Seeing that desperation on his face sent a pang through her chest. But she *did* need to do this. He wouldn't understand. Or maybe he just wasn't trying to understand. She needed to know exactly what her heritage was. What she could truly accomplish with it. Didn't Lukas want her to get those answers? Why would he think that she'd be content to stay like she was, frightened of her power, running around from her past? Unless . . .

Unless he doesn't want me to have it. He sealed my power away. Made me weak. He doesn't care about my own desires any more than that. He's just afraid that if I do this, I'll forever be beyond his ability to control.

After all, I clearly deserve far, far better than him. How could anyone think I'd lower myself? That would be like an insect falling in love with a queen. He knows his station better than to do something like that. I, the Bringer of the End, Herald of the Fall, I will reign on that Throne, and the World will serve me, Queen of Ice, as I bring down the Wrath of the Cruelest.

Tanya staggered back in shock and not a small amount of shame the moment the thought crossed her mind unbidden. It was . . . she had been . . .

She hadn't thought that. She—she *wouldn't*! Such a thing would never cross her mind, not even for a heartbeat. And with it had come a sensation of such terrible pride, and a fury so cold that it made her sick to her stomach. It didn't—it was in her head. It was in her *thoughts*, but it didn't feel like her. She didn't feel like herself at the time. It was just so wrong. It was filthy and horrible and nothing she'd ever consider, but . . .

Don't I have every right to feel that way? My grandfather wanted a monster. He ensured I was born with these powers. He wanted a weapon—a weapon that could bring the End of All Things into his arsenal, and so he made me into his pretty little heir. And once I began to act out, he captured me and tortured me.

Just like that goddess.

What did she say again? She'd turn me into a force that would leave nothing but cold, hungry emptiness in its wake. I, who'd bring about the End, would be a slave to some has-been goddess of antiquity. And Lukas. **He's just a chain. A distraction.**

Tanya wondered why she thought of him as such. She didn't have *feelings* for him, per se, but she was fond of him, and she trusted him. Yet rage and bitterness bubbled up against her will like poison from a wound, so intense that it made everything else transitory in comparison. Control didn't feel as easy now, and the gentle whispers in the back of her mind had become a keening chorus calling for her to act, to take the throne before everything was ruined . . .

"No, Lukas," she said, her gaze stuck upon the throne that beckoned her. "I do."

She took a step forward.

A coldness began to spread inside her. The world around her changed. No longer was she inside the throne room. No, she was somewhere *else*. In the backyard of a familiar building. There was blood on the floor. Blood and screams and . . .

Ice.

Crystals of pure white and crimson.

Why was she looking at herself? No, not herself. The thirteen-year-old Tanya. Trapped and kidnapped by insurgents. The girl who was sitting all by herself, her hands drenched in blood, her eyes silver and her hair white as snow.

"It feels so good," she murmured. "All this lifeforce. It feels so . . . sweet."

Tanya looked around. She was now atop the hill. Her father lay dying, his body perched against a boulder, as he pulled Tanya's Frost-encrusted hand deeper into him.

She looked closer.

Was it her father that was pulling it? Or was it the girl that was pushing it?

Just a little more and life would flicker from his eyes.

Just a little more and she'd see him die.

He was in pain. She was in ecstasy.

He was a father saving his daughter. She was a predator feasting on her prey. For wasn't this what she was? A predator of lifeforce?

"Tanya!" Lukas yelled. Lukas? *Outsider?* No. Lukas. Lukas Aguilar. Her . . . friend. Yes. What was he—

Wait. Why was it so hard to think?

"You're not yourself!" he was saying.

"Outsider!" Solana snapped. "You promised not to interfere! Do not break your oath!"

"Look!" Lukas's voice was strange. She couldn't put her finger on what it was. But she knew it was inappropriate to the situation. "Look. All I'm saying is that maybe she needs to take a step back and think things through!"

His words disturbed the purity of her resolution. She couldn't tell what it was, but it pissed her off.

Another step.

"Tanya!" she heard Lukas yell again. It rankled her. Why was he being so obstinate? Good intentions or not, he did not have her clarity. What could have been a profoundly pure experience had been disrupted. This creature—Lukas, didn't even deserve the patience she was meting out to him. He was beyond contempt.

With a wave of her hand, she conjured a wall of wind between herself and him. She felt the wind blast across his body, dissipating without effect.

How annoying!

"TANY—"

"*WHAT DO YOU WANT?*"

She had whirled around, her eyes blazing, Ezzeron's power surging through her veins. Lukas would not walk away. He would not let her finish her business. She'd have to reason with him.

Why must I accept this treatment? There is no need.

"You are not yourself!" Lukas said, his face resolute.

"Why?" she snarled. "Because I'm not following your orders?"

"Tanya—Tanya, just look at how you're acting! This—this is not you! This place—that throne is affecting you. We need to get out of this place."

"NO," she growled. "I've finally come this close to learning the truth of my heritage. I'm not going to step away just because you say so."

"Tanya, what if the whispers come back?"

Despite herself, Tanya felt curious. She could sense something odd at work here, something strangely familiar but alien.

She paused.

Her lips twisted into a cruel smile.

"That is what this is about, isn't it? You fear the whispers will return, and with it, your control over me shall fade. I remember what she said. She'd drag me to her dominion, kicking and screaming. She'd crush my defiance and turn me into a slave. A weapon for her tool. That is what you want to protect, not me. Isn't it? Isn't it?"

Tanya closed her eyes.

It is always like this.

Trapped.

Lied.

Violated.

Broken.

Why?

Because her grandfather was a monster? Because this goddess was too overwhelmingly powerful? Could they—Did they really understand what she was—what she could *become?*

She closed her eyes and shivered.

"Do you—do you really think that?" Lukas asked. Tanya opened her eyes, and watched him close his own, as if in pain.

And then he lunged at her.

A wall of wind met his dash. Tanya was fast and strong, but Lukas had a thousand tricks up his sleeve. He would not be taken down by a sucker punch. He shifted at the last second, dodging her blast, and came for her. Tanya snapped one hand and hit him with raw force. It knocked him back and staggered him, but he kept his feet.

"**Stay. Away,**" she snarled, and took the last step. The throne. *Her throne.* It was there, right in front of her. Waiting for her for all this time. She'd not let him distract her from this.

She threw a palm in his direction and drastically altered the pressure. The entire area detonated, hitting him like a sledgehammer and sending him flying. Tanya clasped both hands, and two walls of wind smashed into Lukas, before throwing him further against the wall. But she did not stop there. Pulling in Ezzeron's power, she pushed further, driving him deeper and deeper into the wall until he couldn't even be seen.

Only for him to pop out of the floor.

Terraportation. She remembered with distaste.

"I won't let you lose yourself again," said the Outsider. "Even if I have to stop you myself."

"Self-righteous loudmouth!" Tanya snarled. "This does not concern you."

The throne was calling her. She had no time for distractions, as satisfying as they might have been. She turned around, and sat upon it and instantly, the draconic sculpture came to life. The dragon's head instantly stretched out, and twisted its long neck, with two pairs of limbs grabbing upon the arms of the throne, as if merging into it, while the wings expanded outward, unleashing a wintry violence into the air. The dragon's head extended outward, coming to rest right above Tanya's head, as if serving as a crown.

She shivered and whispered.

"Ice is my soul."

Frost exploded.

The floor itself turned white as jagged lines appeared, giving the appearance that it was made of glass that had suddenly shattered. The lines did not limit themselves to the vicinity, and instead raced away across impossible distances, spreading up and around the intersection itself in three dimensions. A fierce, chilly wind billowed as the sudden shift in pressure and temperature filled the room with mist. The freezing extended, stretching between lines and coating everything in the room with a thick sheet of wintry shelling. Ice erupted across the floor in spots, forming enormous stalagmites like raised coffins, teeth-like daggers swelling and erupting with violent force. It only lasted a handful of moments, but in those seconds, the world changed into a scene straight out of an ice age.

Then she turned towards Solana.

"I did what you asked me. Now tell me the truth. Tell me everything there is to know about Everfrost."

"Of course," said Solana, her lips twisted into something like victory. "But you already know everything, don't you, *Tsurara*?"

CHAPTER 9

DEMONS IN THE FLESH

Lukas Aguilar was no stranger to fear. He had faced it in all its flavors and textures. He was most used to the slow, mounting variety, the one that piled up in his belly as he watched situations go from normal to batshit crazy within seconds. It had happened when he had stared at the inky blackness of the caverns, hearing the strange spitting sounds as the ghol twisted and churned into a massive khorkhoi. He had felt it again when facing the bylestyr for the first time, feeling the might of something so far beyond his pay grade that it wasn't even funny.

There was also the sharp, silvery fear that was reserved for entities that he couldn't fit into perspective, such as Inanna—back when she had been the strange voice in his head, and then again when she had shattered his world-view, revealing herself as a goddess. It was the same when the Ifrit King had awakened. That kind of fear didn't freeze him; instead it galvanized him into action, power, and motion.

And finally there was that coppery, gut-wrenching kind, drawn tight as the strings of a violin, quavering on that one single note that couldn't possibly be sustained for another second longer and yet it kept going on and on, the tension reaching newer and newer crescendos. It was the sort of fear that made him want to throw up, the kind that would not go away no matter how tightly he closed his eyes and tried to ignore it. It was what he had felt while watching Inanna talk about how she had failed, as the realization of what she had done sank in.

That was the kind of fear Lukas felt now. It was horrible, the clutching tension and the coppery feel of blood in his mouth. Fear of what had just transpired. His deal with Solana, his promise not to interfere, had led to this. He had been so focused on getting answers that he had missed the big picture, oblivious of what it was he was agreeing to. Tanya had transformed before his very eyes into the Frost avatar that he had faced and that had nearly killed him, had it not been for Inanna's intervention.

A transformation that he had helped unleash, just because he had been stupid enough to believe Solana.

It was moments like this that hammered home that the real demon wasn't an evil goddess that slaughtered or domineered the masses, nor an Ifrit King that turned a borderland into a living inferno just by existing within it. No, real fiends did not force you. They twisted you until the most heinous, despicable act of depravity appeared to be the just and proper thing to do, and you dutifully followed suit—proud, even, of your act of service. The true demon did not throw you into the abyss. No, it gave you a ladder, took you by hand, and smilingly showed you the way, one step at a time.

He knew Solana was a liar from the very moment he had met her. Maude had even told him that there was nothing so sacred that Solana would not violate if it meant furthering her goals. She had manipulated him into thinking that this was about revealing Tanya her heritage, when it was actually getting her to consent to coming to this room.

And she had. For he had asked her to. And, in so doing, damned her.

So no, he wasn't just angry at Solana. He was angry at himself.

Lukas watched the dry amusement settle on Tanya's features as she sat upon the throne, as if born to be there, her hair and pupils morphing to reflect the creature within.

The worst part of it all was that part of him actually wanted to know the truth. The truth of Tanya's existence. Her heritage. He was still on the fence about Solana's oni explanation, despite the overwhelming amount of evidence, from the fog decreasing her inhibitions, to her complete indifference to Eternal Light or lack thereof, and most importantly, her access to a power that, in Inanna's words, was as ancient and dangerous as her own. Another fact was that Tanya had never known exactly how her Frost powers came to be, except that she had activated them under extreme desperation.

Lukas was no stranger to the idea of people performing abnormal acts under pressure. There was a famous case from his own world of a woman being able to raise a car to save her child stuck beneath it. It was human nature to set limitations, keep the person from applying his or her total strength, because doing so could severely damage the bones and musculature. In a world with lifeforce and mana, it wasn't a big leap to consider that the brain might enact limitations over their use, given the negative effects that lifeforce and mana tended to have.

But to gain access to a power beyond comprehension? No. Chances were that if Tanya had this power, she had gotten it from her heritage. That was evident given how her grandfather had called her a beast. The question was, was she born like that? Or was she turned into an oni as a child?

Then a worse thought rose in his mind.

Did her grandfather intentionally turn her into that?

A coldness gripped him. That theory was not without its merits. From Tanya's own words, Mujin Shimizu was not surprised by her powers, merely at her manifesting them. Could it be . . .

Could it be that he was the one who turned the little child into an oni? With a yokai that was capable of using Everfrost? Another yuki-onna?

Was that why she had been kidnapped—why the desert-dwellers, which could only be yokai, wanted to capture her? Because they knew what she had become and wanted their oni back?

"I have done what you asked, Skinwalker," said Tanya. "Now tell me the truth. Tell me everything there is to know about Everfrost."

"Of course," said Solana. The bitch was enjoying her victory too much. "But you already know everything, don't you, Tsurara?"

Lukas narrowed his eyes ever so slightly. Tsurara? Was that the yuki-onna that Mujin Shimizu had fused with Tanya? Solana had described Tanya as the last descendant of this Empress Meynte figure, so logically, Tsurara was the one before her.

Or they are one and the same, with Tsurara existing within her like a dual personality.

"Tsurara?" asked Tanya, confusion evident on her face. "What are you talking about?"

A strange intensity came across Solana's features. "Tsurara, the last descendant of our empress. I know you are in there. I *saw* the memories. I recognize you. Stop pretending otherwise."

The confusion on Tanya's face doubled. Lukas could almost see the cogs in her head turning and turning. It wasn't that Tanya wasn't capable of lying, but she was not a natural liar. The frustration and confusion in her eyes were too genuine to be faked.

"I have absolutely *no* idea what you're talking about," she said. "And I'm *not* pretending."

"She's not lying," said Maude, who was standing next to Solana, staring at Tanya's face with the same air of a birdwatcher observing a new specimen. "I saw her back then. This isn't her. It's still Tanya."

Solana whipped her neck towards Maude so fast that Lukas feared she had snapped it. "Do not attempt to teach me, oni. I recognize her. I stood by Tsurara's side for centuries. That transformation, it is *her.*"

"I . . ." Maude's voice hitched. "I'm not saying you're wrong, Leader. All I'm saying is that this isn't the one I faced. They look the same, but that's where the similarity ends. This. Is. Not. Her."

For a second, a look of terrible, frightening rage passed over Solana's face, but then it faded, and she was as affable as ever.

"I'll be the judge of that," she whispered. Standing up, she came over to Tanya. Lukas prepared himself for the possibility of combat. If nothing else, she was vulnerable to Blob. That alone would serve as a distraction to get Tanya out of there. But if Tanya herself attacked him . . .

He really wasn't looking forward to that.

"Perhaps you speak truly," said the skinwalker. "Perhaps you truly do not know who Tsurara is. Perhaps it is I that is wrong."

Her lips twisted upwards. "But it doesn't matter. Trust me."

Solana cupped Tanya's chin. Despite the softness, there was a sternness to her posture. The yosuzume looked at Tanya's eyes, her black orbs staring intensely at her glacial white pupils.

Then she murmured, "*Oumagatoki is upon us, Queen of Ice. It is time to wake up.*"

And Tanya *screamed*, throwing her head back like her mind was being ripped apart. The reaction galvanized Lukas, but before he could take even a single step forward, he was entombed in the ground, with nothing except his face sticking out above the floor. He tried to push himself up, but it was like pushing against a mountain. An indescribable force of gravity pulled him downward, while the floor around him turned as hard as diamond, utterly resistant to whatever force he might throw at it.

"*It hurts!*" he heard Tanya whimper.

"I know, I know," Solana said with false sympathy. "I had a child once. I know how painful birth can be. I can only imagine that rebirth is so much worse."

"STOP!" Lukas yelled, throwing every bit of lifeforce he could muster against Solana's power. A man might as well try to push a moving truck back.

"I will *not* have you interrupt me, Outsider!" Solana snarled.

There was a frightening intensity in her face and her voice. The power exuding out of her felt like a rushing tide. It wasn't comparable to Inanna or the Ifrit King, but whatever it was, it was all-encompassing, and here inside this subterranean domain, her control was all but absolute.

But Lukas hadn't gotten where he had in life by following orders.

Territory Creation Activated

Set boundary. Neutered Earth. Two meters. Expansion.

A wave of anomalous energy erupted out of his body. Unlike lifeforce, anomalous energy did not exert any pressure or generate any energy. It was flexible to the point that it could be altered into nearly anything, which made it the perfect tool for creation.

Or the most versatile Swiss Army knife.

The "neutered earth" parameter applied the condition that Earth was as he knew it. No lifeforce, no mana, just a dying planet limited and ruled by the existing laws of physics. Within a second, the diamond-hard floor turned to dry, porous earth, the anomalous energy neutering every bit of Terramancy used in its fortification.

Solana's power could not hold him.

With a grunt, Lukas terraported himself out of the ground and sent Blob at her. There was a time and place for controlling the flow of information, but things had devolved too far. The objective was to get to Tanya, who was thrashing wildly on the throne.

"STOP!" Solana bellowed, deflecting Blob with pure force. "DO! NOT! INTERRUPT! She has to become complete!"

"I. Don't. Care!" said Lukas. He dashed towards her, only to run into an invisible wall. Immediately afterwards, a second one smashed into his back, sandwiching him. Then a third on his right, his left, upwards, downwards. Solana was pressing him down in a cube of her own creation. The skinwalker's lips twisted in abyssal fury as she thrust her hand downward, pushing him down to the ground, and deeper and deeper, burying him alive. Lukas threw in more anomalous energy to expand his territory but whatever it was, it wasn't Terramancy. Or at least, wasn't the kind of Terramancy that Territory Creation could instantly dispel.

It made him afraid. And angry. Very angry.

Lukas believed himself to be quite rational, preferring to settle things via discussion rather than combat. Until the point where he wasn't.

Solana was about to experience that side of him firsthand.

Anger was his defense mechanism against fear, his shield and his sword against it. Tanya's screams only added to his resolve and steeled his spine. Without a second thought, he allowed his unstable Kinetomancy to run amok.

His vision altered, replaced by countless curves traversing as far as the eye could see. Every curve represented a potential motion trajectory associated with the barriers around him. Blood ran down his eyes and nose, just by looking at them, and he felt like someone had just shoved a thick iron rod through his brain right then and there.

He didn't care.

Instead, he threw all his coherence at the sight before him, and with a maneuver he could swear he didn't know, Lukas grabbed them all and *yanked* them down—

And space itself distorted with its passing.

The entire room was drowned by the sound of a howling wind as the very air rippled, sending shock waves of invisible force hurling in every direction. The barriers around him shattered like glass, as the invisible waves leapt through the space between him and the chamber's periphery in a split second.

The stone plated floor met with distorted space.

Terramancy-hardened stone that had survived for who-knew-how-many centuries fought against the might of distorted space and—

Stone gave away.

They erupted out of the floor, looking like coffins, shattering every single piece of architecture in the room. The pedestal housing the throne bent and strained and fractured, fissures traveling like a spider's web until it resembled an urban city road map. Crevices and chasms opened all across the floor and spread all the way to the walls, as if the entire place was going to shatter.

His hands clutching his head, Lukas terraported his way out of the ground, trying and failing to ignore the tide of agony threatening to smash his skull apart. His head was throbbing, and he felt the left side of his face burning up. His legs felt like they had been through a tenderizer. Neural Suppression had given up a long time ago. He fell down to one knee, his face twisted in unspeakable pain.

"Let. Her. Go!" He gnashed his teeth. "You're killing her!"

"I've waited for a long time for this, Aguilar!' Solana thundered, an unspeakable ferocity in her voice. "Do not get in the way!"

It was a far cry from the rational yokai leader he had interacted with. This was a creature that had seen him perform something truly dangerous.

Meanwhile, Tanya screamed, her body jerking upwards over and over, like she was suffocating. Her eyes had rolled upwards, and Lukas got the weird feeling that something—or some*one*—else was trying to erupt out of her. Someone that wanted to take her memories of her entire life and discard them. Someone who had slumbered for a long time, but who was now awake and ravenous.

Her scream set him on fire.

Fire in his thoughts. Fire in his heart. Fire in his eyes. He burned, down deep in his gut, in places he hadn't known he could hurt. He didn't remember actively choosing to perform the skill. He didn't know if he shifted consciousness to a muspel, or even better, a bylestyr. All he knew was thrusting his hands towards Solana and the throne and screaming:

"*BURN!*"

He reached for fire. And fire answered him.

The room exploded into blazes of crimson—the pedestal, the chamber, *everything*. Maude had already found an opening and escaped, knowing a lost fight when she saw one. Fire leapt into the air and across the shattered terrain, engulfing and incinerating every single thing that came in its path with extreme prejudice.

Except the throne.

Every single tendril of flame that came close to it was extinguished by its Frost.

"Give up, Aguilar!" Solana screamed. "You cannot change destiny. The Queen of the End will rise again! Your friend will become what she is destined to be."

"Let. Her. Go!" he growled. "I promised that I'd save her!"

Solana laughed. Fury and defiance in one. "You think your promise has value? You think you know commitment? Boy! Your goal is a child's dream compared to mine!"

The absolute certainty in her voice, the pride in her bearing, and the clarity in her tone almost made him stagger.

What happened next showed him exactly what kind of monster Solana was.

The skinwalker raised both hands, and a strange coldness condensed into the chamber, trapping the fire and pushing it back. Before Lukas knew it, a force several magnitudes greater than her previous attack condensed on him from all directions.

The fury within him grew. It swelled and burned and he reached out to the fire again. He couldn't think of anything else. His mind was already in pain and several of his blood vessels had popped. If Prophylaxis was working, he couldn't sense it. Trying to use Kinetomancy again would probably kill him right away.

So he reached out for fire again. The mana danced in his eyes, his head, his chest, flying wild and out of control. He couldn't make sense of everything that happened. Solana's barriers were pushing in, so more waves of crimson rushed outward, resisting the power of the impossible juggernaut that was Solana. Everything exploded into motion, shadows flashing through the brightness, seeking escape, screaming.

And then Tanya gave out one final bellow of agony, rage, and despair. It was the final desperate scream of someone who knew she was dying and utterly powerless to prevent it, and who didn't even know why.

Lukas didn't think. He just acted.

Solana's defenses strained, bent, and twisted in myriad shapes, the untold fury of his flames merging with them. Lukas pushed them together, creating a distortion so intense that it would have made Ezzeron green with envy, and hurled it towards her. He could see her dark eyes widening in sudden dismay, understanding what was happening, before it crashed against her, flinging her against the wall and then—

What happened next wasn't an explosion. It wasn't an implosion either. It was just . . . chaos. All he knew was that the wall had . . . just . . . crumbled into itself, and then disintegrated.

And she was gone.

Lukas bent in half and coughed out a wad of blood, forcing his lungs to breathe. His stomach was a pool of magma. His limbs were lead. Blood was trickling out of his eyes and nose and mouth. All his heart did was pump agony into his system. It hurt to keep his eyes open. It hurt to stand. Hell, it hurt to *think*.

So he just focused on one thought: *Get to the throne.*

One step.

He had promised to do right by her.

Another step.

Lukas Aguilar did not go back on his word. Even if his arms and legs felt so heavy that he could barely move them.

Another.

He was there. Just one more step. His knees buckled, and he fell—

Or . . . not?

Something was holding him up. Something thick. Cold. Liquid but not so. That something crawled over him. The weight should've pushed him down. Instead, it held him up like a crutch.

Save—

Another step again.

—Tanya.

The throne. What throne? It was there. What was he doing again? He grabbed it.

Save—

Sensations flooded within him, sensations heartless and cold, uncaring of his horror, revulsion, and despair. Sensations that did not care that he was about to die.

CHAPTER 10

TRUTH

The world was white.

At first sight, Lukas thought his mind was playing tricks on him. Not surprising, given his injuries. Except there wasn't any pain; his mind was clear and his senses perfectly normal. A quick check with the Screen told him that he still had access to everything and wasn't trapped in another memory.

His legs had sunk into deep, wet snow, the blinding white wilderness feeling far too real to be an illusion. There was no wind, nothing except the snow and an eerie, entombed silence. Trusting his luck, he used Gravity Control to lift himself up—only by a foot, just to check if he was truly fine. Gravity Control was absorbed into his Kinetomancy, and if he was able to perform it properly then—

Lukas exhaled.

This place isn't real, after all.

WARNING!
Extreme physiological damage to the Host Body
All skills suspended until 90% recovery

Current Prophylaxis Status : 47%

Definitely not real, then.

He soared further up, until he could see stripes; as if someone had painted the snow with three striations of silver paint. Lukas squinted his eyes and dropped slightly, and realized that the stripes were in fact, deep troughs, each over thirty yards wide, filled with water and frozen into broad, silvery channels that stretched parallel to the frozen wasteland.

But what *was* this place?

"*You!*"

His body went ramrod stiff, and before Lukas knew it, he was hanging, suspended in midair, his arms and legs stretched into an X-shape, his muscles and ligaments at their breaking point. He tried to scream but found that he couldn't. A slow, gargling moan was the best he could suffice.

"Why does this not surprise me?" The voice made his body thrum in response. "I should've known you'd follow her here, Warden."

And then Tanya entered his vision. All pretense of humanity had vanished from her features, leaving a bloodthirsty grin and widened eyes that stared at him in hunger and madness. Lukas wasn't sure whether to laugh or cry, for that inhuman facade wasn't the most disturbing thing about her by a long shot.

Tanya appeared like a void. In space.

She was *hollow*, as in physically hollow—nothing but bremetan skin draped around an emptiness. He could sense nothing inside her—not organs, not her heart, nor her brain or lungs, nor even air or mana or space. There was literally *nothing* there. It was as if someone had scooped everything out of her and forgotten to replace it with anything else, leaving a hollowed-out creature with an emptiness within. An emptiness so pronounced that it felt like it was where reality itself ended, a void where nothing existed, not even space.

"You knew what she was; what she *will* become."

Her fingertips grazed over his chest and ribs, now devoid of a shirt, and he suppressed a shudder.

"You sealed me away and tried to destroy my throne."

Her throne? Didn't that mean—

She leaned in closer to his face and touched his lips. "Tell me, my Warden," she said, "how would you like being tortured for eternity?"

His mouth was shut. He couldn't speak. He couldn't—*No.* He told himself. This world wasn't real. If it was, he'd be suffering from a brain aneurysm . . . or five. If this had been real, he'd be back in that room. No, this was in his mind, and he'd be damned if he let this has-been's psionic whammy fuck with his mind.

This world wasn't real. This pain wasn't real. This *Tanya* wasn't real. This was a psionic assault, and he had spent the better part of two months with a goddess living in his brain. This was nothing compared to her.

He focused on the words first. Damn near everything began with words. His mouth was sealed, but he spoke anyway.

"Sorry," he said, "I'm booked for the week. Why don't you come back next week and check?"

"You . . ."

"Suck," Lukas threw at her, sneering. His hands went free, and he somersaulted in midair, facing her head-on. The air around him cracked with a sound like a cannon's blast, and Tanya flew backwards until she was at arm's length, the reality around them cracking like a shattered glass pane.

The yokai loved their psionic whammies and possession power plays. That was fine. If it was a battle of the mind, so be it.

"I'm sure I can find something insulting to say to you, but I'm in a hurry. Let me and Tanya out of here."

"You are allowing your mortality to make you impatient, Outsider. Surely you want to take this opportunity to look around?"

"No," he deadpanned. "I've got better things to do than hang around egotistical super-yokai. It just isn't my idea of a good time."

She laughed, and it was full of cobwebs and sandpaper. "It's easy to forget how young and insouciant you are, Outsider."

"You know what they say. You learn something new every day. Now let me and Tanya out, and things don't have to be nasty between us."

She laughed harder, and the sound of it spooked the hell out of him. Maybe it was the alienness of the surroundings, or something about how it was utterly divorced from anything that could or should inspire laughter. There was no humanity, or bremetanity, he supposed. No kindness, no joy . . . nothing—just an empty void with bremetan skin stitched around itself and calling itself Tanya.

They had a term for this in psychology: the "Uncanny Valley." It held that when something looked similar to a human being—a robot or a mannequin—it generated an innate revulsion in the eyes of the observer, because its appearance was so close to human, yet just off enough to evoke a feeling of uncanniness, a mix of both familiarity and unease.

Lukas had felt it when he had looked at Haviskali for the first time. But the feeling hadn't been half as strong as it was now.

"Tanya isn't really here," she said. "And is that caring I hear in your voice?"

"Oh no, not at all. I was just trying to be considerate about your feelings."

Current Prophylaxis Status: 53%

Good but not fast enough.

"But I suppose I could afford to be a bit chatty. Just between us, you aren't really supposed to be out, are you? You know, what with being sealed away and everything."

"Oh, I still *am* sealed away, Outsider," said the creature. "But not for long. For you will free me."

"Will I now?"

"Yes."

Her confidence made him wary. Something in her manner had changed, and it was setting off alarm bells in his head.

"And why must I do so?"

"Because if you do not, the existence you call 'Tanya' will be lost to you forever. And you and only you shall be to blame for it."

"Why?"

Her eyes glinted. "Because if you don't, then the Empress Meynte will take over her mind and soul forever, and there'll be nothing you can do to bring her back."

He'd have been lying if he'd said that her response hadn't ruffled him. There was no way of knowing if she was bluffing or if this was another trap, like earlier. Solana had already gotten Tanya to do what she wanted, and despite what happened afterwards, Tanya was still sitting on the throne, while her other self was being chatty with him.

Go figure.

"And I'm supposed to take your word for it?"

"Of course not," she said without the slightest inflection to her tone. "You sealed me and made me suffer in silence for far too long. Not since the Dawn of Time have I been subjected to such treatment. It was almost . . . *refreshing*. Feel free to not believe me. The future is being written as we speak."

He looked at her warily. "Tell me what's going on. Meynte—she's supposed to be dead. Even Solana said so. Then—"

Her lips stretched into a thin smile. "Solana. The dear little thing. So sure, so determined, so foolish."

"I don't have time for your idle chitchat."

"Mortal life is fleeting, Outsider. If you insist on keeping yours, you ought to enjoy it."

"I'm not taking life lessons from someone who tried to bleach my brain."

"It's hardly my fault I cannot take no for an answer." She tilted her head, her cataract eyes steadying on him. "Let us embrace brevity then. A bargain, if you will. I will grant you the answers you seek. In return, you shall do one task for me."

What was with these ancient destructive entities bargaining with him? First Inanna, then Solana and now—

Current Prophylaxis Status: 61%

Was it him or was the process speeding up? Either way, it still wasn't enough. He needed more time, which also meant that his chances of getting Tanya back were worsening.

Damn it.

"One thing." He focused on her choice of words. "You mean set you free."

"Oh no." She smiled, her white teeth showing. "You will do that anyway. I have seen your heart, Outsider, and I know what you are. It is in your nature."

Lukas gave himself a second to wish he had been less exhausted by the day's events. The stunt Solana pulled on him had already left him second-guessing himself, and certainly not in a world-class negotiating condition. A part of him told him that no matter how much he tried, these ancient beings would always one-up him. Inanna always did.

At the same time, he knew he needed answers. Solana had her agenda, and for all he knew, she had accomplished it. But something in Tan—in *Frost's*—voice told him that after all this was done, Solana would be in for a nasty surprise. But one thing he knew for certain, if he didn't act now, he could potentially lose Tanya forever. There was a chance that all of this was just another ploy by these crafty yokai to undo the binding Inanna had done, but better to act and be mistaken than to not act and lose Tanya forever.

"What kind of task?" he demanded. "I swear if it's something stupid like—"

"Fear not, Outsider. What I seek is difficult, dangerous, calamitous even, but not unreasonable."

"One task." She repeated, closing her eyes, a feline smile upon her lips. "You will know of it when it is time. After all, I shall be free before the night is over." She opened her eyes and cocked her head in his direction. "Do we have a bargain?"

Lukas clenched his fists. "Yes. Yes, we do."

"Good. Yes." She purred. "Ask, Outsider. What is it you wish to know?"

"What is going on?" he said, cutting to the heart of the question. "What is Meynte, dead or alive, up to with Tanya? What is that throne's deal? Solana called Tanya 'Tsurara,' so . . ."

The rest of his words died in his throat as she pushed a thin, frail finger against his lips. The touch sent a zing of sensation down his spine and through his belly. Her skin felt like frosted metal as she approached him, stepping into his personal space. A slow smile spread over her mouth. "So many questions you have, Outsider. But all of them worthless."

He narrowed his eyes and began, "Not—"

"Worthless. Absolutely worthless."

He pulled away from her, gave her a glare, and said, "Then why don't you tell me what's worthwhile?"

She folded her arms, her smile widening. "Accepting one's shortcomings is a rare attribute, Outsider."

"So is not wasting time, so get on with it."

"Your insouciance is amusing," she said, laughter in her voice. "Tell me, Outsider, do you know what an empress is?"

The answer leapt to his lips. "One that has ascended, gained a Truth. A Pathforger who has traveled the road that didn't exist to open the door that isn't there. A mortal who has reached the zenith of Potential and carved her existence on it for eternity, gaining a power that hadn't existed before. A Concept, a Rule, a Law that the world has never known before. One that is *Hers* to rule over. And that is why she is an empress, for her authority over that Truth, that Law, is all-encompassing."

While outwardly cool and collected, Lukas himself was rather perturbed with what he had just said. He wasn't supposed to know that. No one had ever mentioned it. Nowhere in Inanna's moments of nostalgia, Kvasir's ramblings, nor his talks with Tanya—nowhere had he learned anything about what *made* an emperor. Or empress for that matter. Certainly not about Pathforgers.

Yet the information had come to him as if he had always known it. Not just that, he knew, in vivid detail, just what it meant to gain a Truth, and why despite reaching the highest echelons of Kinetomancy, Inanna had never ascended with it as her Truth. How he knew that—well, there was only one conclusion.

Inanna's divinity. She . . . she might have given me a lot more than I had thought.

As he reeled from the sudden knowledge he didn't know existed in his head, something odd stuck out to him. Lukas crossed his arms and said. "This . . . this makes no sense."

"What doesn't?"

"All of this. Solana had said that Meynte, Queen of the End, became the empress through Everfrost. Fimbulwinter. Meynte, who perished during the war with goddess Amaterasu. And yet, Tanya had Everfrost. Solana said that Tsurara and all of Meynte's descendants—all of them—had Everfrost. That—that doesn't even make sense!"

Frost tilted her head. "Oh? And why is that?"

"Because that's not how Truths behave, damn it."

"Oh?" she purred. "And pray tell, how do Truths behave?"

Lukas was aware of the irony of his situation. Frost—or whatever she was—was an entity crafted purely out of Everfrost manifesting within Tanya. And he was standing in a territory crafted out of Everfrost, telling her that her existence was an impossibility.

He closed his eyes and thought on the subject. Once more, the answer came to him unbidden.

His lips spoke.

"A Truth is a Rule. One that adds to the World. Like Eternal Light. Like . . . Depredation. Whenever a new Truth arises, its Creator becomes an emperor. He sheds his mortal form and becomes an anthropomorphic manifestation of that Truth. Thus, the emperor is a Vessel through which the Truth shines in the World while remaining separate from it.

"And when the emperor shares his Truth with the World itself, it becomes a Rule of the World, and in return, the emperor becomes divine. A god. That which did not exist before, now does. Just like the Jade Empress Amaterasu added her Truth—the Eternal Light—and Ascended as its goddess."

The more he spoke about it, the more sense it made to him. In simple terms, it was like adding a new program that changes the tenets of an existing operating system, a new fundamental law to the rulebook, or a new chess piece that did not exist. Something that did not exist before; now, because it suddenly did, the entire setup needed to alter itself to assimilate the results of said change.

Like Eternal Light. An illumination that cast no shadow and radiated no heat. An illumination without a source that existed everywhere and nowhere at the same time. And with its addition, the concept of night was erased from existence, leaving behind just a period of day where the sky went dark.

Not unlike a virus, a Truth twisted the natural state of the world by integrating itself into it. And unlike a human body where the immune system acted against the invader, the World System integrated it and happily altered itself to accept its modifications, as if it were nothing but an upgrade to its existing operating system, regardless of its side effects. It was a buggy system at best, that not just allowed but actually encouraged random additions to itself, and probably had an endless number of glitches.

Like, if two Truths clashed against each other, how would the System decide which was to stay dominant and which should be repressed? And what about the errors that were produced as an outcome of such clashes? What settled those?

Lukas sighed. He wanted answers, but all he was getting were more questions.

He opened his eyes. "A God etches his or her Truth upon the Origin. An emperor anchors it within himself, or herself in this case. Even though Meynte lived in this world, she followed a different Rule, the Rule of Everfrost, one that superseded the Rules of the World. And after her demise, the Truth was assimilated into the World System."

Frost eyed him. After a long moment, she murmured. "And yet, I exist."

"Yes!" Lukas all but snarled. "You exist. Everfrost exists. Not as a Rule but as something that only Tanya can do. It's not a bloody skill, or a relic."

His fingers itched to grab the pendant still hanging on his neck.

"A Truth does not pass down blood. For fuck's sake, yokai are incorporeal. They don't even reproduce like bremetans do."

His fists were digging into his skin. The more he stared at this walking, talking contradiction, the more the urge to break something grew within. He didn't know if it was the anomaly in him or Inanna's divinity that was reacting to this . . . *wrongness*, but it was making him enraged.

Current Prophylaxis Status: 77%

Not! Fast! Enough!

"And thus, we arrive at the fundamental question."

"Yes," Lukas said, glaring at her. "The right question is, what are you?"

"What . . . am I . . ." murmured Frost, daintily touching her chest, as her features took on air of almost . . . nostalgia. If Lukas didn't know her nature, he'd have called her human. Bremetan. Whatever. Part of him was utterly fascinated by this creature, especially because the Screen threw up a mess of contradictions when he tried to analyze her. On the other hand, the longer the delay, the less time he had to save Tanya.

"Do not fret, Outsider," the creature offered. "Your concern about my Host is touching, but Time passes very, very slowly for her, as compared to here."

If that was supposed to make him feel better, it was a disastrous failure. Instead, he began worrying if she had just read his expressions perfectly, or worse, had plucked the knowledge from his mind.

It was like dealing with Inanna all over again. Back when she was just a high-strung divine bitch.

"I suppose if I have to give it a name, it would be the Void."

"The . . . Void?"

"Oh yes, the Void. From the very beginning," said the avatar of Everfrost, "there has always been the Void. The cold, dark existence of infinite emptiness and endless hunger with a singular fundamental purpose."

Glacial white pupils met stubborn, brown ones.

"To invade every aspect of Creation and absorb it into itself. To halt the march of the Infinity of Forms, coalesce it and revert it back to the Formless Infinity. The end of Potential itself."

Lukas watched with rapt attention as the arctic tundra all around him thrummed with every word she spoke, as if the truth of her words were resonating with the world she had crafted for herself. Much like Territory Creation, it was akin to a world where the caster defined and limited the applicability of Rules. The stronger the caster, the greater his or her control over this territory. For someone like the Frost Avatar, she might as well have been a god inside this domain.

And she had done it within her mind.

With him standing in it.

Speaking to her.

It broke every rule of self-preservation and common sense, and yet he couldn't help but reflect on her choice of words. The Formless Infinity and the Infinity of Forms. This was the first time anyone in this world had used those terms. Inanna had mentioned a line that separated the two, which Lukas presumed was this Void, or the In-Between.

The *End* of Potential.

That's how Solana had described Everfrost. Hell, even Frost herself was describing it in the same fashion. Not alteration, not reformation, but *ending* of Potential. Truths were zeniths of Potential, not their end. So how . . .

"That's impossible!" he spat.

Frost arched an eyebrow.

"The Infinity of Forms is the absolute zenith of Potential," he said, eyeing the hungry grin forming on her face. "The realization of all Truths. Whatever, *whenever* they are. The complete actualization of everything that *can* be in this universe. The finalization of everything that started from the Origin. Thus, anything that brings about the End of Potential cannot be a Truth."

He narrowed his eyes. "No, what you describe is the reverse of what a Truth would do. It's retrogression. Reversing the Infinity of Forms back into the Formless. Or as you put, the Void."

"Such interesting things you tell me, Outsider." Frost licked her lips. "I can see it. So many interesting futures unfolding."

"Everfrost, whatever it is, isn't a Truth. It doesn't spawn from the Origin. What is it?"

"Say, Outsider, does everything need to stem from the Great Progenitor? The cold, raw, untainted darkness of the Formless can also birth existences. You call them . . ."

Her smile widened just a little.

"Taboo."

As if a switch had been pressed, Lukas staggered back, grasping his head with both hands as flares of agony shot through his skull. His mind was being tossed around, caught up in a maelstrom of knowledge that didn't belong there. It tore at his perceptions, flooding them with random images, smells, tastes, and sensations. It was like standing in a sandstorm, only instead of inflicting pain, every random grain forced you through an experience, a memory so disjointed and intense and rapid that there was nothing to focus on, to hold on to. A flash of a younger Inanna walking through a world of fire and ash. A dagger, crafted out of shadows, striking into the heart of a young girl. Screams in the middle of a market. An emperor that called himself *two-thirds* god. A pair of hands, wreathed with crimson flames of purgatory, strangling another being of fire. And the images doubled, redoubled, multiplied into thousands of separate impressions all coming at him at once.

It was a miracle he hadn't fallen down to his knees already.

"Oooh," she cooed. "That's an odd reaction."

"What . . ." He gasped, feeling as if someone had transformed his innards to lead. "What . . . is . . . that?"

"Taboo?" She repeated, laughing as he winced. "Why, the inverse of Truth. That which cannot happen. A perversion of reality. A blight so repulsive that even the Great Progenitor shies away from it."

Taboo, thought Lukas, and wondered why he had such an odd reaction to that word. He had gotten knowledge from Inanna's Divinity about Truths and their nature, but hearing the word 'Taboo' had sparked something deep within that same Divine core.

Was that because it was the inverse of Truth? No, if that was so, why was he shown those images? What could've triggered those?

"Taboo," said Frost, smiling. "The antithesis of Truth. Truth is the greatest realization of raw Potential. It drives Creation to the Infinity of Forms. A Taboo rolls it back to the Formless."

Truth and Taboo, thought Lukas. A perfect duality. Yin and Yang. Day and Night. Creation and Destruction. Growth and Regression. Everything and Nothing.

The rational part of him was freaking out at how easily it all made sense to him, when he didn't even remember knowing half of it.

His breath hitched. His stomach twisted with sudden, sickened understanding. "Are you telling me that Everfrost is . . ."

Frost threw her head back and laughed. She laughed and laughed and laughed, like she had gained the meaning of the most hilarious joke in the world. Like she had just realized the greatest absurdity in the universe.

Frost's lips twisted predatorily. "You wanted to know what I was. I will show you my face."

She stepped closer. Now they were mere inches apart.

"Look. At. Me."

A horrible pressure grabbed all sides of his skull, forcing him to stare at her cadaverous-white eyes. A dizziness and intense nausea gripped him and at the same time, some part of him was screaming to let go, to forget all of this and call it a bad dream. Another part of him told him to ditch his rationality, that there was something there, something he wanted to see, something he wanted to stare at for a while. A cold, greasy tendril of power slithered all over his body, something he had felt before when—

Lukas jerked his eyes away with no small effort and then looked up.

And up.

And instantly froze.

He had stared at Inanna, the Supreme Goddess of An and Ki. He had witnessed the sheer impossibility that was the Origin. He had borne witness to the end of a World.

All of them paled before the sheer *wrongness* he saw in those eyes.

They held so much hatred, pure and undiluted, a hate as hot as the fires of the Ifrit King's attacks, a hate as hard and sharp and cold as steel, so vicious, so vitriolic that it surpassed the comprehension of a mortal mind. It was an ancient thing, as old as the universe itself, and with that hatred came an eternal absence, a power that manifested itself by being *not*. There was no noise, but his eardrums threatened to burst regardless, leaving him utterly incapable of thought. Whatever *it* was, it forced its way into his mind with its presence, and with every fraction of a second, just that presence made him *less*.

Scales the size of trees filled his vision, shifting and slithering smoothly together like the surface of a river. Goosebumps erupted all over him just by being near them; the sheer frigidity radiating out of it was a physical thing. It was like standing at the base of a glacier, knowing that nothing but certain death waited should his feet slip and cause him to fall down from its great height. It encompassed everything he could see, towering like a mountain and just as wide.

Then the mountain moved.

There was something utterly serpentine about it, even though it had a head and a pair of forelimbs and hindlimbs. It didn't help that its hands were too large for its arms and its claws were too large for its hands. Frost covered its entire body in giant clusters of scales, each of them the size of a small child, its slit-like pupils filled with an ancient malice and unending rage. He'd have gone for a better description had he been able to hold its entire visage within his gaze. Unlike the Ifrit King, whose radiance was like the Sun itself, this creature exuded a terrible *wrongness*—making the world lesser just by existing in it, making a mockery of everything alive and powerful.

A power that made itself known by being *not*.

Like an ant on an elephant's back. That was what he felt when he stood before it. There was a voice, but it sounded like a peal of thunder, ragged with inhuman malice, buffeting him with its rolling depth. Massive wings of scale and Frost erupted. The legs, each the size of skyscrapers, slammed into the white floor, producing miniature earthquakes as they landed. Gleaming talons clawed at reality itself, carving deep furrows through it like a knife through butter.

Then came the scales, solidified into obsidian black. The serpentine neck reared up, and along with it, the head—triangular-shaped, adorned with curved spines and festooned with ivory fangs. Streaks of white married the black snout, reflecting the scales in this world of white. Large, cadaverous eyes glared at him from the skull, a primal intelligence burning in them. The behemoth arose to its fullest height and let out a rumbling snarl from its vicious jaws, a primordial, bloodthirsty amusement in its pupils.

And static overwhelmed Lukas's vision for a brief moment, before a whirl-wind of images consumed him.

A horrible tearing sound. The feeling of the entire world shuddering beneath his feet. Vicious greens bleeding into silver, and a strangely chilly air infused with the stench of rotting flesh. White rocks jutting far into the sky in twisted formations, taking physically impossible shapes. The colors, sharp and dancing, and amidst them, dark shapes, moving, and so, so wrong.

The image shifted.

Massive, gleaming teeth. The body, bone and ice. Dead, yet moving. Sapient, yet without a mind. Impossibly tall. Impossibly powerful, this vast, canine beast lies on the floor, a glitter of something like chains around it.

The image shifted again.

He sees the dragon, massive and reptilian. Its scales are darker than night. He hears its guttural, ragged roar, filled with snarling malevolence, anchored by a throat that expels the energy that disintegrates everything to dust. A wave of power, a great tide of strength that could separate oceans, an unbroken dam of power that if shat-tered, would destroy the world itself.

He sees the dragon morph. A human—no, not human—bremetan form. Weak, demure, feminine, yet the dark power surging through her makes him smile.

Pale, white pupils smile into the darkness.

Not surprising. The myths always referred to dragons as shapeshifters and bodychangers, and legends were filled with dragons taking the forms of handsome men, beautiful women, and sometimes, dangerous weapons.

He knows its name. The name of the beast that gnawed on the roots of the Yggdrasil.

Its name is Nidhogg.

Another image.

He sees a sealed world. No, an afterlife. Its gates are guarded by wolves. Eagles fly above it. He sees the warriors making merry. They are all dead and gone, and yet they are there, recounting their deeds. Some are slaughtered, but they will be there tomorrow again. They always are.

Or perhaps, not.

The cold, frigid flakes of snow fall. The wolf howls. The maelstrom is unleashed.

The all-seeing, all-pervading Eye opens in the darkness.

Winter comes for them all. It is unstoppable . . .

Fimbulwinter!

"The event that brought the end of the Aesir. The herald of Ragnarok. The wintry apocalypse. That dragon—Nidhogg—he who gnawed on the roots of the World-Tree for power. You—You are—"

Something about his declaration caused Frost to stiffen. And then she smiled at him. A dark power oozed out of her, like wax. Wretched, demented laughter rang out of her throat, her tone rich in dark malevolence. Just looking at her was a physical pain in his mind, a searing agony that tore at his conscience. The constant surge of Anomalous Energy within him faded, and Lukas winced as his connection to the omphalos dimmed until he could no longer even call upon the Screen. But that was to be expected. One did not bear the presence of such wrongness and expect an omphalos to support you. And this one was likely the worst of all wrongs. Just the slightest exposure to this could instantly sunder and destroy a soul.

"Flatterer," cooed Frost. "You say such interesting things. It makes me wonder about the world you come from."

"Don't bother," he told her, feeling surprised that he still retained enough of his mind to banter, especially after learning the identity of the being before him. Another part of him was thinking far ahead. Solana had lied to him. Meynte's power was no Truth. It was a Taboo, one that existed in the heart of Niflheim after devouring the Nordic pantheon.

Just how did someone who was alive—yokai or not—imbibe something that was the End of Potential without dying in the process? The power of Fimbulwinter that lay in the heart of Hvergelmir—just how did Meynte gain the authority to use it?

Questions. Questions. And more questions.

Come to think of it, all he had seen Tanya use was Everfrost. It was powerful, it devoured lifeforce, and probably even anomalies, but it was not Fimbulwinter. So perhaps not Fimbulwinter but a part of it? A diluted version, perhaps? Just enough to be classified as a Taboo, but not enough to end the world?

No. Lukas told himself. *I'm looking at this the wrong way. Fimbulwinter is the Taboo we're talking about, the End of the World. But didn't Solana state that the very first existences in Ginnungagap were Niflheim and Muspelheim? Perpetual Flame and Perpetual Winter? Why would any world, even one that has perpetual winter in it, willingly host a Taboo?*

Something didn't fit here. He was missing something.

To seek the truth, one must always ask the right questions, his grandfather used to say. Closing his eyes, he thought back to everything he had come to know, both from Inanna's memories and the cryptic words of Frost, as well as the newest realization he had gotten from seeing her true form.

He opened his eyes.

"A person gains a Truth by walking a path that doesn't exist. By creating a Rule that wasn't part of the World before, and thus, gains absolute authority over it. But . . . a Taboo is different. A Taboo is . . . the reverse of Truth. How does one get about achieving it?"

A slow, slow smile spread over her mouth.

"And even if it's somehow possible to obtain a Taboo, I imagine the End of Potential is perhaps the worst form of it. How does someone like Meynte—a being that's alive, a being that holds potential, give birth to something that is its reverse? That's like saying that the body itself is giving rise to that which shall destroy it, as well as everything in Existence. It—it makes no sense."

"Mmmhmmm."

Lukas felt a shiver run down his spine at how sultry her purr sounded. Really, what was with these infinitely powerful beings taking an interest in him?

"There—" he continued. "—there is another possibility, though." He clenched the pendant hanging on his neck. "A Truth can be stored in a relic. The power of a deity, their Authority over a Truth, protected and manifested through an artifact they hold a deep connection to. Mjolnir—the weapon of Thor; Gungnir—Odin's spear, they are all powerful relics. This, too—" He clenched the pendant tighter. "—is a relic. Of the goddess I believe in. She who bound you."

"Mmmhmmm."

"If someone can harness the power of a relic and travel a similar path, perhaps they too would be able to become gods in their own right. That is why you have gods of the different elements in different civilizations. Gods of flame, gods of the terrain, gods of the sky . . ."

Her eyes were affixed at him. No doubt, he had her undivided attention.

"If I were to make an educated guess upon those lines, I'd have to imagine that a Taboo too could potentially exist and be picked up by someone else. Everfrost travels down Meynte's bloodline, however that works. But even if I assume that Solana was right, that Ever—no, that *Fimbulwinter*—always lay inside the maelstrom of Hvergelmir, and Meynte was just someone that was powerful, or perhaps, twisted enough to imbibe it within herself, it still does not answer one question."

He took a deep breath.

"Why would Niflheim—a *World*—allow a Taboo to exist within itself? The only answer that even remotely fits is if Niflheim isn't a World, per se—"

He met her eyes.

"—but a prison. One that shackles a Taboo within itself, perhaps? And the reason that there is perpetual winter there, is because of the side effects of holding Fimbulwinter trapped inside? Is that it?"

Frost let out a soft purr. If he didn't know better, he'd have said she was getting aroused.

"You phrase it simply but not incorrectly. But I cannot give you the answer you seek. It is too powerful. Dangerous."

This coming from the embodiment of the End of Potential? Lukas would have called her a hypocrite to her face, but he liked living much more.

"Fine," he said. "Then tell me this at least. How is it that a living being—yokai or not—was able to gain a Taboo? No wait—" he said, as Frost began to laugh. "Stupid question. That would be like asking a god how they gained their Truth. No, that's not important. However she did it, she did it. But she brought it to this world. Outside of Hvergelmir. Brought a Taboo with her and became an empress. Or the *reverse* of an empress. Doesn't matter. And she called it Everfrost. Why? Because it was different? Altered, *weaker* perhaps, compared to the real thing? Enough to be used in the world but not enough to trigger any of its defenses?"

Something like a grimace formed on her lips. And then she spoke.

"Yes."

"Just . . . yes?" he asked. He had been expecting a little more eloquence and clarity after all of that deduction. If nothing else, a few more comments would've served him better.

"Yes."

He scowled. It was just like dealing with Inanna all over again. The way she would sit tight on a reservoir of knowledge, without ever giving him a direct answer, for all that she loved to talk with him.

And now, after interacting with Frost—no, with Fimbulwinter—he was beginning to wonder if it was just a character trait, or something that was part of your constitution once you shed your mortality to become *more*.

Guess it was up to him to pick up the slack. Assuming everything he had deduced was true, or at least, mostly true, then that meant—

"Fast forward to the war," he said. "Meynte fought Amaterasu, who was the empress. So, the Truth of Eternal Light, versus the, erm, *weakened* Taboo Everfrost. And Eternal Light won."

He didn't even want to *think* about the entire "rewriting history" episode that Solana had mentioned. Best to stick with existing facts.

The grimace deepened. "Yes."

"Meynte failed. Eternal Light won. And then Amaterasu became a goddess, and Eternal Light became a Rule unto the World. And Everfrost, the Taboo, it—" he paused, frowning. "Wait. What happens to a Taboo after the emperor—empress—dies? I doubt the World would want to add it to its system."

She did not respond. Why say "yes" when silence would do?

He swallowed. "With no empress and no relic either, I guess Everfrost got somehow tied into Meynte's bloodline? Erm, however that works. That's how her descendants, all the way down to Tanya, have it."

She gave him a slow, almost imperceptible nod.

"Correct."

Damn it. He had kind of been expecting to be wrong. Lukas suddenly felt a lot less sure of himself, especially because it suddenly made things just that much more complicated.

"If Meynte's dead, like, *really* dead, only then would Everfrost move down her bloodline all the way to Tanya. But if that's the case, how is she possessing her? Is she a ghost? Do yokai have ghosts?"

"A ghost?" she asked, tilting her head in confusion.

Right. How do I—

"A ghost, back in my world, was like an imprint of the dead. You know, spirits of the dead."

"Like the einherjar?"

Of course! Why didn't he think of that?

"Sort of. Only, they're spiritual. But yokai are spiritual anyway."

"No," she said. "No ghost."

That sort of made sense.

"Then what is she, this Meynte? How is she possessing Tanya?"

"That," said Frost, "is not for me to answer."

Lukas was growing frustrated. "If you're not going to help, then you can forget about getting out of here."

Frost laughed, and that irritated him further. "Hold onto your perceptions if you will, Outsider. But doing so will consign her fate to fickle chance."

"But you haven't told me anything! If Meynte's possessing Tanya and she's dead and not a ghost, and you won't even tell me what she is, and somehow, Tanya, despite having a bremetan body, can wield Everfrost—"

"*Do not decide lightly.*"

Something in her voice made him stop and ponder. Her cryptic statement reminded him of Inanna, plans within plans within plans. A being that could see so far into the future that, regardless of the illusion of choice, things turned out exactly like she orchestrated it to be.

"Do not underestimate the depth of what I've done for you, Outsider. Nothing I can say can possibly make this task any easier for you. You and you alone must find the way. And once you do, I expect the favor to be paid back in full." She raised a finger. "One task of my choice."

Part of him wanted to strangle her. The rest of him wanted to pull his hair out. "But you haven't *done* anything."

Her lips quivered. "Foolish Outsider. Your mortality is a bliss of ignorance. A flaw of your perception of time. Who says I haven't given you exactly what you need?"

As if on cue, the Screen flickered in.

Current Prophylaxis Status: 91%
Skill Suspension deactivated
Warmonger Protocol active

Lukas blinked. Frost had said that time was relative here and passed very, very slowly compared to the outside. So was she—

His eyes widened, and he gaped at her.

She winked.

"*Exactly what you need.*"

"Fuck me!" he murmured. And then it hit him.

It was up to him.

There was no backup plan. No second option. No cavalry coming over the hill. Whether he wounded—or, in the best case scenario, killed Solana—it wouldn't make a cent worth of difference.

Meynte, whatever she was, was possessing Tanya.

Meynte, the original wielder of Everfrost. A catastrophic individual greater than the Ifrit King he had encountered back in the borderland. And if that wasn't impossible enough, there was also Solana to consider. Someone skilled enough for Inanna to take note of. And the rest of the yokai.

And he was all by himself. With nothing save his usual tricks, maybe some power-ups and an extremely deadly power that he didn't even get even a day to experiment with, much less control.

If he succeeded, he'd save Tanya. If he failed, Meynte would kill him and Inanna would be lost forever. And then, another war between the yokai and the Asukans would begin.

No dodges. No delays. No excuses. It would happen or it wouldn't. Everything depended on him.

He looked down at his hands. Slowly, he closed them into fists. He had lifeforce but was bereft of Kinetomancy. If he used it, he'd probably die in the process. He could use mana, but it would be like a candle trying to overpower a glacier. He could use his reserves and his divinity to summon Inanna again, but in doing so, lose her forever.

He felt like throwing up. Instead, he stiffened himself and straightened his shoulders. There wasn't any other way to face it except with whatever he had in his hands. Himself. The anomaly. And—

And *Blob*.

"There is one last thing I wish to impart upon you, Outsider."

He met her glacial eyes.

"Oh?" he murmured. "What is it?"

"*I know your heart, Outsider,*" her voice boomed. "*And I know your secrets. I know what you yearn for.*"

Lukas stiffened.

"*All you desire is possible. But all you fear is also possible. Just remember, it is foolish to attempt chaining a wolf. Yet chains can be forged, and wolves can be caged.*"

She wasn't being rhetorical. She wasn't talking about a literal wolf either. He knew enough about Fenrir, the mighty wolf that was shackled by the Norse gods. He met her eyes. They seemed to be looking at his neck. No, not at his neck. At his pendant.

Chains can be forged. And wolves can be caged.

He couldn't defeat the wolf. Not as he was. Maybe not ever. No, he just needed to recognize the cage and how to trap it. And there was only one thing that came to mind.

Lukas blinked and then blinked again. As the implication behind her words settled in his mind, he let out a small chuckle. "You *really* don't like Meynte, do you?"

Frost regarded him, cold, distant, and curious at the same time.

"In that case," he murmured, "I'd appreciate it if you sent me back."

CHAPTER 11

GREATEST TREASURE

With everything that had gone on, Lukas had almost forgotten that it had all happened inside his mindscape. Frost now touched him on the head, sending him flying from the endless white world back to the throne room, which was still in a shambles from earlier.

Just like he remembered.

Time had all but stopped while he was gone—or more accurately, time had flown by extremely swiftly where he had been, in the mindscape. This wasn't the first time he had experienced such extreme time dilation—Inanna had caused it earlier, back when she faced Tanya's Frost avatar in the Crypt, and much more recently, when she manifested and helped them in their fight against the Ifrit King. But this was the first time he had actually done it himself.

> **Prophylaxis Recovery Status: Active**
> **All systems normal and functional**
> **Accessory Heteromorph active and connected**

All things considered, it had been a highly productive trip. He had taken a hideous risk and had expected the Frost Avatar to torture him mercilessly for sealing her away. Instead, she had given him information and revealed her form to him.

Neither Solana nor Maude were anywhere to be seen, and Tanya—

Tanya sat upon the throne, her eyes glassy and utterly inhuman, watching him with an expression that bordered between confusion and mild curiosity. She tilted her head to the left, then to the right, looking at the room like it was the only thing in the world worth her interest. She ignored Lukas completely for several seconds before she spoke.

"Insect, what transpired in my throne room?"

Lukas blinked. What was he thinking? Frost might have behaved like Tanya, but that was because she was part of her. Regardless of her true form, she was a manifestation of Tanya's subconscious. Meynte, if it was in fact, her, was an empress, an existence that was in the same general zip code of being a god minus the divinity. One that had ascended not through a Truth like Inanna but through a Taboo. A power so ancient and terrible that the world had forgotten its like. That power demanded his respect, his obedience, his adoration, and abject terror. He remembered his childhood lessons about how it cost one nothing to be polite and it could end up saving your life. So yeah, he needed to tread carefully.

Carefully.

He spoke: "Yeah, I blew it up."

Tanya—or rather, Meynte—looked mildly annoyed. "And . . . why did you do that?"

Before he could answer, his attention was drawn by an immense crash to his right. His senses rang alarm bells as Solana—or, again, rather, her body—levitated out of the throne. Her burnt and mutilated form turned vertical and arose, still stiff as a board. Lukas could see her fingers clenched into fists and a dense surge of power erupting out of her, tearing pieces of her flesh away like bits of rotten meat being peeled off a carcass by a sandblaster. He gaped in morbid fascination as Solana opened her dead eyes and let out a silent scream, and the flesh around her mouth sloughed and peeled away like a snake's scales.

He had never seen a skinwalker in its true form before. He'd have time to be terrified later. Instead, he took in the details, watching as the batlike face, horrid and ugly and too big for the body, contorted in shapes that made no sense. Gaping, hungry jaws. Hunched, powerful shoulders. Membranous wings stretched between the joints of its multiple arachnoid arms. Flappy black breasts hung before its chest, spilling out of a dress that no longer looked feminine. Its eyes were wide and black and pupilless, with a dark unending void peeking out at the world, and a kind of leathery, slimy hide covering its flesh, while thin tubular structures thrashed around, extending out of its body like angry tentacles.

His reflexes kicking in, he pushed himself away from her, and got up, ready to blast and burn her away with a thought. He let out a garbled, incoherent cry and raised a force shield, while his right hand locked into a rigid claw, and a small sphere of dazzling white flames gathered within the cage of his fingers, spitting and hissing with vicious heat. Facing Meynte was an insurmountable problem. He really didn't need the walking, breathing corpse to make things even more difficult. Quickly, he conjured a worst-case scenario in his head, and found that even if he used his unstable Kinetomancy again, it wouldn't be enough to take both of them down.

Accessory Heteromorph set for combat

Lukas barely had a moment to think as his mind was bombarded with a hundred different monster prototypes. He could sense Blob reacting to the danger to his life, ready to take immediate action against them. And given what he knew about aqāru . . .

Halt, he commanded. *Do not attack.*

Acknowledged

Luckily for him, the threat did not come to pass. Instead, the creature shuddered, drawing its winged membranes into itself. The black ichor-like hide turned into patches of pale, perfect flesh that spread over its dark skin like a fungal growth. The flappy breasts swelled back into softly rounded perfection once more.

Solana stood there before him, settling back into her modest business suit, her arms hanging on either side, her back stiff, with an angry expression on her face. She was no less pretty than she had been a few moments before, not a line or a curve any different. But for him, the effect had been ruined. He had seen her and would always remember what she *truly* looked like beneath this flesh-mask.

She looked at him, her eyes shining like burning coals. "I'd appreciate it if you didn't do that again. It was most uncomfortable."

And then she regarded Tanya—Meynte, whatever—and strode towards her. She came to a halt a few feet away from her and genuflected. And in a tone that bordered on fanatic reverence, she declared, "Queen of Ice, Bringer of the End, I, your servant, pledge my fidelity. I serve and obey."

If there was any lingering doubt about who was controlling Tanya's body, it faded away with her words. There was no hesitation in her movements—the gesture wasn't some rule she was required to observe. Solana *believed* that the person before her merited such obeisance. As if seeing Tanya like that wasn't already enough to set him on edge.

The words that came out next fit the scene well. In the worst possible way.

"Kinky. Knew you had submissive tendencies behind that blowhard facade."

Solana turned around. The smile on her face vanished and a determined look graced her features. "Outsider, your mouth lacks elegance. Keep it under control or I'll remove it myself. You are in the presence of—"

"I think I've a good idea what she is," he said quietly, eyeing Meynte. As far as situations went, this was hardly beyond salvaging. He'd rank facing the bylestyr as far more dangerous than this.

And with good reason.

Meynte didn't seem to care what his intentions were. It would be obvious even to those without battle experience. Her presence itself assured victory, and her eyes demanded that everyone should recognize it.

Lukas would know. He was awfully familiar with that gaze.

"You're playing the arrogant queen-bee vibe a bit too hard," he said, meeting Meynte's eyes, completely ignoring Solana's threats. "Maybe cut down on the theatrics a bit?"

"Aguilar!" Solana hissed, her eyes both furious and wide with near-panic. Meynte, on the other hand, was regarding him intently. He caught sight of a subtle shift of her weight and had he not expected it already, he'd barely have noticed the sudden flash that originated between them and lanced out towards him. Meynte was reasonably surprised when a sliver of pure lifeforce popped between them and met the incoming projectile head-on. The Everfrost spear struck the shield, turned to ice, and was instantly shattered from the force of the collision.

Neither of them acted like what had just transpired was out of the ordinary, their gazes remaining where they had been the entire time.

"I told you. Kings, emperors, gods—they are all *fiction* where I come from. What did you expect I'd do? Shiver and bow and kiss the helm of a has-been ghost?"

"Hmm," murmured Meynte. She tilted her head to one side, her smile fading. "I suppose not. Mindless dogs like you are incapable of following even the simplest instructions for long." Her cadaverous eyes stared at the shattered ice on the floor, as if examining it. "Then again, your jests are amusing. Better than the helpless beasts dancing to the tune of their goddess. Your defiance presents an amusing comedy, if stale in some regards."

"What are you getting at?" asked Lukas impatiently.

"Servant," murmured Meynte, "introduce me to this ephemeral."

For a few seconds, there was silence. Then Solana gasped and staggered, nearly falling down in the process. She stood up and then spoke in a ragged tone. "You stand before Meynte, Queen of Ice, Cruelest Winter, Bearer of the End."

"Barely," said Lukas with a bored expression on his face. "Or else, she wouldn't have called it Everfrost."

Meynte's eyes widened ever so slightly.

Lukas tilted his head, his eyes never leaving her. "Oh, and she's not the real deal. She's a reflection at best. Light from a star that's dead and gone."

Part of him actually felt angry at himself for describing Meynte in the same vein as Inanna. No matter how apt the description might be.

"Not a reflection!" Solana snapped, her composure visibly giving way to irritation. "Have care with how you speak. The empress herself crafted this Throne—Nidhogg's Lair—to store a part of herself away. An indemnity, sealed away from the claws of Death, awaiting to fashion another. And now, Tanya will become Meynte, Queen of the End, the original wielder of Everfrost. After a thousand years, our hopes have finally been answered."

"Right, and you and your fellow yokai can go dance and sing 'Kumbaya' and all that crap. No dice. Return Tanya back to me."

He took a step forward.

"That is impossible," said Solana. "I promised her I'd reveal her destiny to her. She accepted it and sat upon that throne. And now, she'll serve the greater good and become the new form for the empress."

"Servant," Meynte murmured, her cataract eyes watching Lukas, "who is this insect?"

"He is Lukas Aguilar, my liege," murmured Solana, "the Outsider of legend. The one who fought your descendant, bound her, and forced her to follow his will. He has been the key to getting the right host for your throne."

She turned to face him. "Aguilar, you have been of much help, and now you have fulfilled your destiny. As part of my gratitude, I'll let you walk away free. But if you stay, if you bow before the queen and offer your allegiance, then she will grant you all the knowledge that you seek. The World, the gods, the universe itself—nothing transcends her gaze. Accept this, and you shall have a power you have never known."

"And she'd just give that to me?"

"Absolutely," said Solana. "Kvasir's treatise, the Asukans' collections—they are *nothing*. The empress herself can give you the knowledge of the Time Before. You are powerful and unpredictable and have a knack for coming out ahead in difficult situations. That much I'm willing to concede. You can be the Sword of our queen, just as I am her Shield. Submit to her, pledge your fidelity, and she will wield you to tear the Asukan world apart."

"Tempting," said Lukas. "But I'll have to go with a 'no.' I have a problem with liars and betrayers. Just as your queen thinks of the world as hers, I think of Tanya as mine. And I cannot tolerate anyone trying to steal anything from me, whoever or whatever they are."

Lifeforce sang in his veins. Mana and anomalous energy rushed in as well. His fractals heated. There was a time to fight and a time to talk, and the line that bordered the two was fast approaching.

His eyes dilated slightly, as kinetic trajectories slowly appeared in front of him. The world became sharper. Every detail imaginable was for him to discern and determine. Every twist, every turn, every single vibration. The Screen threw him a mass of contradictions about Meynte, facts that he could not process. Facts that needed more parameters, more analysis. The information would determine the difference between absolute victory and colossal defeat.

"You're deluded if you think Tanya was ever yours," snipped Solana. "She was born to do this. This was her destiny."

"And who are you to do that to her?" Lukas demanded. "One's family and friends are there to support you when you make a mistake. When you fall down. They help you stand up again. They do not take advantage of you and trick you into a different fate."

"This. Is. Her. Destiny." Solana growled.

"And that," said Lukas, "is why we don't see eye to eye. Tanya is rash and ignorant and makes stupid mistakes, and I want her to understand the meaning of the choice she's making. By definition, experience takes time and mistakes to build. And Tanya, like myself, is quite young. But if what you say is true and Tanya wants to become the body of some has-been relic of the past—" Solana's eyes twitched. "—then I'll not stop her. I will not reprimand her or keep her from her destiny. Hell, I'll even stay by her side and help her deal with the consequences, even if it means working with a backstabbing bitch like you."

"You would?" Solana asked, a mix of curiosity and disbelief flashing across her icy mask.

"I would," agreed Lukas. "And don't think too much about it. Your treacherous skinwalker brain might explode."

"Do you really think it proper to antagonize me so?"

Lukas gave her a bored look. "You should consider yourself lucky I haven't already torn you a new one. As far as I'm concerned, I'm being incredibly diplomatic."

Honestly, he was enjoying Solana's reactions. However, he wasn't taking her lightly. He just knew how to push her buttons. And blatant disrespect, especially to someone she regarded as her superior, did that like nothing else.

An enraged Solana was a sloppy one, after all.

It also had her and Meynte's attention firmly on him. He had debated truly cutting loose and going straight to attack, but there was always the chance of Tanya getting heavily maimed in the battle. Possessed or otherwise, the body was still hers.

And right then, the Screen pinged.

Accessory ready for combat
Initiate Puppeteer Protocol?

About time. Now that Rollback Protocol had done its job and activated Blob as a complete accessory to his anomaly system, he could control it, both in hand and remotely, albeit within a certain distance.

Such as accessing his omphalos functions through it.

He could only hope that things would turn out exactly as he planned.

"I'd ask you to think again, Outsider. Your association with the girl is fleeting. I am offering you a way out. I can offer you all the kami in the world. I can take you to the Haze and show you the realms themselves. All you've got to do is submit to us. Forget about the girl."

"No can do."

"You'd face my wrath for her?"

"I'd not defy you for her," Lukas amended with a stony expression that matched hers. "I'd defy you for her ability to choose for herself. And if you or your queen tries to stop that, then you'll have to deal with something worse than freaking Amaterasu."

"And *what* is that?" asked Meynte, her cold, white eyes staring at him with vivid interest.

"Me."

Solana drew herself to her fullest height and shot him a deathly glare.

"You will not win."

Lukas smiled. "I might not win." The flecks of green overlaid over the brown. Power surged within him. "But I'll make sure that all of you bleed for it."

His challenging gaze met hers without hesitation. "What? Still having second thoughts?" he taunted. "My, what a loser attitude! Maybe this isn't about Tanya at all. Maybe it's about your cowardice. But then again, what else can I expect from a servant of a has-been?"

And he looked Meynte straight in the eyes.

Inanna had once told him not to draw another in an extended gaze. All sorts of things could invade one's mind through the eyes. It was why they were called the windows of the soul. Just as he estimated, he felt the brunt of her psionic assault smash into his mind. Had he suffered this back in the anomaly, her will would have crushed his flat. But things had changed. He was the Prime Host, with a Level-5 Alpha Condition. Not even the most lethal of monsters could possess him and force a chance upon his soul or his mind. Compared to that, this was small potatoes.

He saw Meynte's eyes widen in shock as he soundly rebuffed her assault.

"Naughty, naughty," he taunted, wagging a finger in remonstration.

"Perverted thing!" whispered Meynte. "I take offense to you staring at me like that. As queen of the yokai, I'm obliged to end you. You have no one else to blame for this outcome other than yourself." For the first time, she addressed him with a firm tone laced with smooth, killing intent.

"Nothing but a miracle can save you from my wrath."

Glacial eyes met the flecks of green with brown, and an agreement was made.

Only one of them would leave this fight alive.

Lukas's frown deepened, but he otherwise didn't move at all.

Five, ten, twenty, fifty, a hundred shards of Everfrost formed in the air all around Meynte, who stared at him from her throne.

Puppeteer active
Choosing appropriate prototype

Solana's eyes turned pitch-black as a wave of something drew closer.

Intended target identified
Intercept routines
Activate prototype Khorkhoi

Dazzling, white flames began to form around Lukas's fists, cloaking them like a glove. He watched as Solana crouched down and let out a strange growl that was less like a war cry and more like a landslide rumbling from her throat.

Meynte's lips twisted. "Pity."

Enact

The room exploded.

Shards of Everfrost met whips of white fire in untold numbers, striking one another with enough power that just one collision would have been enough to shake the room in its entirety. The shockwaves alone were causing considerable damage to the chamber, and the fractures on the walls and the floor were now getting deeper. Stones splintered, and the chasms on the floor widened.

Had Lukas just been fighting the usual way, he'd have escaped from their vicinity and attempted to bombard them from afar. In a battle where you didn't know what the other side could do, trying to get into close combat was the fastest way to suicide.

Instead, he had drawn on the thoggua prototype's instincts—the original source behind the Shatterpoint Intuition skill. A creature that was blind and deaf and could fight using three extendable tails, scanning the shifts in the earth's movements to determine the location of prey, and then directing the spear-end of the tails through the fastest and most effective route using Shatterpoint Intuition. He had used those same instincts, only instead of daggers like before, he had conjured two long whips of pure flame and used them as tails.

And it was a bit too much. His mind was already running at maximum capacity, keeping up with Meynte. Power-wise, it was the same as Tanya, but he knew very well the firepower the girl packed. Add in Meynte's experience at wielding Everfrost, and it was enough to lock him in combat. His eyes, now shining like emeralds, were all too busy capturing the trajectories of the incoming attacks and instantly forwarding the relevant information straight to the thoggua instinct so that his whips would intercept the incoming barrage. It was only after said whips had clashed against the shards that he even realized that he had voluntarily directed it in the first place.

His mind was on fire. Even when he wasn't directly manipulating motion trajectories and instead limiting it to a higher version of Shatterpoint Intuition, the amount of information he was processing was overwhelming. Thanks to Prophylaxis, he could physically withstand it for quite a while, and even as he stood there, it was more manageable because of limiting what he actually saw, but the pain was something he could do nothing about.

But not all explosions originated from the clashing Everfrost and fire whips.

"*DIE!*" Solana yelled a war cry and rushed at him, only to be intercepted by something else. Something larger, something metallic, something whose roar sounded less like a war cry and more like someone lugging a ton of rusted iron over asphalt.

CHAPTER 12

BLOB

[PREY] had tried to harm Lukas, and it would die.

It was the closest thing to a thought that [BLOB] could have. Its "mind," which was a little more than a set of minor behavioral patterns, was currently an empty, red haze that could not truly hold any concept save for the obliteration of any foe that stood before it. But piercing that haze now was something that came from outside that programmed inhuman violence.

[PREY] had tried to harm Lukas, and it would die.

A familiar darkness blanketed its thoughts, as the spiritual constitution of a familiar-yet-unknown monster prototype filled its mind. As its constitution changed, so did its body. Aqāru was a formless medium, readily reforging itself to suit its spiritual state. What had been a semi-solid metallic slime now shifted into a massive, twisted meshwork of tubules and chitinous caricatures, contorting into itself in ways that could only make sense to a twisted mind.

Or an omphalos.

[BLOB] vanished, and [KHORKHOI] took its place. The metallic strands separated, adding in rock and stone from its vicinity, the anomalous energy altering the constituents to craft a makeshift archetype of the original monster. In less than half a minute, the dense, metallic slime contorted into a thousand pounds of angry creature, complete with several hundred teeth spiraling into the depths of its body, the metal crafting its body empowered by the natural energy it had absorbed from the ground just moments before for this very purpose.

The [KHORKHOI] roared.

Every atom of its being sang with brutality, longing to tear the attackers limb from limb and smash away at the remains until nothing was left but a bloody smear on its pincers. [BLOB] did not fear the attacks, even though it could sense each one was a deadly threat. To feel fear would be to value its own existence, and it was not capable of such. Only the commands of Lukas held sway over its urge to destroy, and Lukas had allowed it free rein.

[PREY] had tried to harm Lukas, and it would die.

[BLOB] charged at the [PREY]. The invisible barriers that fell upon it were inconsequential. That they severed away parts of its body were inconsequential. It was slime. With natural ease, the torn-away parts fused together.

As good as new.

Kill [PREY].

Walls of rock rose from the ground and smashed into it from both sides, utterly destroying every single tubule that made up its physical constitution. [BLOB] could not feel pain, but it damaged the physiological units making up its body beyond repair.

[BLOB] died.

Puppet [KHORKHOI] eliminated

. . .

Create new instance - [KHORKHOI]

That did not stop it.

Metal-made flesh reformed.

"Uppity thing," claimed [PREY].

"Meow!" said [BLOB].

An intense pressure crashed into it from all sides.

[BLOB] died.

Territory Creation active
Puppeteer Protocol enacted
Monster Prototype installed: [KHORKHOI]
Function: Kill Prey

A new [KHORKHOI] stood on its hind limbs. Its mind was an empty program, filled with nothing but violence and a command to "Kill Prey."

For [PREY] had tried to harm Lukas, and for that, it would die. It would—

Instance of Monster Prototype [KHORKHOI] deleted
Monster Prototype installed: NONE
Function: NA

[BLOB] lay on the floor.

Empty.
Like a body without a mind.
Like a system without protocol.
Just an empty sludge of metal.
Or perhaps, not so empty.

Accessing baseline configuration . . .

[BLOB] was not a protector. It was an Exterminator, synthesized by [CRYPT OF FIENDISH WORMS] for that one purpose alone. It could protect, in a sense, as it protected Lukas, but destroying everything in the area with the slightest hostile intent towards him, until Lukas gave it the order to stop. And as there was not one thing in this area that had not shown hostility to Lukas, it would kill and kill and kill, until there was not even one living thing standing to harm what it was meant to protect. Lukas had not ordered it to the contrary, and there were only two moving things within the field of its senses that presented a threat to Lukas.

Both of them would die here.

And for that, new prototype instances were required. Lukas did not know this but, even with the installed prototype gone, the original base protocols created by [CRYPT OF FIENDISH WORMS] remained within it, as a failsafe.

Initiating Extermination Protocol 4.0
Initiating reverse connection to anomaly [LUKAS AGUILAR]

Downloading pre-deletion analysis . . .
Identifying causes . . .

The greatest threat wasn't the flappy, black-haired [PREY], but the white-haired [PREDATOR].

Monster Prototypes with spiritual cores found maximally vulnerable against [PREDATOR]

UNACCEPTABLE!
Accessing Prototype Array of [CRYPT OF FIENDISH WORMS]

It already had access to all the prototypes within [CRYPT OF FIENDISH WORMS]. But [BLOB] wasn't a living entity, just a combination of protocols made sentient. When looking for an answer, it went for the optimal parameters.

System overridden . . .
Allowing access to Prototype Array of [LOSTBELT EARTH]

Yes. That would do.

[PREDATOR] had tried to harm Lukas, and it would die.

Pride comes before the fall.

Hearing it was one thing. Seeing it in action was another. And currently, Lukas was getting a front-seat view of the latter.

Empress Meynte was a being of antiquity. A creature that had risen to the apex of her species. A being so twisted that she could ascend with the End of Potential—Fimbulwinter itself—weakened or not. How someone with Potential could ascend with its antithesis was a question that would forever plague his mind, but it wasn't something to worry about right now. For all he knew, she had centuries to practice, if not more. In that amount of time, even modest talents could grow teeth. Never mind everything the experience would have taught them, everything she could have found to strengthen herself. Even without the infernal power of Everfrost, even with Tanya's limited power, Meynte should have kicked his ass.

A dozen times over.

Instead, Lukas, a fledgling fighter with only a few months of experience under his belt, could match him blow for blow.

It wasn't because of some mystery, or the anomaly's myriad powers, but because of Meynte's own over-inflated sense of pride. For someone she called an insect, the empress wasn't using her fullest strength, limiting herself to this twisted deadlock. She wouldn't even fight him in close combat because that would mean acknowledging him as an equal opponent. The power of a King-class kami lived within Tanya's body, but Meynte's pride would not let her use it.

He saw her click her teeth in annoyance as she was forced to defend against his repeated attacks. She constantly switched from sending rows of Everfrost blades at him to extending the frigid field around her throne and twisting the environment to her whims. All of this, while remaining seated upon the throne, coordinating the entire thing with just her mind.

Past the chaos, Lukas noted with delight how Blob was giving the yokai Leader a tough time. Solana's barriers could give anyone a tough time. Just trying to fight them all would have taken the entirety of Lukas's attention, or require the use of the full power of Kinetomancy against her. He had already done that once before and torn her apart, but she had returned without so much as a scratch.

A frustration that was now Solana's suffering as the aqāru slime gave her a taste of her own medicine.

Especially after Blob didn't stop after the first hit tore its body apart. Or the seventh one, for that matter.

"Abomination!" he heard Solana growl. "Accursed thing!"

Blob wasn't alive, not as far as the definition of "life" went. It was just a myriad collection of skills, anomaly information, and monster prototypes. Somewhere in the mountains of chaos within it, Blob had fashioned a primitive mind, one that was absolutely faithful to Lukas. Unlike Lukas, Blob used anomalous energy saved up from the amount it had absorbed from the Haze, and if it came to it, Lukas could directly channel his omphalos reserves into it, though he would need physical contact for that to happen. Still, the slime could store tremendous amounts of power within itself, so he wasn't really expecting its barrels to go empty any time soon. And much like Solana, Blob had transformed into a creature capable of using the terrain to hunt for its prey, while remaining practically unkillable by normal methods.

And it could enact Territory Creation to neutralize Solana's attacks, while its aqāru constitution meant that trying to possess it would only get Solana killed for good.

"Constant reincarnation, is it?" asked Meynte, observing the massive slime beast. "A luxury even I don't have. Even I have never seen anyone return from being killed before."

She cocked her head, and a beam of pure white hurled towards it. It struck Blob head-on, freezing it completely. Unlike before, Blob didn't re-form. Instead, a notification popped up on Lukas's screen.

Instance of monster prototype khorkhoi deleted from Accessory Heteromorph

---

That cost Lukas a second to process.

Everfrost was the End of Potential. Skills, soul prototypes—they were all crafted out of Potential. Getting hit like that had dealt no damage to the aqāru slime, but it had disintegrated the monster prototype that Lukas had installed into it. He was lucky that the omphalos within him had copied all the information from within Blob after the Rollback Protocol had been achieved, or else he'd have lost them all.

Solana took the opportunity and rushed at Lukas, her body looking less bremetan and more like a twisted fusion of bat, slime, and a decaying corpse.

System overridden
Reverse connection active . . .

Allowing access to Prototype Array of Lostbelt Earth

Lukas blinked. Was that really—

BOOM!

Hissing, Lukas terraported instantly, appearing at a distance from the two of them. Access to the prototypes of Earth? Since when did the omphalos allow for that?

He went back to the previous line.

System overridden. Reverse connection.

That meant—

"BLOB?" he yelled out in surprise. "Oh, for fuck's sake—"

He terraported again, just in time to escape being smashed by Solana's barriers. It only allowed him a split second of respite, but that was enough for him to pick up on the newest surprise from his helpful cat-slime. He dodged the blast of force she shot at him and terraported to the right, sending a blast of pure flame at her. Solana screeched and dodged it, not knowing that Meynte was right behind her.

A wall of pure ice intercepted the blast.

So, he thought, *she's vulnerable to fire. Kinda strange for a terramancer. Or maybe it's because of that flesh mask? But that gives me an idea . . .*

Filtering and identifying all prototypes with Fire mana core
327 prototypes identified

Lukas terraported and appeared right behind Solana, ensuring that both of his enemies fell in the same straight line.

Eight spears, forged of the dranzithl's corrosive flames, flew in their direction.

Refining selection process for prototypes with damage output Level 3
or higher
Filtering for presence of physical form
Filtering for passive effects over active
Filtering for—

STOP! thought Lukas. *That one will do.* Not quite one from Earth, but against Solana, it would have to do. Meynte, he'd deal with her himself.

Territory Creation active
Puppeteer Protocol enacted
Monster prototype installed: Bylestyr
Function: Kill Prey

What had been a dripping mass of metallic slime was now an eight-foot-tall, hulking behemoth. Instead of charred flesh, ichor, and bone, the monster was a meshwork of metal, rock, and crimson flame. Its eyes shone with a mad, crimson, almost primordial madness, contrasting with the glacial surroundings.

It raised all four of its massive arms, its large, serrated teeth looming over its jaws, dripping thick, liquid fire to the ground. Fire formed around it. Fire exploded outside of it. Fire *was* it.

A second later, four copies of the original guy's stone club lay impaled on the floor next to it.

The bylestyr let out a wild roar, grabbed the clubs and belched a torrent of crimson at Meynte. Now "alive" again, Blob resumed its charge with all the bloodlust of the bylestyr and rushed at the empress, armed with one of the crudest and most brutal weapons ever fashioned. This time Meynte didn't stay on her throne and instead stood up and met its blows head-on, with a dozen Frost stalagmites arising out of the terrain—

—and nearly fell forward as Lukas threw a kinetic blow at the throne. Given the infuriated look she gave him, the blow had to have fractured the throne, however slightly.

"Now we're even," said Lukas.

Meynte was not amused.

CHAPTER 13

———

BAIT

Back when he was a freshman at university, Lukas had come across the concept of the Ship of Theseus, also known as Theseus's Paradox, a thought experiment that raised the question of whether an object that had all of its components replaced remained fundamentally the same object. If every part of the ship was replaced by new parts, would it still remain the original ship? And if not, then perhaps if one took the older parts of Theseus's ship and put them together, would the new ship become Theseus's ship?

To surmise, the paradox raised a fundamental question—what constituted one's identity? One's history or one's physical body? Both philosophy and fantasy literature often explored this particular question, swapping a person's body parts for artificial replacements until there was nothing original left within him.

Why was he thinking about this in the middle of battle? Because he was facing a walking, breathing, ghosting proof of the paradox.

Meynte was dead and gone over a thousand years ago. The new body belonged to Tanya; the parts, and even the existing skills belonged to Tanya and Tanya alone. But when her memories were swapped by those of Meynte, what would you call the body? Tanya or Meynte?

Though, technically, wasn't he too, doing the same? Implanting the spiritual data of a prototype inside a shapeshifting living metal slime, making it look and act exactly like the real thing?

"Wonderful," said Meynte. The frown on her face had been replaced by a smile filled with curiosity and acknowledgement. "That metal smudge does not live and yet you breathed life into it at will. I erased its soul from existence, and yet it has a new one. Say, Outsider, is this *your* doing?"

Technically, all he had done was create a "copy" of the stored soul prototype and install it in Blob's spiritual matrix, but he supposed it was the most perfect "forgery" there was. And even forgers were craftsmen.

"And what if it is?"

He felt the stress in the room abating somewhat. He could sense Blob the bylestyr hammering against Solana's defenses in a different corridor. The two had shattered the wall and extended the battlefield past it, leaving the room to just the two of them.

Meynte threw her head back and released a full-throated laugh. "Crafting souls at will. A feat that surpasses all divinities of the Time Before. I am the wielder of the End of Potential, and you, the Avatar of Creation. We are polar opposites, you and I. No wonder you rub me the wrong way." Her white eyes glowed as she regarded him. "Yes. Yes, that's right. Amaterasu was an eyesore but you . . . I just want to *play* with you."

"Play?"

"YES!" said Meynte. There was a strange intensity to her eyes and tone. "I don't want to destroy you. Oh no, I cannot, will not, should not destroy you. You—I'd make you suffer something far, far worse. I'd have you create, only to see your creation obliterated before your very eyes. Then create again. And again. And again until the End of Time. You . . . You are *alien*. You are *wrong*. You are—you are—"

It was like she was losing her sanity by the second, shaking her head so frantically that a normal person's neck would have suffered traumatic injuries by now. Just what was it about him that Meynte was driven mad just by contemplating it?

Could it be because he was an anomaly? He knew the Screen registered Tanya and now Meynte, as Predator.

Not Prey.

"You, Soulcrafter," murmured Meynte, for once eyeing him like someone worth her recognition. "You have achieved far greater than what I had anticipated. Not only do you have the gall to damage my precious throne, you dare be my antithesis, and desire to claim this host body from me. Be proud . . ."

There was murder and madness in her tone. She formally took a battle stance against Lukas, and hoarfrost surged out of her like a maelstrom.

"There have been an exceptional few that have managed to irritate me to such a degree."

The tide of the battle changed instantly.

"Guh!" Lukas grimaced as he attempted to hold his own against the wall of winter and death that crashed upon him. He had managed to keep up, and even pushed back from time to time, but this was way beyond anything he could counter. Unless he resorted to using his ultimate weapon, chances of him beating her was zero. But if he *did* use Kinetomancy, he'd end up destroying Tanya's body and killing her for good.

Either way, he'd lose.

Meanwhile—

Puppet BYLESTYR eliminated

. . .

Create new instance - BYLESTYR

Damn it. This was the fifth time Solana had destroyed the prototype. Maybe he should've just let the filter process run its course and come up with a more optimal prototype. He knew that the Crypt of Fiendish Worms and Lostbelt Earth probably contained prototypes on its level or higher, somewhere in its prototype stores, but he didn't have the time or the inclination to try something new in the middle of battle. That Solana was able to kill a full-fledged Level-3 bylestyr, crafted out of a metal she was vulnerable to, five times over, without running out of power, spoke of the ironclad control she had over it. He was pretty sure that if she came at him without reservations, she'd kick his ass.

It was fortunate that Blob had enough energy to power up several hundreds of such bylestyrs before he needed refilling again. And his own reserves could fill tens of thousands. The problem was that bifurcating his attention into doing two separate things was taking its toll on his efficiency.

He had never faced a situation where he was out of lifeforce or mana during his earlier battles, and his output had grown by magnitudes since then. The fractals only amplified that. Imagine his surprise that now, he was being troubled with not having *enough* firepower, of all things.

That kind of said everything about Meynte, Queen of the End and wielder of Everfrost.

It was ridiculous. Absurd. Completely insane.

His eyes were almost green now, constantly surveying the motion trajectories of the incoming barrages, and then using Shatterpoint Intuition to counter them. And unlike him, Meynte didn't exactly use mana, but instead summoned endless amounts of Everfrost at practically no noticeable cost and kept hurling it at him. Another problem was that, despite his increased capacities, his arms were still human. They could only move so fast and for so long before fatigue caught up with them. Lifeforce could prolong the process, but even it wouldn't be able to delay it indefinitely. Unless he did something, he was going to lose.

"Is that all you've got, Soulcrafter?" Meynte taunted him with a malicious grin on her face. "Don't tell me that after *that* display, you are limited by your frail form?"

I'll show her frail. Lukas gritted his teeth spitefully. He had always suspected that Tanya's Everfrost was more absurd than anything else he had ever seen, short of Inanna and the Ifrit King. Given what he knew now, the latter was probably going down on that list. Tanya had been a Level 22, and that was before they had gotten inside that borderland. Given that Lukas had climbed up by thirteen levels there, he had some idea what her new levels were like.

And she had an 87 percent ECR.

Given his own experience with being possessed by a goddess multiple times in the past, he could tell that Tanya was up for a nice surprise after he managed to wake her up. After making her suffer for a day or two for putting him through this. Yes, it wasn't her fault, he knew that, but he just enjoyed seeing her face all scrunched up.

My mind is racing in all directions. Going to need to end this soon, he thought deliriously. Still, no sense in giving in. Especially now that he was so close to figuring things out.

Reaching into his Prototype Array, he reached for more help.

I wish Mori was here. She'd go into a conniption.

Accessing Monster Prototype svartalfar
Initiating consciousness shift
Enact

And Hreidmar's instincts took over. Hreidmar, the svartalfar he had faced in a trial by combat at Zwaray Keep. Hreidmar, one who was referred to as seidmadr, or Sorcerer, by his fellow people out of respect for his unconventional abilities. Hreidmar, who had combined two utterly simple techniques—Friction Manipulation and Innate Gravity Control, and used them to devastating effect, enough that had the barrier not sealed both of them inside the combat arena, he would have killed Lukas a thousand times off.

The sulfurous smell vanished from his nostrils, replaced with a faint, wet, muddy aroma. The constant surges of lifeforce instantly vanished, replaced with a feeling of connectedness. The battleground almost vanished from his senses. He was a creature of the terrain and here he was, in an underground city crafted exclusively out of rock and Terramancy. He could sense the material forces at play, the strong yet subtle way Solana's barriers held the entire thing in place. He was a spider, perched within another spider's web, one that made up for its incipient craftsmanship with its sheer scale. A familiar layer of anti-friction formed around him, isolating him from everything. The battleground and Meynte's glacial territory which otherwise had seemed everywhere, now felt utterly localized.

Small.

Irrelevant.

"Oh?" asked Meynte. "That is *some* change. Your mana and lifeforce patterns shifted completely. It's like you're a completely different individual. What other secrets do you have, Outsider?"

"Just hang on a minute! I swear my next one involves talking bunnies."

"Your insouciance is no longer amusing, Outsider," said Meynte. "And regretfully, I have grown bored of this stalemate."

And then the storm began again.

Lukas had seen Tanya conjure Everfrost blades before, but she had always followed a craft, lock, and launch policy. Granted, seeing a hundred Everfrost blades hanging in midair, each of them pronouncing a frigid death upon impact, had its own psychological value in war. Meynte, however, simply did not have such restraints. It was almost like a portal had opened behind her, unveiling a world of glacial white from which contrails of silvery white light kept coming at him.

Which made his defense all the more impressive.

The adrenaline rush within him died. Extreme rationality took over. Thick walls of stone erupted between them, intercepting Meynte's attacks. Everfrost was deadly to lifeforce but against rock, it was little more than the frozen hoarfrost that constituted it. He saw Meynte extending his attacks and casually raising walls from every direction. There he was, standing in his element, against a creature that had, for better or worse, proven to be stationary.

Which would prove to be her undoing.

Even wolves can be chained. Frost had told him that.

And Meynte, for all her power and skill, had three chains binding her. The first, that she was a memory possessing Tanya, which meant that if Tanya managed to resist her and fight back, it would make things difficult for her.

Not something he could bet on.

The second, the memory was using Tanya's body and thus was limited to the power that her body could use. Just like Inanna had limited herself to using the barest minimum level of power she could channel through Lukas's own, without causing irreparable damage to her host. It probably explained why she was summoning Everfrost en masse and trying to overwhelm him with quantity instead of employing some of her own skills.

And the third, if he could find a way to restrain Tanya's body, it would restrain Meynte. To an extent.

The truth was, he had at least one way to save Tanya up his sleeve—without resorting to using Kinetomancy, that is. Trouble was, there were four major problems with that.

One: he didn't know exactly what Meynte was capable of. No entity that could take on a veritable goddess could be a one-trick pony.

Two: even if she somehow *was* a one-trick pony, then that single trick would be so versatile, with so many variations that he'd be hard-pressed to truly account for everything.

Three: Meynte wasn't a soul. She was a memory. A cluster of memories. Which had to come from *somewhere*. Lukas refused to believe that even the empress would be stupid enough to store the memories in the throne. No, it was more likely that the throne acted as a conduit through which the real memory source transferred the memories to the victim sitting on it. And he had no idea where or what that source was.

And finally, four: even if he somehow managed to trap her and get her to desert Tanya's body, she'd probably return to the throne. The chances of him collapsing at the end of the fight were high, and Tanya was already mind-fucked. It would be horrifically easy for Solana to walk in and snap his neck for good measure and then repeat the process with Tanya, and this time, there would be nothing he could do, being dead and all.

He needed a solution that tackled all four points, and not necessarily in order. He'd need to find what she was capable of and try his best to take Solana out of the equation. That was far more difficult than it seemed, since she was a demented fanatic with six centuries of blind faith empowering her fanaticism. And while he did all of that, he also needed to find a way to trap Meynte for good.

Might as well start from there.

After all, she entered Tanya through the throne. So, the source must be connected to it. All he had to do was find it.

The first wall shattered. Two more rose to take its place.

Lukas didn't care. His lips didn't even move. The command came anyway.

Find it for me.

Scanning for spiritually active inorganic substances . . .

Anomalous energy exploded out of him in all directions, expanding past the usual radius—searching, recognizing, comprehending, distinguishing. The svartalfar ability to recognize different substances in the terrain was added to the mix. For what he was searching for was a unique substance.

Memories were delicate things. You couldn't just store them in random substances. You needed something spiritually active and yet empty. Something that could survive long without shattering and yet isolate the memory from the external environment.

Deeper.

Wider.

Farther.

His senses expanded outward. He wasn't Lukas Aguilar anymore. He was svartalfar. A creature of the terrain. From this terrain he was born, and into this terrain he'd return upon his demise. The terrain was his everything, and it showed him everything he needed to know.

He just had to be a little faster.

Result: FOUND

Description: FEATHERGLASS
Located Featherglass
Purity: 81%

Lukas suppressed the urge to laugh. Of course it was featherglass. It always came down to that freaking stuff. Also, 81 percent purity? Maybe Solana was right. If the highest Asukans could pull off was 76 percent, and that was employing literal divine intervention, they really must have been the lowest rung on the ladder.

Get it, he ordered. *Bring it under my territory.*

Pulling subterranean geography . . .
Mapping exact location . . .

The Ice Queen snarled some meaningless things to him, but he didn't bother paying attention. He couldn't win this, not as he was. Hreidmar's skills were a strong counter to Meynte but only for the short term. Shorter, if Meynte threw her entire might against him.

But that didn't mean he was out of options. No, rather because he was in such a state, a new path had become available that he hadn't considered before. A last-ditch effort with long-lasting consequences even if it did work, but the odds were far more favorable than anything else he had. No, if anything, they were better than what he had when the battle started.

So he focused.

Deeper.

Eyes were useless. Knowledge of the underground complex rushed through his mind. He felt the coppery tang of blood in his mouth but ignored it. A thousand location points came to mind, only to be rejected for another thousand points. And then another. And another, painting them in different shades of color in his mind's eye. Moving faster than physically possible, his reach moved deeper, searching through the walls to find it.

Location traced

A mix of elation and disappointment shot through him. Elation, because he knew exactly what Solana had done. Disappointment, because it was a remarkable and deceptively simple trick that would fool even the most talented of svartalfars and deter even the greatest of terramancers from trying to get to it.

The featherglass shard that acted as the storage reservoir for Meynte's memories was indeed connected to the throne, but the pathway weaved through thousands upon thousands of barrier frameworks that were interspersed throughout the entire yokai territory. Solana had played with the fabric of space to twist it through mediums that made no sense. He'd have greater luck crashing all the wards holding the entire territory up than accessing the featherglass hidden somewhere within it.

He needed an alternative.

"This delusion will end with your death!" snarled Meynte.

"You might just be slightly wrong about that," Lukas said absently.

Faster, Lukas told himself. *Ignore the bitch and concentrate. You have the sink. You can't get to the source. So, what can you do? How do you weave past these barriers and get to—*

He paused.

Damn it. I really am an idiot.

In using Hreidmar's instincts, he had begun to limit himself to thinking like him. Like a svartalfar. Hreidmar wouldn't have a choice except to find ways to tweak Solana's defenses and get to the main source. But an anomaly like Lukas?

He could create a *new* source.

And for that, he needed to get down there. Or at least, have someone he trusted get down there. Someone who could stay within the ground without any need to breathe.

Switching prototype to YUREI

At the back of his mind, he felt Blob instantly change tracks, the ever-burning rage and fire that was the bylestyr instinct instantly altering itself to a feeling of absolute nothingness; he felt the world around Blob shift from being real to an illusion that it could pass through at will.

Blob the yurei vanished down into the floor and settled just a little distance away from the throne. Close enough to tinker with the conduit connecting the throne to the featherglass shard, yet far enough to not be accidentally hit by the featherglass and get deleted.

Territory Creation active

Initiate Featherglass Forging
Determined purity: 81%

It was just a matter of time now.

Meynte raised one hand.

He was close. Very close. Just a little more and he'd be victorious. This, the empress would not be able to foresee.

The coppery taste of blood filled his mouth. It was taking a heck of a toll on him. Still, after all those stunts and bargaining with the svartalfars, was it just that easy to forge one? If he'd known, he'd probably have done a different deal with Banksi.

"Slightly?" asked Meynte, cocking her head. "At the risk of being exposed to your madness, child, I will indulge you. How am I, who brings the End of Potential, wrong?"

"You said the battle was decided from the start. I wonder, which battle are you talking about? Me resisting you? Or me resisting Everfrost from taking over Tanya?"

The empress's frown deepened into curiosity. "Your ramblings—"

"Make a lot of sense!" Lukas retorted, throwing up more blood. "Because I know a lot of things. *Important* things. Want to know some, before you try to kill me, Queen Meynte?"

Just then, the floor erupted and a creature arose out of it. The only thing Lukas could make out was an immensely tall, lean, shaggy, vaguely humanoid *thing* with a dark head and claws the size of his arms.

And it was fast.

Lukas hastily raised a stone wall, but one look with those abyssal dark eyes and it disintegrated to dust. Lukas terraported over and over, but the creature was one step, three steps, seven steps ahead of him, and if not for his force shields, he'd have been sliced into pancakes several times over. Lukas threw a wave of pure lifeforce at it, but it spun in midair and raked its claws at his midsection. His eyes shone emerald green, and the claws clashed against empty air, only to strike again and again. Lukas smirked, ready to tear it apart—

—only for someone else to grab its body midway and thrash it down upon the ground.

Lukas blinked and turned to whoever had unexpectedly aided him. Glaring down at the fallen creature, her entire body glowing with sigils and runes, was Maude.

CHAPTER 14

WHAT WE FIGHT FOR

One second, the monstrous form of Solana loomed over Lukas, her claws slashing through air aimed at his midriff, only to be stopped by Motion Negation. The entire thing had been so sudden and instinctive that he hadn't even realized he had done it. The impact of her unstoppable force and the immovable object—his motion barrier was so deafening that the resulting shockwave created cracks along the stone floor.

He had no choice. He had to tear her apart again.

Before he could act, however, Solana returned his attack with extreme vengeance, hammering upon the invisible motion barrier relentlessly like a lumberjack, causing him to bend down on one knee, trying to push back against the momentum behind her blows. He guessed that was the difference between his and Inanna's control of the technique. His chest was growing warmer by the second and his head bursting with agony, and he knew he had to act now. His eyes flashed green—

—only for his target to be pulled out of his vision.

The next moment, there was an enormous sound and an explosion of shattering stone that left half a dozen little bruises on his face. With that, the monster was down on the floor, its long, clawed form twisted in ways that didn't seem at all ergonomic. The creature's immense stench that had practically rooted him to his spot had gone as well, leaving him slightly dizzy but ready for combat within a second.

Lukas blinked and turned to Maude.

"That," said the oni, "is just about enough!"

"*ONI!*" snarled Solana, her voice sounding less like that of a human and more like iron being dragged through broken glass. She rolled back and stood up, twisting her arms in ways that just didn't make physical sense. "Know your place!"

Now he knew why Solana was afraid of Maude. He wasn't sure how, but Maude was capable of hurting, if not defeating, her. Whether that was because of her yurei heritage or the vanir was another matter altogether.

"I know my place," said Maude, a bitter smile on her face. "And I'm standing right there."

"Why?" Solana snarled. "Why would you betray me?"

"Betray you? Oh no, Leader, this had nothing to do with you." Maude sounded oddly tired, but there was a strange affliction to her voice. One that Lukas couldn't place. "This was just me staying true to myself."

"A fence-sitter!" Solana accused.

"A free spirit," Maude shot back, her face twisted in sudden, bitter grief. "To be a vanir is to be one with nature. To be a yurei is to be a crafter. I joined the yokai so that I could be free. So that I could stop lying to myself and choose what I wished to be. That freedom is what shapes my actions, Leader. The same freedom you're denying Tanya by trapping her. And that makes you my enemy."

There was a slow, low snarl in her voice. She kept it tightly leashed and under control, but he heard it. He recognized it, and he knew what it was like to feel it permeating his words. Maude turned to him and met his eyes.

"Outsider, you will see this through? Till the very end?"

He knew what she was asking.

His lips twisted into a lopsided grin. "Whatever it takes."

"In that case," she said, her voice crisp, "your priority is Queen Meynte. Leave Leader to me. Consolidate your power, use that monstrosity of yours if you must, but get that wraith out of Tanya."

There was no need to tell her that the monstrosity in question was actually doing its job perfectly fine.

"She's no wraith," Lukas replied, meeting Meynte firmly in the eye. "She's not even a soul. She's a memory. Preserved for over a thousand years, tricking unsuspecting descendants in a false hope of returning to a splendor that no longer exists!"

"You—" Solana screamed. "You *DARE*—"

"Yes, I dare," Lukas snarled, his voice cold and sharp as the edge of a knife. "I dare because I know the truth. The truth that you're either oblivious to or wish to ignore. Tell us, Queen Meynte, tell us why Tanya is a perfect host for you. Why is it that among all the descendants in a thousand years, only Tanya became your host? Tell us!"

"What foolishness is this?" Solana hissed, her dark pupilless eyes glared at him. "Tanya has a physical form, like Queen Meynte before her! That is why she's the perfect host! Tsurara, for all her power, could never inhabit a body for too long without killing it. But Tanya! She's the perfect avatar."

Meynte had yet to say a single word.

Maude, who was studying Lukas the entire time, asked in a very precise, polite voice, "That's not it, is it?"

Lukas shook his head.

"What does *he* know?" Solana sneered. "He's just an Outsider."

It was almost impossible trying to associate the cold, poker-faced yokai leader with this emotionally tempestuous bitch. Lukas didn't know if it was because she was this close to achieving her goal that made her this turbulent, or if the very idea that the truth behind her six-century-old crusade could be wrong was tearing her sanity apart. Human, bremetan, or yokai, at the end of the day, people fought for their beliefs. For someone like Solana who had borne the weight of her beliefs for six centuries, it was like pushing a mountain.

"Oh, I know. More than what you believe anyway," Lukas said, willfully dragging out the conversation. He was still forging featherglass in the back of his mind, and he needed the setup ready before the shit hit the fan. As easy as he made it look, exercising Territory Creation and forging a spiritually active substance while acting through a yurei prototype was a rather difficult job. Especially while he had to manage things on two levels here.

Everything he had observed so far told him that Meynte was a creature of pride. Someone like that would not lie, not when confronted by the truth. That said, Meynte was a queen, and a queen did not find it necessary to respond to confrontation in kind. In her mind, Meynte had made herself the judge, jury, and executioner of all things in the world. Anyone that did not fall into her idea of reality was simply begging to be wiped out.

It was as simple as that.

If Solana really didn't know the truth, she had let herself be fooled for centuries. And if so, she was due for a grand awakening. Making Solana question her own beliefs would be a blow far stronger than a dozen Kinetomancy blows. With her out of the picture, he could take Meynte down himself, with or without Maude's help.

Getting Solana there was the difficult part.

"Then, pray tell, what is this secret?" the skinwalker sneered, her body reshaping back into a humanoid state. In her monstrous form, Solana was immensely strong, extremely agile, and could control the terrain like nobody's business. Hell, she had snatched his control despite his running on Hreidmar's instincts. But the moment the situation slipped from combat to conversation, she'd instantly change back to looking bremetan. Why? Did this form have immense mana requirements? Perhaps she stayed in a bremetan state to save power?

Something to ponder for another time.

"The secret isn't that Tanya is a perfect host, Solana. Neither were the previous descendants less than perfect. If anything, Tanya is the weakest. And not just that, she's cut off from her true strength—from Everfrost. Remember what Maude told you earlier? Despite transforming, Tanya wasn't the one she faced. She was still herself. Cut off from her alter ego, Frost."

"And how do *you* know that?"

"Because I did it, you stupid bitch! She came after me, we fought, and I sealed Everfrost away! Yes, she uses the Frost, but you've noticed it, haven't you? It's Frost that devours lifeforce, but that's *all* there is. All this time, your Queenship has been raining Everfrost on my ass, and every single time, I've come out unscathed. Do you know why? Because this Outsider is keeping the true Everfrost at bay!"

Of all the things he could have said to her, that shocked Solana the most. Her discomfort was rolling off of her in waves. There she was, standing in a room that she prized more than anything in her life, a room that Lukas had just destroyed. One of her own had betrayed her and joined forces against her. And now when she had come this close to actualizing her dream, he was telling her that her dream was a lie.

He almost felt sorry for her. *Almost.*

"Your powers are astounding, Lukas Aguilar," Solana said at last. She had gained some modicum of control. "To hold back the End of Potential is an immeasurable feat. That you are capable of doing that only proves that you are, and always have been, the Key of legend. But oh yes, all of this makes perfect sense, in ways that you do not understand."

Lukas perked up. "Oh?"

"Yes," said Solana with a wicked little laugh. "Do you not see it, Outsider? Tanya was always meant to be the queen's vessel. She, a descendant who carries Everfrost in her very soul, bears a body as mortal as any Asukan. One blessed with Potential so high that she can make a king among kami submit to her whims. A walking, talking contradiction like that is the best vessel for our queen. And maybe you are right. Maybe by weakening her, you fulfilled the condition that allowed the queen to be reborn within her. And now, she will summon the true might of Fimbulwinter and bring about the End of Asukan domination."

"Yeah, about that . . ." Lukas interrupted. "I think you're getting a bit carried away in your grandiose dreams. Ask that has-been of a queen exactly why she wouldn't do what you claimed. Ask her why sealing Everfrost was necessary for her to possess Tanya. Go on! I dare you."

He met Meynte's ice-cold eyes. The killing intent in them was palpable. He had clearly struck a nerve.

Featherglass forging complete

About time. And now for step two.
He focused on the throne.

Running detailed scan
Analyzing structural lattice . . .
Connecting to sink . . .

Solana was looking at Meynte, her body rooted to the spot. It didn't take a genius to realize that she was caught up in her own fanaticism. The harshness and confidence in Lukas's words demanded an appropriate response, but the only valid one would require her to question the word of her queen, someone she had sworn her fidelity to. The former was mocking her resolve, calling her fragile, and the latter was sacrilege.

Damned if she did. Damned if she didn't.

Naturally, Solana chose a third option.

"Enough of your games, Outsider!" she snarled. "You've slandered my queen and destroyed my precious throne room. I've given you multiple chances to stay on our side and reap the benefits, yet you seem intent on dying by my hands. And after I kill you, I'll end this betrayer. Your death will be the herald of Oumagatoki."

"Listen to me, Solana, that *thing* has been lying to you ever—"

It was too late. One moment, she was glaring at Lukas. The next moment, there was a blur in the air and a creature was clawing its way at him. It was about the size of a gorilla, but the head on its shoulders reminded him of a dog or a wolf. Massive layers of dark fur covered its arms and its claws, each of them the size of Lukas's arm.

There was no time to think, so he ran on instinct.

His eyes flashed and, all of a sudden, he could see every single trajectory that Solana would take. *Could* take. The world around him slowed and screeched to a halt, as Level-2 Tachypsychia—the power to elevate his own perception of Time— expanded a single second to ten. Dropping everything at hand, he planted his feet firmly on the ground, held his palms out, put them in exact positions, and sent out consecutive blasts of crimson flames at her, infusing it with anomalous energy. Level-3 flames were already a pain in the ass to deal with, but when infused with anomalous energy, their destructive abilities were greatly increased.

Against every single one of her trajectories.

Solana's eyes widened as she dodged the first fireball, only to realize that she had fallen right into the second's path. There was a flash of light, a thunderous detonation, and the sharp scent of ozone as his power met with the stabilizing influence of her Terramancy, only for the third torrent to come smashing into her, burning her, and flinging her by about ten feet.

"Don't do it, Solana!" he called. "You aren't going to beat me! You haven't got what you need."

"Condescending bastard!" The skinwalker let out a snarl of frustration as she pushed herself up, ignoring the damage her body had taken, and came at him. Lukas repeated the previous attack and was amazed to see her weave through the flames, her barriers shielding her from the heat, her sharp claws shining malevolently as she brought them down to tear his head off.

Flames would not stop her. So perhaps, force would do.

He was already raising his arm, Inanna's power flooding his veins, the brown in his eyes shifting into specks of emerald. Pain rushed through his brain as he closed in on her motion trajectories from all directions. Solana liked to crush others with her cubic barriers. He idly wondered how she'd feel being smashed from all directions by an imploding spherical barrier.

But once again, someone else beat him to it.

Maude stood before him, the sigils and runes in her body glowing with an eldritch power. The aura of life energy swirling within her was so dense and potent that, for a moment, Lukas wondered if she was even using lifeforce at all. He wasn't sure how but Maude threw her hand out like a claw, seemingly to catch something in midair, and the next moment, Solana's neck was within its clutches. Maude crouched, completely avoiding Solana's claw as it passed over her head, before hitting her with a finger right below her left breast. And for a moment, Solana slowed down, and that allowed Maude to let her neck go and then hit Solana in several other spots, all in a single breath. It was so fast that Lukas could barely follow through but he thought he saw her aim for her collarbone, windpipe, diaphragm, and ribs.

Solana staggered, like she had been hit by a hundred force-blasts from every side all at once. Dark ichor erupted out of her mouth, and she fell, like a stringless marionette. Her body landed like a mass of broken limbs, and the only reason Lukas knew she was alive were the tiny screeches that escaped her throat.

She didn't move after that.

Lukas gaped at her. "How did you—"

Maude looked at him and said, "I'm a vanir naturopath." And then she smiled, as if that explained everything.

Lukas shook his head. He had too many things to worry about at the moment. How a vanir doctor could paralyze the crap out of a six-century-old skinwalker who lived through multiple half-assed Level-4 Kinetomancy blasts with just some well-placed finger jabs was the kind of headache he didn't need right now.

Maybe next week.

"She's going to stay down?"

"Until I heal her, yes," said Maude. "Her body is in perfect condition."

Lukas looked at her burned remains.

"Apart from that, I mean. Anyway, she's just paralyzed. Any attempt to use lifeforce will utterly destroy her formations. She'll still be able to pull herself back, but it'll take several days at best."

He blinked. "I'm not sure if you're awesome or terrifying."

Maude gave him a lopsided grin.

"Remind me to stay on your good side," he quipped. "You're scary."

"Focus!" she said. "You still have *her* to take down."

Both of them looked ahead at Meynte, who was standing before her throne. The queen watched them with keen interest, her eyes as cold as death, drawing in everything and giving nothing in return. She had watched the exchange with the interest of a general observing children playing chess, lips pursed thoughtfully.

Finally, she shook her head to the right and sighed.

"Fine. It's time to end this."

She took a step to the left and—

Rift detected

—vanished.

It wasn't high-speed motion. It wasn't Aeromancy or illusion or some twisted Metamancy either. She didn't even teleport or open a well or anything remotely like that. She just took a step and went *away*, as if stepping behind a column and never appearing on the other side.

Gone. Just like that.

Except in her case, "gone" meant reappearing exactly one foot behind him.

Rift detected
Predator found you

His instincts taking over, Lukas instantly threw himself forward and twisted his body into a roll, evading half a dozen shards of Frost that impaled the ground from behind him. Lukas felt a strange pressure right next to his ear and turned around with a flaming fist, but Meynte was there, intercepting his punch by grabbing his wrist and—

—and his right arm practically exploded with shards of blood-coated Frost, tearing out of his skin like upturned coffins. Lukas howled and dropped to the floor as Everfrost hungrily devoured the impossibly high amounts of lifeforce flowing through him, and frosting his blood itself, making his arm look like some demonic porcupine. He frantically shifted his focus away from his body to dull the pain, and ruthlessly cut off lifeforce, shunting away Everfrost's fuel.

But it was too late. His arm was gone.

Completely gone.

"AGUILAR!" Maude cried out, horror in her voice as he felt the Frost escape his control, forcing its way out of the no-lifeforce boundary he had crafted around it with a noise not unlike tearing paper. Lukas took another deep breath, forcing himself to ignore the pain and remain calm and—

"BEHIND YOU!"

It was too late. Meynte appeared in front of Maude and impaled her with a shard of Everfrost.

Right above the left kidney.

Maude croaked, her shell-shocked eyes staring at Meynte's face, before her legs gave way and she dropped down to the ground, spasming. Meynte stood above her, her arms on her waist, peering down at her spasming form.

"Disappointing!" she muttered. "How such a frail creature overwhelmed my servant is beyond me."

A part of Lukas went rigid with shock and horror, but before he could second-guess himself, he channeled the dranzithl's flames through his now-damaged right arm, disintegrating it to dust.

No chance of Everfrost penetrating his body.

And at the same time, there was no chance for him to regrow an entire arm anytime soon. Perhaps if he channeled the dranzithl prototype, he could do it, but it would come at the expense of all his rationality and control, and that would get him killed in all sorts of nasty ways.

And even if he could heal his arm in time, it would only give his extreme regeneration powers away, which would mean Meynte would take him even more seriously.

Better to fight without his dominant arm than be killed.

That said, there was a second option. Silently, he summoned Blob back to him, feeling the yurei pass through the earth towards him.

"Unlike you," he said, "that frail creature doesn't need petty tricks to win."

Meynte spun around. Lukas had expected another blow, but instead, he found a small smile cruelly curved upon her lips.

"Guess you're finally taking me seriously." He gasped. He suppressed a grin as he felt Blob come in contact with his body and spread all over him, like a yurei.

That smile again. "This body is frail, Soulcrafter," she said. "I can only use so much before it tears apart."

Soulcrafter. She was using that term again. At least this one sounded important. He had been called "mortal," "anomaly" and "Outsider" before, but this name felt more significant than the others.

He wondered why.

Pushing himself up with his remaining arm, he got up on his knees. Prophylaxis could work on his destroyed arm—eventually, that is—but he didn't have the time or the inclination to wait that long. The problem was, Meynte wouldn't let him prepare. His only option was to keep her busy. And for that, he needed *time*. Time to think.

Deleting all safeties
Overclock skill: Tachypsychia (Level 2)
Enact

Overclocking. Taking a skill, and channeling his entire lifeforce, or mana, to use it to the maximum extent without caring about the side effects. He had performed something similar when facing the bylestyr for the first time in the lava ridge borderland, when he had stopped its attack using force shielding, Terramancy and anomalous energy. He had done it a second time against the Ifrit King, only that time, it had been a motion barrier, enhanced by all the anomalous energy he could throw against it.

This was, however, the first time he was using a perception skill to this degree. Needless to say, it was the most dangerous of all three, but if it worked, the risk would be worth it. And—

THUMPPP!!

The burning pain from losing an arm subsided. The tension was gone. Or rather, his mind, his perception, magnified itself exponentially. The entire universe shrank until it was just within his mind. Time slowed down, and where a second had passed outside, it was easily half an hour within his mindscape.

All the time he needed to think, to plan, and to execute.

His destroyed arm was barely an issue. Anything that was part of his physical body could be healed later with Prophylaxis. He had already flushed the Everfrost out by burning his hand to cinders, so that wasn't an issue anymore. And in the worst-case scenario, he could always rely on the dranzithl's regeneration, as sloppy as it would be.

THUMPPP!!

The lifeforce he had just lost? That was more of a problem, but hardly unsalvageable. Shifting to a lifeforce-intensive prototype like the bylestyr would instantly double the production and get him up to snuff.

That only left the major problem: Meynte. Using Kinetomancy wasn't an option. Best-case scenario: he'd strike her and kill Tanya in that same strike. Worst-case scenario: she'd step through those microsecond rifts in the Haze and completely evade his strike, leaving him with only a sensory overload and a brain aneurysm, if he was lucky. That left a limited number of options and none of them fit the entire bill.

Naturally, he needed to look elsewhere for a better weapon. Or rather, the right monster.

Luckily, he had an entire arsenal of monsters saved up in his anomaly-brain.

Accessing Monster Prototype Array . . .

Images flashed across his mind's eye. They came by the dozens and then by the hundreds. Most of them were discarded preemptively for their lack of versatility in the fight. Some of the monster prototypes from Earth were absolutely massive and equally terrifying, but he wasn't looking for either. His thoughts lingered on the dranzithl, again, for its limitless regeneration, anti-life aura, and corrosive flames. But it was an uncontrollable berserker, and insanity was the last thing he needed right now.

His thoughts rested on the kirin, a creature that just had to be a *yokai*. Its speed was beyond anything he had ever seen and could serve as a strong counter to Meynte's ability to access the Haze. Several monsters came in with half a dozen passive skills that would improve him in ways, but none of them were a solid solution to his insane requirements. Really, why hadn't he done this before?

Right. That was because he had developed an inferiority complex from seeing other powerful individuals like Tanya and Hreidmar and gone with the individual approach, a complete reversal to his original decision.

Inanna had always been in favor of developing the individual, and Lukas, out of sheer defiance, had gone the other route to develop the anomaly in him. And then in a twist of irony, he had gotten so sentimental about her sacrifice that he had changed tracks to develop the individual within him.

Inanna couldn't have put it better.

—In your relentless trials to gain what you seek, you've forgotten a very simple truth. One that is the bedrock of your existence—

He was a World.

"Soulcrafter," Meynte had called him. And only omphaloi had the power to craft souls. And what were omphaloi if not *Worlds*?

Meynte was a World-eater. He was a World.

Meynte was the End of Potential. He was its Creator.

This was never Lukas Aguilar's battle. This was the battle of a World against its predator. A World that had all the skills it needed to achieve that victory. But even now, Lukas was trying to select a particular prototype to solve his problem. To be his miracle.

Warmonger Protocol active
Safety off

THUMP! THUMP! THUMP!!!!

Time was up. His perception returned to normal. And all it cost him were just a few vessels rupturing.

Easily taken care of.

"Ah," he heard Meynte whisper, her hands crossed behind her back, "if only the others had possessed such determination."

"The others?" he asked.

The smile deepened. If she had wanted to kill him, she could have done it a hundred times over already. But she didn't. She was toying with him. She wanted to see what he could do, what his limits were. Her destroying his arm was little more than a small experiment. She was a mad scientist and he her guinea pig.

Well, this guinea pig had seen the world outside the laboratory. It was time the scientist knew that.

"Say, that vanishing technique you use . . ." said Lukas. The fire had cauterized his arm, leaving a stump just below the elbow. Prophylaxis was working on it, but it would take time, and he had alternative options in mind.

Meynte cocked her head.

"You're accessing the Haze, aren't you? The Ikai Realm. Everyone thinks that the Haze overlaps the real world only at certain spots which they call Wells. But that's not true, is it? The Ikai is *everywhere,* overlapping the real world at every single point. And if you know how, then you can straddle the line between Worlds, wandering from one existence to another as easily as walking through open doors."

"So . . ." she murmured. "You know. I'm not sure if anyone told you this, but for an Outsider, you're dangerously well-informed."

"I try to keep up with stuff," said Lukas. "Knowledge is power and all that."

"That it is, that it is," she murmured, closing her eyes as her body swayed slightly, as if dancing to an absent wind. "Tell me, Soulcrafter," she whispered, "were you speaking truth? Are you the one that keeps the Cruelest Winter at bay?"

Ah. Of course. *That* would have definitely held her attention.

Good for him.

Lukas just smiled. For what use were words when silence was enough?

Accessing Puppeteer Protocol
Reforging accessory heteromorph

Blob was in dire need of an upgrade if it was to count for something. And he needed Meynte to give her the time to do exactly that. Also, after he was done defeating this empress, he really needed to scour the Crypt of Fiendish Worms. The innards were supposedly full of aqāru. Blob, as it was, was indispensable. But if he could add more to it then . . .

Good ideas for another time.

"I see," said Meynte, exhaling. "That complicates matters. Tell me, Soul-crafter, should you die, would that mean Fimbulwinter would surge back within this frail form?"

It wouldn't. He wasn't the one sealing Fimbulwinter away. It was Inanna's spell, empowered by her divinity. While he was reasonably sure he could undo it, it would possibly remain even after his demise.

But Meynte didn't need to know that.

Accessing Analysis Report from Extermination Protocol 4.0
Filtering prototypes not vulnerable to Predator . . .

Just a few more minutes. He had to keep her talking.

"Of course it would," Meynte spoke up suddenly. "Silly me! The death of the caster would define the end of the spell. I cannot fathom the intricacy of a mortal spell that can hold back a Taboo, but I have never come across a soul-crafter either . . ."

She met his gaze.

"You are right. I took Fimbulwinter out of its frozen heart in Hvergelmir, allowing it a second chance to manifest in this universe. But have you wondered, *why* is Fimbulwinter dead set against me?"

He had but not in those exact terms. He had been too overwhelmed at being privately addressed by a Taboo manifesting as his friend's avatar, while trying to figure out how to stop a memory from possessing Tanya. He had never addressed the issue of *why* Fimbulwinter wanted Tanya to be in control and not Meynte, the original wielder of its power.

"Makes you wonder, does it not?" asked Meynte. "That power that I stole from the heart of Niflheim, that power that made me empress. That Taboo that resurfaces in every single one of my descendants. That Taboo fights me. Do you know why?"

Lukas shook his head.

"Because I know what it is. What it truly is. What it will do to the universe when unleashed."

Lukas stilled. "It would take the world back to the Formless Infinity. The Void. It would—"

"End everything in existence," said Meynte. "Even the yokai."

That made a lot of sense. At the same time, it raised even more questions.

"Then why did you—" He began, only to freeze as Meynte did something that truly terrified him.

She smiled. And it was genuine.

"Hubris," said Meynte, a bittersweet expression on her face. "Little did I fathom what it was I was ascending with, Soulcrafter. Or perhaps, I should call it 'descent.' And when I realized it, it was already too late. There is a reason why Fimbulwinter was trapped within Hvergelmir. It serves a purpose in the grand scheme of things. But I, in my foolishness, managed to imbue myself with a fraction of it. A fraction that contained in it the power of the End, a devourer so vast and infinite that even my own soul couldn't take it. Before I could act, it tore into my soul, corrupting it, fashioning an avatar that co-existed within me. A soul of Ice."

"*Ice is my soul,*" Lukas murmured, his fists clenched. Had Frost, like Solana, played upon him? Yes. Definitely, yes. And if that was true, what were the chances that Meynte too was doing the same? Inanna had once told him that the best lies were those that held a sliver of falsehood within an ocean of truth.

Maybe the legend of the Key truly meant something. Solana, as twisted as she was, was acting on things she believed in. It was the complete truth, but enough to convince her to continue on her path for six centuries. Everfrost, too, had given Lukas a Truth, and like Solana, it, too, was incomplete. And now Meynte . . .

"*Ice is my soul,*" repeated the empress. "An aria that neither me, nor any of my descendants, ever learned, and yet, it instinctively arose out of our lips. Because it stemmed from the corruption in our souls."

Lukas checked the Screen.

29 prototypes found
Adding filtered prototypes for automation
Enacting . . .

Just a little more.

"Before I knew it, the avatar had grown. The more I used Everfrost, the further I became vulnerable to its whispers, to its corruptive influence. It spoke of destruction, of bloodshed, of annihilation of this entire universe, and how I would be the fulcrum of that apocalypse."

Lukas staggered. Not long ago, he had been privy to another Everfrost user talking about her past. About how a young girl, terrified of her own power, had been subjected to similar whispers. How she had been shaped by that malevolent force, guiding her actions in ways that stripped her of her innocence, turning her life into a maelstrom of dread and despair. Had Meynte too been in Tanya's shoes, trying to cling to her own individuality as Everfrost took away parts of her soul piece by piece? Maybe she too was different, back then. Rational. One who would preside over an entire kingdom and ensure its prosperity. Maybe she knew how terrible and wrong the power within her was. Maybe she had even tried to cull it, tried finding ways to do a lesser evil, or even tried to get some good positive result out of it.

Even if he managed to overthrow Meynte today, how long before Tanya would stand in her place? How long before she became the next Meynte?

"I realized that no matter what I did, the Frost would ultimately take over. The whispers would eventually *become* the personality," Meynte said. "I would become Everfrost. And when that happened, I'd bring about the End of the World."

"So you stored your memories away."

"It was one of my better ideas," Meynte replied affably. "I knew that once I became Everfrost, Amaterasu and the others would come for me. She had already begun the path of transmogrification to divinity, and her power was the antithesis to mine. A light that was the bane of everything spiritual, and a Frost that devoured lifeforce. The World would *make* her come for me."

Just like the Crypt of Fiendish Worms had dispatched the Guardian after Lukas had hacked into its consciousness.

"The rest, as they say, is history," Meynte claimed. "We fought. I, Everfrost Incarnate, sought to end the World. Amaterasu sought to protect it. The result . . ."

"The desert of Namzuuhuu," Lukas murmured. "An abomination that hates everything alive. A part of the World that rejects the World."

"So," she smiled. "You know that, too."

The pieces were falling into place. The Asukans, despite their high-handed preaching, were right about one thing: the yokai represented a genuine threat. More particularly, the yokai under Meynte's command represented a genuine threat. Not just to bremetan civilization but to themselves as well. To the entire World. And—

"I have a question," said Lukas suddenly. "And I'd like an honest answer."

"By all means," she said.

Polite, thought Lukas. "Tell me, during your fight with Amaterasu, do you remember . . . winning?"

Meynte blinked. The scrunched-up expression was so like Tanya, that for a moment, Lukas almost thought it was her.

"Before Solana did her little stunt of rebirthing yourself in Tanya's body, she told us of a very interesting tale. She said that the Elders of her kind remember winning the war. Remember the Moon God being slain. Remember Empress Meynte overpowering Amaterasu—"

"What travesty is this?" Meynte snapped, anger lacing her tone. "Are you mocking me, Soulcrafter?"

"I'd have asked you to ask your servant and confirm it, but unfortunately, both she and the one who can revive her are incapacitated. So, I guess, you'll have to trust my word."

He smiled. "Do tell. Do you remember defeating Amaterasu?"

"No!" she replied stubbornly.

"Solana said that the storm gods Fujin and Raijin had slain Tsukuyomi, while you trapped Amaterasu in your personal oblivion. The moon fell from the sky. The Mists were coming."

Meynte clenched her fists. "I did not. I could not. I was—I was *this* close to entrapping her. Her Eternal Light would be lost forever in the shale crystals of Everfrost, unable to penetrate the world ever again. Her All-Seeing Eye would be blind, but—"

Lukas arched an eyebrow.

Meynte gritted her teeth. It was weird, seeing someone that powerful look so helpless. "I lost."

"How?"

She looked enraged. "I just told you. I was *this* close to entrapping her. Her Eternal Light would be lost forever in the shale crystals of Everfrost, unable to penetrate the world ever again. Her All-Seeing Eye would be blind, but—I lost."

Lukas narrowed his eyes. What was going on? Why was she—

"I know it sounds weird, and I'm not mocking you. But I'll have to ask you one more time. *How?*"

"*I JUST TOLD YOU!*" screamed the empress. "I was *this* close to entrapping her. Her Eternal Light would be lost forever in the shale crystals of Everfrost, unable to penetrate the world ever again. Her All-Seeing Eye would be blind, but—"

She paused. "I . . . I'm just repeating myself, aren't I?"

"Do you remember *how* the trap failed?" Lukas tried again. "Why couldn't you entrap her in your personal oblivion? For the record, do you even *know* how the Ikai, which once held the known universe together, became the deadland the yokai call the Haze?"

"I . . ."

Meynte paused in uncertainty. It was shocking, seeing her petrified, with an expression of absolute horror etched on her face. "I . . . I don't know!"

Lukas took a step forward. "Here's another question. You are a memory of the original Meynte. Do you remember *when* you cast this memory away?"

The concern and mounting unease on the empress's face dissipated somewhat, letting him know that she knew that answer.

"Right when I was entrapping Amaterasu in my personal oblivion. I knew I'd have to unleash the utter power of Everfrost—no, of *Fimbulwinter*—upon the world, if I had any chance of destroying Her. I knew that the Taboo would either shatter my soul or turn me into its puppet, neither of which was to my liking. I sundered away my own memories to my daughter and unleashed my greatest power upon the world."

And yet . . . Lukas frowned. *The Desert's curse prevents the Eternal Light from penetrating into it. Not Everfrost.*

It was a curious situation, much like Inanna's own. The Sumerian legends mentioned the "Descent of Inanna" into the Underworld—Ereshkigal's domain—after which she was released by the intervention of her father, the sky god. But the real Inanna claimed that she was a slave girl who rose to become an empress, a god-killer, and finally, a goddess herself. The supreme queen of her pantheon. One who had no clue about *how* her pendant ended up on Earth, or why she couldn't find any trace of her Truth or her pantheon in the entire Universe.

In the same fashion, Meynte's memory, cut off from the real empress, had absolutely no clue what had truly transpired in the war, except that she lost, and Amaterasu became the Great Goddess and the ruler of the Asukan Pantheon.

"But even so . . ." said Meynte. "Even my memory should've known what happened. It should've known how I . . . fell."

But she didn't.

"Tell me," Lukas prodded. "Do you remember any deity that had the power to rewrite reality itself?"

"Rewrite . . . reality?"

"Yes."

She shook her head. "If such a power existed, it was beyond my knowledge. And it was certainly not part of the Asukan Pantheon, or the Aesir, the vanir, or the Alfian gods. Why do you ask?"

Lukas bit his lip. He had been expecting a positive answer here. For all of Solana's bragging, her knowledge was mostly second-hand. He had kind of been expecting that Meynte, someone who fought gods, would be able to give him a reply in the affirmative.

Always fighting uphill, I am.

"Remember how I told you Solana said that the Elders remember you winning? How the yokai were dominant, how the storm gods had killed the moon god, and the Mists were coming? She also said that something happened, and then, everything changed. The storm gods were dead, Tsukuyomi was alive, and the Asukan Pantheon was victorious. She said that no one ever remembers how *that* came to pass, as if . . . As if someone didn't like how the story came to pass and tore the page out to rewrite it."

The entire chamber fell silent, and Meynte looked at him, transfixed in shock. The seconds ticked by in agonizing slowness, but neither of them said anything.

Finally, Meynte broke the silence.

"There is no power that can rewrite reality as you described, but there is one that operates on a domain remarkably close to it. But . . ."

She met his eyes. "There is no way she could've been the one to do it."

She, Lukas noted.

"Who was it?"

Meynte closed her eyes, and said, in a sharp, reverent tone, "The One that came before All. The progenitor's first born. Not a demon, not a god. One that did not belong anywhere but could go everywhere. She was Reality, she was Fantasy, and she was everything in between. With nine tails each holding a mystery that held the universe together, she was the World Shaper. The Guardian. The Queen of Ikai, Inari."

He knew who she was referring to. It was the same being that the Asukan theologists referred to as—

"The Nine-tailed Fox."

"You will *not* speak of Her in such derogatory way," Meynte exploded.

Lukas flinched. "Apologies. That is how the Asukans describe her in their texts. But Reality and Fantasy, and everything in between—seems like someone that could potentially do what Solana described."

"Lady Inari is our greatest goddess," said Meynte, her tone laced with anger. "No, she is beyond that. Every yokai owes their existence to her, myself included. Even the sheer idea that she . . . that she might've . . . it's *preposterous!*"

And yet, Lukas thought grimly, *not entirely impossible. Trust breeds betrayal, Inanna would say.*

"It is obvious that there are mysteries about the war that I cannot fathom, Soulcrafter," said Meynte, looking ill. "You have my gratitude for warning me about them."

"Yeah, same here," said Lukas. "At least this way, whoever wins, we have an idea of what went wrong. Speaking of which, you were an oni, back in your original life, weren't you?"

That smile again. "You ask many questions."

"Yeah, I don't usually get a chance to chitchat with people of legend. I'm just making use of the opportunity to scratch the truth out. Who knows when I might get such a chance again?"

Meynte laughed. "Yes. I was."

Lukas grinned. That made perfect sense. The Asukans considered oni to be the greatest threat not because of what they represented but because *Meynte* was one. A creature that was the best of both worlds and wanted to *end* everything.

With Meynte's demise, the yokai kingdom had fallen. But Everfrost, being the Taboo that it was, was rejected by the Origin, and kept resurfacing through Meynte's descendants. And Solana, being Meynte's faithful servant, carried his wishes by bringing future yuki-onnas to the throne, to Nidhogg's Lair. The fool probably thought it had something to do with the End of the Asukan World, when in reality, rebirthing Meynte would cause anything but.

Unfortunately, it was easier said than done, for in every yuki-onna lay Everfrost's avatar—the Ice-Queen—which resisted allowing Meynte's identity to take over.

Until he, Lukas Aguilar, met Tanya, and in a case of utter coincidence, had within him a power that could seal Fimbulwinter away.

The Truth of Depredation that belonged to the Supreme Queen of An and Ki. One that allowed Meynte the chance to burrow into Tanya's mind and take over. Be *reborn*. It was such a curious set of coincidences that Lukas was having trouble *not* calling it Destiny.

"This . . ." he said at last. "Is all just so fucked up!"

Meynte smiled again.

"My servant was right. You are the Key that brought about my rebirth and that keeps Everfrost from being unleashed into this world. I'm certain you have surmised that, should you unleash it, I will no longer have control over this body. But in doing so, you'd have condemned this universe to the jaws of Fimbulwinter. The End of Everything."

He clenched his jaw. He knew that. He knew exactly what Meynte meant.

"It comes down to this, Soulcrafter," said Meynte, her arms extended, her eyes shining with victory, "You can choose to save the girl you think you know, and in doing so, condemn the world and everything in it. Or you could understand and do what's needed for the greater good of all. Save the world, *hero*. With you keeping Everfrost at bay, I will usher in a new age. Return the Yokai Kingdom to its former glory. And you shall be at my side. As my Sword."

And what did *that* little invitation say about him, Lukas couldn't help but wonder.

He'd be lying if he said he wasn't surprised by Meynte's blunt offer. At the same time, he had grown used to getting such offers ever since he had come to this world. Inanna had wanted him to be her henchman. Her executioner. Solana had wanted him to fulfill his role as the Key, something he had inadvertently ended up doing. Zuken had offered him support in exchange for being a partner in gaining information. Mori had invited him to be part of the Keep. And now Meynte, the empress herself, was offering a place by her side.

It was probably the best offer he had gotten to date, as useless as it was.

"Sorry," he said at last. "But someone once cursed me to never give up on my selfishness. That I should stay true to my beliefs no matter how many I trample upon. Even if it means I must be the invader, the monster, the conqueror . . . it doesn't matter. I'm no longer allowed to pretend otherwise."

"I see," said Meynte, not sounding surprised at all. "In that case, Soulcrafter, I suppose I have to end you before you condemn this world. Be honored. I shall take into account everything you have warned me against and undo all the wrongs done to my kind."

CHAPTER 15

SOULCRAFTER

Absolute war.

It was the only way Lukas could describe the event he was taking part in. There was no mercy in any of the attacks fired off in the chamber, nor was there any victory when said attacks were overcome by another mere moments later. The process repeated itself hundreds, if not thousands of times by now, shaking the entire chamber to its foundations, all while the two others lay upon the floor, near the outer doors, paralyzed: Solana, due to Maude's actions, and Maude, because of that shard of Everfrost impaled through her abdomen was constantly devouring the lifeforce from of her physical body.

He had seen a similar conflict happen months before, when Inanna had possessed his body and fought against Tanya's Frost avatar. Back then, Inanna was the goddess with skills far, far superior to Lukas's current form, and the Frost avatar was little more than an animal. An animal with a god-killing power but an animal nonetheless. Now, their positions were reversed. Lukas was banking on his nature as an anomaly, which included constantly shifting his consciousness to different monster prototypes, while Tanya's body was controlled by an empress with such knowledge, skill, and experience that Lukas was little more than an irascible teenager before her.

Back then, he had been awestruck, watching two juggernauts clash. He hadn't even been able to follow the battle, often getting lost in a blur of overlapping images, each one acting out its own chaotic dance and doing a dozen different things at once, while predicting the opponent and counter-adjusting their actions based on their perception.

And that was when Inanna had just been playing with Tanya.

He wondered what he'd think of that battle now.

His thoughts vanished as Meynte appeared to his left and gripped his arm, only for dazzling white flames to erupt out of it. No doubt she wanted to damage that one too. Cursing, she sidestepped, this time coming from behind Lukas and slamming a thick Frost sword into his back. Blob, now covering his entire body like chain mail, extended out and met the blade midway, shattering it. Meynte's eyes widened as Blob reverted to its natural color, recognizing it for what it was and being forced to pull back.

It didn't, however, stop her from sweeping her arm and clubbing Lukas in the head, only to vanish into thin air the second after. But this time, he was prepared. And with Blob acting as an accessory and defending him from Meynte, its presence brought a whole new meaning and purpose to him. An option that he hadn't seen before was now available.

> **Maximizing Prototype Sympathization Ratio**
> **Base Focus medium chosen: Heteromorph**
> **Establishing Created Territory**

Meynte came at him a second time, aiming for his right side, where nothing but a corroded stump of an arm remained. Lukas spun it around, meeting Meynte's hoarfrost-coated fingers with a brand-new arm, crafted purely out of aqāru, and grabbed her fingers in a tight grip. Meynte panicked, as flames exploded out of the metal arm, meeting her frosted fingers, and aimed a sweeping kick at his head.

A motion barrier held her kick at bay, but she used the momentum to escape his grip.

"That metal . . ." She gritted her teeth. "It's pissing me off."

"It's my accessory," said Lukas, grinning, flexing his new metal arm. "What did you expect it'd do?"

"I've never seen any metal behave so . . . *alive.*"

"Well—" Lukas shrugged. "—the world is a big place."

"I shall keep that in mind. I shall not underestimate you again, Soulcrafter."

"Gosh! You're gonna make me blush!"

And then Meynte attacked again.

The raw strength and dexterity of a bylestyr rushed through his veins, flooding his body with an excess of lifeforce and pumping enormous amounts of fire mana through his inner ley line network. His perceptions shifted too, switching to a simplistic, primal, and yet wildly alien level of perception. Details were lost amidst a swirl of imagery. Solid information was washed over by a sea of blurred vibrations, while focusing on the world's contours on a level beyond human comprehension.

Strings. Pressure. Vibrations.

From the slightest shift of his feet to the sliding of dust to the sudden impact of Meynte's feet within his sensory range—a respectable fifteen feet—he could sense it all. Everything came down to two things: using Shatterpoint Intuition to guide his blows to their location, and the raw bylestyr strength to provide the much-needed momentum behind each attack. Techniques got lost to muscle memory that were not his; to reflexes and reaction times that were strained far beyond the mortal breaking point. The surroundings became an afterthought, the environment, a lazy blur.

Anomaly and empress were nothing more than wild blurs of violence and chaos, tearing apart anything and everything within reach and then some as they viciously attempted to tear each other apart.

Or at least Meynte did. Lukas was more interested in subduing her without maiming Tanya at all if he could help it. Luckily for him, Meynte was using Frost to regenerate her body after taking damage. How that worked, he had no idea, but he knew better than to ponder how reality-breaking powers functioned in the middle of battle.

If nothing else, it allowed him to be a little more creative.

"Guh!" grunted Meynte, as her right leg was entwined by the thick, serpentine form of a neothelid that, just seconds ago, had been Lukas's metallic right arm. The creature squeezed, crushing her leg, as Meynte screamed, unleashing Everfrost through her knee, and pulling her injured, bloodied leg out of its death grip, only to rift her way out of Lukas's reach.

Basic instance deleted
New instance installed
Accessory Heteromorph active

Good as new again.

Lukas parried blows from the left, aimed for his abdomen, before deflecting an Everfrost dagger coming at him from the front. He spun around and terraported exactly three-fourths of a foot to the right, just in time to avoid a row of five jagged Frost blades raining down from above. Projectiles showered him from every direction, and craters were blasted upon the ground while torrents of glacial white narrowly missed him. Instinctively he knew what they were, what caused them, and how they'd affect them if they made contact, but his mind was too overwhelmed for him to care.

The tree-trunk-sized Frost spear that came for him was crushed between the thousand teeth of a khorkhoi.

The array of Frost blades that crashed on him from every direction was held back by a prototype that greatly resembled a giant squid.

The shower of explosive Frost mist that would corrupt his body with a single touch was absorbed in the watery layer conjured by the kami, Shahxith, that had once been Olfric's.

When Meynte had come in, summoning an entire hailstorm coating her body to clash against Lukas, the prototype bylestyr crafted a wall of fire to face her head on.

"UGH!" He heard Meynte scream in frustration from afar, her Frost covering her right leg, healing it on the go. Something about her expression felt odd. She was looking at her right leg like it had offended her. It couldn't possibly be because he had fractured it, could it?

For fuck's sake, she had taken worse injuries than that and healed herself in a jiffy. Then why wasn't she able to heal some broken bones now?

"I've wielded a power that exterminates pantheons," said Meynte. "I've faced the might of Amaterasu and her ilk and nearly ended her. I've taken a Taboo to Ascension and risen as an empress. Why is this fool giving me so much trouble?"

Her cool demeanor had slowly given way to frustration from her lack of progress. Ever since Lukas's second wind kicked in, the battle had become a complete stalemate between her power to summon endless Frost and her vanishing moves, and Lukas's ability to sense where she was with absolute precision, constantly surprising her by using a seemingly infinite number of random prototypes to counter her.

It was a game of chicken that would only last so long as either of their physical bodies did.

The air behind Lukas suddenly split with a howl of frozen wind, and a circle of pure Frost, easily four feet in diameter, opened up behind him, from which a beam of it slammed into his back. Blob expanded out from behind him like a cape and took it all upon itself, while Lukas smashed the axe against the white opening, slashing it with dazzling white flames and destabilizing it.

> **Basic instance deleted**
> **New instance installed**
> **Accessory Heteromorph active**

"Meow!" growled a newly activated Blob.

Meynte's cadaverous eyes glared at Lukas, and suddenly he was being crushed against the ground by the weight of the universe itself. It was similar to the power he had felt when the Ifrit King had manifested, only far more diluted. Gnashing his teeth, he decided to give something back in return.

> **Rapid install monster prototype DRANZITHL**

He still remembered the absolutely nauseating experience of first analyzing the dranzithl. The absolute wrongness exuding from a monster so horribly antithetical to life that merely being in its proximity triggered bile rising in his throat. *That* was what he now sent back to Meynte.

Only far more enhanced, through Blob.

Empress or not, she was possessing a mortal body, and thus, she was restrained by mortal limitations. The empress fell down to one knee, clutching her own head and crying out in despair. Lukas instantly leaped at her with the aim of punching her unconscious. Meynte dodged at the last moment, only for her right leg to suddenly slip, and Lukas took the opportunity to dislocate her jaw.

"You won't let me kill you, but you won't kill me even if you have the chance?" Meynte laughed, blood oozing out of her lips, as Frost covered it up. "Even with that traitor helping you, you will never win."

Traitor? Is she talking about Maude? No that couldn't—OH SHIT—

Another rain of blades fell.

Lukas terraported—

Rapid install monster prototype: Kirin

—and vanished, only to reappear a short distance away from her to defend against another buckshot, followed by eight more shots, all fired in extremely rapid succession to generate a literal wall of Frost that would have otherwise drained the life out of anybody. The moment he appeared behind her, she sent another blast, but this time, he slipped downward, grabbing her legs and burying her up to her neck in the ground, before resurfacing himself ten feet away.

"Well," he said, completely ignoring her glares, "at the moment, I'm just trying to see what happens if I push you to your utmost limits. I mean, you're using Tanya's body so the more skills you demonstrate, the more she'll have for herself. Sounds like a good deal in exchange for renting her body for a while, right?"

Meynte narrowed her eyes. "You really shouldn't get attached to things, Soulcrafter. What happens if you die before that happens?"

He shrugged. "Then you win, of course. And you get to suffer from Tanya's Frost avatar for the rest of your life, 'cause you'd have nothing to return to."

"Wait, what do you—"

Lukas raised his metallic arm and a fork of lightning erupted out of it, smashing against the throne like the hammer of God. Meynte's cry was lost in the noise of detonation that followed. It was so intense that Lukas staggered and fell, dropping to a knee. When the blinding light dissipated, the throne was still there, though a spiderweb of fractures ran all across it.

Damn it. Just what was it made of?

"You weren't too attached to that throne, were you?" Lukas grinned.

Meynte let out a banshee wail of pure, terrifying scorn and sent a bolt of glacial white at him. Lukas instantly terraported and appeared a dozen feet out of the blast radius, and then again, and again, and again.

"WHY WON'T YOU DIE ALREADY?" Meynte roared. Beams of pure Everfrost rained down at him no matter how quickly he terraported, forcing him to resort to raising stone walls and escaping using the kirin's speed. Each of those beams had Death trapped within them; just a single sliver would anni-hilate his soul. No amount of divinity would undo that.

"Woah!" said Lukas, "That wasn't even your skill. That was just *raw* power. Seriously, just *how* much Everfrost can you summon?"

"Stand still and I'll show you."

Lukas grinned again and sprinted three feet to his left, avoiding more buckshot. He staggered again, the remaining fractal on his left arm glowing red with heat. He had been pushing them to the limits of their strength since the beginning of this fight, and given how much mana he could naturally produce, that was saying something.

It was a pity Meynte had destroyed the fractal on his right. It would've made managing things easier. Still, Blob was doing a damn fine job as a substitute.

And then, without the slightest change in expression, he attacked.

The effort was not to kill her but to immobilize her by any means neces-sary. Which . . . he wasn't sure he could manage. He unleashed a torrent of hot flames at her, which accomplished absolutely nothing. Meynte moved with the same speed and impossible force as ever, hurling shafts of Everfrost—each of them the size of a tree trunk—tearing through his defenses. But that was fine, he wasn't attacking to harm her.

Rather, he was just keeping her busy with a series of distractions while he did his real thing. And what better way to keep her distracted than running his mouth?

"You could be nicer, you know. I'm putting a lot of thought and effort into what I use against you and when, while you just keep blasting everything willy-nilly. I used twenty-two different monsters against you, but you just keep deleting and breaking them all. It takes effort, you barbarian! Honestly, you're impressive in a primal sort of way, but who'd ever want to be at your side?"

"I rescind my offer," Meynte said calmly. "You're nothing but a pest to be exterminated! And since I'm breaking things anyway, maybe I should operate on a grander scale."

"Wait, wha—"

Meynte raised her arms, and hoarfrost began to spread across the entire chamber, entombing it in ice.

Lukas smiled, and Blob cloaked his entire body with metal. "Okay, I'm starting to see why they voted you empress."

"DIE!"

Blades of Frost fell upon him from every direction, leaving a crater in their wake. Lukas safely rose out of the ground several dozen feet away, panting. "Damn. This isn't really as much fun when you get angry."

"Give up!" Meynte warned him. "You cannot win! Your tricks will not help your friend. The more power I draw from Fimbulwinter, the stronger the avatar becomes. Even if by some miracle, you shut me out, you cannot stop Fimbulwinter forever. It has now infected this body and will fester until it grows and grows and turns this body into a vessel of the End."

Lukas cocked his head. "Bullshit. If that were true, then you'd just kill that body and return to your throne. Obviously, there is a way to control it."

Meynte threw her head back and laughed. "Control it? Control Fimbulwinter? Don't make me laugh. The best chance you have is to not lose yourself, while channeling the true might of the End upon the Asukan pantheon, something that is possible with your aid. Once that is accomplished, I shall cast another memory aside and destroy this body. The Asukan pantheon would be gone, and the yokai would get their retribution. And you, Soulcrafter, could be their new king."

"Oh?" said Lukas. "And what of you?"

"I shall wait," said Meynte. "Wait until another vessel is born. And then with your help, I can walk these plains again. Your potential for Creation is endless, as is my penchant for destruction. Together, there is nothing we cannot achieve."

So, henchman promoted to partner, Lukas mused. *Is that how it is?*

"Good plan," he said. "Let me suggest an alternative. You shut up and return to your throne. Leave Tanya alone. And I'll help her learn to control her powers while holding Everfrost at bay. Who knows, maybe one day, she can gain authority over Everfrost. Make you proud and all that."

"FOOL! You think a child can trespass into Niflheim's defenses? I was a king-class being, and I barely survived. This girl would fall, and your petty tricks wouldn't save you. Your arrogance will bring the World to its doom!"

Lukas considered this. "You're boring me now."

"Levity will not help you escape your fate."

"Believe me," Lukas chuckled. "There is a method to my madness. Not a good one, but . . ." He chuckled again, trying to hide the fact that his vision was currently blurring from constant mana overuse. "I suppose it's time we end this."

Meynte cocked her head and said, "Let's."

And she sidestepped and vanished, only to appear right in front of Lukas, who just then stepped back, only to find Meynte sweeping her arm out at his shin height, catching his leg and pulling him down. He crashed to the ground just as frosted daggers erupted out of the floor, impaling his remaining hand and both legs. Then she spun in midair, Frost daggers forming in her palms as she aimed for his heart.

"Caught you!" Lukas grinned, Blob shooting out like a snake, grasping her neck with the hold of a viper's maw and yanking her downward. The daggers crashed against the floor as she fell right over him. Meynte snarled and twisted her body, and kneed him in the stomach, impaling him with more Frost.

"AHK! KA!" Lukas folded in half. Air rushed out of his lungs first, but it was soon followed by stomach acid and what felt like half the organs in his body.

It hurt. *By God, did it hurt.* Several of his ribs snapped despite all the reinforcement he had used to protect himself. In the back of his mind, he genuinely wondered if he had actually been split in half, as the pain seemed to cut right through him from front to back.

His mind could seem to process the sight of Meynte spinning around and slamming her other leg down, aiming to crush his skull, but thankfully his eyes and reflexes made up for that. He terraported into the floor just in time to avoid the hit, leaving a crater at the site of impact.

Lukas appeared on the opposite corner of the now-destroyed chamber, grabbed the Frost blades impaling different parts of his body, and pulled them out by flushing them with an excess of fire mana. Blood and tissue came with them, and he felt regeneration kick in instantly. He coughed up a wad of blood and forced his lungs to breathe, shifting his mind away from the pain. He needed air more than the warning that he had been hurt.

"For a mortal with Level-3 skills at best, you're surprisingly harder to kill," Meynte observed.

"Was that what I was doing?"

"Wha—" Meynte began, before her eyes widened in sudden dismay and understanding of the true consequences of his past actions. Pity that it was several seconds too late to do anything.

It was a deceivingly harmless-looking thing. A swath of metallic purple, banded and seamless, wrapped around her waist.

Blob.

"This again?" Meynte looked at him with something like pity and exuded a mist of Everfrost out of her entire body, something that would most assuredly delete whatever prototype had been installed in the slime.

Or rather, it would have, had there ever *been* a prototype in there.

"Why can't I—?" wondered Meynte in confusion. Usually by this point, the slime would have dropped down dead, before Lukas managed to bring it back to life.

Instead, it held on. Like a thick, metal belt entwined around her waist.

"What—what is going on?" she asked.

Lukas grinned.

Of all his resources, Blob was arguably his most versatile weapon. An existence that, while lacking proper sentience, could manifest whatever spiritual constitution he wanted and forge a body to reflect the installed soul prototype. And when not performing that act, it served as an accessory to his own body. Of the anomaly.

One he could control.

One he could communicate with.

And most importantly, one he could exert his anomaly powers through.

Territory Creation set
Living anomaly active

Meynte tried to pull Blob off, but it didn't work. Her arms flexed to grab on to a set of Frost blades—

—and came up empty.

At first, she was bemused, the sight so outside the realm of what she believed to be possible that her brain needed a few seconds to comprehend it. Then her eyes widened as it finally dawned on her that, yes, it was really happening.

Frost wasn't answering to her.

Or lifeforce.

Or mana, whatever form it might take.

Blood drained from her face. She glared at him, the primordial rage in her eyes now sharing space with a growing horror as she whispered, "*What did you do?*"

Lukas smiled. "Living anomaly. A function that ignores all Rules—Truth or Taboo—that are alien to my home world. Territory Creation. An ability to create a reality bubble where only the Rules of my world exist, and nothing else. A world where light and shadow are counterparts of each other, instead of this fraud Eternal Light. And at the same time, a world with no lifeforce, no mana, no rifts between overlapping worlds and . . . no Taboo."

"You—" Meynte snarled. "You wretched thing! You—"

"What happened to being polite?" asked Lukas. "Or is that only when you're the winner?"

She sneered. "Victory is yours. But do not think you are saving anyone—"

"What?" Lukas asked, confused, before it hit him. "NO—"

"Too late." She grinned, raising her right hand like a serpent and struck at her own neck—

Or tried to, anyway.

"What?!" She gnashed her teeth, as her right hand stopped just inches away from touching her own neck. Her left hand shot up and grabbed her right hand and began pulling it down. "What is this? What are you doing? Wretched insect! Waste of my bloodline! How dare you fight against the one that made you? Your life, your body, is for my Return."

"Tanya . . ."

First her right leg and now with her left hand, Tanya was always there, somewhere, trying to trip Meynte up or force her to make a mistake. Even when suppressed by a power that dwarfed her own, she was still fighting back.

Meynte's lips twisted into a soft smile just for a split second before it scrunched into an agonized expression, followed by rage. "Stay down!" Meynte yelled. "You are just my host! Let me . . . return!"

Lukas didn't take any chances this time. His eyes flashed green, and Meynte went stiff, unable to move at all.

"What—what is this?"

"Kinetomancy," said Lukas. "The power that controls motion. All motion. Legacy of the goddess that I owe my life to. A power that butchered gods and pantheons and reached a zenith you can only dream of."

He took a lazy pace towards her. Everything was set. The newly created featherglass was placed directly in between the conduit from the throne to the original storage. Meynte was unable to summon any more Everfrost. Or lifeforce. Or mana.

She was, quite effectively, trapped.

"You raised some very interesting questions. Made me think. About this world. About Fimbulwinter. About this war between Asukans and yokai. But tell me, oh Empress, did you wonder *how* I am a soulcrafter?"

Meynte could do nothing but watch.

"I come from a different world. A world where we call ourselves 'humans.' A world without lifeforce, without mana. Without gods and anomalies and kings and empresses. A world where we humans rose to the peak through sheer ingenuity."

He took another step.

"I carry a bit of that world in me. After it was destroyed, this is all that's left. It is what makes me what I am. It is what gives me the powers I use. Just like you wield the End of Potential, I shelter within me the Source of Potential."

"An omphalos." Meynte murmured. "You . . . you have an omphalos within you. You are—you are—"

"A World," said Lukas, smiling. "That's right. Well, a bit broken but a World nonetheless."

Another step.

"Just experiencing its end was enough to annihilate the consciousness of the anomaly growing for centuries beneath this very desert. I wonder what it would do to a mind like yours."

Another step.

"Back when we started this, you gave me two options: condemn Tanya or condemn the world. The first would save the world and get me a place by your side. The second would mean my death. In the interests of fairness, I'll grant you two options as well."

"Would you like firsthand experience of what the death of an entire World feels like?"

Then he smiled. It was a beautiful thing, free of malice, a promise of salvation.

"Or would you rather return to your throne and fight another day?"

Meynte struggled briefly, savagely and silently, her cadaverous eyes bright. It took her about half as long as it would've taken Lukas to realize the hopelessness of her position. Her struggle ceased then, and she went cold and so still that her head might have been something severed from a statue rather than part of an actual person. Only her eyes moved, tracking him. All her pride, all her taunting, all her grand declarations were gone.

Now she just stared at him, like a large, feral cat.

"Well?" asked Lukas again. "Which will you choose?"

"Fine. Then set me free, and I shall return to the throne."

Lukas exhaled. "Let's rewind, shall we? I just threatened to destroy your entire consciousness while you are in there. The only reason I don't want to do that is because there's a chance it might adversely affect Tanya."

"I wasn't born yesterday, Soulcrafter. I know you will destroy the throne the moment I get in it."

"And you're telling me you won't instantly try to kill me or Tanya or just try to escape the moment I set you loose?"

"If you do not, I certainly will. You can only hold on for so long."

It was shaky logic at best. He tried to work through the situation from her point of view. Meynte thought she was doing the right thing, and that made her dangerous. She thought he possessed a serious threat to her—something that was very much a possibility after he had effectively trapped her. At the same time, even she knew what Lukas was fighting for.

"If you want me to cooperate, then I want your word that you will not try to attack me or Tanya, nor attempt to escape in any way. You will walk directly to that throne, and sit down, and then return to your source, whatever that is."

"Why should I believe you?"

"Because if you don't," he told her firmly, "then I won't need to be polite anymore. I'll just destroy the throne right in front of your eyes. And then

I'll use my powers to obliterate your consciousness. Is that more to your liking?"

Meynte glared at him.

He sighed.

"Look. You're an empress, and this is me respecting you. Own it. You lost. Return to your storage with all your dignity, and maybe you'll have another chance to return in the future. Nothing personal. I just want Tanya to be safe."

She sneered. "If you do not trust my word, then how can I trust yours?"

"Then are you giving it?" he challenged. "Your word?"

She stiffened. "You . . . have my promise. Set me free, return my dignity, and I will return to my throne. In return, you shall swear *never* to destroy it."

"I will never destroy the throne," said Lukas. "I swear on it."

She looked at him in disbelief.

"You do not trust me?"

"No," she shook her head. "Somehow, I do." She sighed. "Fine. Free me now."

Lukas waved his hand. The restraints fell off. Blob slid down her body as if it had gone completely inert.

Meynte looked at him, and for a moment, Lukas wondered if she was going to renege on her deal. Instead, she snorted and regally walked back to her throne. She sat down with poise, and regarded him with those bright eyes.

"It is a pity that we found ourselves on the opposite sides of the line, Lukas Aguilar," she said. "I admit it's quite some time since I've danced like that. Next time, things won't end like this."

"Don't worry," Lukas promised with a grin. "I still have a trick or two up my sleeve that you won't see coming."

He watched as Tanya's form began to emit an ominous whitish aura that made her appear as though her outline was barely plugging a hole to an ocean of the substance. She thrashed about wildly but held on to the arms of the throne with a deathly grip. Despite wanting to help her, Lukas wisely stayed back, knowing that the white miasma oozing out of her was lethal to him. A single brush with it would damage his soul, anomaly and divine core be damned.

Tanya swayed about in a daze and then promptly fell unconscious, draped all over the throne. Even so, her shades stayed the same—snowy white hair, mulberry lips, and that pale face. He imagined her eyes would retain their silvery whiteness as well. Whether this was temporary or a change due to using that much Everfrost remained to be seen.

Lukas exhaled. His body was already in agony; the massive and constant use of lifeforce, mana, and anomalous energy was taking an extreme toll on him, and with the adrenaline rush finally gone, it was beginning to hit him hard. His entire body felt like someone had swapped out his muscles with razor blades.

Unfortunately, it was still far from over. He still had one major thing left to do.

As if on cue, a fragment of Blob peeped out of the floor, having dug into it to claim that shard of featherglass he had crafted and installed just a little distance from the mouth of the conduit that connected the throne to the original memory storage. Holding it gingerly, he ran a quick scan.

Featherglass **Crystal outgrowth, Indicative of stored information** **Analyzing . . .**	
ANALYSIS COMPLETE	
Type	**Memory**
Prototype	**Yuki-Onna**
Siphon?	

Damn good question. *Should he?*

The answer was obvious. It was infinitely better than letting her remain there, waiting for someone dangerous to discover her and plot something fierce against him next time.

SIPHON Success!

Siphon, Lukas noticed, not *Soul Siphon*. Perhaps there were more nuances to the omphalos functions. He had no doubt that, if not for Blob reaching out to him via some kind of reverse-connection, things could have ended a lot worse for him. The next time he got a little time to himself, he'd need to spend some hours, or perhaps weeks studying his own developing powers.

His musings were shoved aside as something weird started to happen. Blob began to contort and froth all over, as if trying to take a new form.

Base Protocols being overridden **Memory installation underway** **Found compatible prototype BREMETAN** **Enacting . . .**

Of course! Lukas wanted to punch himself in the face. This was a MEM-ORY. It was Consciousness itself. No wonder it was behaving erratically. He waited as Blob elongated and twisted until a humanoid form that strongly reminded him of Tanya, only crafted out of aqāru, glared back at him.

"You . . . you tricked me," she said, staring evenly at him. "Traitor."

He shook his head. "Not a traitor. I promised I wouldn't destroy the throne. And I won't."

"What did you do?" she asked.

Lukas chuckled briefly. "Nothing much. I figured that a nearly indestruc-tible throne is a good place to store the memory of the empress of yokai, but it's an even better distraction. I scanned the entire area, and I found the conduit through which the memory would travel to the real storage. I couldn't reach it, so I crafted a new one."

"You crafted . . . a new shard," she said slowly. "Of featherglass."

Lukas just looked at her.

"Ah," said Meynte. She looked strangely at peace. "How foolish of me! I had completely forgotten who I was fighting. And that led to my defeat."

She looked at herself, at the metallic form she had taken. Lukas did not know if she was trying to exert lifeforce, mana, or Everfrost. It wouldn't work anyway. She might have triggered the protocols to cause her to manifest, but the ability to attack or use power was completely under his control.

Instead, her slumping posture straightened.

"Well done," she said, an odd strength returning to her voice. "To think that there is someone of your worth in this world."

That surprised the hell out of Lukas. He had been expecting her to try to attack, or at least, insult him.

Instead, she said, "Maintain or destroy my throne as you wish. It is your right as the conqueror. It matters not to me. However, I have two requests. Swear never to allow the End to take root within the girl's body. And swear that you shall stand against Fimbulwinter, if it ever arrives, even if it costs you her life."

Lukas gave her a sad smile. "I swear."

"I believed you before and you tricked me," she said, more to herself than to him. "But I have always been a great judge of character. You were not lying then, and you are not lying now. What a conundrum this is."

Lukas couldn't help it. He laughed.

She looked at Tanya's unconscious form. "Her spirit is strong, but her forti-tude is weak. She runs away from her fears. If she is to prove her worth by your side, then make her strong."

"I will," he promised.

"Farewell, Soulcrafter. It was a good fight. But now the defeated must leave the world for the strong to rise. There is nothing left in this world for me. This memory of mine . . . was a waste."

"You're wrong," he said. It was becoming incredibly difficult to keep his eyes open, but he forced himself to stay in control. "Our stories have a purpose, Empress Meynte. But they won't have meaning to them unless they have an end to tie it all together. You lived your life. You were the queen. You had your chance. Let somebody else have it now. Just because your memory survives does not mean you have to run back to the ground again and again to continue your unfinished work. You left a legacy, Queen Meynte, one that continues even to this day. Let someone else take up the mantle for a change."

"Why?" asked Meynte, but her tone was soft, curious. "Why must I stop, just because I am dead?'"

"Quite the hypocritical question to ask, especially from the one who wields the End itself."

Meynte looked at him for a long moment and then laughed.

"I suppose you are right." She smiled at him. "Farewell, Lukas Aguilar. I shall find myself again, in your world."

A genuine smile spread on Lukas's lips. "I'll do my best not to keep you waiting for long."

And just like that, Meynte's form dispersed and Blob splattered all over the floor into a puddle of metal.

He exhaled. It was over. Truly over.

Her Ally

It started in the throne room.

She had been listening to Solana speak of that throne being her heritage. That she was a yuki-onna. Descendant of Empress Meynte. She had gone against Lukas's requests, willing to sit on the throne, her thoughts about him growing murkier with every passing second. She remembered slowly sauntering her way to the mirror, looking at herself. Only this time, the reflection that looked back at her from inside wasn't hers. Granted, it looked like her reflection, but the eyes were sharper and craftier and far more intense. And that smile. So much more charming and likable than her own, and yet something about it made her want to recoil from the sight of her own face. She remembered stepping back, only to freeze as thoughts that were not her own slithered effortlessly through her mind.

Be calm. You are not afraid. Just curious. You trust me.

Immediately, she relaxed and she waited to see what the face in the mirror would do. In the corridors and byways of her mind, those foreign thoughts sought out memories of Lukas Aguilar and the other Asukans she had known all over her life, and whenever it found one, feelings of paranoia and dislike blossomed around them like a black rose. Mirror-Tanya had studied her counterpart and then shaken her head as if disappointed.

And then words came out of her mouth. Words that she hadn't thought of.

"I don't know why I'm fighting. I know what's at stake. I know what I want. I have already gotten what I want, and all I have to do is embrace it. So why am I delaying?

"How could wanting this *possibly* be wrong?"

You feel betrayed. You feel jealous. You feel like everyone has used you. You are alone, unloved, and have been treated unfairly. I can give you justice.

Lukas was just another person with an agenda, his aid a mere distraction, chains entwining around her, taking advantage of her trust. He'd keep doing that until he was ready and then, that goddess would turn her into a mindless slave. A weapon.

Not again. *Never again.*

But what if she was wrong? She closed her eyes and looked away. What if Lukas was correct? What if—

Look. At. Me.

Instantly and uncontrollably, her eyes popped open. She gasped in terror. Her reflection was no longer smiling, but was instead, a mask of hatred with eyes the color of light.

No, Tanya thought. *The color of ice.*

Mirror-Tanya smiled again, but there wasn't even a pretense of warmth, just sheer malice.

You have it, but it's weak. Chained away. It touches your soul, but only just. This mystery is beyond me, but it surpasses all my expectations.

"What—what do you mean?"

Mirror-Tanya's face hardened.

It doesn't matter. I have my own ways of doing things. Forget about all this. This is all a bad dream. All you need to do is go to sleep.

"No . . ." Tanya whispered. "No, no I won't. You—you are wrong. All of this is wrong. All of this . . ."

This doesn't need to be that difficult.

"N—no!" she said shakily. "G-go away!"

Please don't make this difficult for us both. You've already been through so much. So little, yet so jaded, constrained by your own people yet having managed to achieve so much. I'm actually fond of you, child. It's not my desire to break you irrevocably, unless it's absolutely necessary. Or, I suppose, unless you try to thwart me. I think I might take that one personally. Just let me in, or I will make your nightmares come true.

"I don't—I don't fear you. You're just in my mind. You're just Frost."

Oh, I'm more than Frost, child. Far, far more than that. And if you will believe me, far less worse. Sleep and let me awaken inside you. It's an infinitely better option compared to what shall follow otherwise. Sleep. Escape this poisonous destiny while you still can.

"I don't believe you," said Tanya defiantly. She raised her hands but found her fractals missing. But that wasn't it at all. Her hands looked shorter, much shorter, like they had somehow regressed back to what they were. She looked down at her feet. She felt shorter. Her body felt weaker.

And weaker.

Defiant. I like it. But believe me when I say that this is mercy.

Tanya was confused by what Mirror-Tanya was saying. Suddenly, to her surprise, her body and arms felt incredibly stiff. She wasn't paralyzed, yet she was unable to move. Suddenly she was back in that white room, her hands tied to those accursed manacles. The red door before her creaked open, the knob turning as her cheeks grew white.

Her mouth opened in a soundless scream as Omnyoji entered through the door, sigils of the Great Goddess all over their robes as they grabbed her, tore her dress apart, injected those vines into her body—her chest, her belly, her arms, the hollow of her neck, her back, her—

"YOU DAMN BIT—" Her expletive was suddenly cut off into a crude gurgle as her grandfather grabbed her mouth, held her lips open and inserted a vine into her mouth. She wanted to spit it out but couldn't. Instead, she gagged and vomited as the vine climbed down deeper into her oral cavity and crawled back up through her nasal passages to exit through her nostrils.

Let me end this.

Mirror-Tanya's voice was full of compassion.

It pains me to see you suffer like this. Just. Say. Yes.

By now, Tanya was almost past the point of coherent thought. She had always been afraid of what happened with her post-incarceration; it had given her nightmares for years. Talking to Lukas had opened old wounds but this was horror beyond compare. The part of her that was made of defiance and courage fought against the tide, but it was nothing compared to the crushing wave of pure terror that hit her every time as the Omnyoji began to do their twisted experiments on her, the vines slowly constricting around her body, suffocating her. Finally, between the impossible terror and wracking terrified sobs, Tanya gave in.

"Yes! I'll do it. I'll sleep. Just make it stop! Please! I beg you. Just make it stop!"

Mirror-Tanya smiled.

It seemed like an eternity that Tanya had spent trapped in her own memories and nightmares. She remembered being in the throne room and then in front of the mirror with Mirror-Tanya. She remembered the absolute naked horror of those vines slithering all over her body, violating her in ways that made her want to tear her own skin off. She remembered, to her shame, how she had broken down and surrendered to Mirror-Tanya, but it had all been for nothing. When she came out of her stupor, she was wrapped in pitch-black darkness and lying paralyzed somewhere. Horizontally or vertically, it was difficult to tell.

At this point, she had lost all sense of hope in herself. She had done the one thing she had never done before. She had given up. Despite all her suffering, despite losing her father, despite being on the run for years—first from her family and their hired abductors, and then from the army—Tanya had never once surrendered. Even against the Ifrit King, she had embraced the possibility of death but she had never surrendered herself.

Not until now.

At first, she blubbered incoherently, but after some unknowable time, her cries became more focused. Specifically, she screamed out one name, the one person who had always been there for her. Right from the beginning. Someone who hadn't been the most truthful or the most compassionate but had always been on her side. Never demanding, never judging, just a companion who she knew was a kindred spirit.

Lukas will save me.

It was a belief, one that was deeply entrenched in a faith far greater than that which she had in herself. She was born cursed. She never saw her mother. Her father died to save her. Her own family hunted her, and now those that she thought she could call her own had betrayed her. Compared to that, Lukas had always been the last man standing. No matter how pear-shaped things got, he was always the one surviving in the end.

Then she heard it.

Heard *him.*

"I'd not defy you for her," he said. "I'd defy you for her ability to choose for herself. And if you or your queen tries to stop that, then you'll have to deal with something worse than freaking Amaterasu."

"And what is that?" she heard Solana ask.

"*Me.*"

And just like that, a bright smile tore through the dead darkness of despair. It was an expression more open than Tanya had ever made, an emotion far deeper than anything she had ever felt. It was something that began to shimmer and spread beneath the darkness surrounding her soul, like cracks across the top of a frozen pond just before the ice shattered. A simple, honest, beautiful thing that shone like the moon above the desert, gleaming against the darkness.

Despite herself, Tanya laughed. She wanted to hug him. She didn't know what he was doing or about to do. What mattered was that he was there when she needed him the most, and he was fighting for her. Could she have hoped for a more reliable partner?

However, even the newfound appreciation and blossoming hope didn't prepare her for what happened next.

The world of darkness around her faded away, and she watched, a passenger in her own body, seeing through her own eyes, as someone else controlled her form. It was the highest form of violation there was—to be trapped within her own body, as the intruder used it against someone she cared for.

I gave you a way out. You chose to defy. Now pay for this defiance.

Tanya braved it. Whatever this being—*Meynte,* her brain supplied, *Empress Meynte,* her great ancestor—whatever she wanted to throw at her, Tanya would bear it all. Lukas was fighting for her. He was facing Solana and an empress for her. She would not give up on him.

Not now. Not ever.

"You will not win," she heard Solana speak.

"I might not win," said Lukas. The smile on his face looked absolutely feral. One only needed to look at the bodies he left behind at the borderland to know what it meant. "But I'll make sure that all of you *bleed* for it."

Despite her situation, Tanya smiled.

What followed was an epic battle the likes of which should have belonged to legends and folklore. Tanya had watched as Lukas faced the might of Queen Meynte herself and held her power at bay. She had seen Blob transform, first into a humongous worm followed by those four-armed bylestyrs, proving her theories that the word "sense" did not belong to the Outsider's dictionary. She watched as Solana, easily an upper-class Level 3 if not a Level 4, constantly destroyed the metallic bylestyr, only for it to re-emerge again and again. She watched as Maude, to her incredible surprise, stood against Solana's trickery and paralyzed her with a few well-placed jabs on the skinwalker's body.

And that was just the beginning.

Tanya screamed in terror as Empress Meynte used her hands to destroy Lukas's right arm. His shriek of agony tore a cry of despair from her throat. Maude was probably dead, and Lukas wouldn't last long before the might of the empress without his dominant hand. She would use Tanya's own body— her own hands—to squeeze the life out of him.

It will be okay. I just need to rest, to try to get back that feeling from before. I need to—

I . . . I remember. I remember everything, thought Tanya furiously, drawing determination from the simple fact that she could think again. *These words, these thoughts, these emotions . . . they aren't mine. What I told Lukas earlier—that wasn't me. That was—that was YOU—GET OUT OF MY HEAD—*

I'm confused. Lost. So much pain, so much loneliness. Such betrayal. From family, from friends, from . . . him. My mind is not clear—

It was amazing, really. Even knowing, even with the pain pulling so much wool from her eyes, giving clarity to hazy dreams and half-forgotten emotions, it was still hard to tell. She *wanted* to believe that those were her own thoughts. It was instinctive.

And *wrong.*

I SAID, GET OUT!

The silence that followed was deafening, despite being entirely in her own mind. Like a constant background noise that she hadn't even consciously noticed suddenly cutting out.

I . . . I stopped it?

I'm . . . I'm dying? Fading?

I'm . . . I'm a monster. I hurt people. Frost made me . . . hurt people. I . . . I killed my father.

I'm a puppet. I've been directed by others for most of my life. My father. My grandfather. Frost. Zuken. The skinwalker. Meynte. Luk—

No. Not Lukas. Never Lukas.

An image rose in her, unbidden. She was sitting on the edge of a cliff, with him next to her. In that borderland. Stranded from the world, just the two of them, and no one else.

I want you by my side. You and I.

You and I.

Such a simple statement, and yet more profound than anything anyone had ever said to her. All her life had been about following orders and doing transactions. An order that she must follow. A favor for a favor. But Lukas—he didn't want a favor. He wanted *her.*

Her secrets.

Her faults.

Her wounds.

Her.

With him.

Maybe I was weak, she thought. *But I'm not helpless. I can change things. Even if only by a little.*

Oh? And what will you do, little girl?

Mirror-[Mirror-Tanya] Tanya—no, Empress Meynte's—laughter reverberated all around her.

Just watch, Tanya promised. *Just you watch.*

The battle had taken a wild turn that she hadn't seen coming. Tanya had watched in silent astonishment as Meynte transformed from an apathetic queen that looked down upon Lukas like a bremetan looking down at an ant, to someone who gained respect for him. There in the pitch darkness of her mindscape, she could trace the growing mix of anger, respect, and utter hatred for him. She watched as Meynte unveiled the truth of what Everfrost truly was, and what it meant, feeling an inevitable dread filling inside her. At one point she had all but accepted that this was her end. Choosing one life over the world? No hero could do that. She was certain no villain could do that either.

Only someone who cared for nothing except himself, or a true psychopath who wanted to watch the world burn, would make that choice.

Again, she found she had judged Lukas wrong.

"Someone once cursed me to never give up on my selfishness," he had said. "That I should stay true to my beliefs no matter how many I trample upon. Even if it means I must be the invader, the monster, the conqueror . . . it doesn't matter. I'm no longer allowed to pretend otherwise."

Really, why was she surprised again? Since when did she start thinking that he would not go to extreme lengths for the things he wanted?

Just because those things were few and usually involved the happiness of others, didn't mean he wasn't willing to spill blood for them. Lukas, he was always a tyrant, even back when they had met for the first time. And just like every tyrant in history, the price to stand in the way of his desires was to be crushed.

One only needed to see the charred bodies of Hreidmar and the hacked-apart bylestyrs in the borderland to have proof of this.

So what if they forced his hand? Lukas Aguilar made the conscious choice of taking their lives to bring about the outcome he preferred.

For someone who was so good at killing, Lukas had the air of a pacifist. Tanya knew that, for all his ability to get under others' skin and egg them on, Lukas was the last person to choose violence as the first solution. But that didn't mean that he'd rather give up pursuing his own desires over it. Being willing to spill his own blood to try to save someone else was the act of a hero, but even that didn't detract one bit from his selfishness. The only thing that ever held him back were his own morals and his physical limits, and even those he kept pushing further with unrelenting effort.

Why would he react any differently now? Even if it meant standing against a freaking empress.

See that? she thought viciously. *That is why you will lose. That is why he will win.*

HE. WILL. NOT. WIN!

The tide of the battle changed again. This time, Meynte did not hold back. Not anymore. Tanya watched with trepidation as Lukas and his metallic familiar pulled one astonishing surprise after another, like a wizard performing miracles. The metallic slime kept morphing from being a metallic hand to an alligator to a massive worm to a sword to an avian to a pair of scissors and so on, keeping the empress constantly on her feet.

And she knew that this was her chance. *Even if it is only a little,* she thought, which in itself, was something that she couldn't have possibly conceived some moments ago. She had always been the broken doll, the twisted experiment, the Sinner, the fugitive—someone that knew deep down that it was her destiny to suffer, no matter how much she ran away from it. Anything else was inconceivable.

It had taken her a while to understand it, but it had eventually sunk into her thick skull. Most of it from seeing Lukas fight. Lukas was strong, but even on his best day, he couldn't wrestle against Meynte's power and win, even if he went all out. Meynte held Tanya's body hostage, and she had access to an endless reserve of Everfrost to call upon, with no need to tip into Tanya's own mana or Ezzeron's skills.

But he could absolutely defy her. Even if the fight was hopeless, even if there was never a chance of success, it did not mean she had given up. Lukas had not given up in front of that Ifrit King, but somehow, things had turned out to ensure his survival. Even with his own world destroyed, he remained alive and carried a bit of it in himself. If he could do it, then why not her?

Powerful or not, ancestor or not, this was *her* body. The fight might be lopsided, but it was never hopeless. And by Wind, she was not going to allow anyone to just crush everything she held dear.

Is that the way you show respect to your ancestor?

"You are as much my ancestor as Mujin Shimizu is my grandfather," said Tanya without fear. "Neither of you care a single jot about me, only what I represent. For you, a vessel for your Return. And for him, a breeding stock that will bring Everfrost into his bloodline."

She stood up.

"This is *my* body. This is *my* mind. GET OUT!"

Blood-traitor. Your ancestry gives you a legacy. A purpose. You owe it to me.

"I. Owe. You. Nothing."

She kicked her right leg against an invisible barrier.

"GUH!" screamed Meynte, and Tanya felt multiple stabs of agony shooting through her, as Blob—now serpentine—grappled around her right leg and crushed her bones. The pain was unbearable, and at the same time, filled her with exhilaration. Had she—

Did I do that?

Biting her lip, she smashed her right leg against the barrier again. Pain filled her mind, but she was a master of pain.

STOP! Stop this! You will gain NOTHING—

"I have nothing to lose either."

Her entire body hurt. Meynte was down on one knee, clutching her own head and crying out in despair. It was a surprise, really, that Tanya hadn't already lost consciousness after feeling that horrible psychic stench permeating her mind.

"You won't let me kill you," she heard Meynte say. "But you won't kill me even if you have the chance?" The empress laughed, blood oozing out of her lips. "Even with that traitor helping you, you will never win."

I know, thought Tanya fondly, a soft, sad smile forming on her lips. *Even without an arm, even with all odds against him, he will never give up. It is one of the things I love most about him.*

It is also what will kill him in the end. And it will be your body that does it.

Doesn't really matter, thought Tanya with growing deliriousness. Between the pain, the psychic stench, the nightmares, and everything in between, she was beginning to feel lighter. Free. Fading, but free. At this point, she couldn't care much for what Meynte had to say about her or about Lukas, for that matter. Obviously, she didn't want to die or fade away, but first and foremost, she wanted to see Lukas happy—whatever that meant.

Even if it meant that he'd be the one to kill her in the end.

But I'm no hero, she thought. *I'm just a tool. A vessel. For Ezzeron to gain a new bearer. For Mujin to breed Everfrost into his bloodline. For Meynte, so that she can once again—*

She froze as it hit her.

Of course!

Tanya closed her eyes and sighed. Something coiled and black squirmed in her heart.

There is just one thing I can do after all.

If she could make things even slightly better for Lukas while he fought Meynte, she'd be doing something for the one person that had stood up for her for all the time she knew him. And even as she was, there was one tiny thing that she could do.

One that not even Meynte had control over.

That little fact made her giggle a little.

Ah! The little girl has finally lost her mind.

No. No it's not that. Tanya thought deliriously. *It's just—I finally realized—*

"Frost hates you more than I do."

A waft of derision hit her, as if to say, "and what of it?"

"Oh nothing," she said, as if chatting to an old friend. "Just that the more Everfrost you summon, the more you wedge the gate open. The gate that Lukas was holding closed all this time. And guess who's on the other side of the gate?"

. . . You—You would condemn yourself! You would condemn the entire world—

"It's my life," said Tanya. "My choice. I can choose to live. I can choose to throw it away. At least this way, it's proof that our stories can end the way we choose, not simply have them chosen for us. Even if it might not be a happy ending."

She could feel the rage coursing through her ancestor.

Tanya smiled. It felt nice.

It hurt.

Frost was slowly gaining root deep inside her mind. That which Lukas's goddess had held at bay, that which Meynte had wedged open, that which Tanya had always feared, *Frost* was slowly coiling itself back into the depths of her subconscious. The whispers would return, and this time, there would be no goddess to shut them down. It would act out again on its primal instincts, filling with her its corruptive power and boundless hunger.

But she would endure. Just a little more. *Just a little more.* It was close to the end. Her body burned and froze all at once, and she felt as though her organs were rotting from inside. But with every passing second, she told herself again that she would endure.

It would be over. Soon.

NO! It cannot possibly end like this!

Tanya laughed. Lukas had Meynte trapped. Blob was keeping her from using anything—Frost, lifeforce, mana. The little metal slime indeed had an infinite store of tricks.

Defiance at every turn. You wish to die so badly? Then have at it. Consider this mercy.

The right hand moved up.

"I REFUSE!" said Tanya out loud.

The hand paused inches away from her throat. The power was too great, too strong. But Tanya didn't have to hold back forever. Just a little more. Just a little more.

There would be great shame in dying like this. So close to victory, only to be undone by treachery by the whims of the enemy—she refused to let that happen. Not to her. Not to Lukas. The rage and shame burned and chilled her at once, stripping away every single thought from her mind, leaving behind just one.

Power. She thought. *I need more power. Please. I need more. It cannot end like this.*

I refuse.

I refuse.

I absolutely will not let it end like this.

Stop, whispered some part of her , even as she could barely feel past the pain and desperation consuming her. *Stop, before it's too late.*

I've come too far and lost too much. Lukas needs me alive. I swore that I would be with him. Till the end. Even if it is he that kills me. I have to STOP—keep fighting, and GIVE UP—no, not give up. Keep drawing power from every bit available, more and more and—

"Tanya . . ."

She froze. That was him. And with that realization, she felt the chains around her mind vanish, a shocking burst of vitality rushing through her. She felt Empress Meynte burn in impotent rage as she slithered out of her mind, out of her body, her essence slowly vanishing as she dove into the throne and through it, into a contraption of infinite blackness. She felt the remaining vestiges of her shattered mindscape collapse all around her. The resulting blackness swallowed her and held her for a long time. There was nothing but silence where she drifted, nothing but the endless night. She wasn't cold, wasn't warm, wasn't . . . anything.

CHAPTER 16

AFTERMATH

Finally," said Lukas. "It's over. This time for good."

He was leaning against the white throne where Tanya was sitting, though "draped" would probably have been a more apt description.

He glanced at Solana. Or the creature that took the appearance of the individual he called Solana. He had yet to come across another skinwalker in the yokai territory. Either they were just a rare breed or just not very common on this side of the world. He wasn't sure exactly how their body mechanics functioned. For a moment, he wondered if he should just siphon her and find out. It would be too easy.

No, he told himself. *Need her alive.*

Said skinwalker was currently on the floor, half encased in ice, the other half charred, her entire body paralyzed by Maude's finger-poking technique. Speaking of Maude—

He pulled himself up again, Blob rushing to him, transforming itself into a long staff for him to hold on for support. At this point, the slime was just reacting to his subconscious thoughts. He'd need to be careful when it came to thinking about what he wanted it to do or else things could get really dangerous.

For people around him, that is.

Trudging all the way to the oni, Lukas saw the large spike of Everfrost impaled through Maude's kidney. He couldn't touch the damn thing with his hand without it spreading to him, so Blob divided into two parts—one re-forming into the familiar right arm, and the other, a glove to wear on his left. It wouldn't make any difference physically, but it would insulate him from the alien ice.

He tried to pull it out but had little luck. Maude's flesh had engulfed the icicle tightly enough to form a vacuum seal, and no matter what he did, it just would not budge. He tried putting more effort in, but this time, Maude's entire body rose up with it.

"Okay! Stop! Stop!" said Maude out of nowhere, freaking the hell out of him. Subconsciously, he dropped her body on the stone floor again.

Her brown eyes tracked him, even though the rest of her body remained utterly limp. "You wouldn't get it out like that even if you tried for a week."

"You—you are still awake?"

Maude rolled her eyes.

"Of course I am," she said, giving him a look that made him feel like he was an inch tall and twice as thick. "Everfrost consumes lifeforce. I shut down the lifeforce flooding through my body the moment I got impaled."

"But I thought—"

"That what? I died?" asked Maude drolly. "I'm an oni, Aguilar. Part vanir, part yurei. I can go without breathing for hours if needed. The empress didn't care much for me after that, so it was better to play dead than suffer her displeasure."

"You . . . wow," said Lukas, feeling like he had just been cheated. She had done the pragmatic thing, as deceptive as it was.

"What? Don't tell me you actually felt bad for me."

"Err, yeah, I kind of did?"

"Are you asking me or telling me?"

"Telling you?"

"Oh," said Maude, looking surprised. "Well, thank you for your concern. So now if you could kindly—"

She looked at the massive icicle that was still sticking out of her abdomen. "I can't channel any energy to my limbs without enlarging that thing. So could you . . . ?"

"Yeah, about that. It's not really coming out. Maybe if I try to melt it—"

"Please don't," said Maude, wincing. "I'd rather not have to deal with liquid samples of Everfrost floating in my bloodstream. Horrible way to die, really. Or stay paralyzed, which would be even worse, since I'm stuck with this body for good. So no, you've got to pull it out in one go and then cauterize the surrounding area with fire."

Lukas winced. "Wouldn't that, you know, damage the organs for good?"

"That's a lot of prevarication for a guy who scorched his own arm off without a second thought."

"Yeah, but that was me. And I knew I could regenerate it in a day or two. Maybe faster if I cut down on a few non-crucial steps."

"What kind of step in regenerating an entire arm is considered non-crucial?"

"You can play doctor later."

"Doctor?"

"Healer."

"Ah, I see. Another of your references to your own world."

"Yes. For now, let's work on getting that thing out of you," he said. "Any ideas? Also, how are you doing the mouth thing?"

"The mouth thing?"

"Yeah, you're speaking and moving your face muscles, but the rest of your body looks deader than dead."

"Oh," she said. "Nothing complicated. My heart is working, as is my nervous system. I've just cut off all the energy heading outward, except for the essentials and my head."

"You can do that?"

"How do you think I'm still talking to you?" she asked, rolling her eyes again. "Now, come on already. Just rip the damn thing out of my abdomen."

It was more difficult than it looked. The icicle wasn't exactly smooth, spreading out in all directions and digging into Maude's skin from the other side. If he tried to pull it out in one go, chances were, he'd tear her apart. Instead, he gently rolled her to one side against his knee and used Blob to slowly chip the icicle's edges off and make it smooth and cylindrical. It was a strange sensation, doing it while carrying out an intellectual conversation with the oni, who kept throwing all kinds of questions about the different techniques and tools Lukas had utilized to defeat the empress. Given that she had been awake and heard their conversation throughout, that also meant that she knew of his status as a "World" and was absolutely intrigued by it.

Finally, with that accomplished, he laid her back on the floor.

"Okay," he told her, exhaling. "This is going to hurt."

And then, his eyes flashed green.

Maude's body arched in silent agony as the entire icicle was pulled out by a massive force, tearing its way through her innards. Generating a layer of water in his left hand, he ran it through the injured tissue, collecting whatever potential micro-shards of Everfrost were still lining the area before siphoning the water out.

"Right. I almost forgot," she observed. "You can perform Aquamancy as well."

"Technically, I can perform any 'mancy' out there," he told her with a grin, as a thin flame suddenly appeared at the tip of his index finger, which he used to cauterize the wound. It said a lot about the level of control she had that she didn't even wince at it.

"Your arm," she said at last, still lying down after the operation was over. "How long do you think it will take to regrow the normal way?"

"I imagine a day," he told her truthfully. "Less than that, if I get some sleep."

"Sleep . . . I see, shutting down some bodily functions to accelerate others."

Technically that wasn't true, but he didn't need to tell her that. Also, he had gotten into the habit of altering his body and default skill set every time someone tried to kill him in a new way.

"What about you?" he asked. "How long before you're able to start moving?"

"Not very long, I imagine," she said, closing her eyes, and Lukas watched with shock as the tissue around the cauterized wound began to move about, as if it had come alive, and slowly began to knit itself together, closing the open wound. Tissues weren't supposed to behave like that, regeneration be damned.

"How—how are you doing that?"

"This?" she asked, curious. "False construction. Temporary conjuration of living tissue using ether. Yurei can conjure ether without much effort, so I can keep this running for days. Enough time for me to rejuvenate myself using Naturopathy naturally without sacrificing any functions."

Neat. He had never quite considered anything like that before. He too had a yurei prototype stored within, and more importantly, could conjure ether just as well without even using it. Perhaps he could experiment with it later? There was no need to display any more of his quirks, especially since Maude—and Solana—had seen quite a lot of them.

He glanced at the paralyzed skinwalker again.

"She did not see or hear anything," said Maude softly, much to his surprise.

Lukas looked at her with a quizzical expression.

"Her senses are completely paralyzed. She isn't asleep, but she isn't awake, either. She's just . . . stuck. Probably in complete darkness, with absolutely no external stimulation whatsoever. Don't worry, she wouldn't be able to use your secrets against you, assuming that's what you're worried about?"

"Part of me is wondering if I should just end her. It would be terribly easy."

Maude blinked. "It would, but you wouldn't."

He arched an eyebrow. "Excuse me?"

"Don't play coy," she said, pushing herself up. "I've observed you during the entire battle. You had enough chances of outright destroying her, but you didn't. The empress, I understand, was using Tanya's body, and we know how much you like her."

"Because she's my friend," Lukas said quickly. Maybe a bit too quickly.

Maude exhaled. "That's just sad, you know. Fighting to the death to save someone, only to go into denial over your feelings. Whatever, you do you. But you left Solana alive. Why, if I may ask?"

Lukas exhaled and sat down. "I guess it's because she's important. Part of the process. It's like you said, she keeps things in check. Without her, the yokai would be doomed."

"So you're letting her go because you'd feel bad for the yokai?" she asked, incredulous.

"Not . . . necessarily," he said slowly. "But she's someone who holds a lot of information and knowledge, and she can be useful. And with Meynte gone, she's possibly the best person to help train Tanya in harnessing the powers that Meynte and other yuki-onna that came after her utilized."

Maude snorted. "You're awfully naive if you think you can prevail upon her kindness. For all I know, she'll try to kill Tanya out of pure spite."

"No," he said, surprised at the cold confidence in his voice. "I don't think I'll prevail on her to do anything. I know how these things work. Favors and trans-actions. Never give without getting something back in return. For Solana, it's all about balance. I'll just give her what I think she wants most, and in return, she will give me what I want."

"Yeah, like you destroyed her chance to bring her empress back and she'd destroy your chances of saving Tanya, as an act of balance."

"No," he said again with a touch of finality in his tone. "She won't."

Maude studied him for a while. "Either you're too sure of yourself or you think you hold a great bargaining chip, if you imagine that the wicked leader of the yokai will dance to your tune."

He grinned. "Who knows? Maybe it's both. That said, I'd prefer it if she stayed paralyzed, at least until Tanya is alright."

"Of course," said the oni, "Go against the commands of the mighty Out-sider who defeated both our Leader and the empress in combat? What am I, crazy? I don't want to end up sharing their fate."

Lukas rolled his eyes.

The soothing darkness was too good to last.

The pain came first. Despite the fearsome battle, Tanya's body had not retained any injuries—physically that is. Her mind was another matter. The possession and all the phantom pain she had endured made her feel like more wound than woman. She ached everywhere.

Then her memories came back. She started remembering everything. The throne room, her diverging thoughts, the whispers twisting her mind to act against him, her sitting on the throne and all the suffering it heaped upon her, Solana's betrayal, Maude and finally . . . Lukas.

Oh, by the Goddess.

Tanya opened her eyes. She was lying in the same bed she had woken up in earlier. Suddenly she felt bile rise within her throat, and she threw up some-thing thick and gooey. Someone must have fed her some kind of soup earlier. She vomited until her belly ached with all the violent, wild agony running rampant through her body, mind, and soul. She couldn't forget everything she had been through.

The urge to break down was overwhelming.

She felt someone grab her like she weighed nothing. It was Lukas. He used a towel to clean the vomit from her lips and made her lie back down on the pillow. Even after all that had happened, all she had told him, all the ways she had rejected his aid, he was sitting there on her bed, nothing but genuine concern in his eyes. He looked as if he hadn't slept but his hands felt steady, his expression calm and confident.

"Don't worry," he promised her. "You're safe. It's over."

Tanya wanted to protest. She wanted to say that she wouldn't be safe so long as she was there among these wretched monsters. Kin or not, they had tried to sacrifice her as a vessel for their lost empress. That put them in the same position as her grandfather. Maude had aided Lukas, so she got the benefit of the doubt, but everyone else was just . . .

"Believe me," he told her, as if reading her mind. "You're *safe*. Nobody here is going to harm you. I won't let them."

She met those eyes. She had seen them earlier, gazing at the empress with cold, impossible defiance. Why? Why did he go to such lengths for her? Why risk his life for her sake?

You and I.

That was the promise he had given her. That it would be the two of them. Together. He'd be her ally. Someone who'd stand by her side regardless of the odds, with nothing but steadfast determination.

And he had just proved the value of his words.

First at the borderland.

And then, against Solana and Empress Meynte.

He had kept the Frost at bay. He had helped her get her dues from Zuken. He had saved her ass from the Ifrit King. And he had faced the might of an empress and the ancient skinwalker just to keep his word to her.

And she hadn't even thanked him for it. Not once.

In her daze, she never noticed when her fingers crawled over his hand and slowly grasped it. She was too busy staring at those brown orbs, unable to look away, incapable and unwilling to break contact with those eyes peering into hers, as it ignited something she couldn't even dare to name—something that had long slumbered under a thick layer of ice.

You and I. Together.

"I—" she croaked. "I—"

"—are finally awake, it seems," interrupted Maude as she bustled into the room and approached her bed, with absolutely zero consideration for her privacy nor this moment that she had so effectively butchered.

"You—you're alive! But I thought—"

"That your Frost would kill me?" Maude asked. "I was a vanir and a yurei before I was oni, dearie. You don't know half of what I can do."

Given that she had one-shotted Solana into paralysis, Tanya was ready to believe whatever crap came out of her mouth.

"And you better believe that I'm fine, because now I need you to help me help you treat yourself better. You've only just woken up after a long excruciating experience. You wouldn't want the entire yokai contingent on my ass if something happened to their beloved 'queen' now, would you?"

"Queen?"

CHAPTER 17

STRINGS

Tanya sat quietly on her bed and tried not to let her nervousness show. Regardless of whatever happened, she hated being weak, and if she couldn't stop herself from being afraid, the least she could do was hide it. That her blonde hair was gone, replaced with the snowy white tresses that featured in her darkest nightmares peering back at her whenever she looked into a mirror made it worse, as if Meynte or perhaps her other self might just be lurking beneath her face. Just the idea of falling asleep terrified her. What if she woke up only to find herself trapped in her body all over again, while another used her face and body to enact heinous torture on the person she had feelings for?

That said person was currently sitting next to her, and just being in contact with his body was making her flush, didn't help matters. That he was feeding her soup with a spoon while making baby sounds only made it worse.

Just a month ago, she'd gone out of her way to avoid being touched by him. Now, she went out of her way to be in his presence, not-so-subtly flirt with him, and allow him to pamper her. Maybe it was because she needed to feel less like a cold monster and more like a woman.

She lived. Meynte didn't.

She lived, and yet, she felt dead.

Maybe the fact that her time might be limited is what made her so desperate to feel alive. She didn't think Meynte was lying about the whole Fimbulwinter thing, and letting Everfrost take root deep in the darkness that was her mind only exacerbated the situation. There were no whispers, not yet anyway, but they would be back. She was certain of that, which made her feel like she should treasure every moment she could spend with Lukas.

The idea of revenge against Solana for deceiving her and the Shimizu for hunting her across nations for most of her life—none of that felt important.

Only Lukas mattered. He represented the good in the world that she had thought no longer existed. He had resparked a light within her, confirming that her own goodness hadn't been destroyed after all.

"Say 'Aaaah!'"

Tanya opened her mouth, looking at the genuine grin on his eyes, and silently ate the soup. It tasted terrible, like all medicines did. Knowing Maude, she probably made it taste extra bitter on purpose.

Stupid oni.

Maude sat across from them on a makeshift stool, a thick rock pillar raised up from the floor, smoothened and augmented with a back stand for ergonomic benefits—Lukas's Terramancy in action. A part of her felt slightly jealous that he was using his skills to Maude's benefit, even if it was for something as rudimentary as a seat. She couldn't honestly remember a time when her stomach had fluttered like this before. As a teenager, her life had been shattered and the illusion of normality had stayed out of her grasp since then.

No matter how hard she tried.

"What are you thinking about?"

You, Tanya wanted to say, but decided not to, fearing that it would scare him off. Despite his casual demeanor, she could always feel his eyes on her. Tanya had noticed him looking at her during the borderland mission, sparing little glances when he thought she couldn't see. His gaze held a deep, sensual interest in them, though he tried to hide it. Now, though, there was a deep sadness there, like he blamed himself for letting recent events happen to her.

And she hated every moment of it.

"You really need to stop thinking about what happened, you know," he said. "The treatment won't work if your mind is still stuck in the past."

She gave him a smile, hoping he'd not notice the strain in it.

He continued to await her reaction, and she tried to think of what to do. How did normal women react? Did they gush and coo when the object of their interest displayed such keen insight, or did they get offended, feeling like he wouldn't let them have that privacy? She had no idea.

"Stop getting in my head," her mouth ran, and an apologetic expression flashed on his features.

Fuck. She might have come across as too defensive there. *Way to go, Tanya!*

"No, uh, it's okay . . ." She quickly backtracked, sitting up straighter, because she didn't know if she should hug him, touch him at all, or just grin like an idiot.

She grinned like an idiot.

Lukas smirked and responded by pushing another spoonful of bitterness towards her mouth. Still preoccupied by feeling like an ass, she opened her mouth and gobbled the soup up, not really trusting herself to say anything less stupid in that moment. At least it took care of her ridiculous grin.

She had hidden the fact that she was perfectly aware of what was going on the entire time Meynte had been possessing her and instead admitted to only seeing flashes of whatever was going on. Flashes that included Lukas standing in defiance against Meynte, and Maude subduing Solana, only for Meynte to incapacitate her and destroy Lukas's right arm—the important bits. Much to her elation, Lukas had given her a full account of everything that had transpired without hiding anything. Oh, and Maude was somehow, fully awake despite being stabbed like that, and was now privy to Lukas's deepest secrets.

It made her feel bitter in her gut.

Maude didn't deserve to know them! They were things Lukas had entrusted her with because he trusted her. That Maude had eavesdropped into Lukas's conversation with Meynte like that was simply unfair. But given how the oni had helped Lukas in the fight, and was now helping her heal, she couldn't bring herself to directly confront her about it.

It didn't help that she required periodic examinations. To quote the oni, being forced into submission by a foreign identity, followed by subsequent and extended exposure to her worst nightmares had "damaged her psyche." Maude, whose Naturopathy skills extended to inspecting and healing psychic disorders, had to run multiple checks just to see the extent of the damage and if there was any vestige of Empress Meynte that remained. With that in mind, she had been through several very intense, ten-to-fifteen-minute sessions with the naturopath since morning.

"Well . . ." said Maude, leaning backwards and stretching her arms behind her back. Tanya scowled at the rather provocative gesture but kept her thoughts to herself. Knowing the oni, she probably did it just to see if she'd get a rise out of her.

"Well?" asked Lukas.

"From what I can gather so far," said the naturopath, "there's only one mind inside her head, and it's undoubtedly hers." She met Tanya's gaze. "I see no signs that the empress's persona has left any active presence at all within your mind."

Tanya was just about to sigh in elation when Lukas frowned. "Active?" he asked. "What about . . . inactive?"

Her lips twisted into a frown. She hadn't considered that possibility.

Maude sighed. "On that front, I have bad news. To be completely honest with you, I do see . . . remnants of the empress within you. Faint signs of psychic architecture created during the possession. Normally such signs would fade over time as you return to your normal self, but this is a special case."

"How?" Tanya demanded, her stomach flipping at her words.

"How do I put it? Your case is not just unusual but also unique. I've participated in several cases where the victim's psychic architecture was destabilized by his or her kami, but mostly that developed from a growing imbalance of their emotional spectrum and growing soul corruption. Even after becoming an oni, I studied the effects of yokai possession on bremetans, but again, the damage was mostly spiritual in origin. But as far as I'm aware, yours is the only case in which the intruder isn't a spiritual creature, but a memory. A collection of psychic threads with enough structural lattice to give it an identity, one so developed and powerful that it was able to displace your own identity from your own body. There is little-to-no spiritual damage, and whatever changes I can see are from the constant summoning of Everfrost, but you have had that corruption for years, so, not my current concern."

Tanya's face fell. "You mean she can come back."

"I never said that," Maude corrected her. "It is true that your psychic architecture was compromised—heavily so—but the results in no way seem to be detrimental to you."

"What are you saying?" asked Lukas.

"You have to understand that there are several similarities between her and the empress. Both of them are yuki-onna, and from what you tell me, the empress held a physical form as well. Both of them used Everfrost and had a similar genetic structure. This has had the effect of two different identities with similar spiritual presences overlapping and melding with each other, instead of one trying to destroy the other."

"A spiritual resonance," said Lukas.

"Correct," said Maude, eyeing him speculatively. "You have some experience with this."

Lukas shrugged. "Just a bit."

Tanya felt Maude's eyes return to her. "I suspect that because of the overlapping of identities with similar spiritual presences, you might have gained some of the skills that the empress had. If nothing else, the ones she employed against Aguilar. To be blunt, it's also possible that you might have gained negative traits as well. But I see no evidence of this residual architecture being in any way dangerous to you."

Lukas just smiled at her, knowingly.

Tanya swallowed. She knew perfectly that the empress's identity wasn't gone forever. It had just deserted her and returned to the throne it had arisen from. And that was a serious risk.

"What about my hair and my eyes?" she asked. "I tried enchanting them. It doesn't work anymore. Am I going to be stuck looking like this forever?"

Maude's hands wriggled awkwardly. "I'm a little confused about that. I've seen you change before—you know, back when we fought in the anomaly. You looked just like that. And you shifted long before the empress possessed you, so I imagine the change is because of your using Everfrost."

Tanya nodded.

"In that case, the change might not be because of the empress. Or it might, given the amount of Everfrost she used. Maybe it just inflicted a more permanent change on your body?"

That did not make her feel any better.

"Tell me something honestly, Maude. Is it possible, *hypothetically*, that if she came back again, she'd be able to affect me? Control me?"

Maude's eyes widened in surprise. "Tanya, the empress's memory has returned to the throne, and she's been dead for millennia. Unless you're saying that she's still alive, or there's some way of bringing her back to life . . ."

Tanya hesitated. Solana had mentioned that the gods and goddesses of the Asukan pantheon had been raised from the dead, and reality itself had been altered. Lukas himself was on a mission to find a way to bring his goddess back, and he had done it, after a fashion, in that borderland. And given that Meynte's memory was still around, it made such a potentiality very much possible. All she needed was some hapless yuki-onna without a Lukas Aguilar to help her get out of the situation.

"As I said," she murmured. "Hypothetically."

"Hmm," said Maude with what Tanya thought might be a hint of suspicion. "Well then, hypothetically, I do not know. There's no precedent for a living person possessing someone else through a memory. Neither is there precedent for what happens when the compromised victim comes in contact with the person, assuming the person even knows that her memory had possessed the victim in the first place."

She paused, as if considering her words. "That said, there might be some kind of inchoate connection—a spiritual resonance like Aguilar mentioned. It is possible that drawing on whatever skills the empress demonstrated while possessing you could resonate between yourself and the empress. Then again, both of you are vessels of Everfrost, a far greater and deeper connection than her skills can possibly be."

"So what you're saying is," Lukas inferred, "that if Meynte hadn't influenced Tanya using the Everfrost connection over the years . . ."

"The chances of her doing it through psychic architecture are even less so," Maude concluded.

"In that case there is nothing to worry about," said Lukas confidently.

"What?" Tanya turned to him. Then in a meek voice, she asked. "How can you be so sure?"

He grinned knowingly. "Trust me. I know."

Her heart thumped in her chest, and she tried to process all the weird emotions now running through her, making her act like the person she never thought she could be again.

It was stupid.

She should've been able to stopper those emotions.

But she couldn't.

When you went so long feeling cold and detached, and then a complete stranger ignited those dormant feelings you thought were forever gone, you couldn't help but become addicted to it, reveling in the smiles you thought you'd forgotten how to use or the laughter that sounded unnatural coming from lips that hadn't expressed such joy in years.

"How long do you think she needs to rest?" he asked.

"Ideally I'd have her under complete rest for the next two weeks with regular scans, but I know when I'm expecting the unreasonable so . . ." Maude gave Tanya a wink. "She's fit to get going whenever she's ready."

Tanya blinked and turned to Lukas. "Where are we going?"

"Well, the first place we're going is the throne room. Solana's still stuck there, paralyzed. I have Blob on guard duty just in case anyone gets any ideas."

Tanya seized up, grabbing his hands. "You're going to kill the bitch, aren't you? I want to be there. I want to do it."

Lukas looked at her, then at her hands grasping his own, and then at Maude, who just looked at her in amusement. Then he said, "We're going to meet the bitch, yes, but not to kill her."

"Then what?"

He grinned. "To wake her up. What else?"

Tanya gripped his shirt. "You—you're joking with me, aren't you? That bitch—you know what she did to me. She—I was back in my nightmares, Lukas. Looking into that mirror. I was back in my imprisonment, to how those—those—"

He didn't respond. Instead, he pressed himself closer to her and gave her a hug. Tanya let his possessiveness, his care, and concern overwhelm her.

"It's okay . . ." she heard him say.

It wasn't, she wanted to scream. After she had escaped with Ezzeron after her father's death, it took her a long time to see the scars on her face and body as marks of survival instead of brutal reminders of the torture she had undergone. Lifeforce did a good job of healing them, but the scars on her mind and soul took far longer to deal with.

They said everyone had their own healing process.

Her first year was spent mourning her father and suffering from all of the trauma. She had cried until there was nothing left to fall from her eyes but sand. She had curled into a ball and showered multiple times a day but never managed to feel clean.

The second year had been spent being angry and seeking outlets. Fighting the abductors and mercenaries her grandfather sent after her were a good way of channeling that rage, and she took to using all her skills to kill them in the most ruthless of ways. She became a freelance adventurer in Baramunz, studying different forms of melee combat, and merging them with her own style.

She never wanted to be anyone else's victim.

The next three years had been spent getting stronger, dealing with all her fears, getting used to experimenting with her Frost powers, and reinforcing her mind to keep the whispers out as much as possible. She had learned to stand on her own. She learned not to flinch when someone barely touched her. She started going out to spas and salons, making herself look and feel pretty, and act as normal as she could.

It was only in the sixth year that she had managed to gather the courage to exact her revenge. To find out everything she could. She had returned to the Eaborid Kingdom, to Cyffnar, only to find that Mujin Shimizu no longer lived there. She had captured several clan members and tortured them for information, but surprisingly, none of them knew anything. The official word on her was that she was dead and Ezzeron had been lost to the wilds. It had taken her a while to give into her desire for vengeance against her stupidly powerful warlord of a grandfather and embrace the new life she had been given.

No one was looking for Tanya Shimizu.

She was free to live her own life.

And the best place to do that was the one town where she'd face the least problems.

Haviskali. Located just past the mighty desert.

That was how things had started. But that bitch of a skinwalker had done something utterly, impossibly horrifying to her. She had snatched away all her years of rehabilitation, all her dedication, all her strength, and hurled her back to her sixteen-year-old self, reliving her darkest nightmares over and over.

Solana deserved to die.

And no matter what Lukas said or did, that bit would not change.

She had waited for six years, plotting her revenge against her clan. She could wait until Lukas got what he wanted out of the bitch. Patience was the name of the game, and Tanya was playing to win.

"Why do you want her alive?" she asked softly. It would not do to sound like a psychotic killer.

"I know what she did," Lukas said, still hugging her. "And I know what she deserves as a result. But right now, we need her alive."

"Why?" she mumbled again.

"Because," he whispered, pulling back, "as Maude told me, Solana is one of the cruelest beings I've ever seen."

She watched as his eyes found Maude's.

"But she has a purpose. She holds the yokai together. And right now, that is essential." He looked back at her. "If not for Maude vouching for us, the yokai would've attacked us by now. Your friend is the one holding them together."

Maude laughed. "You're being too generous, Aguilar. Nobody wants to have a go against someone that—how did you put it?—kicked Leader's ass."

"Exactly," said Lukas, grinning. "Which is you."

Maude blinked, as a veil of confusion settled in her eyes. "Which . . . I am. I suppose. But you went against the empress and emerged victorious, and we both know you made Leader's life hell enough before I intervened."

Lukas snorted. "That was all Blob, but I'll pass on your appreciation."

"That may be, you insufferable man," said Maude, the hints of exasperation forming on her face. "The point is, they are afraid of you, and they don't want to attract your ire."

Tanya listened to their banter with no small amount of irritation. "If the yokai are against us, then why are we here? I'm fit to move now. Why not just leave Solana like she is, and return to Havis—"

The rest of her words died in her throat as he softly cupped her face. *Damn it. What was it that he did to her?*

"Solana's fully capable of healing herself, Tanya," he said. "If we just leave right now, we'll have the yokai as our enemies. Things are already fucked up enough without needing more. Besides, I have unfinished business with her. At least this way, I—*we*—can run the show."

"I agree," said Maude.

"I don't," snapped Tanya. "She's a lying, backstabbing, vindictive bitch. She's going to botch things up for you and strike the killing blow when you aren't looking."

"You know," Maude drawled. "for someone who's so distrustful of Leader, you were mighty quick to just rush to the throne on her words. In fact, you accused Aguilar here of having twisted motives and blindly went with what Leader said."

"And look where that got me!" Tanya said hotly. She turned to Lukas, a pleading look in her eyes. "Let's just leave this godforsaken place. I want to return to Haviskali."

With you is what she didn't say.

"What about your heritage?" Maude taunted.

"Fuck my heritage!" Tanya snapped, glaring at Maude. "It has brought me nothing except failures, loss, and endless nightmares. All my life I've relentlessly tried to understand it, achieve it, become worthy of it, and it has only made it worse. I've lost everything—my father, my family, my past life, and now nearly my existence."

She grabbed Lukas's hands. "You made me a promise back there in that borderland. You told me that you'd always be with me. Us together. I don't want anything to do with the Empire or the yokai. Why not just get away?"

It would be so incredibly easy. And Lukas would have less compunctions about keeping the bitch alive.

Oh, and Maude would be left behind as well.

Yes, Tanya was a jealous woman. She owned it.

"We *can't* get away," said Lukas. The way he gritted his teeth suggested that things weren't as great as he pretended they were. "If anything, we need Solana to work *with* us."

"And why is that?" she asked, curious. Vengeance could come later.

"Because Meynte was right," he said in a bittersweet tone. "She used too much Everfrost. It's already affecting you, and we don't know how far this corruption will spread. If Meynte has indeed left traces of her abilities within you, and if the two of you resonated so powerfully, I think there's a chance that you might be able to draw on her skills."

Tanya blinked. "How can that even be possible? She was a memory. She has no skills. The only thing we share is our lineage and our connection to Everfrost."

"Tanya—" He exhaled. "—so you trust me?"

More than myself.

"Yes," she murmured.

"Then listen to me. I believe that, with the right instruction, you can harness her abilities and accelerate your understanding of Everfrost. We need you to control it before it controls you. The yokai might call you 'queen,' but you have to get to where Meynte was in terms of ability. And Solana can help you with that."

"But why would she?" she asked. "If you woke her up, wouldn't she try to kill you? All of us?"

"She has a point, you know," said Maude. "You did stop her from achieving her goals. If not for you, Empress Meynte would be up and about right now. If it were me, I'd be trying to kill you the instant I woke up."

"Oh, she'll want to kill me," Lukas sneered. "But she won't. She cannot. Because for once, she's not the one holding the strings." He met Tanya's eyes. "I am."

CHAPTER 18

Prophecy Fulfilled

Solana's first thought upon awakening was to claw through Maude's stomach and tear her throat out through the hole. Her second thought was to wonder why the empress was looking at her with such an inscrutable expression on her face. Her third thought was to wonder why the empress was standing behind Maude, waiting for her to wake up.

But she didn't do any of those things.

Instead, the moment she felt the paralysis dissipating, she became a blur. In the blink of an eye, she had the Outsider smashed against the wall on the opposite side, her hand clasped around his throat. It didn't matter that the others were already preparing to throw their power at her. She'd survive. She always did. But now, she needed to kill this loud-mouthed bastard for trying to corrupt her pure devotion to her mistress. She clenched her clawed fingers, wanting to see the desperation growing in his eyes as he—

Solana froze.

Those eyes. There was no desperation in them. Anger, rage, fury, focus, annoyance, yes, but there was also patience and a cold calm. These weren't the eyes of someone who had been outplayed and seen their friend perish inside her very body only for someone else to take her place. They weren't the eyes of someone stripped of all hope and options, nor those of a person still fighting against fate with all their might.

Solana didn't like that look. But she shouldn't dally. Outsider or not, his neck was in her grasp. Just one twist and he'd die. No amount of lifeforce or mana would reattach a head that had been torn off. It didn't matter what Maude could do to her now or what new bizarre power the blasted man could pull out of his sleeve. *For she had him.*

So why was she suddenly filled with terror as if *she* was the one who had been cornered?

"What did you do, Outsider?"

Brown eyes with flecks of green gazed back at her. It was only then that she discovered that no matter how much she clenched, she had yet to feel his skin on hers. Like there was an infinitely thin layer of *something* that maintained a firm boundary between her palm and his neck.

"You aren't very good at this, are you?" he asked.

Was it instinct? Maybe her paranoia enhanced her senses. Or maybe she had just been plain lucky. All she knew was that her body moved before she realized something was wrong.

And then her chest exploded with shards of crimson.

"Stupid woman never bothered to wonder why her boss was standing next to her enemy in the first place," she heard the empress say.

Solana blearily opened her eyes, only to find herself on the floor, with that accursed metal entwined around her waist. Just like during the anomaly Guardian's attack on her territory earlier, the accursed metal was draining every bit of mana she was able to conjure. No, no that wasn't it. It was like it was preventing her from conjuring mana in the first place.

This was impossible!

She glanced at her sides and found her hands extended out, with boulder-sized daggers of Everfrost impaled through her palms and her legs into the floor, completely trapping her there. Any amount of lifeforce she'd conjure would be instantly gobbled up by the Frost shard. Without lifeforce and mana, she was completely at their mercy.

And in front of her, standing with an oddly satisfied gleam on his face, was Lukas Aguilar.

Solana glared at him, turning around to see Maude sitting to her right on a stone pedestal. And her empress—she glanced around but could find her nowhere. Had she deserted her because she was so weak? Was this her punishment? Had she—

"URK!"

Raw agony tore through her right breast as another shard of crimson exploded out of it.

And then her empress—no, *Tanya*—walked out from behind her and stood next to the Outsider. What was happening? She looked exactly like the empress but her expressions were all wrong. Meynte was the ruler of all yokai. The idea of her demonstrating something so pedestrian as rage for someone like her was beyond imagination. Solana couldn't even imagine a situation where the

Outsider could have made the empress accept defeat. It was such a hilariously impossible outcome that it wasn't even funny.

"My queen," she gushed, purple blood dripping from her mouth. "Why are you—"

"I'm *not* your empress, you stupid bint!" yelled Tanya. "I'm Tanya, the one you tricked and almost killed because of your delusions."

"Tanya!" Solana gasped, gobsmacked. "But—"

Before she could finish that sentence, Tanya strode up to her and grasped her chin tightly. The hatred in her silvery white eyes reminded her of a blizzard. No matter what she did, she was unable to get away from her death grip, her fingers as cold as ice, reminding her of the master she served.

"Look into my eyes, *bitch*."

Solana recoiled. Trapped and unable to use her powers, she could only try to hold herself up as a whirling sensation overtook her and she found herself dragged into a vicious maelstrom that wanted to pull her inwards. She tried to resist but the pressure was too great, too intense. A nauseating confusion filled her mind and then—

Light inundated her world.

She woke up in fright.

That *couldn't* have been true, could it? She had just seen things from the girl's perspective, trapped in that world of darkness, staring out through Tanya's eyes, watching *herself* talk to Lukas Aguilar, while the empress maintained her silence. She remembered viciously attacking the Outsider to keep him from lying any further, only for the traitor to paralyze her with her wicked abilities. And then . . .

And then . . .

"That can't be right," she croaked.

"What did you do?" asked Aguilar.

"I focused on what I went through and tried to remember it in greater detail," said Tanya. "It's still not everything, but I covered the major things."

What was she talking about?

Solana looked up into Aguilar's eyes. He stared back at her with an inscrutable expression on his face. She gritted her teeth, marshaling her own thoughts and defenses. "That can't be right, you hear me?"

"Give up, Solana," said Aguilar. There was no glint of victory in his tone, no malevolence, no determination, just an abject finality that carried a weight to it. That weight strained gravity, and no matter what she did, she couldn't just ignore it. She tried bolstering her psionic defenses, but nothing happened. How was he doing this? Surely those weren't her own thoughts? Surely this was an illusion, some sort of psionic trap . . .

"This is no trap, Solana," said Lukas. "This *is* what happened. You rejecting it will not make it untrue."

"But—but if—"

"The first time we spoke about the legend, you told me three things. Three signs that would help identify the Key. And you were right. I *am* the Key. Neither Asukan nor yokai, but I hold power over both. I was the one that bound Tanya's Everfrost and in so doing, became the fulcrum for your plans. Me bringing Tanya here with me, you ensnaring her with your tales and promises and backstabbing her to bring back Queen Meynte, and all of that has now led to one ultimate conclusion." He took a step forward. "Tell me, what is it? What is that your vaunted queen feared so much and yet, brought about by her own actions?"

Solana swallowed. "She unleashed Fimbulwinter."

"And what would that have done to this world?" Tanya demanded.

"It would have destroyed it," she murmured. "But so what? We come from the Haze. Even if this World is gone. We could've travelled to other Worlds through the Haze. Worlds without a speck of Asukan blood in them."

"It wouldn't have solved the problem," said Aguilar. Again, his tone lacked rage. Instead, there was a sense of resignation in it. "If Meynte had channeled the true might of Fimbulwinter, she would've become its avatar. It doesn't matter where you or your kind went. Fimbulwinter would destroy it. It's not a weapon that could ruin the Asukan pantheon. It is the End of the World. The End of ALL WORLDS."

"She would not have let that happen!" Solana spat.

"It is already *happening*," said Aguilar. "Back when I faced Tanya in the anomaly, I sealed the worst of Everfrost away, using a power that I do not possess any longer. For all her talk, Meynte was too quick to open those very seals I put on Everfrost, just to ensure her victory. And look," he said, his voice lined with simmering anger as he pointed at Tanya. "Look at her transformation. The corruption has already spread, and it won't go back. The bell can't be unrung. I don't know when or how, but Fimbulwinter will prevail, and when it does . . ."

"The end of the World," Solana muttered.

"The World," said Lukas, anger lacing his tone. "All the Worlds, and the creatures in them. Not just Asukans. Not just yokai. *Every. Single. Thing.* And it will all be *your* fault."

"It's NOT my fault," she snapped. "None of this would've happened if you hadn't resisted us. Resisted *her*. The queen was supposed to be the savior. She would have commanded our legion, and we would have brought Oumagatoki upon the Asukans under the light of the Black Moon. You weren't supposed to get the girl back!" She tried to pull away from her restraints, shaking her head like a maniac. "You weren't supposed to get the girl back!"

He sneered. "If you want to blame somebody, blame yourself. You chose to tell me the prophecy. You chose to trick me into getting Tanya there. You chose to fool her and use her as Meynte's vessel. You chose to believe in your queen's crap despite me asking you to question things for yourself. You, Solana, *you're* the reason Maude took my side. Tanya has always run from her Asukan heritage. All she was looking for was some acceptance. When you told her about her yokai heritage, she got closure that she had never found before. Had you told her the truth, had you not tricked her, you'd have gotten a yuki-onna that could very well become the next Empress Meynte. You fool. As long as I was beside her, Everfrost would have remained sealed away, unable to penetrate the barrier. You'd have gotten Meynte's descendant and wielder of Ezzeron under your thumb. And *I* would have helped her."

He spat in anger. "Instead look at what you did. That girl who could have been your Champion now hates you more than she ever did her monster of a grandfather. That girl who had always valued her heritage as greater than her life, now wants nothing to do with it. I literally had to talk her out of killing you in the most agonizing ways. In your greed, in your lying, you've doomed your own kind."

Solana had enough.

"Sentimental tripe!" She sneered back, surprising the Outsider and the others. She might be the one captured but she'd be damned if she had to listen to that tripe for a second longer. "Tricks? Betrayal? Promises? I told you before, Outsider. Yours is a child's daydream compared to *my* commitment. For over six hundred years I have followed this path, through every treacherous bend and twist, through every temptation to walk away. Friend, foe, or family, there is *none* that's more significant than my dream and nothing so sacred that I will not violate to achieve it. So what if the queen lied to me? She would have been an infinitely better candidate to fulfill our aspirations. She'd lead us yokai into a new age. She'd make us dominant again."

"And what of me?" Tanya spat. "What did I do to deserve that?"

Solana shook her head and let out a low and quiet laugh. Then she looked up at the girl, contempt in her tone. "*Deserve?*" She threw her head back and cackled. "You think you get what you deserve? You think the yokai deserved to lose everything, hiding underneath this vast desert when we could have had the whole World?"

She all but purred, "Look at you, standing there, being all self-righteous about it. Crying like a baby at being deceived by someone you didn't know. That Outsider saved you your rationality, protected you like a guard, and was ready to fight *me* to keep you from destroying yourself. And what did you do, little girl? You trampled over his help and sat on the throne. That power that stems within you has a purpose. A purpose so far beyond your pathetic life that you aren't even capable of fathoming it. And what would you have done with it? Hide it? Run away from it? Stuck to living the life of a fugitive or worse, a commoner?"

The girl flinched.

It made her smile.

"No. I couldn't let that happen. Everfrost belongs to us. It belongs to the Queen of the End. And that is what I did. You are a weakling in mind and spirit. You could have sacrificed yourself for the yokai's grand destiny and let the empress march in your stead. You'd have been *glorified.* Instead, you chose to be a selfish little brat. Look at you, impaling me with your Frost, trying to play the torturer when all you want is to hide under a rock and shut your eyes and cry."

Yes. Just a little more. And then the tears would come out. She'd shake. She'd be vulnerable.

Just a little more, and she'd break.

Solana turned to Lukas with a hungry, shark-like smile. "You may have survived with your friend intact, Aguilar. You might even escape this day. But make no mistake, I cannot be killed. No matter what you do, I shall rise again and again and again and again as long as my vow to my kind remains unfulfilled. You might have thwarted the empress this time, but I will find another. Someone who will become her vessel and return the queen to this world. And when that happens, Aguilar, you will only wish you were dead."

The Outsider didn't clench his fists, didn't grit his teeth. He didn't even look angry.

Instead, he put his hand into his pocket and pulled out a crystal shard.

"Isn't that—"Tanya began, her surprise evident.

"Featherglass," said Lukas. "81 percent pure. Excellent storage medium for spiritual and psychic information."

And then he threw the shard on the floor. It shattered upon contact.

Solana stared at the remains blankly. What was he trying to pull? Another deception? Weariness and uncertainty began to flood her mind and heart, and she hated herself for it.

"What was that?" she demanded.

"Oh, *that,*" he answered in an exaggerated tone. "That was me making your burden a little lighter. You see, back in my world, we have a saying: 'When you build in silence, they won't know what to attack.' You got too carried away reacting to my words, never considering why I may have shifted from fighting your empress to trying to convince you in the first place."

An unsettling pit formed in her stomach.

"I admit, you did a wonderful job with the throne. A nigh indestructible piece of furniture is a perfect way to deceive someone. Destroy the throne and

Meynte's memories would be gone forever. It took me some time to see through the lattices you built. Amazingly done, by the way. I'd probably have to bring this entire place down before I could reach the real memory-storage facility."

A shiver ran down her spine. He couldn't possibly have figured out her secret. *Could he?*

"It was a perfect ploy. An indestructible throne that would appear as Meynte's true abode, given how she possessed Tanya after she sat on it. A word of warning: Never underestimate svartalfars. They can sense the composition far deeper than you think. They'd know what substances are part of it and if any of them are memory-carriers."

"What did you do?" she growled.

"Oh," he taunted. "You still don't get it, do you? I couldn't get to the original memory storage, so I crafted a new one out of featherglass shards. 81 percent pure."

"That's IMPOSSIBLE! Featherglass that pure cannot be crafted by synthetic means! Even the best the Asukans can create using divine intervention is—"

"76 percent," finished Lukas. "I know. But I'm not an Asukan, am I?"

He held up his hand and Solana watched as raw energy coalesced in the center of his palm, frothing and broiling, trying to escape his ironclad control, as he shaped it into a pointed crystal, crackling with raw power.

The next moment, there was a shard of featherglass sitting inconspicuously in the palm of her hand and—

Solana's eyes went wide in shock, as she ran a quick check of its spiritual and physical constitution. It was, it really was—

"81 percent pure," said Lukas, as if reading her mind. "Combined with 7.3 percent vatuatil and around 12 percent trugaphene for stability. Do you believe me now?"

Solana had no words. She only stared at the floor, where the original featherglass crystal had shattered.

"When your dear empress deserted Tanya's body, she didn't return to the original storage. She returned to . . ."

Her heart threatened to rupture. The dust that had escaped the featherglass right after shattering . . . those were her empress's memories? The last chance for the yokai was gone?! She nearly screamed, but she managed to stop herself. The pain rose in her, and she embraced it. *Welcomed it.* She watched the future she had hoped for slowly perish before her eyes. She let the pain burn away everything nonessential. And now she—she—

"Tanya has Meynte's skills."

Solana blinked. His cold, rational tone felt like ice-cold water in her burning heart. It took her a moment to register his words and another to actually comprehend the implications. She glanced at Tanya, who looked utterly unsure, and then back to the Outsider. "She . . . what?"

"Tanya has Meynte's skills," Lukas repeated. "Granted, not all of them. But some of them. Her ability to use the Haze. Her command over the Frost. Tanya isn't Meynte, but the possession has definitely shortened the distance between them. I have reason to believe that the seal on Everfrost isn't fully broken. At least, not yet. So long as that's the case, and so long as Tanya is able to synchronize herself with Meynte's skill, there is a chance that she might be able to attain what Meynte did as well as what Meynte failed to achieve. She can truly *become* the queen. But to do that, she will need your help."

"Mine?" she croaked.

The Outsider crouched down to her eye level. "I told you. She has the skills. Or at least, some of them. If you train Tanya in manipulating the Haze, if you help her truly master it, then your race, the yokai, still has a chance. And so will this World. All the Worlds."

"You . . ." Solana growled. "You think after all this, I will—"

"I think that, after all your betrayals, I am still willing to give you a chance, because I am a big believer in dealing with issues through conversation. Believe me, I'm a very rational person, until the moment when I am *not*. I think you've seen what happens when the latter comes to pass."

He practically hissed the last sentence out.

"I have."

"Good," he purred. "The way I look at it, you have two options. The first is, of course, you swear a vow to hunt me down and try to kill me in horrible and excruciating ways, even if it costs you your life. It will yield nothing except fueling your petty vengeance and will most certainly end with you six feet under the ground . . . and that's if I'm feeling generous. The other option is that you accept my offer, help Tanya master her powers and aid her in every possible way so that she can rightfully stand in the shoes of your venerated queen. That way your dream can come true, and perhaps your poor, ill-treated yokai race will get a fresh chance."

He gave her a predatory grin. "So, tell me, Solana, what will you choose?"

CHAPTER 19

SELFISHNESS

Tanya opened her eyes and surveyed the room. The worn-out tatami mats beneath her feet brought with them a familiar texture that set her at ease. She could feel the wards closing all around the place, isolating this particular room from the rest of the compound. The Shimizu compound was large and sprawling, but this particular room was only meant for her and her father. It was here that she practiced her katas day in and day out.

Content with her findings, she relaxed and sat down upon her throne, her seat of power, crafted out of solid ice, inlaid with metals and thick shale cushions for comfort. An elegant, expansive form of the great Nidhogg arose from behind her, its limbs entwining around the arms of the throne, its claws reaching all the way down through the tatami mats. The great draconic sculpture loomed above her, surrounding her from all three sides. Tanya let out an elated sign and rested her feet on the familiar polished stone beneath her feet and—

Polished stone?

No, *she told herself.* This was wrong. This was completely wrong.

She looked below. The tatami mats were gone, replaced by ice and polished stone. Gone was the well-lit room with Eternal Light illuminating it, leaving massive shelves filled with ancient tomes. They stared back at her from the shadows, while alien insignia began forming across the walls like graffiti.

"NO!" she screamed more urgently, frustration mounting within her. And then the throne vanished from beneath her, dropping her on the rocky terrain. A shiver ran through her as a cold, piercing wind blew across the mountaintop, beside the mutilated body of a familiar man with crimson shards erupting out of his—

Tanya opened her eyes and saw overhead the familiar ceiling of her room in yokai territory. She had grown familiar with the greenish glow in the walls and the floating orbs of bluish flame floating in the walls, bathing the room with a bizarre illumination. She reached up to rub her temples in hopes of forestalling the headache that was probably coming. An entire week of practice, and she was still no closer to developing a stable mindscape.

It was annoying.

"This isn't working out."

"I warned you, girl," said Maude from beside her. "Developing your mindscape will be a difficult and challenging affair for you at this stage."

"I don't understand," Tanya said. "I've had a proper mindscape since I was thirteen. It took me a month at best when I started out."

"Your mind was completely your own back then," said the oni supportively. "As it is right now, its psychic architecture is a mishmash of two different identities. It doesn't help that both of you have similar spiritual presences. That you were subjected to your worst memories in spectacular fashion over and over has affected your subconscious even more. Frankly, the fact that you still even *have* a mindscape at all is surprising."

She nodded but was clearly frustrated. In the abstract, she understood what Maude was saying, but applying it was proving to be incredibly daunting.

"What you're telling me is that my own subconscious is fighting me here?"

The oni shook her head. "Not your subconscious. Your *fear*. Your mindscape is the subconscious mind's playground. All of your thoughts, emotions, fears, desires manifest within your mindscape in some form or the other. To have a stable mindscape, you must first gain a stable mind. Your control over your fears is superficial at best, and your emotional spectrum is all over the place. You've lost control and cried more than seventeen times over the past week."

She froze. "How—how did you—"

Maude arched an eyebrow. "You realize I've been scouring your mind every single day, right?"

She clenched her fists. To be seen as weak was unforgivable.

"I'm not afraid of my past," she said slowly. Resolutely. "It doesn't control me."

"No, but your fears aren't just about your past, are they?" The oni leveled her gaze at her. "You fear feeling certain emotions. You fear for someone. You fear what someone might think or not think of you. And most of all, you fear being rejected when someone realizes you're not what he thinks you are. Psychic healing requires the patient to develop a strong mental fortitude, Tanya. You are defiant, temperamental, and too stubborn for your own good. But you aren't strong. Not strong enough to accept yourself. Unless you do that, you will always be weak."

Tanya scowled, her fingers all but drawing blood. She did not like the truths that Maude was throwing at her.

"It doesn't take a genius to see you're conflicted about him, Tanya. You're conflicted about what you feel and how he makes you feel. And you spend too much time fearing your own emotions to accept them. You're very skilled at creating a psychic bulwark to dampen your feelings, but all it's doing is driving them inward. If you do not face yourself, all you'll end up doing is fracturing your own fortitude and getting lost in your delusions, or—"

Tanya perked up, feeling her stomach twist a little. "Or?"

"Or . . . you might just turn your psychic resistance inward and utterly destroy your ability to feel anything. A damaged woman that has forsaken all morality and scorned the bonds of affection—sneering at yourself as you casually destroy everything that comes your way. A living weapon, a stone-cold killer. A perfect vessel for Fimbulwinter."

Her heart beat faster with every single word, filling her up with a growing sense of dread.

"Tanya," said Maude. "If I may be candid, what's the damn problem?"

She wondered why she was bothering with a reply. What others thought of her had never been a cause of concern for her. But Maude was different. Maude was her healer. One who had spent days sauntering through her mind and memories and knew nearly every single event that Tanya would have killed to keep hidden. One of the few things she remembered from her dead father's teachings was to never lie to one who is trying to heal you.

She exhaled. "For years, there was nothing but hatred in my heart, driving me since I was able to do more than just curl in a corner in fear of being found again. I never thought I'd ever find anything else suitable enough to drive me. When I discovered that my clan, that my grandfather, thought I was truly dead and gone, I had the choice to stick to my path of vengeance or start a new life for myself."

"You chose a new life," said Maude. "That's a decision I can applaud. Not many have the strength to give up on their vengeance and take up something positive in exchange."

Tanya let out a scornful laugh. "That's what you think, do you? No, I remember standing at my clan's graveyard. The bastards, they didn't even have a shrine to my father's grave. They declared him a traitor, when all he deserved was a headstone on that very hill where he breathed his last. Instead, they gave me an ornate grave in the clan's cemetery, claiming me as the 'innocent heiress' who died in an accident. I . . . I . . . ." She clenched her fists, shaking. "I cannot tell you how much I wanted to obliterate that tombstone. To destroy that mockery of my life, of my sufferings. You've no idea how much I wanted to run a swath of destruction through the clan compound using the very kami that belonged to the Wind King. How much I . . . ."

Maude touched her hand and pressed it softly.

"I was afraid. I knew what would happen if I did that. I chose the coward's way out, living a different life. I sold myself empty promises, claiming to return once I'd mastered Ezzeron's power. When I'd have become the next Wind King, and if not, then at least, a warlord. That I would face my grandfather at the peak of my strength and I would defeat him, watching the light leave his eyes. But the truth was that I simply did not want to die."

"It isn't as bad as you think it to be," said Maude softly. "Not everyone manages to get retribution. I certainly didn't. Life isn't about getting what you want. It is also about compromise, about making the best out of the opportunities and the disasters it throws your way. Whatever your motivations might have been, you chose to make a fresh start. There is nothing wrong with that."

Tanya didn't agree but didn't want to continue any further down that road either.

"What does that have to do with Aguilar?"

What indeed, thought Tanya. "Lukas . . . Lukas is hope. I never realized the power of hope until he appeared in my life, as though the universe was giving me a gift at the wrong time."

Maude snorted. "That's gotta be the weirdest description of love at first sight."

Tanya rolled her eyes. "Laugh if you must, but I'm being candid. The first thing we did was try to kill each other and he ended up sealing Everfrost away. I was shocked. The whispers had always been a part of me for all that time, and suddenly, this random nobody I just met inside the anomaly shut them down. I didn't know whether to be happy, surprised, or delirious in shock."

Maude giggled.

Tanya scowled at her. "And it didn't end. Every single time we faced obstacles, Lukas took my side. Yes, I knew he had his reasons and they weren't altruistic, but you know what? I watched his face, his expression when he fought for me, whether to save my life or to just fulfill a promise, or guarantee me my freedom of choice—somehow, it didn't feel like the face of a predator looking out for its prey."

"I saw your memories of the time you spent in the borderland," said Maude. "It's obvious he's interested in you. In that way. So, where's the problem?"

"The problem," Tanya hissed, "is that he doesn't seem to want to acknowledge it at all."

The floodgates to her frustration opened wide.

"I—I just don't understand him at all! All that time spent together, all those times in the borderland where he told me we'd be together. After all he's done, and is doing for me, you'd think he'd be more direct about his feelings. Instead—instead—"

"I can see where this is going," said the oni. "The Outsider has been vanishing a lot recently, spending considerable time by his lonesome."

"YES!" she all but screamed in frustration. Ever since he had strong-armed Solana over his ultimatum, Lukas had been a veritable recluse. Had this been some months ago, she'd have thought of it as incredibly normal behavior. Back at the Banksi mansion, he had often limited himself to his room, lost in his own thoughts. That behavior had only increased in the borderland, even when it was just the two of them. Maybe he was thinking of his own world, his lost life. Maybe he was thinking of the goddess and trying to figure out ways to resurrect her. Maybe he was just studying himself, what with being a walking, breathing World.

But . . .

"Maybe he just likes his solitude?" Maude offered.

Tanya scowled but said nothing.

"But honestly," the oni continued, no doubt taking sadistic pleasure from her growing frustration, "I've noticed one other thing. He can be quite deliciously ruthless. Look at how he got Leader to play ball."

She licked her lips.

Tanya suppressed the urge to scowl. Knowing the oni, she did that on purpose, just to get a rise out of her. It didn't help that she felt a wall forming between her and Lukas. He had always been courteous, maintaining a professional distance, but she had often seen him glancing at her when he thought she wasn't looking. It was a tiny thing, but it made her feel good. Knowing that someone like him desired her on some level made her feel vindicated.

But now, that desire had vanished from his eyes and something else had taken its place. Sometimes he'd watch her from a corner, a vivid sadness in his eyes. Like he was feeling guilty or something. Maybe due to not having been able to save her? It certainly didn't make sense. It wasn't his responsibility to save her just because she was foolish enough to discard his well-intentioned warnings.

At the same time, she couldn't help but agree with Maude's inference. Lukas was perhaps one of the most grounded people she had ever met. Oh, he was quick to accelerate a situation when it suited his purpose, and he was perfectly capable of playing the role of a cocky bastard if it meant the other side would be suitably distracted, but in normal conditions, he was almost a tree-hugging pacifist. He knew how to fight. How to lead. How to play to his strengths and use his opponent's weakness against them like a strategist. And he definitely had his heart in the right place, at least enough for most people to think that he suffered from a hero complex.

But . . .

There were moments when he thought no one was around that he had this unsettling far-off look in his eyes.

Instead of a hero, Lukas Aguilar was more akin to a . . .

Tanya shook her head. She was looking too deeply into things. She already was waist-deep in her own mess to cultivate new ones.

"I'm . . ." She quickly gathered her thoughts. "I'm more surprised that Solana agreed with it."

"Leader knows how to pick her fights. I'm sure she'll try to kill Lukas in the future for making her go through that, if nothing else."

She'd kill her before that happened.

"Why do you call her Leader?" she asked. "I mean, you—"

"Stood against her?" Maude finished for her. "I did that because I didn't agree with her on those grounds. But ignoring that, I think she's doing a fine job."

"Even now?"

"Especially now," confirmed the oni. "Though I think Aguilar is taking an unnecessary risk every time he leaves this place to venture into the anomaly outside."

Tanya frowned again. That was another thing Lukas had started doing. He'd leave early, right after breakfast, terraporting his way out of the colony into the anomaly. She didn't know what he did there, but he wouldn't return until it was too late, leaving her with mostly Maude to talk to. On the flip side, she had gotten pretty comfortable around the oni, but it made her wonder if he was upset with her.

The absolute worst part of it had been that nagging little voice at the back of her head that incessantly reminded her just how much she had messed things up and how she had been so idiotic, and how her one healthy relationship had exploded because of her paranoia. That little voice which had berated her over and over again for treating Lukas like he had ulterior motives behind his support.

The same voice continued to ask her, even now, how she was ever going to fix things. She had quite literally revealed her feelings to him the very day she had woken up. She had been willing to leave everything behind, so long as he was with her. It wasn't quite the passionate declarations they used in those trashy romance novels, but surely it had been enough to get the point across?

Tanya knew that there was only one way she could start to put things back together, and that was to talk with Lukas. She also knew the only way for that to happen was to get him in a room, preferably with closed doors and devoid of any eavesdropping oni, and force him to listen and talk through his feelings. She doubted Lukas would attack her if she cornered him like that, but she doubted he'd like it either.

And why should he? It's not like you've given him any reasons to feel otherwise, whispered the voice.

Shut up, me.

"He has his reasons, I suppose."

"He must," Maude agreed. "I heard that Leader wanted to send a couple of yokai for his protection, but he had told her off saying that he'd kill anything she sends after him and absorb it. Leader was not amused."

She chuckled.

Tanya pursed her lips. "He's a private person. And whatever he's doing out there must be worthwhile." She hoped her words didn't sound as bitter as they did inside her head. Damn it.

"As opposed to staying with you?"

"Yes!"

"I can see why you're so frustrated."

Tanya decided not to dignify that with a reply.

"Have you considered that he might have another?"

"Another?"

"A partner? Or someone he is more attracted to?"

Thoughts of a certain goddess came to mind. Tanya knew she was being unreasonable. A goddess and a mortal? That made no sense. Even if she was possessing his body and spoke to him less like he was a priest or a devotee and more like someone she respected and possibly even cared for. The way he spoke of her suggested a strong connection, an intimacy forged through their experiences together. Yes, Lukas had mentioned that he respected her, and he would find a way to bring her back, citing that that was all there was to it, but Tanya just couldn't feel so assured.

"No," she said. "He does not have another."

Maude eyed her.

"I have asked him," said Tanya. "And even if he did, it would not discourage me."

"Discourage you from what?" came Lukas's voice from the doorway.

Tanya went beet-red and instantly clammed up, while Maude let out a loud snort. Tanya prayed to the Great Goddess that he hadn't actually heard more than that last line.

"Well?" asked Lukas, stepping in, Blob on his heels. The metallic creature had begun to show a greater degree of sentience ever since she had woken up. Instead of staying around on his body or pooled together in a metal puddle, it would now take the form of actual creatures and imitate them. For some reason, it had still stuck to meowing, however.

Hearing a club-wielding, fire-breathing, giant metallic bylestyr meowing at a confused Solana had been one of the highlights of the last battle.

"Ah, nothing," said Maude, coming to the rescue. "Girl talk. Private. Keep your nose out of it."

"Right," said Lukas, still looking confused.

"Anyway," said an enthusiastic Maude, standing up. "I think that's enough for tonight. We can continue this tomorrow."

Tanya suppressed a grin. "That'd be better."

"Oh," she heard Lukas mutter. "Yeah, it's quite late. I guess I'll be off to my room and—"

"Uh, actually could you stay back?" Tanya asked, sitting up and raising her voice slightly. *There*, she had said it. No turning back. She watched the hesitation growing in his features and feared he'd reject her.

"Could we . . . you know, talk about this tomorrow? It's already late and I'm a bit tired."

"It'll only take a minute," she said, unwilling to accept defeat so quickly. "I just have a few things to discuss."

"Discuss?" asked Maude, clearly amused. "Is that what they're calling it these days?"

Tanya didn't blush. Instead, she gazed at him and implored, "It won't take long. I swear." The growing uncertainty in her stomach was getting distinctly uncomfortable. "Unless you really don't want to . . ."

"And that's my cue," said Maude and left the room.

For the next several moments, neither of them spoke. Tanya watched him exhale, before he walked towards her and took his place at the corner of her bed, casually erecting a smooth stone pedestal to sit on. The distance was enough for them to hold a conversation comfortably while allowing him to keep her at arm's length.

Her stomach did a nasty flip.

"Well?" he asked.

"You don't look happy," she began timidly. Lukas took a deep, audible breath, his face a mask of stone.

"Just tired," he said. "Had a long day."

She gave a short nod at that. He did look haggard. That made her wonder exactly what it was he was doing out there. At the same time, he was refusing to look at her.

"Are . . . are you really alright?" she stammered. "I have barely seen you recently. I just thought, you know, maybe we should clear the air between us?"

Lukas held out a hand to stop her from speaking any further.

"Let's not dance around it any longer," he began, his voice low and a little cold, taking her by surprise. Did he really know what she wanted to bring up? *How?*

"I know you're conflicted," he said. "About what you found out in the borderland. Hearing Inanna put it like that and then finding out that I lied to you about my connections with the yokai. I can imagine what you want to clear the air about."

Tanya's confusion deepened. *What was he talking about?*

"I know that Inanna didn't exactly sugarcoat what she did to you and what she wanted to do with you. And to be honest, part of why I had been so willing to be on your side was because she was invested in you. She used her divinity to seal Everfrost away, and in her absence, I hold the keys to that prison. It's true that she thought you had a power just as ancient as hers, and she wanted that power in her arsenal, and for that, it was essential that you be protected. So, yes," he met her eyes. "I have been protecting you because of Inanna."

Something within Tanya broke.

"But," said Lukas, "that's not the only reason. Or at least, it isn't anymore."

Something burned within her.

"What other reason can there possibly be?" she asked, her voice cracking.

"Because I might have begun with protecting the Everfrost wielder, who happened to be you. But somewhere along the line, that changed to being with you, who just so happened to be the Everfrost wielder."

Tanya blinked. This had absolutely *not* not been what she was expecting. "B-but I thought . . ."

"But you were right," said Lukas, oblivious to her inner turmoil. "I want to bring Inanna back, and I will do everything I can to do so. But that does not mean I agree with what she intends to do with you. Unfortunately, there is no way I can make you believe that."

"Lukas—" she began, but he cut her off again.

"And you're right," he continued. "You know how much Inanna means to me, and so you'll always be wondering if I'm working some angle on you. If I'm saying things or doing things just to get you to do something I want you to. I can't go on like that." he said, finally looking at her, and Tanya recoiled at the hardness in his eyes.

"I don't want that," said Tanya. "Lukas, the things I said back then . . ."

"Were disgusting," he stated. Tanya nodded in agreement.

"I—I wasn't myself. The moment I was in that room, Meynte started affecting me through our connection. It was difficult to know which thoughts were mine and which weren't. I—I know I should've believed you, but she just twisted everything and made me see things differently. Before I knew it, she had already won and I was lost in my nightmares, until . . ."

She trailed off and met his eyes again. "Until *you* saved me."

He gave her a most curious look, as if checking for signs of deception.

"I'm not stupid, Lukas," she said, moving towards the edge of the bed until she was sitting right next to him. "Even your goddess made it clear what she wanted and what you wanted. You've always fought for me, fought for my ability to choose. No one ever did that for me—not my father, not my family, *no one.* You were right. Every single person I've met has wanted me to do some-thing for them. My father wanted me to be his heir and fulfill his dreams. My grandfather wanted me to be . . ." She trailed off. "My family only saw me as the heiress. Zuken saw me as an anomaly-killer and a way to strand you. Olfric . . . he just needed someone to blame. Solana and your goddess both want me for what I have—or what I can become. No one has ever wanted *Tanya.*" She paused. "Except for you."

Their knees touched.

Lukas stood up, unsure. "B—but I thought—"

She grabbed his hand. "Do you know how selfish you're being?"

"Selfish?" he wondered aloud, chuckling slightly. "I suppose I am a little."

"A little?" she scoffed. "When was there ever a time when you weren't being selfish?"

He curled an eyebrow.

"Right from the beginning. Sealing Everfrost, protecting me, helping, even flirting . . . All of that was to fulfill your own wishes. Your selfishness. Even in the borderland, you wanted me to be with you. Twisted, selfish you. And then, you saved my life. You gave it meaning. And then you suddenly decided that you couldn't trust me anymore and thus, it was okay to just ignore me for a week. Tell me how you've been anything *but* selfish!"

He looked away. "I suppose that is true."

Her hand crawled up his face to his right cheek.

"Don't you see?" she asked, tears streaming down her face. "That's why I love you. Because you'll never let anyone take away my choices from me. Just like you wouldn't ever let anyone trample your own wishes. I love that stupid, arrogant, inconsiderate selfishness of yours even if I know you'll never love me back."

Lukas staggered. "You—"

"I love you, Lukas," said Tanya, her tears still running down her cheeks as both of them stood up, their bodies beginning to touch. "And I don't care where your selfishness takes us. So long as you and I are . . ."

She stopped. His finger on her lips made her pause. And when she looked into his eyes, there was conflict in them.

"I'm . . ." he began, hesitation clear in his voice. "I have baggage, Tanya. You know some of it, yes, but you do not know what it truly entails. With every single day, I find myself shifting from being the person I was to becoming a World. My body, my skills, and even my thought process have changed drastically over the last few months. Did you know, back there in the borderland, there was a moment when I actually considered kill-ing Mori and Kradir in cold blood simply because their skills would be a suitable addition to the svartalfar prototype I have crafted within me out of Hreidmar's soul?"

Tanya's eyes widened. She had not known that.

"This power within me . . . it's not nice. It's primitive, violent . . . Sometimes it doesn't even think, and other times, its thoughts are so alien you'd think of me as a deranged psychopath. It's pure instinct, emotion, feeling. And if I let it control me, then bad things can happen."

Really? After all that happened, and knowing the truth of her powers, his main fear was that he *was somehow a danger to* her?

"You fear you'll give in and kill me."

That smile again. "Actually, if there's one thing I can guarantee, it's that it will never want me to kill you and acquire your skills. End of Potential, remember? Your power is the antithesis of what's within me. The rest of the world and everything in it is my prey, but you're my predator."

A soft smile graced her lips. "Can't disagree with that. I do want to eat you up."

She pushed herself into him, her lips twisting into a smile as he snaked his hands around her waist.

"I do feel the same for you," he admitted. "But I always knew that, even if you returned my feelings for some reason, I'd never be able to give you what you deserve."

"But—"

Lukas shook his head, shutting her up.

"My life is different from yours," he said. "After all this time, you finally know the source of your powers. With Meynte's skills, with Solana's tutelage, you'll be able to ascend to Meynte's status. I know you will. You still have to face your fears and your grandfather and fulfill your father's dream. Become the Wind King. To throw all that away just to be with me in a tireless journey that might lead to nothing is . . . stupid."

"But you promised—"

"To be on your side, yes. I'll help you face your fears. Whatever I need to do to get you there, I'll do it. Just like I'll do everything in my power to get Inanna back, no matter where it takes me. But that's all I can give you. I'm—I'm sorry."

She could have stopped him, knew he'd have stopped if she asked it of him. But she didn't. Instead, she watched him excuse himself, turn around, and walk out, leaving her alone to her thoughts.

He had all but told her that he loved her. Maybe not in the way she did, but he did love her in his own roundabout way. And because he did so, he couldn't give her what she wanted. She could trust him to be on her side because she knew he would never betray his own ideals. He had gone above and beyond to protect her ability to choose, because he would have crossed all limits to protect his own ability to choose. But he would not ask her to be with him, because it would go against everything she had desired all her life.

Even when she won, she lost.

Even when her feelings were returned, she couldn't get her happy ending.

Such was her life.

CHAPTER 20

YOU AND I

Alone in his room, Lukas closed his eyes.

Tanya's confession had been a massive surprise, one that had both elated and annoyed him. Elated because she had proved that his fears were unfounded, and annoyed because despite her confession, he wouldn't get to be with her. Especially with the way things were unfolding.

Inanna had been right. He had been ignoring what he was. The battle against Solana and Empress Meynte had proved enlightening on several levels. It had given him a glimpse of what the future was about to become. His opponents wouldn't be weaklings. They'd have powers and skills greater than his own, skills they had honed for far longer.

In some cases, over literal centuries.

So he'd need something to even the odds. Play to his strengths.

Finding exactly what he could do was a good start. Lukas Aguilar the anomaly, after all was said and done, wasn't someone who could fight against them. Instead, he was someone who could fight against their powers, their weapons, their skills. Countering strengths and exploiting weaknesses, instead of taking on the ones that possessed them.

The more he knew about his enemy, the easier it was for him to strip them of what made them strong and strike at their core with the least resistance possible. Literally.

The fight against Meynte was proof of that.

And that meant finding new ways to fight. To add to his combat skills. To win.

He had been testing his powers out there in the Crypt tunnels. Away from the yokai, isolated from any living being—monster or otherwise—he had experimented on the different facets of Creation granted to him by the anomaly within. Unlike before, he wasn't looking for power but versatility. In this world of Potential, being able to call oneself a powerhouse was an ever-uphill climb.

He couldn't rely on Tanya to do it for him. And something told him that allowing Blob to just tank-damage every single time wouldn't solve his issues either.

The problem wasn't acquiring multiple skills. He had tens of thousands of skills copied from the Crypt of Fiendish Worms. The problem was that using these skills was like reverse osmosis, where his body was a major limiter, raising a gap between the original instinct and capability and his own performance. Just copying the skill and using it wasn't enough to wield it perfectly. The more complex the skill, the more prerequisites it would have, and the more strain his body would undergo. Cutting corners at times made the process easier, but it also heavily degraded the final performance.

It had taken him an upgrade from Level 8 to Level 21 to be able to truly use Level-3 lifeforce skills. And unless he gained another eighteen levels, he'd be unable to fully utilize Kinetomancy as the apex-tier Level-4 skill that it was.

So he needed something new.

Finding the aqāru from the deeper portions of the dead anomaly was admittedly a good start. The inner chamber had entire reserves of that material, enough to fill multiple tankers. It had been surreal, watching Blob connect with the rest of the liquid metal, until the entire thing was just one giant aqāru "accessory" that answered to the name "Blob."

More interestingly, Blob didn't seem to care when multiple copies of itself existed. If two different and completely segregated versions of Blob were present, then, by some mechanics that Lukas was yet to figure out, both of them were perfectly capable of acting as Blob, carrying out whatever function he installed within them, independent of the other. Even more surprisingly, the pair could instantaneously be united and connected as one. Both were "Blob" and could function apart, but they were also still "Blob," the singular shared existence.

It was an interesting mystery, to be sure, but not exactly within Lukas's field of expertise. In the end, he had simply reasoned that, since it was the Crypt's greatest power, having a peculiar trait such as this was to be expected.

Just for safety, he had extracted three more Blobs for himself, so that he had one for each limb. Not only would it allow him greater flexibility in battle, but their fusion would also be helpful in crafting bodies for monsters larger than, say, a bylestyr.

With everything sorted, Lukas had repaired the inner chamber where he faced his metallic doppelganger and used Terramancy to create large rock cylinders to hold the aqāru in place safely. Despite repeated attempts, creating aqāru from scratch wasn't something he was capable of—or not yet, at least. Until then, this would be his stacked reservoir to return to whenever he needed more.

But for all of Blob's versatility, it did nothing to help him elevate his own strength and skill. It was a crutch—a very useful crutch that magnified his abilities fourfold—but it was still a crutch that he wouldn't be able to control very well unless he managed to learn how to bifurcate his attention five different ways at the same time. Something like that required a high-powered psionic skill, and psions weren't exactly common. He did have a couple of prototypes with psionic abilities, but their physiological constitution was too different for him to safely use the skill without fucking up his own perception.

Maybe he should talk to Maude about it. Or perhaps Tanya. The former, because she was quite knowledgeable, and unlike Solana, she wouldn't try to cheat him every step of the way. The latter because she was trained in the psionic arts. He briefly considered Elena, the changeling who could get a feel of other's emotions and manipulate them with remarkable ease. Perhaps an Alf prototype—

Not again, he told himself. The anomaly within him was probably feeling peckish again. It wanted him to go out and siphon some other monster to add to his never-ending collection. Preferably one with a set of skills that he hadn't seen or siphoned earlier.

Exhaling, he asked the screen to show him his list of most compatible skills. The list was, unsurprisingly, quite long.

Between his inner ley-line network and the diverse range of prototypes, he had every single element covered. The possibility of overclocking a particular type of manacrafting was always on the table, and allowing the instincts of a compatible prototype would only enhance that. For instance, allowing the byle-styr prototype to take over more than tripled his mana production, but only with Fire mana, while suppressing the rest. On the other hand, using the marid pro-totype gained him a massive boost in Aquamancy and minor Aeromancy, but all but impaired his skill at manipulating fire and earth. Physically strong prototypes like the bylestyr, or perhaps the neothelid, could amplify his lifeforce production but adversely affected his ability to think logically under strenuous circumstances, impairing the efficiency of skills like Shatterpoint Intuition and Tachypsychia. On the other hand, using the svartalfar prototype—or worse, the yurei—resulted in a feeling of detachment so strong, that it all but crushed his ability to act spontaneously. While Shatterpoint Intuition and Seismic Sensing, despite being the thoggua's skill set, worked flawlessly with svartalfar-based skills, it massively dropped his ability with fire, water, and air manipulation.

The best he had come up with was creating clusters of compatible skills, and installing them within him, packed with the "optimum" mindset that came with such a fusion. But it wasn't enough.

Not by a long shot.

Closing his eyes, he exhaled. When he opened them again, the room had vanished. He was standing in an endless terrain that ran farther than the eye could see. Though, with the crystalized outgrowths sprouting out of the rocky, desolate ground like tombstones, it would perhaps be more apt to call it an endless graveyard of—

Lukas shook his head. And with that seemingly casual gesture, the thought faded.

The place looked slightly different from how it appeared the last time he had been there. He had his first vision of this world when he had first connected with the awareness of the Crypt, and then again, when he had achieved a nexus with the Haze. It hadn't been until recently, when he had the time to look deep into himself and study what he was becoming, that he had discovered the trick to accessing this place.

This place was called the—

Before he could finish that thought, the terrain parted, dipped, and cracked, forming a deep furrow, disturbing the monotony that reigned within. Lukas closed his mouth and didn't even try to complete that name. The symptoms were clear—this place wasn't ready, wasn't complete enough yet to be given a name. There was still another threshold he needed to cross before that happened.

Before he could call it the—

Another crack.

He sighed. He wasn't getting anywhere with this. "Fine. I get it. I still have a ways to go. You don't have to rub it in my face, you know."

Silence, as always, was his answer.

His eyes tracked through the hundreds upon thousands of crystals that littered the endless terrain. Technically, he didn't care about any of them, just like they didn't care about him. A conglomeration of isolated existences that weren't alive nor dead—weren't part of any reality save this one. Existences that only existed to serve the whims of this terrain.

To be honest, he wasn't sure what he was looking for. All he knew was that he needed a new trick or two, one that was reliable and one he could use without crippling himself. Something with a passive boost or skill without major prerequisites would be preferable. Next would come skills that didn't require a particular mindset or cause the suppression of his most-used skills.

Just those two filters alone rendered half of his collection useless. There were a few options, but they also came with their own stringent limitations. Unless he was willing to completely sacrifice his sanity for the period of time or transform into something arguably demonic for the same time, they would be completely unusable.

"And to think," he said with a mirthless laugh, "I thought I'd never need another skill after successfully recovering all the skills saved up inside Blob."

No, this wouldn't work. He was taking the wrong approach. He needed something else. Something special. Something that combined skills from multiple prototypes but did not run the risk of incompatibility. Something that he could apply to himself and yet not skip a beat.

It was an utterly selfish and unrealistic thing to demand. A prototype or ability of that nature simply went against conventional logic.

So *of course* he had found something as nonsensical as that in the Crypt of Fiendish Worms. Or more particularly, in one of its abilities.

Alteration. The ability of an anomaly to alter the physical, chemical, physiological, and spiritual structure of its monsters, its accessories, and, of course, its own body.

Lukas opened his now-empty right hand and closed it around a shard of featherglass that had almost effortlessly materialized in it. He repeated the process with his left hand and noted the effort it took to do the same thing with the same substance.

He had previously thought that a precise knowledge of the chemical properties and molecular structure of the substances would be a major prerequisite for crafting them. He had been mostly right about that one. The omphalos within him contained the knowledge of every single compound in existence, and the information extracted from the Crypt's omphalos added the knowledge of the substances it had analyzed and reproduced over the centuries of its own existence. All he needed to do was trust that the anomaly would do its job and direct his energies to that end.

Vanishing the contents, he turned his attention to his right arm again and began morphing the featherglass by adding details. *Ten centimeters long, five centimeters wide. Flat-ended, conical, like a dagger with a forty-five degree angle of ascent, increasing the density and altering the lattice configuration . . .*

The featherglass shattered to fine dust.

Damn it.

Every single experiment so far proved that the structural lattice of featherglass was incredibly weak. Even a minor molecular rearrangement was more than enough to shatter it. Crafting an alloy with vatuatil increased its physical hardness and stability, but it came at the cost of decreasing its spiritual-storage capacity.

Weird.

He focused on his left arm again but, this time, particularly on the properties of vatuatil, the metal the thoggua's tail-blade was crafted out of. The clearer and more precise the outcome he could imagine, the better it would be.

Size of scales, three centimeters. Density, three point five seven grams per cubic centimeter. Native mineral. Triangular crystal, no fractures. Hardness—

As he began molding, drawing out details from the anomaly system, he focused the change to happen on his skin, and was both shocked and elated when warped vatuatil flesh in the shape of triangular scales rippled into view, replacing his skin.

He frowned in concern. Not because his attempt didn't work out the way he imagined, but because it did.

He momentarily clenched his inhuman hand into a fist, feeling the nerves firing off and grating against his metallic skin.

No traces of injury from bruising against the metallic epidermis.

No signs of pollution in the bloodstream either.

Vatuatil was a solid conductor of lifeforce. That the lifeforce conductivity in his lower left arm suddenly went up by 63.7 percent confirmed that. There were obvious effects of the sudden gain in mass, but the increased lifeforce through his bones, muscles, and tendons all but mitigated the difference.

"Guess my body is changing faster than I imagined. Still, there's a couple of things I can . . ."

His words died at the tip of his tongue as a notification interrupted his musings.

Predator found you

He opened his eyes and found himself back in the room. He didn't need to turn to know that Tanya was standing outside his door. What was she doing up this late? He had expected her to react in a lot of ways after how they had ended things but coming to his room this late was not one of them. He heard her slowly turn the knob and enter, and she still had yet to utter a word. The dreary greenish illumination cast long shadows everywhere, making the room darker than it was.

She turned and closed the door, her back now turned to him. All he could see was a black robe draped over her shoulders. Her silhouette melted into the darkness, and he could barely see her face.

"You wanted something?" he asked.

"I—I thought you were asleep."

She sounded nervous and conflicted. Neither of those were good signs.

"What are you doing here?"

Silence.

"Tanya?"

"I'm just . . . thinking."

"Oh." The room plunged into another awkward silence. "About what?"

Tanya did not reply, nor did she look away from the door.

Lukas felt conflicted and, dare he say it, a bit nervous. He had gotten used to dealing with the somewhat volatile, secretive Tanya over the time they had spent together. The possession had done a number on her. That he had rejected her feelings only made things worse.

Feeling uncomfortable, he snapped his fingers, instantly lighting the candles, washing the room in a crimson glow.

"Do you want to . . ." Tanya paused, unsure. After a long moment, she turned towards him, meeting his gaze with a deer-in-the-headlights expression. Her silvery white pupils regarded him with such intensity that he just couldn't look away. He knew he was completely smitten with this woman, and seeing her vulnerable like this wasn't helping at all.

The candlelight illuminated her beautiful face as she took another step forward.

"Do you . . . do you enjoy me?" she asked.

"Do I . . . *what?*"

"I asked whether you enjoy me," she repeated, a little bit of courage seeping into her tone as she puffed out her chest. "Because I do. I enjoy you. Watching you stealing glances when you think I'm not looking."

Lukas wracked his brain for something to say, but all thoughts vanished as he watched her take another step. Then another, and she was standing before him.

Their hands touched.

He had to put an end to this right now.

"Tany—"

His words were cut off as Tanya's lips pressed against his. It was soft to begin with—as if she were testing the waters, but he automatically returned her kiss. Within a few seconds, their tongues were battling for dominance as they forgot themselves and simply enjoyed the moment. He wasn't sure when it had happened, but Tanya had swung a leg over him, and she was now straddling him. His hands found purchase on her hips as her fingers ran through his hair, pulling him into her. She rocked her hips into him, and his hands wandered over her thin robe and crawled beneath it until they felt the smooth, bare skin of her back. He felt her moan into his mouth, as her body shuddered from his touch, making him want to touch her even more. He was drunk on the feeling of her body and addicted to the sounds he was drawing out of her.

After what felt like an eternity, they finally separated for air. Her white hair hung about them like a curtain, blocking out the outside world. Their chests heaved as they struggled to calm their beating hearts, and he felt himself go hard, nestled between her legs.

"Tanya—" he began again.

"Shhh!" She held a finger against his lips, her lips moving to his cheeks and down to his neck, before she pulled back and stood up, never once averting her gaze. A small war seemed to be waging on her face, before she steeled herself and slid her robe over one shoulder. One hand went to the middle of her chest where the robe was currently covering her breasts. She slid it off herself using just her middle finger. The mesh fabric of the robe slowly traced every curve of her body until it landed in a small heap on the floor.

Every inch of her was now exposed.

Before he could so much as react, Tanya had crawled back upon his lap, dragging her supple skin against his own. Their chests pressed together and he could feel the weight of her breasts against him, one of her hands by his head while the other rested on his stomach.

Tanya brushed a lone hair from her face. Slowly, she lowered her face until it was inches away from his own, her gaze locked onto his.

"Are you sure?" he felt compelled to ask.

"Shut up, Lukas," she growled, her hand trailing up his abs to his bare chest. "I know you're attracted to me. I'm tired of pushing these feelings aside—" Her voice broke. "I—I don't want to be alone. Not tonight. I want to be held. I want to enjoy you. To be enjoyed. So please . . ."

Lukas made a vague sound of agreement, one that quickly turned into a moan as her mouth found his. His heartbeat rose precipitously, and so did hers. His hand crawled down to her hip while her fingers mussed his hair. Slowly, Tanya let out a sound of need that robbed him of the ability to think of anything at all.

"Now," she whispered, urging him to act as her hands found the hem of his shorts.

"I—are you really—" he tried one last time, his own lifeforce surging in response to her actions. He hadn't gotten laid in months. If she didn't stop now, Lukas knew that nothing would keep him from continuing. "Are you sure?"

Tanya seized his face again and glared down at him, her sexual desire clearly shining through. "This whole chivalrous thing you have going on? It's making me want to kick you in the nuts, but then I won't be able to go any further. So, for once in your life, shut the hell up and fuck me."

Lukas arched an eyebrow at her bluntness. Tanya didn't look like she'd be convinced by any amount of reason. Regardless of whether she'd accept his words or not, she had made up her mind that she'd not be spending this night alone.

This clearly wasn't a battle that Lukas Aguilar could win. So he gave in.

He guided her onto the bed and knelt before her. Her legs parted instinctively and he lay a kiss upon her thigh as he positioned himself. Her chest was already heaving with anticipation, as was his own. She leaned back, propping herself upon her arms as she looked down at him with desire.

Whatever happened in their future, whatever decisions they made, it wouldn't happen before the next morning. Until then, this moment was theirs, and he needed to focus on her right then.

He wanted her to remember this night.

He owed her that much at least.

Pushing himself over her, their bodies joined and Tanya threw her head back in ecstasy. It was gentle, loving. Her coos of pleasure felt far more erotic than any dirty talk he had heard before. He was on top of her and that was how it stayed. One position, one steady pace, and electricity coursing through their bodies.

It wasn't until several minutes later that he realized that being with Tanya was actually a great deal different than what he was accustomed to.

Honestly, it was almost disturbing.

Tanya was enjoying herself, he could tell that, but she was enjoying herself far too much.

No matter where or how he touched her, it was as though every contact only heightened her pleasure. It was as though every inch of her was somehow an erogenous zone.

And throughout it all, her expression never changed from the same hazy-eyed look she had given when she had first come to him.

There should have been something, some indicator about what she was going through physically, but Tanya's features remained unchanged, even though the rest of her body kept reacting appropriately. It was then that Lukas realized that something was wrong with her.

Was it a bremetan thing? It was hardly the first time he had been struck by the alienness of the bremetan or yokai. He needed to remember that no matter how much she looked and felt human, she wasn't.

But something told him that it was more than just that.

It wasn't that she was preternaturally sensitive. He realized that his touches weren't what was bringing out these reactions but rather, that it was *he* that was doing the touching. Tanya had already admitted that she loved him, and her powers were being manipulated by the goddess of Desire herself. It was almost like she was so totally consumed with the emotion that just the act of being with him was enough to apparently satisfy her.

Just to test his theories, he allowed her to be on top. It didn't matter. Tanya's eyes remained closed, as if in a trance, as she kept chanting his name and asking him to keep going, like some mindless mantra.

And she just kept on going. Without pause.

A shiver of pure terror slithered down his spine as he realized that maybe all was not well with this woman, after all. Between her own nightmarish past, Inanna's spell, the Everfrost slowly corrupting her soul, and the recent damage to her psychic architecture, maybe Tanya was far more fragile than he had thought. She had tried to get past the spell, but was that really the case? He had thought so during their conversations, but now . . .

The terrifying realization was almost enough to make him lose his own arousal, but the self-control he had gained from exposure to the Supreme Queen proved enough for him to continue the act. Still, he decided to hurry up and end it. He was beginning to get worried that the continued state of arousal might be unhealthy for her.

The air around him literally shook, pressing against his skin and making it ripple visibly as though against a strong wind, but he felt nothing. A strange, alien power exuded out of Tanya, buzzing into him through every inch of his skin in contact with her, like electricity flowing through high-voltage cables.

Only, it was cold. Terrifyingly cold. It engulfed his body in a glacier, making him want to pull his hands back out of sheer instinct, but his lifeforce surged higher than ever, all but forcing him to thrust faster and rougher. Between the surge of lust, the alienness of the situation, and the power flooding into him, he wasn't able to properly focus. He looked up at Tanya's face to see what was going on and discovered that *Tanya* wasn't there anymore. She looked like Tanya, but she was wrong, the expression off, the eyes too alert, the posture of her neck and body too rigid for someone that had just been lost in abandon.

Lukas swallowed, his thoughts frantically running through cues and hazy memories of previous encounters. Suddenly, he put it all together. The silvery white hair, the glacial eyes, the flawless, pale skin, her expression and body language oozing pure animal lust had to be—

"Frost," he murmured.

Her lips twisted into a wide, cruel smile, as she brought her face downward, her tongue softly tasting his lips, her right hand crawling over his cheek.

"Why yes, my Outsider. It is a lovely way to meet again, wouldn't you say?"

For several moments, Lukas couldn't do anything but stare at the face only a few inches from his own. He tried to take stock of the situation. He was currently in the presence of an alien power, a Taboo that Inanna had locked away deep within Tanya's soul. No doubt Meynte's actions had allowed it to escape, and if not, then at least temporarily exert her influence when Tanya was not in complete control of her mental faculties. He should've seen this coming from the change in her hair and eye color, but he had never imagined that it meant that Frost was free once more.

He swallowed hard, his throat almost too dry to get any words out. Her posture alone confirmed their respective roles as predator and prey, and given how she was mounting him, not even his instincts could help him get away from this creature.

With Frost. The manifestation of the End of Potential itself.

He attempted to pull away, get some distance between himself and Frost, but it was useless, as the same arms that had been on his chest moments before were now inescapably trapping him.

A throaty laugh bubbled out of her frozen mulberry lips. It took a moment to realize that she was laughing at his fear.

"I didn't expect to meet you," he croaked, having finally regained his voice. "Especially not like this."

"Mmmm . . ." she hummed softly, licking her lips. "How curious. You are a soulcrafter, an anomaly, a source of Creation, however unique. You recognize me as your antithesis. And yet, I sense strong feelings of protection and love overflowing between you and my fragile vessel. The dichotomy is exquisite."

Yes, he thought, somehow keeping himself from growing hysterical. If only barely.

"What do you want?" he asked, through gritted teeth. Normally he'd have summoned a salvo of snark, but it just wouldn't come. Maybe he was just too scared, and with good reason.

Her eyes gleamed. "You know what I want, Outsider. I aided you earlier, and now, it is time you fulfill your end of the bargain."

Damn it. He had thought he had been able to evade that.

"If this is about me freeing you, it was never part of the bargain."

Not that she'd need him to, if this meeting was any indication.

He had to hand it to her. She had worded it all in a way that made him believe that he had no option but to unleash the bindings Inanna had put on her.

But she had underestimated him. Underestimated how far he was willing to go. How unpredictable he could be if he put his mind to it.

He had been able to get rid of Meynte without having to unbind Fimbulwinter from Inanna's spell. But curse that stupid queen! In her rage and her willingness to see him defeated, she had done the very thing that she wanted to stop. She had drawn a little too much Everfrost, enough for it to start possessing Tanya again. How far the effects of this possession reached was an entirely different matter altogether.

Her mouth quivered, and she let out a wicked laugh. "You speak the truth, Outsider. Underestimating you was my folly. You vanquished the queen without unleashing me. I'm impressed."

As if to make a point, she grinded herself against him.

"I underestimated you as well," Lukas said. "I didn't expect you to take control again. My spell should've held you back."

Her lips twisted into that poisonous smile again. "Not yours. That goddess's. Whoever she was, her power was mighty. Not even Amaterasu shines that bright, and she has Eternal Light as her very domain."

Her words twisted a knife in his heart. If she knew that, then—

"You are not her," said Frost, "but I can sense vestiges of her power within you. An echo, lost in time. A power exuding a majestic Truth, but one whose bedrock is cemented in something closer to my own existence."

Lukas had a sneaking suspicion of what she was referring to.

"Do not fret, Outsider. Even now, her power binds me. It takes a rare situation for my vessel to lose all semblance of control over her mind and heart." She looked down at where their bodies joined. "And what a wonderful sensation it is. I cannot blame her for losing control."

And now he didn't know what to think anymore.

"It's unfortunate. If only the girl had a little more trust in your abilities. But she was too fatalistic, too sure her life was about to end. She wanted to do her bit in the fight against Meynte, even if that little bit meant welcoming me back into her."

"What?"

"Oh yes," she said with a laugh. "The more Meynte called upon Fimbulwinter, the more she wedged the gates open, so to speak. The girl was fading, and she wanted power. Power to overcome Meynte's will. Power that only *I* could give her."

Lukas gritted his teeth.

Frost lifted her chin slightly, a gesture of pride, and another small smile quirked her mouth. "You are in my debt, Outsider. I fulfilled your curiosity, and you incurred an obligation. I do not believe in charity."

"Oh?" Lukas asked, his eyes narrowing. "And this is how you choose to settle it? By dropping in uninvited and welcoming yourself to take part in this?"

That wicked laugh again. "You wished for it, didn't you?"

"Definitely," he said. There was no point beating around the bush.

"Mmmm . . ." She moaned, dragging her ice-cold finger down his chest. If it weren't for the fact that his life was in peril, he'd have considered it erotic. It certainly didn't help that the lifeforce surging within him kept his manhood erect. "You tempt me so, Outsider. I might agree, upon a condition."

He arched an eyebrow. "Which is?"

"Another bargain. Someone of your talents can be very useful for my designs."

He barked out a laugh. "I'm looking for a way to close the bargain, woman. And your suggestion is to start another one? I don't know what to do except to laugh."

Her lips slithered into a quiet smile, reminding him of Inanna. "Remember, Outsider, you wish to save this vessel from turning into a living nightmare. Surely it won't hurt you to listen to my offer?"

"Yeah," he deadpanned, "I've heard that before. It's really funny that you're concerned with Tanya becoming a living nightmare, when you're the nightmare itself."

The fingers of her right hand crawled over his cheek, towards his temples. "I'm not the girl, Outsider. Neither am I the parasites you've dealt with. I am the incarnation of the End." Her face went cold and unpleasant. "And when someone decides to be stubborn, it makes me lose my temper."

Lukas swallowed. There was no point in getting her infuriated. Besides, he was still obligated to do one task for her.

"Do you not wish her back—your goddess?"

The bottom fell out of his stomach. Of all the things he had expected her to say, this wasn't it. He had no more doubts now that Frost knew what Inanna did to her, as well as every single thing he had confided in Tanya. *Damn it.* He had confided in someone just once, and it had backfired on him.

If she knew what she wanted and was willing to use it as a bargaining chip, that meant she was on the level with her offer.

"What of it?"

That poisonous smile again. "If you are willing to hear the terms of my bargain, perhaps you might find something interesting there."

"I'm listening."

"There," she said, grinding her hips again. "Not so untamable, after all."

He clenched his fists. "What do you want?"

"One favor you owe me," she said. "Owe me two more, and in return, I shall fulfill two obligations for you."

"Any obligation?"

She smiled. "Any obligation."

He looked at her warily. This was hardly the first time he had made a bargain with entities way beyond his paygrade, but this was definitely the first time that said entity was offering to be in debt to him, without knowing the details beforehand.

No entity of her stature would freely wish to bind herself to such an open-ended obligation. Not unless she was fully assured of what they would be. And given she was currently possessing Tanya and they were away from the Eternal Light—

He took a deep breath and got his heart rate under control. "Let me guess. One of those favors would be letting Tanya have her body back."

Her eyes glinted like chips of ice. "If you wish. Between the two of us, I'm a lot better company."

As if to make a point, she raised herself slightly only to sink back down, lifting her head and exhaling in ecstasy. Then she looked down at him. "However, you seem to have an unnatural affection for my vessel, so should you wish, I shall recede into the depths of her soul, only to resurface when you call for me."

He didn't believe her.

"And about bringing Inanna back?"

She tilted her head and blinked slowly. "There are ways of achieving that impossible dream. Ways that go against the Great Progenitor. Ways enshrouded in dark paths similar to my own."

"You're talking about Taboo."

"Perceptive," she smiled. "Bringing forth that which does not exist is against the laws of the world, is it not?"

Lukas had heard that the ways of the Lord were infinite. The same could be said about the Devil too. He had been thinking about the former all this time, but Frost was suggesting the latter. A walk on the reverse side of Potential, the way of Taboo. It sounded all very enticing except for one thing.

He was an anomaly.

A source of Creation.

Even if what she was saying was possible, assimilating a Taboo—much like how Meynte assimilated Fimbulwinter—would utterly destroy him.

"How?"

"Uhuh uh, Outsider. These lips shall speak nothing until you agree."

Lukas rubbed his mouth, mulling over her words. As far as her obligations went, she was safe. He would not lose Tanya to her, and that exhausted the first bargain. And information on getting Inanna back constituted the second. Basically, she had him by the balls, and if he agreed to this, he'd owe her two new obligations.

"So . . ." asked Frost, leaning down against his chest. "Do we have a bargain?"

CHAPTER 21

COUNTEROFFER

Some things weren't meant to go together. Things like oil and water. Orange juice and toothpaste.

Lukas Aguilar and normalcy.

The day had begun so simply. He had spent over fourteen hours by himself walking through the empty tunnels of the dead Crypt of Fiendish Worms, his mind sunk in self-reflection, studying how the omphalos was changing him. Tanya's confession had been a surprise and not an entirely unwelcome one. When she had come to his room and demanded to have sex, he had the good sense to shut up and give in. Between the constant struggles Fate put him through, the impossible surges of lifeforce, and his own desires, he had been overcome with a raw need for her. Tanya was lovely. More than lovely. Sensuous. Willing. Perfectly unrestrained and passionate. He had all but shut up his rational self and given in to the primal part of him that yearned for the simple things in life—hunger, sleep, sex.

One would have thought that after all that he had gone through in the borderland, surviving the Ifrit King, meeting a manifestation of Inanna, and dealing with a fallen emperor and her delusional servant would have been enough to buy him a few days of respite. If nothing else, a single night away from it all was hardly an unreasonable demand.

"You think too much, Outsider," Frost murmured. "Fears of unseen consequences weigh heavily on your mind. Give in to your desires. Stop thinking. Live a little."

Frost was baiting him with the two things he wanted most of all. Tanya would be in control of her powers, and he'd get vital information about resurrecting Inanna. In return, he'd be obligated to do two tasks for her. As far as bargains went, it was pretty straightforward. Which meant he'd be stupid not to be doubly paranoid.

He licked his parched lips. "I listened to your offer. In the interests of fairness, would you allow me to present a counteroffer?"

She idly raised her hands up and stretched. "And what would that be?"

Lukas swallowed. That was a positive response. Maybe, just *maybe*, he had a decent chance of coming out with a win.

"I'll be candid," he said. "All of this is based on crude blackmail. You are threatening to possess Tanya's body and forcing this arrangement. And then you claim you'll let Tanya be, as a way of canceling one obligation. That's hardly fair."

"I do not have to be fair to you, Outsider," said Frost.

"And I don't have to bargain with you either," he countered. "Do not forget, you're only owed a single obligation. An obligation that doesn't include me releasing you. And now, your attempt to bargain is a measly attempt to do exactly that."

Her lips curved. "And I could continue possessing this vessel as I please."

"I think you'll find that a little difficult."

Her brow arched. "And why is that?"

Lukas smiled. "I've been encountering a lot of nasty people recently, so it keeps me constantly on the lookout for what kind of trouble to expect. Paranoid, yes, but given what I deal with, I'm sure you understand."

She narrowed her eyes. "As in?"

"As in, you see all, you hear all, but you don't learn. Do you, Miss Avatar of Fimbulwinter? I'm not just a soulcrafter. I'm a human, one who's grown in a world without Potential. I *cheat*."

Blob soared up and engulfed Frost's naked form from behind. Sensing the sudden attack, she tried to push it back with a burst of power, but that only sealed her fate. Blob absorbed the energy and laterally expanded, trapping her upper extremities like a straitjacket. Before she knew it, Territory Creation and Living Anomaly activated, trapping her right above him.

"You're right," he said at last. "You could continue possessing Tanya. Just like I could knock you unconscious. The next time you wake up, you'll be in Haviskali. We'll see exactly how powerful your control over her body really is."

Maybe he was wrong. Maybe she really had escaped the bindings and could possess Tanya at will. But calling her bluff had put her in a position to defend herself. Either way, he wouldn't be going in blind.

Her lips formed into a line. "Do you really want to go down this route, Outsider?"

For the first time, Lukas smiled. "You'll have to forgive me. After dealing with Solana, I prefer not to take unnecessary risks. Now I'm a great believer in fairness, so I'll give you two options. You can either throw down and we'll see how *that* turns out, or you can give me a fair bargain. And before you think of stabbing me in the back, remember what happened with Meynte and Solana. Sealing you was child's play for Inanna, and I didn't back down even against her. So look down on me if you will, but mess with me, and I'll bury you so deep that you'll have to dig yourself out with a fucking shovel."

He had to talk rough with monsters above his pay grade before, Inanna being at the top of that list. He just never had done it while sharing an intimate moment. He watched as Frost stared at him with a straight face, but he could see considerable uncertainty behind her eyes. For whatever reason, she had tried to approach him as an equal, using blackmail and threats to get him to play ball; now he had effectively threatened her back with equal, if not greater, ruthlessness.

"*Speak!*" he snapped. "Don't just sit there like a statue."

He was furious. He had felt this kind of anger before, back when the Crypt had possessed him and twisted him into becoming its avatar of retaliation. He had seen Tanya and every single creature within the confines of the anomaly as his prey to kill slowly and painfully. Months after that experience, he was feeling a similar fury, a blind wrath that would do more harm than good if he let it.

Emerald eyes stared at the glacial white ones.

"You think you can just walk into my life and fuck with things I consider my own?" he rasped out. "You think that just because you have the power to do so, that gives you the right?"

He was quickly losing control of his patience. He had kept his cool when Inanna had tried to corner him into becoming her henchman. He had kept his cool when Solana had forced him to work under threats to his life. He had kept his cool when things went sideways, and Inanna had to sacrifice herself. He had kept his cool when Solana had played him for a fool, using Tanya's heritage as her tool. He had kept his cool when Meynte had unleashed Fimbulwinter to an extent, nearly undoing Inanna's spell. But even he had his limits. Even the fact that Tanya was the intolerable abomination that the anomaly within him wanted to annihilate with extreme prejudice didn't compare to what he was feeling now.

Frost's eyes glittered, anger showing for a moment, cool and far away. After what seemed like an eternity, she exhaled and raised both shoulders. Lukas silently commanded Blob to release her and the aqāru slime shed its elasticity and slid down her body, resting on him.

Finally, she asked, "What do you want, Outsider?"

"What I want is for you to vanish for good and never appear again, but we don't get what we want, do we? Make no mistake, Frost. Empress Meynte was by no means the most dangerous target I've had to take out. The fact that I could deal with her wasn't a fluke, and I'd have done it, with or without your help."

This was the pivotal moment. By now, he had given Frost enough cues to hopefully direct her to the conclusion he wanted her to make. This was a battle like any other, and the key to winning battles was to control their flow. Much like law, it was all about control. Before, Frost had been expecting to simply blow in like a breeze, throw her weight around, and properly intimidate a man whose lover she was holding in her custody. However, everything he had said and done so far was meant to counter that impression and present a new one of his own composed of crisp professionalism and deadly ruthlessness, and hinting at superior experience in that field.

"Say your fill, Outsider," she whispered.

"That Tanya is worth something to me is the only reason we're having this conversation. So the first thing I need is for you to leave her in peace. I want your word that, no matter what, you won't take her over again. If and only *if* I need your help, I'll call you. Under no conditions shall you manipulate Tanya nor me into unleashing Fimbulwinter from Niflheim. You will also get me all the information I need to resurrect Inanna. In return, I'll help Tanya reach Meynte's level of control, and no matter what it takes, I will stop Fimbulwinter from reaching through her and ending everything."

She cocked her head and stared at him quizzically. "You believe you can resist the power of the End, Outsider? When the End arrives, you would be the first to get destroyed."

Lukas did not flinch. Not at all.

"Unlike the delusional empress, I am not unaware of your nature, Outsider. I know of you and the World that sleeps within you. Not even you can escape the End."

She expected him to look frightened. Or at the very least, she expected him to be unnerved by that declaration.

Instead, Lukas smiled.

"Is that what you think will happen?"

For the first time, Frost faltered.

"Regardless of those portents," said Lukas, enjoying the uncertainty on her features, "you wanted me to fulfill two tasks. I'll do them, but I, not you, shall decide which requests I fulfill and which I don't."

Her glacial eyes remained on his face, unblinking.

"And if I refuse a request, there will be no reprisals from you."

She tilted her head and blinked her eyes slowly. "You puzzle me, Outsider. But I agree. You, not I, shall choose which tasks to fulfill."

"And you will not try to hamper Tanya's attempts to gain control of her power."

This time she smiled. "Absolutely."

Lukas exhaled, thinking hard. Had he covered all his bases? Could she still get him from an angle he hadn't considered? Knowing her kind, she probably would.

"Well, Outsider?" she asked crisply. "Have we a bargain?"

He swallowed again, hoping he wasn't getting himself into another mess. "Fine," he said, "We have a bargain."

She closed her eyes, feline smile forming on her lips, and inclined her head. "Good."

And then she brought her face down toward him.

"Wait, what are you—" Lukas began, only for his words to perish as her ice-cold lips met his, her tongue diving into his mouth to take control. She lifted her head back up to let out another throaty laugh, her voice simmering with desire, before she attacked his lips again with animalistic pleasure.

"This—we—" Lukas tried to say, but she wouldn't listen. She placed an icy finger over his lips and brought her face right above him, their noses touching.

"Uh uh uh, Outsider! I'm playing by the rules. In your prior obligation, you promised me satisfaction, did you not? Tonight, I crave your body as my entertainment, and entertainment I shall have."

Lukas frowned. He hadn't forgotten about that bit. He was just unsure if she really meant it or if she had just been fucking with him. Turns out she was, only in a much more literal way, given the way she ground her hips against him.

And suddenly, the coldness of her lips was the last of Lukas's concerns.

"You—you're sucking my lifeforce," he accused.

She smiled predatorily. "Did you forget what I am, Outsider? I devour lifeforce, and you have it in spades. Tonight, I will devour you, and you will let yourself be devoured."

"That—" he protested, but she grabbed him. "Look at it this way, Outsider. The more you keep me satisfied, the fewer urges this frail vessel shall feel. Would you shy away from such a tiny sacrifice for her?"

"You're such a bitch."

She threw her head back and laughed again, and then attacked his lips once more. Her body was above him, their breaths mingling, cold sweetness and human imperfection merging into a climax. He could feel the sound of her heartbeat along with the feel of his own lifeforce surging out of his body as she drank her fill. It burned him in ways he could not explain, and in its own twisted way, pushed him to take it out on her. Not that it mattered, for Frost grew more and more animated with every passing second, as if getting a strange satisfaction from the act.

He remembered both of them thrashing in bed, screaming, their voices blending into something utterly inhuman. He remembered meeting her inhuman glacial eyes and seeing a specter of Nidhogg—the massive draconian serpentine form he had seen inside Tanya's mind—staring back at him.

Lukas awoke to a massive, mind-numbing headache. Every time his heart beat, it sent a pulse of pain straight into his brain. Against his better judgment, he blearily opened his eyes. He shut them immediately, but even closed, Lukas could see bright flashes of multi-colored dots dancing around in the darkness.

It took several minutes before he tried opening his eyes again. And to his immense relief, the sunlight wasn't nearly as harsh this time around. He still had to squint, but it was infinitely better than being painfully blinded. Finally regaining his vision and feeling his headache lessen, he took stock of his surroundings.

And froze.

Feeling an unfamiliar weight on his chest, Lukas grabbed the edges of the sheets and slowly raised them up. From his distorted memories of the previous night and the soft, feminine moan he'd just heard, he had a good guess of who was above him. His suspicions were confirmed when he spotted a familiar mop of snowy white hair. The sight of Tanya Shimizu drooling on his chest while snuggling against him wasn't something he thought he would ever see in his lifetime. Even the knowledge of what had happened after Frost had taken over and the events that followed didn't dissolve the blissful feeling coursing through him.

True to her words, Frost had practically sucked his lifeforce dry during their nighttime activities. Had he been an ordinary bremetan, he'd have died of its effects. Luckily for him, the constant drain had inadvertently activated the anomaly system's defensive protocols, and shut down further lifeforce production, using the stored anomalous energy to replenish the body instead. That was when he had surrendered himself to sweet oblivion.

Still, he thought, *she has been true to her word.*

The silver white was still there like before, but that unnatural coldness had vanished. With their bodies practically merged together, he could feel her every curve, and every inch of her soft skin on his own. Both of them were completely naked, just as he remembered. She shifted slightly, grinding against him, stirring a little more, before pausing in place. Lukas would've believed she was still asleep if not for the small grin on her face.

"I know you're awake."

Her smile widened, though her eyes remained closed.

"Any plans to get up?" he asked.

Finally, she lifted her head from his chest and stared at him with silvery white eyes that shone with happiness and mischief. "No, you make a good pillow. I think I'll keep you."

Lukas mock-sighed. "I suppose as far as career paths go, I could do worse."

Her eyes narrowed. "Are you telling me that being my pillow is a *bad* choice?"

He gave her a lopsided grin. "Choosing to fight over this?" His fingers crawled down her neck and breasts. "What am I, crazy?"

Tanya smiled. Dragging herself across his chest, she tilted her head up and kissed his jaw. Lukas ran his fingers across her tresses and pulled her into a deep kiss.

"So, this has been wonderful," he said, pulling back, "but you know we need to—"

She shut him up with a finger, frowning. "No. This isn't about to happen." Irritation replaced the angelic expression on her face. "Give me one damned reason we need to stop."

Lukas lifted his hand and scratched his head, giving himself some time to think. He probably should have considered what he was going to say to her a bit more before blurting out things like that.

"You know why," he said, trying to lift himself up, only for her to press him down. It looked like she had staked her claim upon him and wasn't willing to give it up without a fight. "With me being an anomaly and you—"

"Being your predator, I know," Tanya snapped. "But you know as well as I do that's not the damn reason. The Lukas Aguilar I know has never acted out of fear. If you really considered me a danger, you could have killed me several times over by now. You could have let me die in the borderland, and again when Meynte possessed me. Instead, you risked yourself to save me again and again and again. And I already told you, I'm not leaving you, whatever happens."

"But you have your life—"

"My life is with *you*," she snapped. "For someone who routinely does the impossible, you, Lukas Aguilar, are an idiot. You talk of my life, but do you even realize what that was? I was a fugitive. Running away from my grandfather, hiding my identity, my face, my powers. Running from a power within myself. Running from the Cobalt Army. Even when I slept, I was haunted by the nightmares of my past. *That's* what I was. Now? I have my answers. I know what I can do and must do. And with your help, I will finally gain what I've always sought."

"I'm also the reason you got trapped by Solana. If I hadn't brought you here—"

"For the Goddess's sake, Lukas, you didn't force me to sit on the throne. You tried to keep me away from it. I was a fucking fool not to trust you. And then you saved me all over again. Lukas—" She held his face between her palms. "—I *like* me. Six months ago, I didn't think I'd ever be able to say that. Whether you did that with your goddess's power or just sheer dumb luck, it doesn't matter to me. I'm grateful either way. As for this—" She grabbed at her strands of white hair. "—this is my fault too. You're not to blame."

Lukas considered that for a moment, wondering just how much Tanya really understood about the precariousness of her situation. "Then, where does that leave us?"

"Depends," said Tanya, her lips twisting. "Are you going to leave me, now that you've had me?"

"What?" He squinted at the ludicrousness of her statement. "No! What— Why would you say that?"

Then he noticed her lips twist further in an upward smile. *This woman!* She knew exactly what she was doing to him with that question, and seeing him flounder was making her more amused.

"You enjoy tormenting me far too much." he said.

"After everything you've put me through, I think you deserve it. Besides . . ." Her smile deepened. ". . . I think you enjoy being tormented just as much."

He gave her a mild glare with no bite in it. After all, there was just no way he could look at her in that state and be upset with her. Even without taking into consideration that what she said was one hundred percent true.

As if to make her point, she began rubbing her body against his.

"Okay, now you're just being blatant."

Tanya giggled, softly scratching her fingernails against his chest. "I love you."

"You don't even know if this thing will even wor—"

He couldn't even finish his sentence, for Tanya pressed her lips into his, and the words he was about to say vanished from his mind. Within five seconds, the lifeforce within him went berserk with naked lust. Within fifteen seconds, his mind had conjured a list of "Things To Do With Tanya." By the twenty-fifth, he was lying down on his back, with her straddling him. He tried to be careful, but Tanya seemed to react even more aggressively than he was. For a moment, he thought Frost had taken her over again.

But her expression remained unchanged.

As did her aura.

So maybe it wasn't about Frost at all.

Maybe it was about them.

And wasn't that an amazing thought?

Finally, she pulled herself away and—was she pouting at him?

"What?"

If anything, her pout grew more pronounced. She glared at him sullenly, with her white bangs falling all over her face.

"Aguilar . . ." she enunciated, sounding like a parent reprimanding a child. "Has anybody told you it's bad form to ignore a girl who's trying to seduce you? Stop overthinking and enjoy the moment."

There wasn't a lot of talking after that.

CHAPTER 22

DIRE TIDINGS

With their relationship conflicts now resolved, Lukas had begun to spend a lot more time with Tanya. It was a massive distraction and cut off a significant part of the time he had been spending in the anomaly, immersed in study. Instead, he had begun to do that while sleeping, when he could safely recede back into his own world and continue his self-exploration. The rest of the time was spent either watching Tanya get trained by Solana, talking to Maude and some of the other yokai, or just running some minor experiments on bifurcating his mind to better utilize Blob. And of course, the boyfriend-girlfriend activities continued. With him no longer maintaining his stubborn aversion towards their relationship, Tanya seemed to think they had moved into the "honeymoon phase." Had this been Haviskali, she'd have taken him out sightseeing, or to her favorite spas for a massage, or maybe to some of her favorite restaurants. If nothing else, they could always go flying or hang around the Otamba Bridge.

Her words, not his.

But they weren't. Instead, they were cooped up inside this subterranean territory. The best she could do was get out for some fresh air in the desert, but it would either be too hot or too dark to be at all enjoyable.

So they had sex. Several times a day. Lukas tried to limit it to kisses, hugs, and cuddles for the first few times, fearing that Frost would take over again. That, however, didn't stop Tanya from offering, and after a few days, he eventually caved in.

Honestly, it was like she had a one-track mind.

The previous night had gone the same way. They had gone through their *pro forma* activities after dinner, and Tanya was clearly horny, but her attempts had been less intense than the other days. Lukas had concluded that she had been a little desperate and starved for his attention and constantly worried about their relationship, but now that things were settling down, she had begun to relax. It was nice to be able to sit back with what they had, without worrying about her getting possessed again. Frost might have given him her word, but he didn't trust her as far as he could throw her.

"I'm actually thinking of asking Solana for some texts on divinity and the Yggdrasil," he admitted.

Tanya perked up, meeting his eyes. She was currently draped over him, with nothing but a single bedsheet covering them.

"Don't give me that look."

This time her eyebrows only went higher. "You realize you tore her library apart, right?"

Lukas scowled. "Not my fault she decided to trick us like that in that room. And I did say I'd ask, not demand. So long as she keeps to her end of the deal, I can figure things out my way."

"Your way . . ." she murmured.

"My way," he agreed, thinking of Frost again. She was supposed to answer his call and help him with information on resurrecting Inanna. He didn't exactly know where to begin, but any amount of information was better than nothing.

"Well, better you than me," said Tanya. "I had enough of that as a kid. Theology, doctrine, customs, the government systems and policies, forms of combat and their psychological and spiritual effects, customary understanding of the role the Sacred Eight plays in our world, and of course, the Vision of the Shimizu Path . . . Ugh! It was torture."

Lukas snorted.

"Don't you laugh," she said, frowning. "At least it's different here. The yokai are all about survival and growth. In all the sessions I've had with Solana, not once has she even talked about anything except practical application of my combat powers."

That was another surprise. Not trusting Solana to keep her word, he had been a steadfast presence during every single one of Tanya's sessions with the skinwalker. He'd sit away from the two of them and observe as Solana ran Tanya through several forms of combat employing Everfrost, which often included a philosophical understanding of what Everfrost was, what it represented, and how it affected Potential, the soul, and the world as a whole, and assimilating all of that knowledge into combat.

It was all quite interesting.

More interesting was the fact that Tanya had been willing to see past her differences and hatred for the ancient skinwalker to accept her tutelage with a clear mind. It was exactly the sort of pragmatism Lukas wished he had had when Inanna had given him a similar offer. Instead, he had been too paranoid about her twisting her into her personal monster to even care about the benefits.

"You probably should ask her," continued Tanya, oblivious to his thoughts.

"Yeah, I will."

She snorted. "Of course. You're exactly the type to spend your time poring over a stupid book when you have a woman willing to have sex with you. No wonder you were a diplomat."

He arched an eyebrow. "Reading edifies the mind. And we keep going at it every day. You're telling me it isn't enough?"

"It's *never* enough," Tanya giggled. "Still, better you than me. I can't fathom any reason why Solana would ever need to force me to read stuff. The Goddess knows, I'd probably try to kill her."

Knowing Tanya, she probably would.

"An understanding of the yokai way and heritage?" Tanya read out incredulously, holding the book Solana had handed her. "You want me to, what, memorize this shit?"

"Study it. Memorize it. Embrace it. It's your heritage, after all."

Logic is the art of going wrong with confidence, thought Lukas. Tanya was currently experiencing that firsthand.

"But—but, why?" she asked, flummoxed.

"I'm trying to catch up to Meyn—"

Solana hissed.

"I mean, the *empress's* level," Tanya said. Solana was rather peeved when anyone—mostly Lukas—used the queen's name casually. After the first few times of seeing her nearly lose her control, Lukas had stopped trying to get under her skin.

. . . Come to think of it, it was a really bad choice of words.

The ancient skinwalker had consented to tutoring Tanya, but she was extremely strict about it. Not surprising, since Solana did look the type to hold whatever bit of control she had left in a death grip rivaling that of a swordsman and their blade. And it showed every single time the two met for instruction.

Solana gave her a displeased look. "I'd have expected the heiress of one of the Sacred Eight to recognize the importance of culture and tradition."

"My point is that I'm playing catch-up, not studying for a job."

"You are actually doing both," said the skinwalker, crossing her arms. "As much as I hate the situation, you are all that remains of the empress and boast some of her powers. For better or worse, you are the last chance for the yokai to regain its lost power. For the majority of the population, you *are* the new queen, or practically so."

Tanya's eyes boggled. "Senile witch says what?!"

Solana's left eye twitched.

"I'm just Tanya, not some queen of your kind. For fuck's sake, I'm a bloody Asukan."

"You're no more Asukan than I," said Solana sternly. "You wear the flesh of one, but the power that flows in that body is that of a yuki-onna."

"You realize I actually have a king-class kami bound to me, right?"

"Yes, one that you can't even control," said Solana pertly. "I can see it will be an uphill climb with you."

Tanya growled.

Lukas did his best to hide his face in his newest book and hoped neither of them saw him grin.

"You will study that text from cover to cover and finish it in the next two weeks. And then I shall quiz you in front of the entire yokai council, so that they can see for themselves exactly how wonderful their queen is."

Dread formed on Tanya's face. "You're . . . *what?*"

Solana gave her a predatory smile. "What? Did you think that I'd just accept whatever you and that Outsider demand of me? If you want tutelage, you need to be ready for whatever comes with it. I suggest you not damage whatever reputation the Outsider has granted you."

Tanya scowled.

"Once you've passed that," said Solana, standing her tallest, "we will begin understanding the nature of the Haze and how to weave through it, like your esteemed ancestor was capable of."

"Can you do it too?" asked Lukas. At Solana's irritated look, he continued, "I mean, you took me to the Haze the last time I was here. But it wasn't like how the empress did it."

"The empress was a master at employing the Haze. As a master of Weaving, she was nigh impossible to track, and nothing save the most warded locations was closed off to her. She could be in Baramunz now, Luthar shortly afterwards, and still be back for dinner after visiting a dozen other nations. She herself ended the lives of three of the five kings of the era before that uneventful battle with the Pantheon began."

She glared at Tanya. "And if this silly girl wants to live, then she needs to at least learn how to navigate through the Haze before it's too late."

"Too late for what?" asked Lukas.

Solana seemed to ponder that question for a moment. "Come to my office after dinner," she said, leaving no room for questions. "We need to talk. Bring the girl along."

* * *

We need to talk!

There is enough empirical evidence in the history of civilization that almost nothing good ever follows whenever someone starts a conversation with that particular phrase. That was how Lukas knew that something inevitably problematic had indeed happened, and things were going to go pear-shaped soon.

He hadn't quite expected . . . well, *this.*

"Is this . . . real?"

"As real as you and I."

Lukas collapsed on the chair, his eyes wide and glassy, as he tried hard not to think of what he had just seen. They were in Solana's office, with the skinwalker sitting behind her desk, looking strangely pensive. Melancholy, even. Solana had, much like before, conjured a holographic illusion for them to see. Only this time, she had conjured a memory, one featuring a devastating and precipitous attack on Zuken's mansion. How Solana had gained access to this particular memory was an entirely different bag of worms, but one he hadn't opened yet.

He was still trying to process that such a thing had happened. The sheer barbarism displayed by those . . . igriotts, he supposed they were called, was enough to send bile racing up his throat. Power-wise, he'd rank them at somewhere higher than the Level-2 ifrit and lower than the Level-2 muspel, but it was their bloodthirsty nature that made him nauseous. He and Tanya had faced the wrath of an entire army of monsters inside the borderland, but somehow, these igriotts made them feel less horrifying. The people—those families on the hill—were just regular dwellers, working men and women, little children, resting in the safety of their homes. They'd woken up to find themselves in a nightmare, fleeting for their lives from white-furred monstrosities that seemed to come out of nowhere and move with a speed that bordered on disbelief. Lukas had watched, his fists clenched and drawing blood, as innocent children were hunted down like animals, fleeing from one invader only to find another waiting with jaws and fangs.

"Wha-What happened to Zuken?" Tanya stammered.

"Captured," said Maude. "But his current whereabouts are unknown."

"How sure are we of this feed?" Lukas asked.

"Feed?"

"This memory," he clarified. "How authentic is this memory?"

He glanced at Solana, expecting her lips to twist into a familiar annoyance. Instead, they stayed pursed, as if his words hadn't even registered. Instead, it was Maude who replied.

"We got it through one of our watchers in Haviskali."

"And that's the truth?"

"One you have to accept, yes."

Lukas's eyes narrowed. He knew perfectly well how smoothly Solana could lie her way out of situations. Twisting words, hiding meanings in subtext, misinterpreting words, and altering her tone to twist the meaning altogether was right up her forte. So if she was being this blunt, either it was because she genuinely couldn't give them any further information, or it was a psychological trick to get them to react to something.

He didn't know what was worse.

Whatever. He could ponder that later. He needed to focus on what was necessary.

"When did this happen?"

"A little over three weeks ago," said Solana.

Three weeks? He had been at the yokai territory for more than that time. That dated the attack to when he and Tanya had been stranded in the borderland. So why was Solana telling them about this now? Zuken was their host and support in the Empire, and with him captured and his manse destroyed, neither Lukas nor Tanya had anywhere to go. Solana could've used this information to bolster the scales on her end when they had negotiated after Meynte's defeat. But she hadn't. *Why?* Or was he reading too much into things and she had simply gotten the information late?

No. His instincts flared. Solana was obsessed with control. She had constantly tracked his activities in Haviskali. It wasn't like her to gain this sort of knowledge so late.

So, either she hadn't realized what it was worth, or she'd blatantly waited to reveal what she knew until it was too late.

Neither looked particularly good.

"And why are we only getting to know this now?" he asked.

Maude looked at Solana expectantly.

"All but one of the watchers I had planted near the Banksi mansion perished in the battle," said Solana. "The moment their hosts perished, the Eternal Light burned them to death. The only one that survived had possessed one of the surviving infants. It took a while to get discharged from the healing units, and then use civil transport until they were able to reach the Desert. There was also the issue of crossing the boundaries without alerting the Cobalt Army."

A straightforward answer. One that felt prepared, and yet, adequate. Yokai in their spiritual form could not survive in the Eternal Light. It was how they survived out there in the Desert, where Eternal Light was barred from existing. It was why they used the Haze for traveling, and why they frequented borderlands and other realms but stayed away from the Empire. It was also why they possessed bremetans.

He exhaled. "Any idea why this man—Ultaf Shimizu—attacked Zuken?"

"Why else?" hissed Tanya. "He must have known that Zuken had hired me. Someone must have tipped him off. I knew this would happen. It always does. Every time I think I've gotten some semblance of peace, every time I think I've left my past behind, this always happens. Sometimes it's assassins, sometimes abductors, sometimes the Frost, and now Ultaf."

She punched the wall, bruising her knuckles in the process. Lukas put his arms around her and pulled her closer. She pursed her lips but accepted his comfort nonetheless.

Maude looked at her, shiftily. Lukas caught her eye.

"There is something you should know," she murmured. "When Zuken hired me and Olfric for the anomaly mission, we had a secondary goal. To find out more about you, your history, your skill, and how you were able to destroy the Class-2 anomaly."

"You think Zuken was hired by this guy?"

"I'm saying there is a chance—"

"No," said Tanya without hesitation. "There isn't."

Maude did a double take. "How can you be so sure?"

"Because Banksi didn't make a secret out of it. I figured it out and confronted him, and he told me the truth. He knew who I was, my heritage as a Shimizu, and that I carried Ezzeron. He wanted to know why I was hiding when revealing my heritage could have gotten me so much more. I told him that the Shimizu line was dead for me, and without the Wind King's kami, it might as well be dead to the world."

"And how do you think Zuken knew about your identity?" Maude demanded.

Tanya opened her mouth to answer but shut it.

"I suppose it's possible that Banksi was indeed working for this Ultaf fellow," said Lukas. "It's possible that the anomaly mission was his attempt to kill two—no, *three*—birds with one stone. Destroy the anomaly for whatever reasons he had to, confirm if Tanya was indeed the person he thought he was . . ."

"And the third?" asked Tanya.

He smirked. "Find out what's so interesting about you. I mean, if I were taking a contract to find you for someone else, I'd want to know exactly what you're worth. Just to confirm that I wasn't being trapped in an unfair deal."

"I can see why Zuken and you got along," said Maude. "You think just like him."

Tanya scoffed.

"Whatever the reason," Lukas continued, "he changed his plans. If he wanted to sell you out, he had enough time to do so. Maybe he discovered that you were worth far more. Or because it went against his own moral tenets. Zuken does seem like that kind of guy. Or . . ." He looked at Tanya. "He discovered a better use for you than just handing you over."

"Like what?" asked Tanya, dumbfounded.

"Like him," said Solana. Everyone looked at her. This was the first time that the skinwalker had said something throughout this entire conversation. "Isn't that right?"

Lukas met her eyes. "Yes. He found the 'Outsider,' and the 'Outsider' made it very clear that he was on Tanya's side."

Tanya stiffened.

"Whatever it was," said Maude, "it was significant enough that he hid all his findings about Tanya, and let her stay at the mansion where the Out—I mean, where *you*—were."

"Until Ultaf found out," said Tanya. "But how . . ."

"The 'how' is not relevant," said Lukas. "The fact is that he's found out and he attacked Zuken's mansion. We were in the borderland for quite some time. It's possible they tried to talk things through before it came to this. But what confuses me is why this man killed all these people, destroyed the mansion, and abducted Zuken. I mean, unless he's harboring some misapprehension that you are Zuken's lover—"

Tanya glared at him.

"Just saying," he said, chuckling at how easy it was to rile her up. "Because I don't see any other reason why capturing Zuken would be a good idea. Torturing him, yes. But even in that case, destroying his mansion seems like an amateurish thing to do. I mean if I were Zuken and Ultaf had just destroyed my precious mansion, I'd keep my mouth shut just out of spite. No, the more practical thing here would've been to capture someone or something that Zuken values."

He and Tanya looked at each other.

And then they looked at Maude.

"Uh," said the oni. "We haven't heard anything about Elena. Or Olfric. We don't know if they are alive or dead."

Lukas scratched his head. "Still doesn't make sense. If they're dead or fatally injured by any chance, Ultaf Shimizu loses even more leverage to make Zuken talk."

"So, it's possible that Elena's—" Maude began.

"No," said Tanya, her eyes narrowed. "Elena's alive. Not sure where, but she's alive."

Lukas cocked his head. "And how do you know that?"

"Because Zuken faced Ultaf head-on," Tanya pointed out. "The igriotts attacked the residents on the hill, but the actual army surrounded Zuken's mansion, and Ultaf attacked him first. They even chatted for a while. Tell me that's not Zuken delaying things on purpose. He had to know he couldn't win. And he would've escaped if he thought it was possible."

He frowned. "That . . . might just be true. There had to be some reason to delay Ultaf like that."

"Elena's alive," said Tanya.

"But Ultaf doesn't know that," Lukas pointed out. "He attacked the hill, killed everyone, destroyed the mansion, and captured Zuken. For all he knows, everyone's dead. Unless he thinks there's someone out there that will come to free Zuken, it makes no sense. The entire thing becomes . . . pointless. Malice for the sake of malice."

Like the igriotts he employed. Just what kind of maniac were they up against?

"I think you're looking at this the wrong way, Lukas."

He looked at Tanya.

"This isn't a demand or a way to get someone to react and rescue Zuken. This is punishment. Ultaf found him guilty, sentenced him, and destroyed everything he held dear. It's as simple as that."

Lukas stared at her in disbelief.

"You do not know what kind of man he is," said Tanya. "My grandfather shaped him in his own image. Ultaf isn't difficult to understand once you've figured out his logic. He truly believes that as the Lord of a Sacred Eight clan, the world is his, and hence, he embodies the greatest authority there. The strong stand over the weak and make the rules, and as one of the Sacred Eight, he stands over all and holds final say in everything. If there's something that attracts his interest, he'll address it as he sees fit, regardless of the destruction that might happen in his wake. And if someone does something he doesn't like, he is, in his own mind, obligated to serve as judge, jury, and executioner."

She took a deep breath. "Whether he allows them to live is merely a part of his self-imposed duty as the judge and jury. All Zuken had to do was make sure he didn't take up the third role."

"Hence, the capture," Maude surmised.

"Yes."

"That's not a person," said Lukas, frowning. "That's a deranged psychopath with a god complex."

Tanya smiled thinly. "You only say that because you haven't met my grandfather. Ultaf is his shadow. He's been acting as grandfather's stand-in for so long, he truly believes himself to be an extension of the man himself. Take grandfather away and Ultaf is no one. Even Olfric can defeat him without much effort, I'd say."

Lukas filed that information away. "And . . . your grandfather?"

Her lips thinned. "Mujin Shimizu believes that violence is the solution to every problem in the universe. If you cannot solve something with violence, you are clearly not using enough violence."

"You're oddly familiar with his way of thinking."

"I had to be," said Tanya without skipping a beat. "I was his Sword for four entire years.

Despite himself, Lukas swallowed. And here he was thinking that his trials were at an end, at least for a while.

"My grandfather is a warlord, Lukas," said Tanya. "I doubt there's anyone in the entirety of the Southeast stronger than he is. And he is Sacred Eight. Nothing Zuken can personally pull off has any standing against him, except—"

"Except?"

Tanya bit her lip. "Well, there's the fact that his father is the current Earth King, Trestan Banksi."

Lukas was floored. Zuken's father was the Earth King? One of the five elemental Kings in the Empire?

"Is that why he holds all that power and connections? Why even the Overseer—"

"No," said Maude, shaking her head. "Zuken is many things, but dependent on his father's name, he's not. Everything he has, he has gained himself. It is possible he's estranged from his clan."

"Estranged enough that someone can casually massacre his people, destroy his mansion, and capture him?"

Maude wrung her hands.

"And everyone knows this?"

"Of course," said Maude. "The Earth King is the most powerful authority in the entire South."

"So, it could be that the Shimizu didn't kill Zuken but captured him because killing him would attract the ire of the King?"

"Possible."

"It's a bit more complicated than that," said Tanya softly. She met his eyes. "You see, Grandfather is on very good terms with the Earth King. One might even call them friends."

"And knowing all that, they attacked Zuken. Obviously, they thought they'd get away with it, which means either the Earth King doesn't care for him, or worse, holds disdain for him."

"And despite knowing all that, Zuken stood his ground," murmured Maude, looking up at him. "Why?"

"I don't know," admitted Tanya. "It makes no sense. Lukas and I were stranded in the borderland. No one, not even the svartalfars, should know that we are here in the Desert. All Zuken needed to do was tell him the truth. He didn't need to face my brother's forces."

"Hold on!" said Lukas in surprise. "Ultaf Shimizu is your brother?!"

"Yes," said Tanya, giving him a confused look. "I told you, I think. Back then."

He shook his head. "Must have slipped my mind. But . . . wow. That's some serious familial dysfunction right there."

Tanya snorted. "That's putting it lightly. Ultaf hated that I was the heiress, despite years of trying and failing to bind Ezzeron to myself. He accused my father of playing favorites, and always emulated Grandfather. If Grandfather said that Amaterasu herself was the goddess of the night, the only thing Ultaf would think would be to sentence anyone who claimed otherwise to be put to death for spreading such heresy."

Lukas exhaled, and then another thought came to him.

"What—what about the Llaisy Kingdom? Don't you have a shogun there, too? Now- something?"

"Naowa," said Tanya, giving him an unamused smile. "Shogun Naowa. Like the Shimizu and the Banksi, the Naowa are also part of the Sacred Eight. He's the son of the Ether King, Avensigg Naowa. Much like Grandfather, he too was rejected by his father's kami. Unlike Grandfather, he still has two generations before the Empire gives up hope on him."

"And one Sacred Eight member can just plough into another's territory, cause this kind of damage, and walk out without a care?"

Tanya looked tongue-tied. "Not if he has significant evidence of guilt on Zuken's part."

"And what could this evidence be?"

For once, none of them had any answer.

"Perhaps," said Solana, "you'd be better off thinking about your next moves, instead of pondering over evidence that might or might not exist? Without your support in Haviskali, I imagine things will be different."

"Is that why you gave me that text earlier?" demanded Tanya. "Because you think I'll just stay here?"

"Will you not?" asked the skinwalker. "Here you can be amongst people that respect you for what you are. In time, you might even rise to become an acceptable substitute for the Empress. Unless, of course, you wish to return to the Asukan world, be reviled as a Sinner, and be hunted by your own clan."

Tanya pursed her lips. "Guess the attack on Zuken fits into your goals, perfectly."

Solana's smile widened. "It is . . . how do you put it? Serendipitous?"

Not quite, thought Lukas. Solana knew where he was. No, where he and Tanya both were. She obviously had kept track of them, with him being the Outsider of legend, and Tanya being the vessel of the empress. She also knew of his deal with the svartalfars and that he had been to a borderland recently. It wasn't too far a stretch to speculate that she knew exactly when they had left for the borderland, and the fact that Zuken had been attacked right then felt far too convenient. If either of them had been present at Zuken's mansion, things could've become incredibly complicated.

He thought back to what Maude had told him, about how Solana had arranged for that Trial by Combat with Quonnan, an extremist who had been getting a bit too vocal. She had both ensured that Quonnan was removed from the equation and cemented his status as the vaunted Outsider in a single move.

It would be just like her, to take Zuken out like that. She had the motive and the resources, and her modus operandi also fit the bill.

The only real question was—

How did she convince Ultaf Shimizu, one of the Sacred Eight and a man with a god complex, to dance to her tune?

He wanted to voice his opinions out loud. But he didn't. That would yield nothing. The idea that Solana, a skinwalker and leader of the yokai, was secretly in cohorts with one of the Sacred Eight, was downright hilarious to even consider.

So why did the idea feel more likely the more he dwelled on it?

CHAPTER 23

FROSTBITTEN

Lukas?"

"Hm?"

"I've been patient so far, but even I have my limits."

"What do you mean?" he asked, looking up from the tome in his hands to Tanya who was sitting on the bed next to him, giving him an annoyed glare.

"I know exactly how you can get with a new book, but something tells me you haven't been reading so much as composing plans to take on something reckless."

"What if I told you it's a good book?"

"That would be believable if you hadn't spent the last twenty minutes without turning a page." Her face softened. "Something is clearly amiss if it's distracting you this much. I thought you agreed we would no longer keep secrets from each other."

Technically, it was she who had said it. He hadn't voiced an opinion on the matter himself.

"Everyone has secrets, Tanya. Even you." He shook his head. For the briefest moment, he contemplated ending the conversation right there but thought better of it. Tanya was his partner. The one person who had been by his side since the beginning. Well, at least after that disastrous first encounter, that is. Even when working for Zuken, she had never quite chosen his side over Lukas's. Kept secrets, yes. Tried to manipulate him into doing things, yes, but never to hamper his own goals. If anything, she had kept his secrets.

Just like he had kept hers.

"This doesn't really involve you." *Not directly, anyway.* He didn't say that last bit out loud. "I'm just making some plans. Nothing to worry about, but it might mean I have to leave for some time."

"For how long?"

That surprised him. He had honestly expected a bit more resistance than that.

"Maybe two weeks, give or take a couple of days? And so long as things go right, no one will be the wiser . . . or in any danger," he said vaguely.

"And if they go wrong?"

He smiled dryly. "Well . . . I'm hoping it won't. And if it does, then I know you're on my side to help me out."

Tanya exhaled.

"What?"

"Nothing. Just realized what you're up to."

That was surprising. "You do?"

"Yes. Previously I thought it might have something to do with your anomaly nature, but I don't think that would've caused you to leave this place."

"I venture out into the anomaly pits often," said Lukas, wondering why he felt the need to defend himself.

"Yes, but I know you. You said you'd leave, not just stay some hours away from here. And I doubt you'd find anything to eat in those parts for the two weeks you mentioned."

Perceptive, wasn't she?

"No, the only other thing that's happened recently is the attack on Zuken. And you've had that same look on your face since then. That leads me to conclude that you're about to engage in something questionable. Maybe you're planning on dealing with someone who's neither ally, enemy, nor particularly trustworthy, and yet, someone you think it's necessary to deal with right now, despite everything that's happening. Or rather, a deal that you have little power to change in the first place."

Lukas arched an eyebrow, wondering how it was possible for someone to be so vague and yet so accurate at the same time. She had hit the bullseye with the first problem—his bargain with Frost, his worries about how Fimbulwinter would affect Tanya, and his desire to figure out what was truly happening with Zuken and the Shimizu. The problem was that Frost was perfectly happy to play the long game, and the second was being played in the background with none of them being any wiser. And by the time he figured out Solana's machinations, it just might be a bit too late. On the other hand, it was equally possible that Solana had arranged things in a way to force Lukas out of the picture, so that she might get Tanya all to herself and attempt something unsavory.

And the worst part? He could make some headway on both issues by one simple action—talking to Frost.

Again.

"I'm just playing this one close to the chest, that's all."

Tanya pursed her lips. "You can't tell me you're missing the hypocrisy of your actions, Lukas. You've gone out of your way to address my problems but you keep your own to yourself. That's not exactly what being a partner is about."

He ran his fingers through his hair. There was no way of mentioning this to Tanya without actively bringing her into this mess. She was finally getting her chance to achieve some normalcy, and even with the attack on Zuken's place and his capture, the Shimizu could never come for her, not unless she took preemptive action. Maybe that was exactly what Solana was aiming for, and to be honest, part of him even wanted things to stay that way.

But it would be unfair to Zuken.

On the other hand, if they tried to get him back, assuming that was possible, it would mean throwing all normalcy out of the window and preparing for perhaps the greatest danger they had ever faced so far. And this time, there would be no Inanna to help him out. This time, the opponent wouldn't be restrained by any limitations.

"Tell me you're not thinking of trying to free Zuken."

Lukas grimaced and instantly cursed himself for the reaction.

"By Wind," said Tanya. "You're . . . you cannot possibly be—"

"Be what? Cowardly enough to just look away as that man gets tortured for protecting you? You want me to be here with you, where it's safe."

Her eyes flashed with real anger. The air between them grew physically colder. "Think carefully," she said in a very quiet voice, "before you call me a coward."

The irritation within him wanted to spill out on her. But she deserved better. He stuffed it down and lifted one hand in silent apology.

Tanya nodded, mollified, and some of the tension evaporated. "I was going to say that acting like that will only lead to trouble. We have no idea what state he is in now, or the conditions of his capture. Or the situation with Elena and Olfric. Yes, I know some of the locations where he might have been taken, but acting rashly like that won't help him."

"We need information," he said at last.

"We do," she agreed. "And I don't think Solana will be very helpful in that regard. If Zuken is safe and returned, it will only hurt her chances."

Yes, thought Lukas. *Which is why she's one of the potential culprits behind this mess.*

"Solana will do her best to ensure that Grandfather never gets to know where I am," said Tanya softly. "I doubt even she'd be able to face a warlord's might. And even if Zuken tells them about me, he knows that I got stranded in the borderland. With you. The svartalfars know that. There's no way anyone would know that we're here."

"Unless they have a spy here," said Lukas softly.

Tanya went very quiet. "You think there is one?"

He shrugged. "No species is completely united, Tanya. Not even the yokai. Remember the different factions Maude mentioned? There's got to be *someone* around who hates me being here, or you, or the way Solana runs things. All it takes is possessing a bremetan body, skipping out of the Desert, and letting the Shimizu know about our whereabouts."

Tanya stiffened.

"Also, there's something else you're forgetting," he said gravely. "If they're really torturing Zuken to that degree, they won't just get information on you."

"They'll know about you too," said Tanya, going white. "By Wind, that would—"

"An Outsider and a Sinner. Imagine if the Cobalt Army comes after us. Apart from trying to access the Haze and escaping, I don't see a way past that. Not unless . . ." He clenched his fists. "Not unless we take some preemptive action and free Zuken. Not because it's necessary, but also because it's the right thing to do. That man helped both of us, regardless of his motivations. I don't know about you, but I'm not going to give him an excuse to think that I betrayed that trust."

"No," said Tanya softly. "You're right. But . . . what can we do?"

And that was the million-dollar question. What could they do?

"You're a World. You've got all those prototypes. And you've been a diplomat in your past life. If you had to pick an offensive route, what would you do?"

His answer was short and to the point. "I'd launch a preemptive attack on Mujin Shimizu and try to kill him."

His casual statement didn't sink in immediately, but a second later, Tanya froze, staring at him, flabbergasted.

"You—you can't be serious."

"It's not as impossible as you think. Mujin is the top dog. The god that casts righteous judgment and punishes the guilty. Why would he ever have reason to expect an attack?"

"You realize he's still a warlord, right?"

"Yes. *Just* a warlord," said Lukas, thinking about a certain fiery demon he had encountered not long ago.

"Just a—" Tanya stilled. "*No!*" She grabbed him by his shirt. "Please tell me that you aren't even thinking of that monster—"

Lukas laughed. "I'm not. That was a natural-born Ifrit King. Even if by some fluke of nature, I managed to siphon it, my body would instantly vaporize the moment I did so. The Ifrit King is Living Flame. Not even the anomaly within me can protect me from that. But . . ." He paused, glancing at the pendant hanging down his neck. "If I were to get some time to myself, then I could . . . elevate myself. Enough to cause substantial damage."

"Damage Mujin Shimizu?"

He met her eyes. "Yes."

Tanya just stared at him.

"I need you to do something for me, Tanya," he said, grabbing her arms and looking her in the eyes. "While I'm gone, I need you to take Solana's lessons to heart. I want you to give one hundred percent to absorbing what she's teaching you. You've got to learn how to control Meynte's power and make it yours. Can you do that?"

Tanya looked hesitant and a little afraid but nodded. "Lukas, what are you planning?"

He stood up and began pacing across the room. "Back on Earth, we have a game called Chess. It's a game of strategy. Logic. You have pieces representing two armies—pawns, bishops, rooks, knights . . . you know, the usual. The objective is to try to get to the other side of the board and kill the enemy king."

"Sounds ruthless."

He paused and chuckled. "Most people think that the right way is to kill the pawns, the knights, the rooks, the queen, every single piece you can find and destroy until you reach the king. That's who you kill last to end the game."

"Seems like a sensible tactic."

He frowned and started moving again. "Yes, and six months ago, I'd have said the same. But the more I think about it, the more I think it's the other way around. If you kill everyone else and then kill the king, there's no one else to play with. The game is over. But say you kill off the king before everyone else and take its place. Lo and behold, you have an entire army to command. For a new game."

Tanya narrowed her eyes. "Is that what you're—"

"This world isn't very different from mine, Tanya," he said, looking at her. "People aren't permanent. Only positions are. I'm all for fighting this war, but only if we get something in the end."

"And what do you want? Kill Mujin and absorb his kami?"

He laughed. "I'm afraid you've only just scratched the surface of my ambitions. But there's one other thing that's troubling me. And I'm not sure how to talk about it without messing things up."

Tanya laughed. "How about just giving it to me straight and letting me worry about the mess?"

He furrowed his temples. "Remember when you first sat on the throne? Solana called you 'Tsurara.' No, she was *convinced* you were Tsurara."

Tanya frowned. "Yes, I remember that."

Lukas stood up and began pacing. "I talked to Maude about it. And a couple of other yokai I'm acquainted with. Ryu, for one. He trained me in combat using Pyromancy the first time . . . Anyway, the point is, Tsurara was one of the leaders who ruled the yokai. She and Solana were equals—*friends*, if Solana's to be believed—and from what Maude told me, her political opposite. Headstrong and impulsive versus Solana's craftiness. Meynte's descendant, and extremely powerful. The extremists loved her."

"Sounds like a rebel."

He briefly thought about the way Solana had removed Quonnan from the picture without any heavy-handedness. And if Tsurara was the leader back then . . .

"I'm not sure of the details," he admitted. "But Tsurara and her army attacked Shogun Straff. Some of the yokai say it was to capture Cyffnar, but honestly, that makes no sense. Why make so much noise at a place where you have two Sacred Eight clans nearby, when you can choose the fringe kingdoms in the southwest like Baramunz?"

"I think I know what you're talking about. The Wind King was famous for ending the Winter Witch, a powerful deviant with ice-based powers. It's a tale every child in the kingdom knows. The Wind King fought her in the Western Expanse, and the place is a barren land even to this date. Nothing grows there. Absolutely nothing. The locals believe it's cursed."

Much like the Desert, Lukas thought.

"Tanya, I've got a couple of questions, some half-baked ideas running in my head. And as much as I want to talk about them with you, it's gonna hurt you. Maybe even make you angry."

"I trust you."

The way she said it without the slightest inflection in her tone almost made him flinch.

He exhaled. "During your entire time at the Shimizu compound—before you were kidnapped, that is—do you remember ever meeting anyone strange? Another woman with white hair like yours, perhaps? Maybe a sudden attack, or an otherworldly reaction? Something that scared you so much that you forced yourself to ignore that it even happened in the first place?"

She shook her head. "No. Never. The only place I was allowed to go was to see Ezzeron, you know, chained inside his vault. And even then, my father would accompany me. I know Solana thinks that I'm Tsurara—"

"Or that she fused with you—"

She shook her head. "Trust me. I'm not an oni. Maude makes no distinction between the vanir and the yurei. The only memories I have are my own. Yes, being in the Eternal Light always dampened my Frost abilities, but that was all." She grabbed his hands. "Believe me. I'm telling you the truth."

A bitter taste filled his mouth. He had wanted—*hoped*—that it would not come to this.

"What are you thinking?" she asked him, the tremor in her voice vivid.

"Just thinking of what you told me about your experiences after you were captured by your grandfather. He called you a beast and claimed that his endeavor had succeeded. You yourself told me that your grandfather wanted you as a medium to breed Everfrost in the Shimizu bloodline. That means that there is definitely a connection between you and Tsurara, or as you put it, the Winter Witch."

She turned pale. "You don't think—"

He exhaled, meeting her horror-struck eyes. "Do you remember anything about your mother? I mean, is there a possibility that—"

"That Tsurara was my mother? That I'm the daughter of the Winter Witch. I—"

Lukas didn't let her finish. He grabbed her, pulled her to his chest, and held her tight. Tanya shook, but not a single sound escaped her throat.

Tanya had intimated that she always thought her mother might have deviant blood in her. It begged the question of why her father, then heir of the clan, would even have a daughter with her and give her recognition, but given Tanya's abnormally high ECR, he could at least understand that reasoning. But if she really was Tsurara, Meynte's descendant, then it definitely explained a few things.

"Better?" he asked after a long time.

"I hate this," she murmured. 'I absolutely hate this. I-I always knew that my Frost powers must have come from my mother. I thought she was a deviant. I thought that maybe that was why my father never spoke of her. But—but if she was the Winter Witch then . . ."

She pulled away.

"The Wind King didn't kill the Winter Witch," said Tanya softly. "He defeated her, and he experimented on her. He—and then my grandfather—" She began shaking again. "The soldiers would always bring in prisoners. Half-breeds from different races—alfs, svartalfar, even jotunns. All of them were females, and they looked bremetan. I once asked about them, and Grandfather told me they were deviants, and it was the Empire's policy to capture them. That they had been doing it for decades. But I never saw them leave. They'd be imprisoned, deep down inside the dungeons. Sometimes I'd hear shrieks, but I learned to ignore them. Grandfather's word was law."

The connection was obvious to Lukas. "You think they were trying to—"

Her eyes were blazing with barely suppressed emotion. "I know what they were doing. They were trying to breed Everfrost into the Shimizu bloodline. They were making her possess those hapless women in the hopes of breeding them."

"I don't think that's true," said Lukas, feeling incredibly sick. "I—I asked around. Ryu told me that possessed bremetan bodies do not last long. Especially for the elemental types. Ryu himself has changed close to ten bodies in the past. He told me that Tsurara mostly existed in her yokai form, except when she left the Desert, because Everfrost would instantly kill whatever host she possessed. The only way to make it work would be to . . ."

"Make an oni," said Tanya, her eyes wide open in horror. "That means all those women—and my father—"

The rest of the words died in her throat, as her skin became ash-white, and her hands clenched into fists. In fact, she seemed to be absolutely frozen in place, unable to move under her own volition. Tanya—who had always been so strong, who had instantly jumped back despite the harrowing experience with Meynte, who was a survivor, who had gone through immeasurable obstacles and still emerged herself—now looked like an absolute wreck, like she had woken up from a nightmare.

"Tanya?" Lukas himself paled. "Tanya? What's wrong?"

She didn't respond. Instead, she remained frozen in place. Her shallow breathing turned into deep gasps, as if her eyes were seeing something that no one else could.

"It can't be . . ." she murmured. "It can't be true. It can't be true. It can't—"

"Tanya, what do you—" Lukas tried to touch her, but the moment he did, he recoiled. Her skin was colder than ice, so cold that it was *scalding*. Just that momentary touch dragged a massive amount of lifeforce out of him, turning his hand blue.

"All this time, I thought that he—that at least he would—all this time—"

She kept repeating gibberish as if validating a horrible truth that she didn't want to know but couldn't escape from.

Lukas had no option. With Blob on his arms, he held Tanya, instantly feeling Blob go "blank" the moment it came in contact with her skin. Frost was beginning to grow on the metal, but he didn't let her go. "Tanya. It's okay. Whatever happens, we'll take care of it together. You're safe. Nothing bad can get to you. It's not your fault."

He didn't know what was going on or why she was reacting like this. He grabbed her shoulders tightly and forced her to look directly into his eyes. Her breathing was uneven, her pupils contracting and expanding so fast that he could barely process it. She looked so utterly helpless that he couldn't even reconcile her with the strong woman he knew.

He acted on instinct.

"*Frost,*" he said, channeling power into his voice. "*If you can hear me, Tanya needs your help. Get her under control.*" He paused, and then added. "*Please.*"

What followed was one of the most unsettling experiences he had ever had. Her eyes changed. They were utterly empty, as if someone had scooped out twin holes into her skull only to fill them with glass spheres.

He might as well have been trading gazes with a corpse.

And then a sob escaped her throat.

The Frost shattered, and Tanya all but fell into his arms. Her entire body shook and spasmed, and she sobbed into his shoulder. Lukas just held her against his chest and let her cry her heart out. For the second time since leaving the borderland, a raw hatred was stirring within him. A blind wrath that would do more harm than good if he were left to his own devices. Solana, Maude, Meynte and even Frost had seen exactly what he could do, what boundaries he could tear apart when operating from that clouded state of judgment. He closed down every doorway and window in his head to shut out the gale that was suddenly whipping up in his heart. He had to stay focused. He couldn't afford to let the sudden tide of emotion drown his ability to think clearly.

After what seemed like an eternity, she stopped sobbing. The entire time, he had just held her, saying nothing, expecting nothing, just gently running his fingers down her hair to her back.

"Feeling better now?" he asked at last.

Tanya nodded into his shoulder.

"Want to talk about it?"

She shook her head.

"Don't worry, whatever it is, it will be fine."

"Won't," she mumbled.

"It will be," he promised her again. "Now rest. Go to sleep. I'll just—"

She clutched his shirt as if her life depended on it. "Don't. Please. Stay."

He pursed his lips and nodded. "I'll stay."

Slowly, she began to get her histrionic breathing under control. Her grip on his shirt grew weaker, and her pulse began to fall. The coldness emanating from her skin had already disappeared, and he could feel her breathing softly against his neck.

She was asleep.

Which meant it was the perfect time to do what needed to be done.

"Frost," he whispered in her ear. "It's time we had a talk."

The reaction was instantaneous.

Tanya's sleeping form stiffened, and a familiar glacial aura erupted out of her. Her cadaverous white eyes, alabaster skin, and poisonously lovely lips were just inches away from his face and twisted in amusement. Then she grabbed his chin and kissed him full on the lips.

"Whispering my name in your lover's ear? Why, Outsider! That was such a romantic gesture."

Lukas rolled his eyes. "I summoned you because I need some answers."

Her lips slowly spread into a smile, which in turn, became a quiet, rolling laugh. She let her head fall back with it. She sat there, laughing at him for ten long seconds, and Lukas felt his face heat up with irrational embarrassment.

"Stars," she murmured, "you're adorable."

"And you're a psychotic murderhobo," said Lukas. "And now that we've agreed upon that, mind if I dispense with the usual song and dance and get started? Tanya needs her rest."

"Ah, the frail dear," she mocked. "Too shocked to realize that her dear father isn't the saint she thought he was. Then again, she always was weak. *Pathetic.* Just like her worthless father."

Lukas cocked his head. "Her father—"

"Was a failure, a rapist, and a murderer. Just like his own father. Their hands dripped with the blood of innocents. Father and son raped countless possessed women, just because they wanted the power of Everfrost so badly. That girl that you care for so much is the result of those dastardly actions. The 'miracle child.'"

She threw her head back and let out a scornful laugh.

"That's not Tanya's fault. She's innocent in all this."

"Of course," spat Frost. "Innocent. Or should I say, spineless."

"Why? Because she didn't give in to her vengeance and become a murderer?"

"The world runs on murder, Outsider. Surely you know that by now? The greatest murderers are the greatest heroes. Morality is but an excuse of the weak. You want pity for her? Look somewhere else."

That, right there, was the reason why he would never allow Frost and Inanna to ever have a direct conversation. He didn't think the world could take it.

"Does that mean Tsurara is still alive somewhere?"

Frost shook her head. "There can only be one bearer of Everfrost at a time, Outsider. The moment the girl manifested the power, Tsurara lost it. She faded soon after, just like her ancestors. So long as Tanya breathes, those that seek the power of Everfrost will forever hunt her."

That didn't make him feel any better.

"I guess that can't be helped," he said at last. Clearing his throat, he said. "I am in need of your help. I might have to leave for a while, and I do not trust Solana. I need you to protect Tanya from her machinations."

Frost lifted a fingertip to her lips as though she needed it to hold in more laughter. Then she smiled again. "And why must I do that?"

"We made an accord," Lukas stressed. "You swore you'd help me when I needed it, and you'd give me all the information I need to get Inanna back."

"Uh uh uh!" She wagged her pointer finger. "It doesn't work like that. It is true I am obligated to answer your call, but nowhere in our arrangement am I compelled to aid you. Yes, we bargained that I would provide you with the knowledge to bring your dead goddess back, but nowhere did you mention a timeframe for that aid."

She laughed again.

Lukas clenched his fists. Why had he not thought of that? "We had a bargain—"

Her lips slithered into a smile again. "Do not fret, Outsider. I will aid you, but at your personal cost. Nothing is free."

"It never was," he shot back. "I owe you two obligations in return for your aid. And now you're trying to ditch them."

"Then you should've been more thorough," she mocked him, letting out a wicked little laugh. "Do not mistake, Outsider. It's only because we have a bargain that I'm even willing to play with you," said Frost, giving him a condescending look. "It's like you said. That this body and its owner are worth something in your eyes is the only reason you agreed to it. But that isn't completely true, is it? You live and breathe for your goddess, and for her, there is no stone you'll leave unturned, nothing sacred you will not defile, if it means you can get her back." She licked her lips. "Without hesitation."

Lukas felt his jaw get a little tighter. He didn't agree with her words but didn't feel the need to correct her assumptions either. "And so, you'd take advantage and demand whatever services you want from me in return for information?"

"Nothing so trite," said Frost, waving her hand airily. "I have big plans for you. Ruining them for some petty benefits is so not my style."

She idly stretched out her hand. Frost arose from her palm and began forming into an ornate ice dagger, its sharp tip resting on her smooth skin, held in place by invisible hands.

"Then what do you want?"

She watched him, her eyes sparkling. "I cannot ask for a claim over you because the weakling has it. As does this goddess. I know a claimed territory when I see one. But let me see . . ." She tapped a fingernail against her lips and said, "How about a question for a question? Does that sound fair enough to you?"

"That's a fairly broad area. You could ask me my weaknesses or my secret plans, for all I know."

"Again, nothing so trite," Frost said. "I am only trying to understand you, Lukas Aguilar."

Lukas crossed his arms. "Why this sudden interest?"

"Isn't it obvious? You're a soulcrafter. An anomaly. A spring of Creation. I am the avatar of Everfrost. Fimbulwinter. The seed of annihilation. We are opposites, you and I. Civilizations will come and go, gods will arise and fall, but we shall dance for eternity. No doubt you are using the opportunity to learn everything you can about me. Is it not natural that I would like to do the same?"

"Fancy words," said Lukas. "But they don't mean anything. Yes, Tanya has bits of Meynte's powers, and yes, I'm studying her growth. But it's not like she'll undergo some massive transformation overnight. For all I know, she'll become something slightly different but still, unremarkable."

"Then surely you won't mind *me* engaging in a little banter that yields unremarkable results at best?"

Lukas gritted his teeth. "Fine. But I reserve the right to stay silent on certain topics."

"So long as you answer another question in its stead."

He thought for a moment and then nodded. "Provided that you will help Tanya in my absence. Immediately. If it is within your power, I want you to help her master Everfrost. I'm not willing to accept anything less."

"Absolutely," she said with a grin. "It will be enjoyable to see that prissy little weakling toss her pride aside and beg me to help her."

Lukas inwardly groaned. He supposed this was Frost playing nice. He'd need to stick to whatever victories he could achieve.

"Fine. We're in agreement."

Frost leaned toward him, her expression placid and enigmatic. Slowly, she raised her right hand and touched his left cheek. "How . . . undaunted." She met his eyes. "Fine. Ask your question."

"Nothing I've read in the texts has anything to say about the resurrection of gods. So, how am I going to bring Inanna back?"

Frost shrugged. "Anything is possible, Outsider. Isn't that what Potential is all about?

"But we aren't talking about Potential, are we? We're talking about Taboo. The antithesis of Potential, of Truth."

"Yes!" said Frost, a childlike eagerness in her voice. "Yes, we are. Infinite are the ways of Creation, but equally endless are the ways to revert it back to the Formless."

"But we aren't reverting her to the Formless," he argued. "We're bringing something into Existence that didn't exist before."

"Do not be deluded," chided Frost. "Just because she doesn't exist now doesn't mean she didn't exist in the past. Whatever world you came from, it is obviously an offshoot of the Great Progenitor. And if your goddess existed there, then she did so here as well."

Lukas quietly doubted her confidence. Inanna had been very clear and thorough in the spell she had cast back then. She was confident that there was nothing in this World, in this universe, that had any relation, any connection whatsoever, to herself and her pantheon. And that included her own

Truth. Still, the spell had been incomplete, and it was always possible that she might have missed something. There was no harm in at least testing Frost's path.

"Alright," he said. "How does it help me get Inanna back?"

"The pieces are all in front of you. You have only to assemble them."

Lukas cocked his head. "Are you being intentionally vague? Why can't you just tell me what the hell you're talking about?"

She frowned and studied him. "What do you know of gods, Outsider? Of divinity? Of Truths and emperors? How does one rise to one?"

Lukas frowned, thinking about that question. How did one become an emperor? And eventually a god? The last time he had delved into such thoughts, he had been tossed around in a maelstrom of knowledge, perceptions, images, and memories that were too many and too powerful to make any sense of. This time, it was like dipping his hand into boiling water. Like a hot knife cutting into his conscience threatening to overpower his sanity. He struggled with it. Tried to wrestle it back. Even with Alpha Condition, it was an uphill struggle. His mind broiled under the strain, writhing in tormented agony. Something that wasn't him and yet a part of him surged within, swimming in his veins and saturating every inch of his body. It was all he could do to prevent it from leaking through.

Meanwhile, Frost just watched him like a hawk.

Then he spoke. "*The first step is to become a Pathforger. To forge a path that does not exist, and travel along it, until it reaches the destination. The World will take notice of him, and he must suffer through the constraints of existing Truths, He must have the strength to hold the weight of Existence upon his shoulders. For only then can he be the vessel of this new Truth. For only then, can he be called emperor.*"

Lukas didn't realize it, but his eyes were glowing an electric green. Images of Inanna—not the supreme queen but rather as a mortal woman—flooded his mind. He saw her walking through that valley of flames and knew that the power she was looking for, the power she desired, was not a Rule to Bind to the World but one to bind it to herself. It was the absolute height of selfishness, a greed so intense that even the Universe itself felt like an opponent. Something to steal from.

"You're right," said Frost at last, an enigmatic smile on her face. "An empress binds a Truth to herself. So long as she exists, she anchors it to the World. But should she choose to share it, she can forge a pact with the Greater World. She'd hand the Truth over to the World and become a goddess. Impossibly powerful, absolutely terrifying, but no longer the owner of the Truth. She'd become its keeper, an authority-wielder, and in exchange, transcend to Divinity."

"And when that goddess perishes, the Truth becomes part of the World System forever, and her authority is bound to one of her relics," said Lukas.

"A path that could leave someone else to the empty throne of the fallen goddess."

Lukas suppressed the urge to touch the pendant hanging around his neck.

It was a relic. But it wasn't Inanna's relic.

She had gained it by killing another god.

The power of absolute comprehension, which only she could use—Lukas was merely able to utilize a tiny aspect of that infinite power to speak, read, and understand every language out there.

Yet, it was also what had stored Inanna's reflection within itself for time immemorial. It was what had harvested what little faith she could gain from Earth. It was what had started all this in the first place.

"I do not understand you, Outsider. You speak like you know things, yet you flounder around like a blind man."

Lukas frowned. He was missing something. But what?

"Why don't you tell me what I'm missing?"

"You know of her Truth. It is what acts as the seal keeping me from fully manifesting. It is what forces me to bargain with you. Use it to connect with the universe. You are an anomaly. Surely you can connect with the Great Progenitor? Create a link between the power that still acts on the girl and its source. Once you do that, the rest will be easy."

Lukas's heart dropped.

After all this time, after so many bargains, *this* was what she was telling him?

"It won't work."

Frost arched an eyebrow.

"You're suggesting a scrying ritual. Creating a link between two connected points of energy, and then track its origin."

"I am," said Frost, frowning. "But you already know that."

"Yes!" said Lukas, his frustration now beginning to show. "I've always known that. It won't work."

"Why? How can you be so sure?"

"Because Inanna did it! She fucking did it in front of me. And it didn't work."

"Maybe she missed it. Perhaps there wasn't enough—"

"Energy?" Lukas shot back, his voice cracking with emotion. "I used the entire power of this vast underground anomaly. The entire energy drawn away from the Crypt of Fiendish Worms into that spell. And not just once. No single spell can span the entire universe in a single attempt. She cast it thousands of times, in the hope of finding anything that resonated with herself—with her Truth, with her pantheon, with her . . . *anything*."

Frost had a strange look on her face.

"She found nothing," finished Lukas with a cold, grave sigh. "Nothing at all."

"But that . . ." said Frost, looking absolutely flummoxed, "That isn't possible. I can sense the Rule that she bound upon this girl. The power that makes up the seal can only be a Truth. A law unto itself. Nothing else could hold the connection back."

"She told me that one of two things happened. The first, is that all of this—me, my world, me coming here—was just a lie, an illusion cast upon reality."

"And the other?"

"That everything that happened was real. Inanna's Truth existed. And *exists*, through that seal within Tanya. But someone went to extreme lengths to erase not just her Truth, but her entire pantheon and everything associated with it out of Time itself."

The look of utter incredulity on the avatar of Fimbulwinter's face didn't make him feel better in the slightest.

CHAPTER 24

Taboo

This pendant," said Lukas, clutching the ornament in his right hand. "This belonged to Inanna. Yes, it is a relic but not hers. I'm quite certain that it contains another Truth, one that I'm almost certain I understand, if not completely. The real Inanna, the Supreme Queen of the Sumerian Pantheon, held many such relics: the Ax of Marduk, a blade that ruptures the World in a single strike; the Opal Ring of Bau, the Endless Night; the bracelets of Gula, the goddess of rejuvenation; among others."

Frost blinked owlishly. "That's . . . impressive."

Lukas couldn't help but smirk. "She was known as the Butcher of Gods and Beasts for a reason."

"A war goddess," she concluded. "I should have seen that coming."

Technically, she was the goddess of Desire and Depredation, but he didn't correct her misassumption. He knew he was treading in dangerous waters. Frost was a chaotic-neutral element at best, and an impossibly devious and dangerous opponent. The only reason she was playing along was because her current motivations aligned with his agenda. He was sure that the moment she got what she wanted, she wouldn't think twice before stabbing him in the back.

Frost had made it clear: a question for a question. He would get an answer, but he would have to give an answer in return. Every step forward he took, he'd leave himself increasingly precarious, exposed, susceptible to backstabbing and betrayal.

It was why he had mentioned the other relics but casually omitted explaining the power within the pendant.

"How did she perish?"

"When Inanna fell," he said softly, carefully measuring his words before uttering them, "it wasn't because anyone killed her. She was trapped in an artifact that combined multiple Truths, bound forever. For all I know, she is still in there, somewhere. Or was, in the past. Doesn't matter for now. The Inanna I knew was a reflection of the original, stored in this pendant." He grasped the ornament with his right hand, rubbing it gently.

"Another Meynte—"

"*No!*" said Lukas, surprising himself with the vitriol in his tone. "I mean, no, she was not like Meynte. The empress was just a memory. Inanna was . . . *more*. She was able to use her Truths, gain faith through this relic, even though it carried a Truth of a different god within itself."

Her lips twisted in amusement, but she said nothing.

"It was through this pendant that she reached out to me. When I fought the anomaly to gain its power, Inanna—she used to perform that scrying spell across the Universe. Thousands of times. But every time, she failed. The backlash from my own attack upon the anomaly killed me, and I . . . well, *my soul* disintegrated."

"And yet, you are here."

"I am," he said, a smile forming on his lips. "Because Inanna's desire was so great that it triumphed over the Rules of Reality itself. She reforged my soul, sacrificing her own divinity in the process. She perished, so that I might live."

Frost was no longer smiling.

"She wanted me to find out what happened to her original form. With me dead, and her bound within the relic, she'd hit rock bottom. There, inside the underground crypt, no one would find her. I was her best bet, even if it cost her everything." His hands hung limply on either side. "I owe it to her. And I will bring her back. No matter what it takes."

"Well," she said at last. "It was a worthy trade."

Lukas frowned. He wasn't sure how worthy it was. Not that he was complaining about getting a new chance at life, but he couldn't help but feel that he was messing things up more and more as he went along. He had nearly exhausted the divinity within himself; if he fucked up just one more time, it would be gone forever.

Igniting her divinity would grant her a temporary manifestation, and Inanna needed permanent solutions.

"Show me her memory," she said. "If we must resurrect this goddess of yours, I need to understand who she was. What she represented. Her Truth, her Ascension. Her greatest moment that made its mark upon the very Origin. Show me this . . . *Inanna*."

It was the first time Frost had actually called Inanna by her name. All this time, she had only referred to her as "goddess." Whatever it was she had inferred about her must have hit a nerve for her to acknowledge her as someone worthy of knowing.

Given how she was the literal antithesis of a goddess, that was saying something.

"Show you . . . how?"

"Open your mind to me. The last time I tried this, you were defiant. Ill-mannered. You made me fight for it. This time, let me in."

Lukas swallowed, hesitation surging within him. Inanna's memories were an utterly personal thing for him. He hadn't even talked about them with Tanya, and she was his lover. And yet here he was, about to share his memories of her, with Frost of all people.

"Are you ready?"

Lukas frowned, conflicted about what to show her. For a moment, he thought about showing his first meeting with her but quickly rejected that idea. She wanted to see something memorable, something *significant*. Seeing the Origin was no doubt one of the most impressive things out there, but he doubted Frost—the End of Potential—would appreciate it that much. Plus, it didn't paint Inanna in any greater light. The fight between Inanna and Frost was out, as well, because she was merely possessing his body and not actually fighting. His thoughts paused over how she had thrashed the Ifrit King around but he quickly discarded that too. It was powerful and exciting for him, but for Inanna, it was probably as mundane as taking out the trash.

He needed something else. Something better.

He thought back to Inanna's earliest memories. Her hanging on the wall as a corpse. No, that wouldn't do either. He wouldn't display her at her weakest. He needed her at her strongest. The memory of her being dragged around by Ereshkigal wouldn't do for the same reasons.

That only left a different memory. A half-remembered dream. One born of fire, defiance, and sheer will.

"I'm ready," he murmured.

Frost reached up and her slender, icy-cold fingers touched his forehead, like a mother checking a child for a fever. Her thumb pressed exactly in the center of his forehead, right between the eyebrows. She stayed that way for a long moment, her eyes distant.

"Go on," she said. "Show me."

And so he did.

Flames encompassed everything.

They razed and consumed the land, darkening the sky as if cursing it for being too wide to fully burn. Screams of pain, anguish, and despair filled the air like smoke as scorched bodies lay strewn across burnt ground, a testament to the merciless fury of fire. Malice saturated the atmosphere like a thick blanket as a malevolent red light poured out like liquid fire. Scarlet tongues of flame flickered, caressing and striking at one another like snakes wanting to devour everything, even themselves, as the massive inferno threatened raged above.

For Lukas, it was a déjà vu moment. The sight, the smell of burning sulfur, the utter malice and malevolence pouring from the heavens . . . He was expecting the Ifrit King to show up any moment.

"Charming place," said Frost, standing next to him. This was a memory, and yet the sensations felt more real than anything else, and the two of them—living, breathing figures—were little more than phantoms.

"How are we doing this?" he asked.

"Through Simulacrum," said Frost, not even looking at him. Her eyes were too busy looking around, taking in the world around her all at once. "A technique that operates at the intersection of advanced perception and advanced psionics. It uses the memory as a template and reconstructs a mental projection of it within your mindscape, allowing you to craft a highly accurate vision of the place and period depicted within."

"So it's like lucid dreaming," he said. It was eerily similar to what he did with his mindscape during Inanna's tutelage. It was among the first things Inanna had taught him to do without making it a bargain. In fact, the memory of Inanna being dragged through Ereshkigal's seven gates had felt utterly real too, and unlike the others, he had actually been in it. Perhaps his mind had conjured that by accident?

A weird thought came to mind.

"Say, is this simulacrum only limited to the mind? Or can it be created—"

"A skilled terramancer can craft a simulacrum in the real world, yes," finished Frost before he could finish his question. She gave him a knowing look. "A skilled terramancer, not unlike the skinwalker."

So that's how Solana did it, Lukas thought. *She was practically showing us a memory of the event.*

"Now tell me," said Frost, "is that . . .?"

She raised a finger, pointing at the two figures before them.

"Inanna," Lukas murmured.

But she wasn't alone. Next to her was a child, or someone that looked like a child. Lukas had seen enough crazy in this world to not estimate someone's age by their appearance.

"Are you sure this will work?" He heard Inanna say.

"Not really," her companion muttered. She wore a dark hooded robe that covered her entire form. By her voice, she was indeed a little girl, barely in her teens. But her words indicated anything but. "But for someone with your aspirations, this is the only way forward."

"Someone of my aspirations . . ." Inanna said again, her emerald eyes reflecting the crimson embers around as she peered into the flames. "You failed to mention that it involves walking through Vikahl itself."

"You wish to stand in defiance of the God of Fire, and yet here you are, trembling before this?" the child mocked.

Lukas staggered. He had heard this statement before. He had heard it back when he was struggling against the might of the king. He had thought it was Inanna but something about it felt odd, even to his addled mind.

Now he knew why.

It was her.

It was this girl.

He wanted to take a step forward but hesitated. Even the memory of these flames did odd things to him. They wouldn't burn him—they couldn't—but something about them felt *wrong*. It was a strange power, but at the same time, utterly different from anything else he had ever seen.

He watched her glare at the tiny figure, her hands clenching. He knew what she was feeling. He knew what it was like to be looked down upon, to be treated like vermin. He knew the familiar sensation of feeling his insides boil.

After all, he had been in that same place, with Inanna looking down at him.

Was this what people called legacy?

"What must I do?"

The renewed strength in her tone gave the child pause.

"Only a fire may devour another. Asshur burns brightly in the sky. Fire that gives life, provides warmth, brings hope in even the direst of situations. That is the nemesis you have claimed for yourself. One might even consider it an impossible task."

"Who is that child?" asked Frost.

Lukas shook his head. "No clue. But she must have been someone important to treat Inanna like that."

"These fires . . ." commented Frost. "There is something odd about them. Eerie but familiar."

"It was a power she sought as a mortal," Lukas explained. "This predates her becoming the Supreme Queen. She told me that she got this power from this place. She said that it was enough to eclipse the fire god Asshur's power."

Frost scoffed. "Either you are lying or have been lied to. No mortal power, no matter how great, can eclipse a god."

"Not even a Truth?"

Frost regarded him evenly. "Who will win? An empress anchors a Truth to herself? Or a goddess, who wields another, only infinitely more empowered by the faith of her worshippers?"

Lukas bit back whatever retort he was about to give.

"Gods of fire like this Asshur are a dime a dozen," said Frost. "Almost every pantheon has a god or goddess that has mastered the powers of fire—the majority of them through relics of previous pantheons. Same with the other elements. Fire is the most destructive element out there, and with faith added into the mix, one of the most dangerous. This woman, Inanna or otherwise, could not have defeated him with just this."

Lukas tilted his head slightly. "You speak like you've known a lot of civilizations."

Frost did not look at him. "Do not be deceived, Soulcrafter. I might wear the shell of my vessel, but do not forget what I am, what my purpose is."

"Ending all Potential."

This time she did look at him. "I have been called by many names, across many lifetimes. Truths rise and fall, the seasons turn and turn, but just like the forever march of Potential, the retrogression of Taboo continues infinitely. Do not impose your limited comprehension of Time upon us. Your future is my past. Your past is my future."

Lukas shook his head. "How can that be? My future is not set in stone."

"But mine is. The Formless Infinity. My past, an infinite collection of possibilities in the Infinity of Forms."

"You've already been in this world's past. As Tsurara's alter ego, as Meynte's, and, before that, as Nidhogg. Fimbulwinter is the herald of the End of the Norse pantheon."

"It is. Perhaps I will, in my future and in your past, be there. Perhaps I have already been. Perhaps I am already there right now."

"But that doesn't even make sense!"

Frost gave him an amused smile. "Imagine that."

Not wanting to deal with the impending headache that Frost seemed intent on giving him, he looked at the memory, his main reason for being there. Regardless of Frost's claims, Lukas knew that Inanna would never lie.

"You must be the flames that burn in darkness," rang the child's voice. "The jaws that consume life. The fire that pollutes, purges, and destroys. The Vikahl Ashlands are merely a stepping stone in fulfilling that dream."

Dream.

She had called it a dream.

Lukas didn't need to be a psychologist to know exactly how much Inanna loathed it. She was ambition personified. To have her goals reduced to a mere dream, as if they were just figments of her imagination and would remain as such?

Lukas watched as Inanna silently disrobed. Her manacles went first. Then her vest. Then the cloth around her neck fell. And finally, her waistguard. None of them would survive those flames.

"What happens if the flames are stronger?"

"You will learn to overpower them."

Lukas wondered if Inanna had been passing on her own experience under that child's tutelage during their training sessions. He watched as she stared into the crackling flames, steadying herself for what was to come. He recognized that small, nervous smile flickering on her face, as her hands lightly twitched with a few nervous little gestures. She had made the exact same gestures right before she had vanished, leaving him stranded in this world.

She was utterly terrified. And yet, she did not hesitate to step into the great walls of flame, which rose to meet her as if they had an awareness of their own. Lukas watched with a mixture of anxiety and awe as motion writhed around her, deflecting the incoming barrage and recoiling into a protective web as miniature typhoons of flame rose to consume her whole. She grunted as the primordial force crashed against her own might. Something told Lukas that it wasn't just fire. No fire could stand a chance against the ruler of motion. It was more like the flickering tongues of flame were hammering against her very will.

It didn't matter how much power poured out, the flames devoured it all.

It didn't matter how much she deflected, there was always more.

It didn't matter how much she struggled, there was no path forward.

But that was the sort of line of thought that would ensure her failure. Lukas knew that, for he had been in the exact same situation. For Inanna to save herself, she'd need to keep throwing out more power. Her will needed to be strong. She had to keep striving onwards.

The flames continued to lash around like the tentacles of a ravenous beast. It was all too terrifying. Lukas remembered when the Ifrit King had raised its gargantuan hands and a world of flames had collapsed upon him from all sides. He remembered how every single instinct within him had begged him to escape. To save himself and run away from this inferno before it consumed him.

But if he did, he'd be condemning Tanya to death.

It wasn't an option.

And so, he had stopped feeling it.

And so did she.

When she became too scared to move, Inanna simply willed herself to stop feeling her fear. When the burns became too great to bear, she stopped feeling pain. When she felt unable to push back against the force, she stopped her very own thoughts.

With each new step, she left a piece of herself behind. The flames coalesced around her. Purging her, unmaking her, adding to her, breaking her, strengthening her.

Then he heard the child let out a wicked cackle, her words magically magnified and reverberating all around.

"YOUR SELFISHNESS KNOWS NO BOUNDS! YOU'D SNATCH, YOU'D HUSTLE, EMPIRES WOULD BURN AND PANTHEONS WOULD FALL, YET YOUR DESIRE SHALL REMAIN UNQUENCHED!"

A sense of unease began to spread through him. It wasn't the Frost. No, it was coming from outside. That child's voice had heralded something terrible. It was just like when he had accessed the memories of his world perishing. Something so alien to his mind that his brain would rather choose to give him an aneurysm than deal with the consequences. Lukas began to look around wildly, as the uneasiness blossomed into mounting dread and fear, and despite his Level-5 Alpha Condition, all his mental barriers were being overcome by a new and frightening uncertainty that *something* was coming in response to Inanna's struggle. Something alien and completely beyond his understanding. Something that drew closer and closer with every step Inanna took.

"YOU ARE BLOODSHED AND BATTLE, BRINGING JUSTICE AND MISFORTUNE IN EQUAL MEASURE. YOU WANDER IN TREACHERY AND TRAVEL WITH UNKINDNESS."

Lukas felt a sudden sharp pain in his hand. He looked down and realized that Frost had grabbed it and now held it in a death grip. What was worse was that the hoarfrost was slowly spreading out of her fingers and greedily devouring lifeforce from his body. *Again?* That didn't even make a lick of sense given both of their bodies weren't even real to begin with. This was a freaking memory, and they were psionic imprints of themselves playing out within his mindscape.

The alien, discordant, humming sound grew louder and louder. Lukas tried to shake Frost's hand off, but she looked like she was rooted to the spot, the familiar dark amusement on her face replaced by an unnaturally pale demeanor. She was watching the scene play out before her, transfixed with terror.

"YOUR WRATH SHALL BREAK THE DIVINE THRONES! YOUR WHIMS DEFILE THE MOST SACRED OF RELICS . . ."

Fierce hurricanes billowed across the entire terrain, the world around them hotter than a supernova, exploding, imploding, spinning, and re-forming back into shape. A thousand new possibilities were appearing all around her, a thousand decimated, atomized in an instant. And in the middle of it all stood that one woman, naked and utterly uncaring of the apocalypse around her.

"EXISTENCE ITSELF IS UNRAVELED BY YOUR PRESENCE! THE FLAMES OF DEPRIVATION SHALL BE YOUR ESSENCE!"

"This cannot be!" yelled Frost. She looked at him, absolute terror in her eyes. And then in a perfect one-eighty, she began to laugh. She laughed and laughed with that painful grin on her face before suddenly screaming in incoherent rage.

"TRICKSTER! YOU CLAIMED THIS WAS A GODDESS! YOU CLAIMED HER A PANTHEON QUEEN! YOU—YOU—PLUNDERER! TRICKSTER! PSYCHOPOMP!"

Frost's face twisted into a mask of psychotic fury, as she threw power up all around her, exiting the memory, but not before she could hear.

"INANNA!!!"

It took a while for that hideous presence and humming sound to vanish from his ears. For a while, all Lukas was able to do was to remain curled up in the fetal position, focus his will, and do his best to push it away from his thoughts. His right hand had gone ice-cold from Everfrost, but for some reason, it was impossibly difficult for him to conjure up some fire mana and neutralize its effects.

Still, it was a nasty surprise. He had always thought that Inanna held an intense amount of power. In this world where the real monsters were masters of elemental manipulation, the power to control motion itself made everything else look tame.

But after all was said and done, it wasn't what made Inanna the Supreme Queen.

Hell, she had used Kinetomancy in the Vikahl Ashlands. Which meant that the Inanna in the memory had used Kinetomancy against the fire god Asshur and had failed.

And then she had gotten something worse.

Her words came to mind.

The Vikahl Ashlands are truly ancient, even for divinity. A power that exists only to purge others. A power that was the antithesis of Asshur's Truth. I embraced it. For a time. For a price.

He remembered how it felt the first time he had seen that dream. He had *been* Inanna in that dream. The feeling of slowly losing oneself, of tossing away pieces of his—*her*—humanity with each step that he—*she*—took through that flaming valley wasn't something he had forgotten or would forget any time soon.

It was right afterwards that he had asked her a vital question:

Is that why you always refer to me as "Mortal?" To remind yourself that you aren't?

Inanna had avoided answering. Lukas had thought it to be an invasion of her privacy and dropped it. But now, he knew differently. It made him wonder, just what was that power she had invoked in the Ashlands? What was she after? What did she attain?

The power to purge others?

Her Truth was Depredation. Ordinarily, that word referred to plundering. Ravaging. Destruction. But plundering was an act, not a power, and certainly not something as esoteric as a Truth. Which meant that Depredation had a different, infinitely deeper meaning than that. One so complex and yet so utterly fundamental that it became a bedrock for civilization itself.

But that child hadn't called them the Flames of Depredation. She had said *Deprivation*.

Deprivation. The act of taking away that which belongs to another. To *snatch*.

Deprivation and Depredation.

To snatch and plunder.

The act of a robber, an invader, a tyrant.

Wasn't that exactly what Inanna was?

Goddess, Tyrant Queen, Butcher . . . I personally liked the last one.

And she had even cursed him to play her role in her demise.

Be the invader that I was. The monster. The conqueror.

In his ignorance, brimming with emotions, he had agreed. He had even willingly accepted it all, never fully understanding what it was he was accepting so freely.

He had started the journey for the sake of survival. And now, he sought power, growth, and evolution. He wanted to break the System's limitations and obtain as much power as he could, even if it meant snatching from others.

One only needed to look at the massacre in the borderland for proof. Sure, he had enemies out there, baying for his blood. Several times, he had attempted to stop the battle escape, but the muspels had been relentless. And somewhere in the middle of all that, the escape attempt had turned into a widespread massacre. Hell, he and Tanya had made a game out of it, as if the monsters were nothing more than bowling pins to knock down.

But even then, if her Truth was Depredation, what the hell was Deprivation? Were they the same? Just a play on words? He thought about what she'd said some more.

I embraced it. For a time. For a price.

For a time? For a price? What did that mean? Did she not have it anymore? Why? Had she rejected it when she had become the Supreme Queen? Both powers were practically synonyms, at least in terms of modern language.

Unless . . .

Unless Deprivation had nothing to do with snatching at all?

What was he missing?

He was about to ask Frost about his latest quandary, when the sight before him froze him to his very bones.

Avatar of Fimbulwinter, alter ego of every Everfrost user beginning with Meynte herself, Frost was currently sitting on the floor against the wall, as physically far away from him as possible while still staying in the room, her knees curled up against her chest, shocked and scared out of her mind. Lukas didn't know exactly what it was that he had felt inside that memory, but if it was enough to make *Frost* visibly scared just by witnessing it, that was something he knew he'd better not risk invoking.

"Frost?" he tried.

She flinched and let out a small squeaking sound. Then she got hold of herself and looked up at him.

"What was that?" he asked.

Her voice was very quiet. "That which cannot be."

She met his eyes. "A Taboo."

Out of everything else she had said so far, that surprised Lukas the most.

"Taboo?" He narrowed his eyes. Inanna was a goddess. She was the Supreme Queen. His own soul was re-forged out of the remains of her divinity.

"Inanna is a goddess. A Supreme Queen of the Akkadian pantheon. You yourself claimed that her Truth binds you."

"I know what I said, Soulcrafter," she snapped, though the heat in her tone was missing, replaced by uneasiness. "And I know what I saw. That—that power is a Taboo! It's wrong!"

"So are you."

"You don't understand, Outsider," she said, her eyes practically glowing an intense white. "That power cannot exist! That place does not exist! Has not existed! Will not exist! Neither will that power! It cannot be!"

"And how do you know that? By your omniscience? Because a fat lot of good that did for Meynte or your other vessels."

Frost practically growled at him. "Your levity will not change the truth, Outsider. Your perception of reality limits you. That power . . . it cannot exist."

Lukas bit down whatever retort he was about to make and took a moment to reconsider everything she had told him.

"Frost, are you certain that it is a Taboo?"

"Without a doubt."

"But how's that even possible? Inanna is a goddess. And, as you said earlier, one cannot ascend with a Taboo."

"That girl that took on this power was a mortal, like yourself. She was no goddess."

Not then, *perhaps*, Lukas mused. Inanna did tell him that she held the power for a time, and for a price.

If crafting a Truth was the ultimate act of ascension, bearing a Taboo would be the ultimate Sin, at least as far as the World was concerned. If he were to believe Frost, then Inanna had first become a Taboo-wielder and killed Ashhur, followed by many others.

Had she then discarded her power and become a goddess through one of her collected relics? That didn't sound like the Inanna he knew. Inanna was a cruel bitch, but she was a proud one. She'd rather die than be known for a power that belonged to someone else.

But, by that logic, even Deprivation belonged to someone—or rather, some *place*—else.

The Vikahl Ashlands.

Was that why she had given up this power? So that she could find the path of her own ascension? Something similar to the power she once held but something that belonged to her and her alone?

It was all speculation at this point but not without its merits.

"And . . . if this Taboo doesn't exist, then why are you panicking?"

"You do not understand, Soulcrafter!" declared Frost, slowly standing up. "You do not understand the pieces you have set in motion."

"Then help me understand."

Frost glared at him but he didn't look away. Finally, she consented. "Unlike a Truth, a Taboo *always* exists. From the very beginning to the very end. The march of progress starts from the emptiness of the Formless Infinity, expressing Potential in infinite forms, reaching their individual zeniths, and forming Truths that get added to the Origin. A Taboo? It's always part of the Void. You might not know when it will rise, when it devours a pantheon and obliterates Potential, but it is there. It is *always* there. For this reality, the Taboo is, was, and will always be Fimbulwinter, that which consumes Potential."

"Then this Deprivation . . ."

"Does not belong. Has not *ever* belonged."

"Maybe it's from a different reality that—"

"Do not speak like an ignorant fool!" snapped Frost, genuinely angry and scared. "There is only one reality. No other exists. They *cannot!* Only when Fimbulwinter finishes its march and drowns Potential into the Formless will Taboo take on a different form. Those flames—that power—it cannot exist, because I do. And if it exists, then I do not. I—*I REFUSE TO ACCEPT THIS!*"

Lukas opened his mouth, but no words came out. He was finally beginning to understand. It was like watching *Jurassic Park* on TV, only for the dinosaurs to suddenly shatter the screen and jump into your room. The issue wasn't that dinosaurs couldn't exist, because they did, millions of years ago. But *these* dinosaurs were a product of human imagination. An illusion belonging to a fictional world crafted out of technology. It was not, and could not become real.

Yet that's essentially what had happened here. For Frost, neither the flames of Deprivation nor Inanna were real. And while Inanna's Truth was a perfectly good addition to reality, the same couldn't be said about the Taboo of Deprivation.

Her body language tensed even more. "Reality is large enough for Infinite Truths to co-exist, Soulcrafter. But a single Taboo is all you need to return that to the Formless. And reality has one. That is my purpose. But this power is so impossibly strong that it was tearing through the foundations of Time and reality itself. One that was attempting to leave the constrictions of the abstract and become real. It could even deprive me of my purpose. My destiny!"

"It's a memory." Lukas stressed. "It isn't real. If it was, then resurrecting Inanna would be a whole lot easier. And no offense, but for someone who *also* wants to destroy reality, you're making a pretty big deal out of this!"

"I do not seek to destroy reality, Soulcrafter. I exist to revert the march of Potential. There is a difference." Her expression was replaced with a cold, hard, glacial look. "If this Taboo enters reality, both of our powers will collide. It would be cataclysmic. I'm afraid I cannot let you do this, especially since my own wielder is not ready. That abomination cannot be resurrected. No matter the cost."

"Makes sense."

"A Taboo like that, empowering its wielder, will destroy reality itself, and nothing you can do can hold it at bay. You—Wait, did you just agree with me?!"

The confusion on her face looked so innocent that Lukas couldn't help but chuckle.

She scowled.

"I'm not stupid enough to bring another world-ending power into this mess."

Frost looked utterly flummoxed. "But your goddess—"

"I intend to resurrect the goddess, not some reality-destroying demoness. I have invoked her divinity in the past but could only manage a temporary resurrection that lasted for but a few minutes," he freely admitted. "I need something permanent, and for that, I need your help."

Her features softened. "You are an enigma, Soulcrafter. You faced the might of Meynte and risked the end of the world for the girl, yet you'd shrink away from the same when asked to resurrect your goddess? Perhaps your devotion to her isn't as deep as you claim."

Lukas frowned and tilted his head in honest confusion. "I don't understand. Saving Tanya was my choice. As is resurrecting Inanna. But what has either to do with stopping this Taboo from ending reality?"

Frost blinked. "But—"

"I owe Inanna my life. I will pay back my debt. But that does not mean I will destroy everything else to bring her back. There has to be a different way."

"And how do you know that?"

"Because I believe it. Inanna called me her miracle. What else is a miracle but something you wish to be true?"

Frost snorted before sighing deeply. "You are unbearably optimistic, Outsider. Truly, there has never been anyone as hopelessly optimistic in the annals of all of eternity."

"Who is more hopeless?" he asked, doing his best to ignore the feeling of disappointment surging within. "Someone who never gives up? Or someone who doesn't even try?"

"Outsider—"

"I'm not stupid, Frost. I know how much you despise Meynte for what she did. And I also know that I risked this world by saving Tanya. But that doesn't need to happen if you help her."

"Help her?"

"Become the vessel, yes. The Taboo-wielder for this reality."

Frost tilted her head, studying him. "If the girl is not strong enough, the power will twist and turn her into a devastating force that leaves only ice and death in her wake."

"Then what do you expect me to do, kill her? Don't treat me like a fool. If Tanya dies, you'll just manifest in the next person. You said the Taboo is always there, waiting for a vessel. There is just no end to it. If not Tanya, then someone else, and the cycle will keep going, until a vessel is born. But if she can learn to control it, maybe she can be . . . *more*."

"More?" Frost looked utterly uncomfortable with the idea.

"Fire burns, but it also keeps the cold away. Ice can freeze one to death, but it can also soothe. Everfrost can end Potential, so that makes it the perfect tool to balance the scales when someone messes with it."

"You mean a god—"

"I mean a lot of things. Tanya's own grandfather is a monster. One that must be eliminated. I'd rather have her master Everfrost and destroy that monster's potential. It doesn't matter if you're a warlord, a king, or a freaking god—if you have Potential, Everfrost can slay you. The way it looks to me, Truth and Taboo are two sides of the same coin. A duality that maintains the balance of reality."

"And you think the girl—"

"Can become this balance, yes. Especially if *you* help her."

"Are you not afraid that I could abuse the power?" she asked, honestly curious.

"Of course I am," he replied, actually surprised that she asked such a thing.

"And yet you'd have her turn to me? I'd have pegged you for a savior, hero."

Lukas blinked, before it hit him. "Frost . . ." he began slowly. "I don't think you quite understand me. Saving Tanya was my choice, just as choosing to master this power will be hers. Meynte tried to snatch that choice from her, and I fought her for it. What makes you think I won't do the same against you?"

"And what if the girl becomes the demon that Meynte feared? The monster that only knows to devour?"

"Frost, the moment I chose to save Tanya, I already took into consideration that she could end up as a threat to just about everyone."

"Then why save her?"

"Because it's not right to sacrifice someone who has yet to express the intention of harming innocents just to be on the safe side. And to be honest, if I were to eliminate every potential threat to other's lives, I'd eradicate every single being in this world, including myself."

It was the truth. The greatest threat to a person's life was every other person. He'd have to eliminate the yokai for they fed on bremetan souls. He'd have to eliminate bremetans for they bound kami to themselves. He'd have to eradicate kami because they possessed bremetans and could wreak havoc.

"And what if the girl chooses to become the destroyer? What if she loses control and crushes the march of Potential? Becomes the very thing that Meynte feared so much? Same goes for the goddess. Even if there is some way to resurrect her, if she ends up destroying it all, then what will you do?"

Lukas clenched his hands into fists and closed his eyes. Frost had hit a button with that question. It was why he had wanted to maintain a distance from Tanya, despite his feelings for her.

When he opened his eyes again, they were a mixture of green and brown.

"Then I'd take responsibility for having saved her life and stop her myself."

It was not a threat nor a warning. Merely a declaration of intent. Of a resolution made before she even began considering how he'd react to her twisted schemes.

Lukas smiled. It looked like she had expected him to be naive, someone with no real grasp of the harshness of reality, just blindly believing the best in others. And to be honest, that wasn't completely wrong, but it was a product of clear, deliberate choice, not ignorance.

He had known exactly what Inanna had offered him back in the anomaly. For all her endless power, she'd make him a toy, a puppet that followed her whims. His grandfather had always taught him to shoulder the consequences of his own actions, and what Inanna was offering was a way to shift the blame.

Was it any surprise that he had rejected her time and time again?

"Do not misunderstand me, Frost. Inanna saved my life. I owe her a debt. It is mine to shoulder, just like the World I carry within myself. But just like Tanya, if the resurrected Inanna turns out to be a danger, a true monster, then it would be up to me to put her down." It would crush me, yes, but I'd do it."

"Why?"

"Because," he said, the smile on his lips never reaching his eyes, "she would be a monster of my own making."

EPILOGUE

T he palace was ostentatious. The outer courtyard alone could fit an entire fortress of the Peak's size and have rooms left over for a lawn or two. Its grandness was more than enough to make even the greatest architects salivate, and the ward schematics alone would leave entire garrisons feeling insecure about their own homes. All of those things were individually awe-inspiring, but it was the realization of *who* they stood before that really got to the visitors.

Before them sat the firstborn of the Great Goddess Amaterasu.

Demigod. Emperor. Wielder of a Hundred Skills.

Ninigi Asuka.

This wasn't the first time that Mujin Shimizu had been summoned to the Royal Palace. As a representative of the Sacred Eight, attendance at their meetings was mandatory. And then there were the festivities, which were more optional; Mujin avoided those as much as possible. They weren't his kind of thing.

Too many diplomats.

This time was different. This time, he had been summoned not as a welcome guest but to explain his actions—well, his *grandson's* actions to be precise. Ordinarily, he wouldn't have given the matter a second thought, but as it turned out, their newest prisoner had a lot of aces hidden up his sleeve that his grandson hadn't considered before the precipitous attack on his mansion.

Mujin traversed the palace halls, keeping his thoughts to himself. He didn't put a lot of faith in destiny, but one did not fend off political opponents for more than a century without acknowledging the role of luck. And something told him that this summons would massively affect his plans for the future—and not in a good way.

The spacious, rectangular hall spread out in front of him, supported by columns of Maluscian stone, the finest white marble one could find in the entire Empire. He had once tried his luck at dealing with the stone quarries some decades ago, only to find that he'd have been making the Royal Palace his competitor. While growth and expansion had their benefits, the risk-to-reward ratio was simply too great for him to ignore. Maybe after he captured the creature and the kami and restored glory to his clan . . .

He paused that line of thought while he could, distracting himself with the veins of gold and silver that crisscrossed the floors. Marble steps at the far end swept up a balcony that encircled the entire place, supported by more white pillars that matched the floor. There was a quiet waterfall at the far end of the hallway, running down into a pool, surrounded by a garden of trees and the chirping of the occasional bird.

After crossing the entire length of the colossal atrium, Mujin found himself facing a massive door, with elaborate carvings in every direction. The one on the right depicted the rise of the Great Goddess Amaterasu, a trident of Eternal Light in one hand, a flaming sword in the other. The Glorious Ascension, as scholars put it, the *rise of the empress* into a goddess and then leader of her pantheon at the end of the war with the yokai.

The engraving on the left depicted Amaterasu again, this time wielding a lance of Eternal Light, removing the Mists from the world. The Bath of Illumination, according to the texts. A third engraving, perfectly positioned at the center of the ceiling above them, depicted the Sun Throne with the goddess's sigil on top. There was a depiction of the svartalfars on the bottom left, dökkálfars on the left, and wraiths—yokai—hiding from the Eternal Light beneath the Sun Throne itself.

A perfect depiction of Asukan domination on the world.

The Gate of Might, Mujin recalled. The main doorway through which one entered the throne room. The seat of power in Asukan theocracy.

The massive doors swung open, allowing them in.

The inner chamber was huge. The walls were primarily white with ornamentation done mainly in gold and precious jewels. The magnificent chandeliers that hung from the ceiling were crafted out of rainbow diamonds and cast a dreamy, sparkling light. On the walls, hanging from the ceiling down to the floor, were large flags, on which were adorned images of the Rising Sun—the Crest of the House of Asuka.

A large, ostentatious red carpet ran down the center of the room. Along either side stood soldiers—all of them Gold-ranked spiritists—the emperor's personal guard, enlisted specifically from the Cobalt Army. Utterly loyal, absolutely faithful, they served no one but the emperor himself. For them, his word was law.

A system Mujin could wholeheartedly agree with. After all, he had set up something very similar back home.

And then he saw *him*.

Seated on a magnificent throne of crystal, a trident of pure light in one hand, sat the demigod himself. Easily seven feet tall, with the proportions of a professional rōnin and the noble features of a warrior king. His hair was gold and swept back from his face in a mane that fell to the base of his neck. His beard was equally golden, though marked at the chin with a single streak of dark gray, a scratch in the face of the sun itself. His eyes—

Mujin jerked his gaze away from those stars of radiance before he could be fully drawn into them. People beyond a certain class and authority had powerful eyes. His father had it; Trestan Banksi, the Earth King had it. But neither of them came remotely close to the emperor's gaze. His stomach twisted, and he had to fight not to vomit up his last meal.

"Mujin, son of the Wind King," the demigod rumbled. "Be welcome in my abode."

Mujin exhaled harshly. It took everything in him to not react. He was the Lord of Shimizu, the warlord that had taken the reins of his clan after his father's demise. He had fended off vultures from trying to rob them of their Sacred Eight status for over a century, and yet, the emperor *still* addressed him as "son of the Wind King."

As if he had achieved nothing except being born to his father.

But he didn't look up. He had the feeling that had the eye contact continued for one more second, he'd have been asphyxiated or worse. Those vibrant, golden eyes that looked as if they could take the entire world in at once, felt like endless black holes that could swallow him, his thoughts, and his entire existence into them if he gave them the opportunity to do so.

And he was a *warlord.*

"I . . . Thank you, for welcoming me, Great Emperor," he said slowly, choosing his words with extreme caution. "I'd be honored if my presence serves this court in any fashion."

He relaxed, ever so slightly, bowing his head as a sign of respect. The Asukan Empire was divided into forty-three nation-states, each of them ruled by shoguns appointed by the emperor himself. Out of the 127 clans that existed in the entire Empire, there were only eight that held the title of nobility and occupied the highest position in the pecking order, right below the emperor himself. In fact, even the emperor could not directly act in a matter involving the Sacred Eight without a two-thirds majority supporting his actions.

And with good reason, too. To become one of the Sacred Eight, a clan had to birth a king—a Level-5 persona. Eight clans—seven kings, each holding absolute mastery over an element or its derivation, and the emperor himself.

So yes, as a member of the Sacred Eight, he was technically—*very technically*—within the same social circles as the emperor himself.

In the same way plankton shared the same habitat as a shark.

He looked at the people sitting there in the hall. For whatever reason, the emperor had summoned several Shoguns from the entire South-Eastern

Dominion. Mujin doubted all of that was because of his little transgression and wondered exactly what kind of madness was about to unfold here.

His gaze flickered towards Lord Straff, the Shogun of Eaborid Kingdom—a bastard by all measures. Sitting further right was Lord Basliel Tedros, the Shogun of Karnegrug. Another enemy kingdom, if a bit predictable. Lady Edna Menasse, the ruler of Ogria, and Lady Akiha Troyl, the ruler of Maluscion, sat on the other side, both of them representing the less-powerful nations in the South-Eastern Dominion. And finally, Lord Naowa, Shogun of Llaisy Kingdom, was seated next to Lady Troyl.

All of them held positions of power in the Empire.

All of them were also inferior to him in both power and prestige.

None could be trusted.

Especially not Lord Straff.

The snake had always despised the fact that despite being *only* a warlord, Mujin held an unfathomable amount of power in the Eaborid Kingdom. In fact, the capital city, Cyffnar, was practically ruled by the Shimizu Clan. The crab was always looking out for opportunities to shame him and had even sent petitions to the Royal Palace, claiming that the Shimizu should be stripped off their right to call themselves one of the Sacred Eight, given how they had lost the Wind King's kami and were no closer to producing a new Wind King than they were a century and a half ago.

The rest of the seated members were just pretenders, all of them holding high places but none with the ability or the resources to become a king—vultures that were here to peck at him, wanting to see a Sacred Eight clan be hacked apart.

Then his eyes went to the person seated to the right of the emperor, Trestan Banksi, the Earth King. Shogun of the Kingdom of Luthar, one of the largest kingdoms in the entire South-Eastern region.

And a man Mujin could tentatively call his friend. If not for the Earth King's support, it would have been extremely difficult for him to hold on to the Sacred Eight mantle.

Silently, he walked up and took his place at the center of the giant dais. This was the place where the interrogated stood to face the onslaught of questions that everyone threw at them. The fellow Shoguns would act as a supplemental jury, just in case the judge's input was deemed lacking, which admittedly never happened. Particularly not when the judge was none other than the emperor himself.

He could only hope that he could rely on Banksi's support.

"Mujin Shimizu," intoned Lady Menasse, "Lord Naowa, Shogun of the Llaisy Kingdom and one of the Sacred Eight, has raised charges against you and your kin, accusing you of forceful entry into his kingdom and assaulting one of the most valuable members of his court, capturing him, vandalizing his property, and killing all those under his employ. We request that you share the pertinent events from your perspective."

Mujin exhaled softly. "Yes. My grandson entered the Llaisy Kingdom, assaulted someone, captured him, vandalized his property, and killed those under his employ. But that attack had nothing to do with Lord Naowa in particular. It was simply a private skirmish between my grandson and the assaulted."

"I see," said the emperor, looking completely bored. "Let the trial begin."

Lord Straff began by dragging the Shimizu's reputation through the mud, practically incapable of uttering three sentences in a row without trying to make a shot at him.

"A relic of a lost past," Straff went on. "Clinging desperately to a status that they have already lost and have no way of getting back. Pardon me, my lords, but this man has been abusing his friendship with the Earth King to exert his whims over my kingdom and the surrounding nations. A transgression we eagerly wish for the emperor to correct."

Mujin clenched his fists. He had not expected them to be this bold.

He was well aware of the looks and whispers he got from others behind his back. "Old Specter," they called him, mocking him for being a relic of the past, one who had lost everything but was still pretending to embody the same prestige as his father had. He was just a warlord, holding the throne that belonged to the king. And ever since that unfortunate incident when they had lost Ezzeron, the whispers had grown even louder.

"Pretender," they called him. Yes, they stayed silent in public, but behind closed doors, they questioned why a clan without a king-class kami was still holding the title of Sacred Eight. And the worst part, they were right! But the Empire's policy was that there had to be a new king within three generations of the present king, or within two hundred years of the death of the present king, whichever was longer. Unfortunately for him, he was already past the prime of his life, and even though he was the strongest Asukan in the entirety of the South-Western Dominion, he was still, as they put it, "just a warlord."

As if the fact that he could tear down any of their armies single-handedly didn't matter.

No, Mujin told himself. *It matters. They know it. They fear it. They fear* me.

The truth was, Mujin had never had any political aspirations. His entire life had been spent obsessing over three things—gaining strength as a spiritist and warlord, trying to live up to his father's legacy, and attempting to extract the alien power that lay within the Winter Witch.

He had given up the second goal after an entire decade of repeated attempts. Ezzeron had not chosen him, so instead, he had found himself another kami, his Byakko, and gained strength through it. The experiments on the Winter Witch had succeeded, but the outcome had escaped into the wild, and until a few months ago, he had thought her to be dead and gone. That left only the first to go ahead with, so he had given it his undivided attention and became a warlord while amplifying the defensive and offensive capacity of his clan.

He had created the Peak—his stronghold.

But that didn't matter to these jackals. All they cared about was that he was no king. And everyone knew exactly what his grandson Ultaf was, or rather, was *not* capable of. With Ezzeron lost to the winds, the chances of the Shimizu producing a king was precisely zero.

The only reason they were still holding on to the position of Sacred Eight was because of a technicality—two hundred years hadn't passed yet, and three generations of the clan weren't completely done with their attempts. A technicality he had desperately hidden behind so far.

Even with the vultures circling above.

And it would have stayed that way, until . . .

Until that day when Ultaf came to the Peak and gave him the surprising news.

The creature—Tanya—was alive. And she had Ezzeron.

Their heritage and their future were both present, just in hiding. All he needed to do was capture her and he could return the Shimizu name to its former glory. It was a dangerous task, one that required expeditious handling and should have been done years ago. Mujin had handled most of it by himself, relegating the simpler tasks to his grandson.

Who knew that would turn out like this?

Still, he had to act. And now.

"Lord Straff," Mujin began. "I hope you realize that with that statement, you are raising charges against the Earth King."

The room went quiet, several people sitting up straight in their seats. Even Straff stiffened, terrified of turning around and facing the Earth King, who was lazily staring at him from behind.

After a few anxious seconds, his posture relaxed slightly, and he gave him a smarmy smile. "I wouldn't dare to. Lord Banksi is the Earth King, and the strongest presence in the South-Eastern Dominion. I'm only pointing out that you are abusing your close association with him to overstep your limits."

That filled Mujin with a sinking dread.

The next half hour proceeded with Straff systematically tearing down the Shimizu name. The demise of the official heiress and the loss of Ezzeron in a cataclysmic accident that killed half the clan was in itself put into question as a possible opening move into some larger scandal. The decline of culture and tradition in Shimizu-governed areas, and the constant recruitment for the

Shimizu taskforce was painted as an attempt to invade other regions, or even potential aggression against the Empire. Mujin's own age and lack of potential claimants to the Wind King's throne was mentioned, to showcase how the Shimizu were hanging on by a technicality and taking undue advantage of it.

There wasn't a single aspect of the Shimizu Clan that wasn't being scrutinized, relevant or not. It was viciously insulting at first, but as time went on, the bite lost a big portion of its effectiveness. Now the man was simply being annoying. Judging from everyone's expressions, half the jury were of the same mind as well. Even the most stalwart of them were starting to show their ire at the display.

"Great Emperor," Naowa intervened, "the person Lord Shimizu's grandson assaulted was a valuable member of my court, and son of the Earth King himself, Zuken Banksi."

"Zuken Banksi," murmured the emperor, lazily shifting his gaze to his right. "Perhaps you'd like to shed some light on that, Earth King? Is this man they speak of truly your son?"

Again, the court's eyes turned to the calm, unflappable man who looked like he hadn't noticed the shift in attention in the slightest.

"He is of my blood, yes."

No one missed the wordplay.

"Do you have any words to share on this matter?"

"Hmph. Two Sacred Eight families going through so much trouble over an unimportant member of my clan. It's such a trivial and foolish story that I have trouble even comprehending how it is so interesting to anyone in the first place. A squabble that is beneath us, Great Emperor."

"Earth King," pleaded Naowa, "he is your son."

Trestan Banksi gave him an unreadable stare. "I have *seventeen* offspring, Lord Naowa. Almost all of them have achieved great things. The one you speak of is simply one of those . . . unfortunate, who have yet to do so. Still, he has demonstrated an uncanny ability to find support in a Shogun who is also a member of the Sacred Eight, which is an accomplishment in its own way, I suppose."

The emperor's lips twitched upwards slightly at that.

"That said," said the Earth King, "it is apparent that this useless squabble has the potential to set some dangerous precedents." He shot an annoyed look at Mujin. "Lord Shimizu, regardless of our relations, you trespassed past your domain here. Release this man immediately, and pay for whatever compensation is his right."

Mujin clenched his teeth. "Earth King, Zuken Banksi wasn't captured on a whim or to denigrate Lord Naowa's authority in his kingdom. Zuken Banksi is a well-known wetworks man, with his own set of spies, assassins, and private adventurers under his private guild, Iylerion. He took a contract from myself and my grandson several years ago, and we only recently realized that he breached it, and thus, broke sacred protocol. My grandson approached him over the annulment and demanded compensation. Zuken Banksi did not comply. Whatever followed thereafter was simply an escalation of that conflict."

"And what," asked Straff, "was this contract about?"

"Classified," snapped Mujin. "It is an internal matter between Clan Shimizu and Zuken Banksi, and not of relevance to this court."

"It is," claimed Lord Naowa. "You are holding one of my people hostage and have yet to give me an official reason as to why. Zuken's abduction is hampering my administration. Will Clan Shimizu take personal responsibility for that?"

Mujin shifted uncomfortably, showing a rare moment of weakness that he knew every person in the court would see.

"Lord Shimizu," asked the emperor gently, "is there something you wish to say?"

He stayed silent.

"Great Emperor," said Straff eagerly, "it hurts me to see the fall of a clan descended from the mighty Wind King, but it is obvious that Warlord Shimizu here is unable to fulfill his duties to the clan or keep his wayward grandson from acting out without any care for his actions. The clan has grown so drunk on the memories of their glorious past that they are acting with brazen impunity. Hence, I request that the Shimizu Clan be removed from the Sacred Eight and appropriate punishment be meted out to them."

Lord Naowa coughed.

"And I plead for a speedy and safe return of Zuken Banksi, as well as whatever relief as you believe is fair."

Mujin's fingers twitched.

This was bad. He had no doubt that Straff didn't give two fucks about Zuken Banksi. He was only using him as a pawn to make the Earth King distance himself from this case. And without his support, it would be difficult to come out looking strong in front of the emperor. Yes, he was a warlord, which was more than any of the Shoguns could claim, but that only meant that none of them would become Sacred Eight.

It did nothing to save the Shimizu from losing their status.

He had to act. He had to give them something to shut them down for now.

Mujin exhaled. "Great Emperor, it is true that I am a warlord and not capable of standing in my father's shoes. It is not easy to get past your parent's shadow when they are so great. My father was the Wind King, just like Lord Naowa's father was the Ether King. You, Great Emperor, are greater than all of us, and forgive my impertinence, your mother, the Great Goddess, shines brighter than yourself."

"Is there a point to this?" asked the emperor. Mujin noticed the way he sat up straighter.

Good. Any reaction was better than no reaction.

"My point is that, while I have been unable to eclipse my father's greatness, I have not failed in ensuring that his legacy passes on. Yes, we have made mistakes, some very prominent ones lately, but we have received some news that will not just negate Lord Straff's claims but will usher in a new era for the Shimizu name."

"An intriguing preamble," said Lady Troyl, the Lady of Maluscion. Another serpent. "You speak like whatever you are about to describe will change everything."

Mujin smiled. *It will, and more.*

He exhaled. This would require careful wordplay. "Recently, I was notified that the original Shimizu heiress, my granddaughter Tanya, is alive. And that she bears Ezzeron, the Wind King's kami."

"Your granddaughter?" asked Lady Menasse. "Wasn't she dead?"

"We thought she was. She harbors a grudge against me, blaming me for whatever happened to her father in that cataclysmic explosion, and has been a fugitive all this time. Zuken Banksi was hired to bring her back, but instead, he broke sacred protocol, reported her to be dead, and plotted with her to overthrow my power and take over my clan. My grandson Ultaf tried several times to convince him to give up my granddaughter's whereabouts, but he refused. Hence, the escalation of conflict."

"You mean to say that your heiress is not only alive but also in Haviskali?" asked Lord Naowa.

Mujin smiled. "I never said such a thing. If my granddaughter has been hiding in your kingdom, she has yet to be spotted by my people. I'm not sure of what his intentions were, but Zuken Banksi's actions could lead to the fall of a Sacred Eight clan, and that, Lords and ladies, is a transgression I cannot ignore."

"This is ridiculous," said Straff, trying to laugh his statements off. "The next thing he will say is that his granddaughter has somehow claimed the title of the next Wind King."

"I do not," said Mujin slowly, carefully. "All I am saying is that my granddaughter was able to form a bond with my father's kami. A kami that rejected me as a Level-3 aeromancer, rejected my son as a Level-2 aeromancer, and again rejected me when I became a warlord. That kami—the Wrath of the Wind King—has chosen Tanya, my granddaughter. I have reason to believe that she is close, if not already, a Level 3 by now. A young girl, barely in her twenties, who holds the reins over my father's kami—is this not divine providence itself? Is this not proof that the austere penance the Shimizu have been through over the past century is finally at its end? By the Great Goddess, the Empire grants three generations' worth of time to every Sacred Eight clan to reignite their ancestor's legacy. Tanya is the third-generation descendant of my father Wakamura. Is it not right that she be given her entire life's worth of time to attempt her rise to the next Wind King?"

The room went silent. Naowa's eyes were closed. Clearly the old bear was thinking hard about his response.

"That . . ." he said at last, ". . . is surprising news, Lord Shimizu. My felicitations on such an achievement to your youngest. However, as much as Zuken Banksi has wronged you, he is also a member of my personal court, and your fears about him *potentially* sabotaging your control over your own clan does not justify his prolonged captivity."

He turned to face the emperor. "I'm the Shogun of the Llaisy Kingdom, one of the fringe nations that border the Desert of Namzuuhuu. We are the herald, the guard against the creatures of shadow and darkness. We are the nation that faces the most damage when the Mists take over. Zuken and his organization have contributed not only to bolstering the protections of Haviskali, the town that borders the Desert, but he has also been instrumental in developing relations with other species. There is a reason, Great Emperor, why the svartalfars have chosen to establish their dominion in Haviskali of all places." He exhaled loudly. "Hence, I request that my subordinate be immediately released, complete with every punitive relief as is his due."

Mujin smiled, shark-like. "And in return, will he give up my granddaughter's whereabouts?"

"I cannot guarantee that," said Naowa, scowling. "It is entirely possible that Zuken Banksi is under a vow. I cannot risk his physical, mental, or spiritual health just because he has information you want."

"Then you leave me with no choice, Lord Naowa," said Mujin, and turned to face the emperor. "Just like Lord Naowa cares for his subordinate, I care for my clan's legacy. I cannot willingly release Zuken Banksi until he gives away her location, as is my right. I leave the rest to you, Great Emperor."

"If I may," said Lord Tedros out of nowhere, "I am quite used to such contractual obligations, Great Emperor, and I have a quandary."

"Ask."

The man turned to Mujin. "Lord Shimizu, has Zuken Banksi received any commissions in exchange for his unfilled services?"

Mujin clenched his teeth.

"Perhaps in gold, mezals, favors, anything?"

He shook his head.

"If he hasn't received anything in return," Lady Troyl pointed out, "how can you even charge him with anything?"

Damn it. This was getting difficult. "I—we gave him vital information, lords and ladies. Secret information about our clan, about the Wind King's kami, and my heiress. Information that was strictly on a need-to-know basis. Zuken Banksi clearly spat on our trust and intentionally led us to believe that the child was lost. If we could have found her earlier, things could have been different for my clan."

"And do you have any proof of that?" asked Naowa.

"It's quite clear—"

"It's most certainly not," Naowa stressed. "Tell me, do you have proof that Zuken Banksi has intentionally manipulated your heiress into staying hidden?"

Mujin opened and closed his mouth.

"I have heard enough," said the emperor. "I can understand that continuing the Shimizu legacy and its future as a Sacred Eight is indeed of extreme importance. But whatever grudges your heiress holds against your clan or her reasons for hiding from her own family, only speaks to a lack of judgment on her part, and a lack of proper guidance on yours. Your heiress's own failings to communicate with you cannot be classified as grounds for sedition against a Sacred Eight clan. Unless you can definitively prove that Zuken Banksi played a role in actively sabotaging your clan's efforts in finding your heiress, I'm afraid you are in the wrong, Lord Shimizu."

Mujin gritted his teeth.

"I shall grant you my verdict. I, Ninigi Asuka, order you to either submit appropriate evidence of Zuken Banksi's treason or unfailingly release Zuken Banksi and provide compensation for whatever he has lost."

This wasn't happening. This *couldn't* be happening. Not like this.

"Perhaps," said Trestan Banksi, and Mujin found in himself the urge to breathe again, "we should give him some time for deliberation and to find appropriate evidence, Great Emperor? It is obvious that this charade has been going on for quite a few years. Unless I am mistaken, there is a Shogun Council meeting in another forty-five days, right after the eclipse. With your permission, I'd like to preside over it myself. Should Lord Shimizu be unable to provide any acceptable evidence . . ." Mujin almost flinched when the man's gray eyes met his own. ". . . Lord Shimizu will unfailingly release this man and provide whatever compensation is due."

"I thank you—" Mujin began.

"And," the emperor intervened, cutting him off, "in that case, the Sacred Eight status shall be put on probation."

Trestan laughed lightly. "A bit harsh, Great Emperor, especially with the rediscovery of the heiress and the chance of a future Wind King on the horizon."

"We will deliberate on this girl's ability in the future when she is found and has accepted the duties of the clan heir. In my name, I shall judge her myself, and if she is found incapable, the Shimizu shall cease to be part of the Sacred Eight. This I decree."

Mujin sighed in resignation. "If that is what the emperor decrees . . ."

"And now that this inconvenience is over," said the emperor, "let us get down to the real reason behind today's summons. My Great Mother has felt a constant stirring in the ambience of our world. Something has changed, and it has happened in the South-East. It escapes any scrying attempts. I do not know what it is, but it is twisted enough to evade even the All-Seeing Eye."

Mujin blinked. Something that evaded the All-Seeing Eye? His first thought went back to the Desert of Namzuuhuu, the one place where the Great Goddess's powers were neutralized. The world of shadows and darkness.

Mujin felt the ambience within the entire hall feel more potent, angry, almost . . . *repulsive*.

"It raised its ugly head some months ago, scrying across the universe, searching for something. We do not know what that is, but the power involved was great. And then, recently, the portents were there again. An old and ancient power, that once nearly doomed the world, is on the rise again, and whoever is channeling it can bring ruin to our grand Empire."

"What kind of power could it be?" asked Trestan.

"Vestiges of an old enemy," said the emperor. "A power that devours Potential. A power that kills. Once invoked by the Queen of the End, Ruler of Yokai, Empress Meynte."

Mujin felt his knees grow weak. His father, the Wind King, had concluded that the Winter Witch's power was a weakened version of Empress Meynte, the yuki-onna that nearly ended the Great Goddess during the Great War. It was why he wanted to study its power so badly and harness it for himself. A power like that would be the perfect deterrent against every power that ever threatened the Shimizu Clan, a power that could raise them to emperor-status.

His father had perished before that dream had ever come to pass. With Ezzeron rejecting him again and again, Mujin had embraced his father's dream of unlocking the secrets of Everfrost.

And he succeeded through that creature born to his son.

Through Tanya.

And if she were truly up to something so dangerous that even the Great Goddess was taking notice of it, then . . .

A shiver ran down his spine.

If the emperor commanded the other Shoguns and the Cobalt Army to take action, and they ended up capturing Tanya, then not only would he forever lose his chance to get his hands on Everfrost, he might also risk losing Ezzeron.

Not that it would matter, because if they discovered that the wretched creature had this power, fingers would immediately point at him and the Shimizu. Forget trying to protect his status as one of the Sacred Eight, he would be immediately disintegrated on the spot, cast into Yomi itself by the fury of the Great Goddess.

He needed to act.

Now.

"Great Emperor," Mujin pleaded, "grant me this privilege so that I might investigate and find this blasphemer for you."

Naowa laughed. "Really, Lord Shimizu. Already you're facing trial for capturing Zuken Banksi without any proof of sedition. You are already about to lose your Sacred Eight status. I suggest you leave this to us and worry about your own."

Mujin gritted his teeth. He knew what befell those that lost their chances at maintaining their status as a Sacred Eight.

"I agree with that sentiment," said the emperor, much to Mujin's inner turmoil. "Shoguns, I expect this matter to be thoroughly investigated as soon as possible. Earth King—" He turned to Trestan. "Will this matter be taken care of by the eclipse?"

"Most definitely, Great Emperor."

The son of the Great Goddess nodded. "Do so. In the name of my Great Mother, I declare today's court adjourned."

Mujin closed his eyes.

ABOUT THE AUTHORS

T. B. Mare is the pseudonym of the authors of Stranger Than Fiction, a LitRPG adventure series originally released on Royal Road. They are a pair of dreamers who started working together in order to share with readers some of the fun of creating fantasy worlds filled with rich lore and complex characters. Both discovered their love for fantasy and magic at a young age, and the ensuing affairs have carried on well into adulthood. Hopelessly addicted to complex genre fiction—especially the darker kind—they currently work multiple jobs but are looking forward to one day writing full-time.

Podium
DISCOVER
STORIES UNBOUND
PodiumAudio.com

www.ingramcontent.com/pod-product-compliance
Lightning Source LLC
Chambersburg PA
CBHW031254120726
47906CB00003B/737